RO. CW01086192 ... J1

Also from Five Leaves

King Dido

With Hope, Farewell

The War Baby

So We Live: the novels of Alexander Baron
edited by Susie Thomas, Andrew Whitehead and Ken Worpole

Rosie Hogarth

Alexander Baron

*Introduction
by Andrew Whitehead*

Five Leaves Publications

Rosie Hogarth
Alexander Baron

Published by Five Leaves Publications in 2019
14a Long Row, Nottingham NG1 2DH
www.fiveleaves.co.uk
www.fiveleavesbookshop.co.uk

ISBN 978-1-910170-68-7

Printed in Great Britain

Introduction
Andrew Whitehead

"I have always loved London", Alexander Baron once declared. He relished above all the unnoticed, superficially ordinary back streets from which he sprang. It shines through in Baron's novels of the city. *The Lowlife*, a cult classic published in 1963 about an obsessive gambler, bears a striking echo of the street on which he grew up, Foulden Road, where Stoke Newington edges into downmarket Dalston. *King Dido* (1969) shows the imprint of childhood trips to visit grandparents in Spitalfields and Bethnal Green. *Rosie Hogarth*, his most compassionate evocation of the city, gets beneath the skin of an inward looking working class community in Islington, a stone's throw from Upper Street and the Angel. Of these London novels, *Rosie Hogarth* — published in 1951 — has the most profound sense of place and moment, and though hitherto the least regarded it is the most deserving of a new readership.

In all these novels, the principal characters are flawed, in many ways unattractive, yet the reader warms to them. They are portrayed with an affection that extends to the grimy streets that moulded them. Alexander Baron was not an exponent of London noir, but he enjoyed the more difficult aspects of the city. In that he was like the young George Gissing, one of Baron's favourite writers, who was ensnared by London and intrigued by what most would regard as the more humdrum of its localities. But where Gissing was appalled by the lack of a cultural aesthetic in plebeian London, and never seemed to care much for those he wrote about, Baron displays a rich empathy with his key characters. The reader feels that this novelist cares about his cast.

Rosie Hogarth was the first of Alexander Baron's London novels, published when its author was 33. The setting is precisely located, a stub of a street close to Chapel Market: 'two short rows of two-storey cottages, once pleasantly rural, now blackened and neglected, with ... a barber's shop on one corner and a public house ... on the other'. The folklorist A.L. Lloyd, writing in the year the novel appeared, described this hidden away corner of south Islington as 'one of the last atolls of the old-time cockney life'. Of the terraced houses around Chapel Market, he remarked:

> *these have not the forlorn abandoned look of many London back streets. Something of the old elegance stays with them in the cut of a doorway or the harmony of a terrace-row. The face may be smudged but the air is still there. They are streets of character, lived in by people of character*

That rings true of the street Baron depicts, Lamb Street, and there is still a faint echo of a proud and assertive cockney culture around Chapel Market today. There was no Lamb Street in this part of Islington – but there was and is a Baron Street precisely where the novel is set, a coincidence perhaps, but quite possibly a street name that excited the writer's curiosity or even suggested the name under which he wrote.

Alexander Baron – known as Alec Bernstein until he began to be published – seems never to have lived in this part of Islington. But he knew it well, and has the confidence to take the reader into the parlour, the pub, the workplace, the music hall, the crowd, and the rituals and pains of courtship. Baron's familiarity with and empathy for London, and his sharp appreciation of its social geography, is one of the delights of *Rosie Hogarth*. He describes the city as 'an archipelago of life' where 'boroughs are like separate towns':

> *The millions of Londoners are really broken up into tens of thousands of little clusters of life. Each is*

gathered round some centre, perhaps a street, perhaps a block of buildings, perhaps a market, perhaps a public house or a Working Man's Club ... Within each of these little hives people live for each other as well as for themselves, and life generates a comfortable warmth. But the man or woman who tries to settle in London without gaining admission to one of these little communities ... is on his own, and he can go mad or die for all anybody cares.

Jack Agass, the novel's central character, has fought across Europe and worked in the Middle East, but once back into Lamb Street, his world is very constricted: working as a shopfitter near Kings Cross, making occasional forays in the West End, but rarely more than walking distance from his moorings.

The gradations of working class London are keenly observed. At one point, Jack Agass visits Hoxton, 'hurrying through narrow, dirty streets that were all stamped with a squalor that was foreign to Lamb Street'.

To Jack, whose upbringing had imbued him with the outlook of that section of the working-class whose proudest possession is the word 'respectable', it was always unnerving to come here. The people in the 'respectable' streets hated these slums and their inhabitants as a reminder of their own origins and of the depths into which personal insecurity or some wrench of social change might one day plunge them again.

Jack is not ambitious or a social climber, but he has savings and a certain status. That goes, by and large, for Lamb Street — scrubbed, thrifty, decent working class.

Jack's fiancée, Joyce Wakerell, a strong-willed Lamb Street girl, has dreams of moving on and out, musing of 'a little house, somewhere in the outskirts'. When she visits a one-time neighbour who has moved into a new

7

estate in Hackney, she's entranced. "It doesn't seem like London, does it? ... It's all so clean, and — oh, all that grass and flowers. ... If I lived here I'd be afraid it was a dream, and that I might wake up any minute and see dirty black walls again." When her brother, a teacher, and his wife condescend to visit Lamb Street, however, it's a painful comedy of social manners in which the author shows greater sympathy for the home side.

Ever present in *Rosie Hogarth* is the shadow of war, the subject which first prompted Alexander Baron to turn to novel writing. *From the City, From the Plough* (1948) made his reputation and many regard it as his best work. It is a raw and powerful account of the "poor bloody infantry" experience of the Second World War, first waiting for D-Day and then fighting doggedly inland from the Normandy beaches in the summer of 1944. It draws heavily on Baron's own wartime experiences. The novel sold in huge numbers. Two years later, *There's No Home*, set in Sicily in 1943, again borrowed from Baron's war record. It established the author's ability to portray strong female characters, evident also in *Rosie Hogarth*, which served him well in his career as a screenwriter of TV dramas.

Rosie Hogarth was, in creative terms, a change of direction — from life in uniform to civvy street, from the camaraderie born of shared combat to the more enduring sense of community in post-war, austerity London. Yet the lasting impact of six years of conflict is a constant refrain, shaping both the novel's characters and the urban landscape. In the opening pages, Baron establishes that Lamb Street has been disfigured by war, and that four years after its end, Jack Agass has not been able to regain his bearings. Agass is almost Alexander Baron's contemporary and from what can be gleaned of his war record, it echoes the author's — fighting in Sicily and through France. Agass, unlike his creator, is an orphan of war, the First World War. Lamb Street has been his adopted home, and a happy one, but the flying bomb which has left a gash in the street also killed Kate Hogarth, the woman 'he had grown up to worship as a mother'. That loss and the shock of hearing that Kate's daughter and his childhood friend, Rosie, has — according to street wisdom — taken to selling sex troubles him deeply.

The novel is the story of Jack Agass's post-war return to Lamb Street, his re-absorption into a caring (but at times cruel) community and his awkward courtship. All this is finely observed. The community, the neighbourhood, comes to life even more than the principal figures. As with *From the City, From the Plough* — and in sharp distinction to his later novels, *The Lowlife* and *King Dido*, which focus on ill-at-ease individuals — it is the assembly of characters that makes the piece. And in *Rosie Hogarth*, that ensemble is entirely gentile. Baron resisted being pigeon-holed as a Jewish writer and was resolutely secular in outlook, but his Jewish background was an important part of his identity. Of his novels, *The Lowlife* and even more so *With Hope, Farewell* (1952) are about being Jewish in a not always welcoming city. Several others touch fleetingly on the Jewish experience — but not *Rosie Hogarth*, his first literary depiction of London.

Alexander Baron's Lamb Street is largely apolitical. There's an occasional expression of class loyalty, most notably in the street's generous support for the Republican cause during the Spanish Civil War, 'one of those blind and beautiful upsurges of human solidarity that sweep their class from time to time'. Rosie's brother, Chris, gives his life to the labour cause, simply slogging it out on the doorstep when his health is too frail, but to little evident result. The street's only communist, the mockingly named Mr. Prawn, is depicted as marginal and ineffective.

This makes the final twist to the novel all the more unexpected. An introduction is not the place to explore this denouement in detail. Suffice it to say that the

9

closing pages of *Rosie Hogarth*, in their account of the title character's life and politics, bear witness to what was then a recent and turbulent episode in Alexander Baron's own life, his break with the Communist Party. As a teenager in north London, Baron became active in the left and was quickly won over to communism. Although he never held a party card, Alexander Baron was for years, in effect, a full-time communist activist and an acolyte of John Gollan, later the party leader. He became prominent in the Labour League of Youth, a target of party activity both as an aspect of the 'popular front' approach and as a potential source of recruits. He was editor of the League's paper *Advance* and later of the Young Communist League's *Challenge*.

Much of Baron's as yet unpublished memoirs, compiled in the years before his death in 1999, is given over to his association with the Communist Party. It demonstrates how deeply he was immersed in party activity — 'very heaven, it was, to be a Young Communist at this time', he wrote of the late 1930s — and how he never quite made peace with his own past. By his own account, Baron had easy access to the party's headquarters in Covent Garden and was on familiar terms with national leaders of what was a small but influential movement. He clearly enjoyed the subterfuge and manipulation practised in pursuit of party goals. After his enlistment in 1940, Baron recorded, the 'army gradually replaced the Party as the object of loyalty'. But it was another seven or eight years before he made the final break. At one point in his memoirs, Baron talks of a 'rendering of accounts' with the Communist Party. It's likely that the final section of *Rosie Hogarth* was part of that accounting process.

Alison Macleod and her husband, both communists, got to know Alexander Baron well — they were all active in the left-wing Unity Theatre — at just the time he was turning his back on the party. "I never could get Alec [Baron] to admit where he got her from, Rosie Hogarth", she recalled recently. "There were lots of people slightly

10

like her. I just didn't think he had got it quite right." The closing chapters don't fit easily with the rest of the book. The style is laboured and at one point becomes a Shavian-style dialogue about politics and society. It's tempting to see some of Rosie Hogarth's political attitudes — her display of what her interlocutor describes as 'bloody cold, hard arrogance ... like polished granite', and her disparagement of Lamb Street as 'a slum of the spirit' — as the author's acknowledgement of his own erring ways when under Party tutelage.

The intrusion of the Communist Party into *Rosie Hogarth* is a little like its impact on Alexander Baron's life and career: memorable, intriguing, but perhaps not the major chord. Baron's first London novel is a warm, embracing account of a city emerging from the travails of war and of a working class culture struggling to find new form. There is just a hint of romanticism and nostalgia in Baron's depiction of Lamb Street. Yet *Rosie Hogarth* stands as a tender evocation of a working class community. It is one of the best London novels of its era written by one of the defining London writers of the last century.

Andrew Whitehead

Part 1

Chapter 1

FOUR YEARS AFTER THE WAR ENDED, Jack Agass came home to London; and within four weeks he was engaged to be married.

He arrived in town on a lovely May morning. He was badly frightened when he walked out of the railway station, but no-one would have known it. He was a man of medium height, with broad shoulders which betrayed the trace of a Cockney roll when he walked, and a merry face. His thick black hair, cut short, the shiny red swell of skin over his cheekbones and his twinkling eyes made his age hard to determine; at twenty he had looked older than he was; now, at thirty, people often told him that he looked less than his age; and in ten years' time he would probably look no older than he did today. He was not unattractive; his skin and eyes were clear, his body solid and strong; but he was one of those men who are too indecisive of expression to be distinctive. Women always thought he was laughing at them. His friends never knew when he was angry, or scared, or unhappy, and never offered him the sympathy which he might have enjoyed had his face been more expressive. Wherever he went he was considered good company, but in the midst of his many acquaintances he remained watchful and reserved behind his smile. Sometimes he would think, with a feeling of terrible depression, "An orphan I was born, and an orphan I will remain till the end of my days." Then he would think of the years, the precious and beautiful years, that he had spent with the Hogarths. But that was all past; and the past, the past....

"You're barmy," he said to himself, standing outside the railway station and struggling to free himself from one of his reveries. His grin broadened as he wondered what the chaps he had been working with for the last four years, or the blokes in the battalion before that, or the Lamb Street boys among whom he had fought and played football in his adolescent years, would have said at the knowledge that Jack Agass, beefy Jack Agass, was a Dreamy Daniel.

However, he could not deny the fear that fluttered inside him. He had been through battles, tackled a burning oil tank and faced a riot of Arab labourers, without anything being awakened inside him but the sense of sport or of anger; but whenever he set out alone on a journey, or arrived alone in a new place, he was like a scared child at heart. At such times it seemed to him that life was all journeying, that the years would slip by, that place would follow place, and he would never settle. Today he was frightened because the London that had bred him was as strange to him as any of the places in which he had been during the ten years since the sweet dream of the old, placid life had ended.

He waited in the taxi queue with an enforced kind of patience. "Where's all the taxis, nob?" he asked an old porter, who was passing.

The old man pushed his cap back and scratched at his white hair. "Gorn to the races, I reckon. That's where the money is these days. That's where I'd be if I 'ad any sense, 'stead of 'umping baggage about for a lot of fat-gutted ferts as ought to be helping me, at my age, instead of me sweatin' for them."

Several minutes elapsed between the arrival of each taxi. When Jack's turn came the porter loaded his two tin trunks and canvas American travelling bag up beside the driver. "Where to, mate?" he asked.

Jack named a popular and moderately-priced hotel in the Strand. He rummaged in his pocket for small change and found none. He put a crumpled ten-shilling note into the porter's hand. "Here," he said, "pick the right treble and you can make your fortune with that."

"You want to look after your money," said the old porter. He peered up at Jack. "Seaman, ain't yer?"

"Nah. Gentleman of leisure." The porter's guess was not an unreasonable one. Jack was wearing the only suit that he possessed apart from his Persian kit, the cheaply-cut suit of grey flannel with broad white stripes that he had been given on demobilization four years ago. In spite of the hot climate in which he had lived since then he had filled out, and with his red face and powerful limbs, he burst out of the tightly-fitting clothes like a farm hand on Sunday or a sailor ashore.

The taxi moved off, and he leaned back to enjoy the unfamiliar comfort — he had ridden in cabs less than a dozen times in his whole life — and to look out through the window at the spectacle of the streets. The fear had gone, and in its place there was a tired, flat feeling. At the beginning of his journey he had spoken of 'going home,' but the sight of the London streets did not arouse any feeling of 'home' in him. He forced himself to notice the gay window displays in the shops, the crowds on the pavements, the way in which the afternoon sunlight made the streets seem even more spacious than they were, the girls in their light Spring frocks. He muttered stubbornly to himself, "This is a bit of all right," but his smile was strained.

He was abashed by the splendour of the hotel. The glittering swing doors, the thick carpets and the deferential servants were all new to him. He had only come here because he had heard his colleagues out on the Gulf talking about it, and because he was still slightly intoxicated at the thought that there was more money in his wallet than he had ever before possessed. He spoke humbly to the door porter, pulled himself together and was aggressive to the reception clerk; by the time he encountered the lift attendant he had recovered his balance sufficiently to crack a joke.

He wandered about his room, trying the taps and the wardrobe doors. He lay down on the bed, sighed, stretched out his arms and shut his eyes.

This was his first time in London since the Spring of nineteen forty-six, when he had been demobilised from the Rhine Army. He had come hurrying home — yes, on that journey, too, he had thought of it as 'home' — full of hope that he would find his way back to the old life and settle down. London had been like a foreign land, the faces all blank to him, the crowds hateful, everyone hurrying to and fro about him. The whole place seemed to be asking him why he had dared return. Back in Lamb Street, Mrs. Hogarth, the woman whom he had grown up to worship as a mother, was dead. The family was scattered. The house had been bombed, and there was only a patch of waste ground, all weeds and puddles and old iron, where the lovely years of his youth had been lived. He had asked what Rosie Hogarth was doing these days, and somebody had told him. There seemed to be nothing for him anywhere. He thought of joining up again, but that was more than he could stomach for the time being. He could not understand the discontent that had seized him, and tried to overcome it. He imagined that he was the only one to feel like this, and told himself not to be a fool; until, by chance, he met an old Army friend in the street.

His friend, who had an air of alcoholic recklessness about him, saw him first and seized him by the arm. "Here, Jack!" There was no other attempt at greeting. "You used to be game for a lark."

Jack said, "Eh? Hallo, Fred."

"Hallo. Jack, let's clear out."

"Out of where?"

"Of Blighty."

Jack grinned and said, "You're drunk." He was filled with astonishment that others felt as he did. The repressed despair in him turned into a physical excitement. "Where would you go?"

"Oh, anywhere. Italy. It was all right there. Australia."

Jack took his friend's arm. "You come and cool off. You just haven't got used to it, that's all." He was arguing with himself. "You'll settle down."

Fred said, with great violence, "I tell you, Blighty's like a rotten apple. One bite and you've had it."

"You come with me," said Jack patiently, and Fred followed him.

A few weeks later the two of them sailed for the Persian Gulf. An oil company was undertaking a big construction project there. Fred was an engineer and Jack a shopfitter by trade, and each was employed to supervise and train native labour, Fred in the installation of machinery, Jack in the building of living quarters. They signed on for five years; the pay was good, and there was a bonus of fifty pounds a year.

He had not been abroad long before he regretted his flight from England. He realised that he had given way to a fit of despair and run away from a fight — an unforgivable weakness to him. In Persia he found none of the colour or adventure with which he had hoped to drug himself. They dwelt in ugly huts in the midst of a torrid desolation. Life was a round of sweat, dust, flies, boredom and short tempers. The only relief was in hard work, which Jack had always hitherto been able to enjoy but which in these surroundings soon became tedious.

As each year went by he reminded himself that he had lost a year which he might have spent in settling down. This was not a career. At the end of it there was nothing for him but some money and the uncertain chance of a similar job in another remote corner of the earth; year after year, with his life running to waste all the time.

All the longing he had ever felt — as a child in the Orphanage and as a roving soldier — for a stable, predetermined life, came back to him. He would, in the life of which he dreamed, have a home of his own; at work, and in the lonely nights, he furnished it room by room, down to the last china ornament. He would have a wife, and there would be no more pursuing a succession of strange women for a relief that was only of the body.

Thus the struggle continued between the two qualities which his life had planted in him — restlessness and the desire for rest; until, with four of the five years gone, he could wait no longer. A fit of desperate resolution seized him, he drew his bonus and savings, three hundred and eighty pounds in all, and came — that mocking word slipped into his mind again — 'home.'

What was he to do now? He would have to go back to his trade; at thirty, it was too late to begin learning a new one. But what else? Here were all these millions of people living around him. How was he to make some of them aware of his presence? How was he to find a home for himself among his fellows?

The temptation came back to him (it had visited him several times during his return journey) to solve his problems by joining the Army again. At least he would find friends there, and an ordered life. But he had promised himself to make a fight of it this time, and he put the Army out of his mind except as a last resort.

He washed, changed his shirt and went downstairs. He had a meal at the hotel and regretted it, for he felt uncomfortable sitting alone at a table confronted by an unfamiliar array of cutlery and silver and a menu that he could not understand. He tried to be hearty with the waiters, but secretly he was cowed.

He spent the evening wandering about the streets, still telling himself that this was 'a bit of all right'. He had a few drinks and saw a dull film. He returned to the hotel early and went to bed.

London, for all its reputation and its civic institutions, is an archipelago of life, not an island. Its boroughs are like separate towns; people who live in one may spend their whole lives without venturing into more than a couple of the others; to those who live on one side of the river the part of the town beyond the opposite bank is as remote and unknown as San Francisco. Even the boroughs are not communities. The millions of Londoners are really broken up into tens of thousands of little clusters of life. Each is gathered round some centre, perhaps a street, perhaps a block of buildings, perhaps a market, perhaps a public house or a Working Man's Club or any one of a thousand different organizations. Within each of these little hives people live for each other as well as for themselves, and life generates a comfortable warmth. But the man or woman who tries to settle in London without gaining admission to one of these little communities (and it is not easy, for the more closely-knit each is the more hostile it is to the stranger) is like a lonely traveller wandering, as night gathers, across the vast deserted moors, mocked wherever he looks by the clustering lights of villages. He is on his own, and he can go mad or die for all anybody cares.

Jack, pondering over his plans in bed, was instinctively aware of this. To whom could he turn? The Orphanage? — It had an After-Care Committee of kindly and well-intentioned people, but the idea of approaching them after all these years seemed ridiculous. There were one or two people he had known in the Army; and there was Lamb Street.

He fell asleep feeling more contented, and in the morning he went back to Lamb Street.

Chapter 2

A HUNDRED YEARS AGO the borough of Islington lay on the rural fringe of London. Even the maps of fifty years ago show it as an outer suburb. Today the Angel, its heart, is one of the funnels through which the life of London thunders. It pours streams of traffic from the suburbs into the central shopping districts; a black tide of cars bound for the City and lorries going to the docks rolls unendingly down City Road; while the cars, lorries, carts, coaches and bicycles heading out of town charge in such masses along Upper Street and Essex Road that several times a day the whole confusion grinds to a standstill, traffic lights blink frantically and in vain, a hubbub of hooters and angry voices succeeds to the growl of engines, and policemen sidle among the press of vehicles, shouting and gesticulating until the black tides are on the move again.

The roads that meet at the Angel are as ugly as any in the ugly sprawl of London. They are broad and dirty, lined with shops whose variety of shape, size and architectural style is a monument to the malignant ingenuity of small minds, and among which the merely shabby are less offensive than the garish shrines of up-to-the-minute salesmanship with which they alternate. Huge hoardings dominate and depress, the pavements are so filthy with drifting dust and scuttering litter that it seems as if all the waste paper in London must have been blown to this one crossroads, funereal queues block the pavements outside half-a-dozen cinemas, fun fairs discharge their screech and blare upon the passer-by, and even the patch of sky that shows pathetically between the rooftops is crawled across by a sweep of trolleybus wires.

But a hundred yards away, in the back streets, there is a quietness and serenity that keeps the traffic's roar at bay and even holds sway over the crying of babies and the shrill chatter of women that ascends from basement windows. Here the pattern of the past is still discernible. Broad roadways; big houses in raised terraces with long gardens, unexpectedly pleasing the eye — despite the grime and decay that have assailed them — with their simple and imposing pediments and their well-proportioned windows and doorways; spacious and pleasant squares; trees to relieve the grey and black monotony with their clouds of fresh green foliage; and the song of birds.

Why these streets and squares are so quiet it is hard to imagine; for the sedate merchants, their ladies and their carriages, have long vanished from them; the poor have swarmed in to take their places; every house is crammed with families from basement to lofty attic; tired and haggard women talk in groups on the street corners while they rest their laden shopping bags for a moment; their children teem everywhere, screaming out of windows, howling on the steps and swooping across the roadways like flights of sparrows; and the bray of conviviality resounds from the public houses. Yet tranquillity prevails. It is only in the little side turnings that connect these larger thoroughfares that dirt, noise, overcrowding and the sense of haste come into their own; in each of these little streets a constant din of altercation and neighbourly intercourse echoes across the narrow pavements.

Lamb Street, where Jack Agass had passed his life between the ages of eight and twenty, is one of these. It consists of two short rows of two-storey cottages, once pleasantly rural, now blackened and neglected, with — at one end — a barber's shop on one corner and a public house, The Lamb, on the other.

23

Jack had slept late, and it was almost midday when he reached the corner of Lamb Street. His home, with the Hogarth family, had been in the corner house on the left-hand side. Now, where it and a half-a-dozen other houses had stood, there stretched a rough expanse of waste ground, bounded by ragged ends of wall. Among the craters and green hillocks the course of foundations could be traced; rusty coloured clumps of wild flowers struggled towards the light between the weathered tracks of brick, overgrowing the scattered boulders of masonry and springing up in wild hedges through the cracks they had forced in patches of concrete flooring. Almost half of one of the two rows of houses had vanished; the street looked as mutilated as a man with one leg. It also seemed much smaller than it had when he was younger. A flying bomb had dropped on the street corner in December, nineteen forty-four. He had been in the Ardennes at the time, with one of the British divisions whose rest had been interrupted by Rundstedt's last offensive; huddled, in greatcoat and woollen wrappings, in a slit trench beneath snow-laden undergrowth, looking out over silent white slopes. When he had read the letter that told him that Mrs. Hogarth and a score of his old friends were dead in a common grave he had felt for a moment as if water were freezing suddenly throughout his veins; and the recollection of it came to him now, for a second, not as a memory in the mind but as a repetition of that feeling.

He had seen the bombed site once before, when he came back to England in nineteen forty-six. It had been silent and abandoned then, and he had not let himself linger to look at it. Now it was different. A great stack of new bricks, red and bright, stood in the middle. Some distance away from him a lorry was backed up on to the pavement, and men were unloading planks. Farther away, labourers were digging a trench; the clink of their picks and the sound of their jesting seemed distant and dream-like in the morning sunlight.

He asked one of the workmen, "What's up, nob?"

24

"Building job. Block of flats. For the council. Why? Lookin' for a place to live?"

Jack grinned. "I might be, soon."

"Well, you won't get one o' these. If you hurry up round the Town 'All and put your name down, you might get one before your youngest great-grandson gets wed."

"Don't give 'im 'opes," grunted another labourer as he passed, "I wouldn't like to see 'im wait a 'undred years, then die of disappointment."

"I used to live here," said Jack. He was eager to talk to people of his own kind. The burden of loneliness lifted from him when he heard his own cheerful voice, and the voices of others speaking to him with warmth. But the workmen had passed on. He felt the cold creeping into him again, in spite of the day's warmth. He was dismayed at the thought that a great red building would spring up on this corner, that dozens of families would move in and would not even know who had been here before them. It had been such a happy house. It had always been full of laughter and gusto, and Mrs. Hogarth had reigned over it like a smiling queen. These workmen were building over his memories; it was as if they were trampling on a cherished grave.

A mob of small boys came charging past him. He did not know any of them; they had all been born since he left here. They looked the same as the children of his own day, each boy's hair close-cropped with a pudding-basin fringe, each pair of dirty legs bursting out of a pair of ridiculously-small breeches, their faces lit at once with innocence and jungle cunning; vociferous, pugnacious and tireless as wild colts. Their leader screamed, "Come on, Lamb Street!" They streamed after him, whooping and screeching.

A memory came to Jack like a revelation. He was filled with gladness: He seized one of the boys by the arm. "Here, where you off to?"

"You leave us alone. We ain't doing nothing."

"Steady, boy," said Jack, "you ain't frightened of me,

25

are you? I'm a Lamb Street boy myself."

The child looked at him warily and muttered, "I don't know yer."

"I used to live up the corner, with Mrs. Hogarth. I been in the Army."

The boy asked eagerly, "Was you in the Commandos?"

"No, the Queens."

"Got any cap badges?"

"I might have. Not on me, though. Where you off to? Street fight?"

"Yus. We an' arf gonna whop 'em."

Jack beamed with delight. "Here, it's not Bennett's Buildings, is it?"

"Yus. They come round 'ere the other day. Dit'n 'arf kick up a stink, they did. Broke free winders. They an' arf gonna cop it this time. We got some big boys wiv us, from White Lion Street."

"Well, I'm blowed,"Jack gloated, "that one's still goin' on, is it? Many a fight with Bennett's Buildings we had, in my time."

The boy looked hastily along the road to make sure that his companions had not yet vanished from sight, cocked his head on one side and whispered in a hoarse and confidential voice, "Got any froopenny bits, mister?"

"What for?"

"Go to pictures wiv."

Jack gave him a shilling. In place of thanks the boy uttered a violent, "Oo!" and dashed away up the street.

One of the two workmen had returned, and Jack said to him, "Well, that's one thing that hasn't changed. Except we never used to beg for money when I was a kid. We used to pester people in the streets for fag cards, but money! Blimey! Our mums would have beaten us black and blue if we'd tried that on."

"Ah," answered the man, "little devils they are. Run about like a mob of wild animals, they do. Can't do nothing with 'em. It's the war, I reckon. We used to be glad of a penny when I was a kid. If you give 'em one now they throw it at you. Takes 'alf your week's wages to keep the kids in sweets and pictures."

Jack continued on his way. There were few people in the street — the men were still at work and the women busy over their stoves putting the finishing touches to the Saturday dinner. He saw no-one that he knew. Strange babies sunning in their pushcarts scowled at him suspiciously. Their big eyes, following him, made him feel embarrassed. His heart sank as he walked on between the little black houses. He should have known, he told himself, that it would be like this. The bomb had killed some of his friends. Others had been scattered by evacuation. Young men had gone to the war, some to die, others to return, marry and move to new homes. He wanted to admit defeat and hasten away.

He began to whistle and quickened his step. Some of the front doors were closed, some were open to reveal dark and narrow hallways. Surely there was still a welcome for him behind some of these doors? Which? He thought of knocking at one or another of them, but the fear of coming face to face with strangers deterred him. There, half way along on the opposite side, was a house that he knew well. The window-box filled with glossy red geraniums must surely mean that the Wakerell family still lived there! He glimpsed a stir of movement behind the curtains of the upstairs window, and thought he saw fair hair. That would be Mrs. Wakerell. He slowed down, in the hope that he would hear the window slamming open and a familiar voice calling after him. He looked back. The movement at the window had ceased. Perhaps it had not been Mrs. Wakerell. Even if it was, perhaps she had not recognized him. Perhaps, after all these years — but he did not see how they could have forgotten him; he remembered every one of them so clearly. Perhaps she had not thought it worth her while to greet him. After all, why should she? She would say to her family tonight, "Guess who I saw walking up the street today? Jack Agass! At least, I think it was." And that would be all.

Disappointment and nervous relief mingled in him as he walked on, although his watchful smile did not change. He was not looking around him now, but was smiling fixedly at the pavement a little way ahead of him. There was an impulse of resentment at work inside him, against the indifference of these walls and windows; he wanted more than ever to take flight once again to the ends of the earth. He was nearing the other end of the street. On the right was The Lamb, on the left the Jubilee Gents' Hairdressing Saloon (Beniamino Leone, Prop.), He could not go across to The Lamb yet; there were still ten minutes to go before it opened. Besides, there was something — again, it was only an instinct, working in the lower levels of his consciousness — that made him hesitate to meet Mick Monaghan, the pub's proprietor. He could give himself no reason for this. What had happened to Rosie Hogarth, he told himself for the hundredth time, was no concern of Jack Agass's. Mick had always treated him well enough. People had a right to live their own lives. He must forget all this nonsense. While his mind made its reasonable decisions a little serpent of hatred continued to constrict his heart. He decided to go into the barber's shop, to see if old Benno was still there.

"JACKie Agass!"

At the sound of the voice, and of the hasty slap-slap-slap of footsteps coming from behind him, he turned. He felt stifled with surprise and happiness. Mrs. Wakerell, seeing that she had attracted his attention, stopped running and stood panting for a few seconds.

"Jackie Agass," she said at last, "where d'you think you're going to?"

Jack was unable to do anything but grin stupidly at her. She had recovered her breath now. "Walking right past like that as if you were a stranger!"

"I was just having a look round," he croaked. He stared at her in fascinated recognition. He could remember her, in his childhood, as a handsome, matronly woman. He had seen her, during his brief stay in nineteen forty-six, when she was assuming the more massive proportions of middle-age. But now her dimensions were overpowering. Huge bosom, broad hips and bulging legs all tapered down to a small pair of high-heeled shoes above which it seemed impossible that the whole mass of her would maintain its balance when in movement. Her cheeks were rouged, she wore a pair of rimless *pince-nez* and, to complete the haughty air which in the old days had earned her the title of Queen Lizzie, her dry, bleached hair was piled up high like a pompadour wig. His voice came back to him. "How you keeping?"

"As you see me," she replied with equanimity. She folded her arms and rested them comfortably across the upper slopes of her bosom. "I have my little aches and pains, but who doesn't? Where did you pop up from? I thought I was seeing a ghost when you walked by. I knocked at the window but you didn't hear me. I was just washing, so I couldn't show myself or come down after you." She smiled benignly, and said with sudden fondness, "How are you, boy? Seen any of the Hogarths yet? How long you back for?"

"I'm back for good," said Jack, "I hope. I haven't seen anyone yet. How's the gov'nor?"

"He's all right. He's still working. He'll be home in a half-hour. Joyce'll be home, too, any minute. Remember her?"

"Just about."

"Oh, you won't recognize her. She's quite the young lady. Come in and have some dinner with us, Jack."

"Oh, I dunno." It was partly out of shyness that he hesitated, partly because he liked to be urged, and reassured that the welcome to which he had looked forward was genuine.

"Oh, come on, Walter'll never forgive me if I let you go. And I want to hear all about what's been happening to you. There's no point in just standing here in the street, is there?"

"I reckon not," said Jack, "to tell you the truth I'd be very glad to say yes."

"Well, come on then." She moved back towards her house, as stately as a towed balloon. Jack walked, humbly and gratefully, at her side.

Chapter 3

IN THE WAKERELL'S LITTLE KITCHEN, Jack sat very primly at first, daunted by the furniture which hemmed him in, by the presence of the uncommunicative Mr. Wakerell, by a wary and unrecognizably-grown Joyce, and by the stiff and spotless white tablecloth that brushed his knees.

As the meal proceeded he felt more at ease. It was years, he told Mrs. Wakerell, since he had sat down to such a good feed. What could beat a plate heaped with big and angular potatoes, all baked so stiff and dry that they resisted the fork as if they were coated in brown varnish, with a mountain of cauliflower that oozed the warm water in which it had been boiled, a great plank of Yorkshire pudding and a slice of roast beef? For years, in his military and civilian travels, people had tried to tempt him with foreign delights, but he had always stubbornly maintained that 'there's nothing like good old home cooking,' and here it was. All his shyness fell away from him as he described to his hosts the horrors he had witnessed.

"I went into some place in France once," he said, "and they asked me if I wanted a bit of fish. Well, I thought, here's a bit of all right. And when they brought it, guess what, there was all yellow stuff over it, and — here, you won't believe this — he paused for effect — "they said they'd cooked it in wine!"

"Go on!" said Mrs. Wakerell, incredulous. She paused with her spoon upraised. "Rhubarb plain or with custard?"

"Custard please. And in Italy once, they tried to give us octopus. Octopus soup. With spaghetti and stuff."

Mrs. Wakerell made a little grimace indicative of well-bred distaste and said, "Oogh!" She consoled him with one of her queenly smiles. "Never mind, you're home again. You won't have to put up with any of that muck any more."

Jack settled back in his chair, letting his cup of tea steam on the table in front of him, feeling replete with food, warmth and the happiness of being among friends. Mrs. Wakerell was talking of her schoolmaster son Fred, of the magnificent fortune he had had in marrying the daughter of a prosperous grocer, and of the glories that she hoped would ensue. Throughout the meal it was Mrs. Wakerell who had done most of the talking. Those of her neighbours who described her as 'standoffish' were unjust to her. She was not a snob; she was friendly with everyone; but she always managed to give the impression that she was bestowing her friendship as a royal favour. The air of benign superiority with which she moved among her acquaintances derived partly from her own origins — her mother had been a lady's maid among the gentry — partly from pride in her son's status, and partly because her husband, a warehouse foreman, was the only man in Lamb Street to wear a bowler hat.

Her husband Walter was, for his part, neither her partner in pride nor (as might have been supposed) her meek underling. He was a man of hard-bitten appearance, shorter than his wife but sturdily built, who loped about through life with a perpetual blue-jowled scowl on his face. Jack, who knew him of old, was aware that he was not the misanthrope that his expression suggested, but a man who had withdrawn into himself and who was able to maintain, in a life totally lacking in physical privacy, an inner privacy in which he pondered over a variety of mysteries. Occasionally he would emerge from his reveries to utter some unexpected compliment to his wife or, with his friends, to venture some heavily amiable remark.

Joyce sat across the table, quiet and watchful; one of those girls who at one glance seem ugly, at the next attractive. She wore a pair of glasses in a frame of pink shell; the sunlight flashed on the lens, hiding her eyes from Jack and at the same time making him feel that he was under intense scrutiny. Her hair was unnaturally fair, the product of childhood bleaching, and hung straight in a long bob. She was twenty-four years old, with a solid, shapely body and with a strong, heavily-boned face like her father's that matched ill with her hair.

Jack cast a furtive glance at her from time to time; he had a speculative eye for every woman he met these days, for he was in a hurry to settle down. He did not know what to make of her. He could not decide whether or not she attracted him, and he was puzzled by the defensive air that underlay both her silent obedience to her mother and her seeming indifference to him. He tried, out of curiosity and to fulfil his duty as a guest, to draw her into the conversation. "Got any boyfriends, Joycie?" he asked.

Joyce shrugged her shoulders and smiled faintly at the tablecloth.

"Where's your tongue, my girl?" her mother demanded. "Pawned it to pay for the pictures? And why don't you take those glasses off when you're indoors? She don't need them, really she doesn't."

Joyce jerked her head back as if about to make a retort. Twin bolts of light flashed across her glasses. She subsided, and said, "I'm doing the washing up, not going in for a beauty contest. Here," she added, turning to Jack, "Finish up the cheese and I'll take the plate."

"I asked you a question,"Jack persisted.

"And I heard you."

"Well, have you?"

"Hundreds," said Joyce, beginning to put the plates together, "didn't you see the queue as you come up the street?"

"Can't say I did. Perhaps I need a lend of your glasses."

"Per'aps you do. Mind your big feet." She squeezed past him with a pile of plates in her hands. He smiled up at her in the moment that her face was close to his, and was surprised by the sudden blush and the searching, hostile look with which she responded. "Open the door, someone," she cried quickly, "I haven't got a spare pair of hands."

When Joyce had set down the plates in the sink and closed the scullery door, Mrs. Wakerell said, "Our Joyce is a smart girl. She's got a quick tongue, but that's because she's got plenty up here." She tapped her head. "I don't say it because I'm her mother — I'm not in the habit of praising my own, but plenty of nice chaps 'd be glad to have her. It's just that she doesn't give them any encouragement." She paused for breath, and went on, "She takes after me there. Many's the visitor used to come to the house where my mother was in service, and used to say, 'There's the real lady of the house.' They meant me." She returned, with an effort that showed itself in her voice, to her subject, "That girl's particular. No larking about at the street corner for her. She's the kind that waits for Mr. Right to come along."

Mr. Wakerell had moved his chair nearer to the open window and was filling his pipe. "Broody, that girl," he grunted, "sits at home moping for want of company, then snaps your head off when you talk to her."

"All she wants," Mrs. Wakerell went on serenely, as if she had not heard any interruption, "is the right chap. A nice, steady chap. And you take it from me, it'll be a lucky man that gets a girl like that."

Jack began to feel uncomfortable again in the silence that followed.

"I suppose you'll be looking up the Hogarths," said Mrs. Wakerell.

"Yes. I heard from Nancy now and again while I was away."

Mrs. Wakerell leaned from her chair to open the

scullery door. She called to Joyce, "Fill the kettle up again, dearie, when you've taken the hot water. There's some hankies under the sink you can wash afterwards." To her husband she said, "I thought you were going to do some weeding this afternoon."

"Plenty of time," said Mr. Wakerell, in a deep voice that was clogged with repletion, "let the grub go down a bit first. Besides, it'll get cooler out there in an hour or two."

His wife settled back in her chair, hands in her lap, like a queen on her throne, and turned once more to Jack. "Now, that was a surprise if you like. A big fat lump like her getting married. And well past thirty, too."

"I don't know," said Jack, "you couldn't ask for a better girl than Nancy. She's a real winner. And she was only —" he calculated — "she's only thirty-six now, and she's been married two years."

"Two years and three months. It was just after I went up the hospital with my piles. Wonders they did for me. I've never had a day's trouble since. Everything goes through like butter. It was going out to work that gave that girl her chance. And plenty like her. In the war, all this doing your bit in the factories. Still, he's a nice chap. Hard-working. She was married in a plain, two-piece costume. My advice, that was. 'White wedding,' I said, 'at your age? Don't ask for trouble, Nancy dear. It's not as if your dear mother was still alive.' I dare say if you asked her she'd thank me for that advice today. Not that I ask for thanks. Joycie! —" she raised her voice with disconcerting suddenness — "don't be stingy with the soap flakes. There's another box on the dresser." She reclaimed Jack's attention with a gracious smile, "No use spoiling the ship, I always say."

Jack took refuge in a somnolent "Ooerh!" which he uttered with a great stretching of his arms. He hoped she would regard this as a compliment to her cooking. "It gets you, don't it?"

Mrs. Wakerell pushed a chair forward. "Put your feet up, dear. Our home is yours, you know."

Mr. Wakerell took advantage of the proffered chair to put his own feet up, and contributed to the conversation the mysterious words, "Nice kiddie."

"Yes," his wife resumed, as if she had heard a prompter's voice, "a lovely little girl they've got. It all goes to show, doesn't it. Her husband's twice the size of her, big as she is. And ten years older in the bargain. And there they go and have a beautiful kiddie like that, eighteen months old and like a little doll."

"I know," said Jack, "Linda Jean. Names they think of nowadays! Nancy sent me a photo."

"It's funny," mused Mrs. Wakerell, "how a family gets scattered. A lovely family like that. It used to be a pleasure to see them all together. And now look at them, all over the place. Ah, well, that's life." She shook her head and popped into her mouth a cube of sugar from the bowl on the table. "That family died the night Kate Hogarth died. That bomb was like the crack of doom for the Hogarths. Isn't it funny? — all in a second — a bang, a cloud of dust — and there's nothing left of all those years of life — no more house, no more Kate. And no more family, either — look what happened. Within a twelve-month poor Chris was dead of the consumption, and no wonder, if you'll excuse me speaking plainly, with that Italian wife of his sucking the life out of him. And Alf marrying that slut from The Lamb." She crunched the sugar vigorously between her teeth. "And Rosie!"

She fell silent, her head inclined and her eyes full of thought. The heavy breathing of three people was the only sound in the little room, but in Jack's ears it seemed to be drowned by multiplying echoes of Mrs. Wakerell's last words.

"It's funny —" she was speaking again, and he looked up as if from a disturbed sleep — "I always thought it might have come to something between you two."

He heard his own voice, gruff and reluctant. "What two?"

"You and Rosie."

"No." At moments like this his tongue seemed to be swollen to twice its normal size, and — what with the difficulty of controlling his breath — it was hard to speak articulately. "I don't suppose either of us ever give it a thought. More like brother and sister us two, I reckon." He marvelled at the calm words that he heard coming from his own lips. "After all, we were brought up together."

"Ah, well," Mrs. Wakerell sighed, "I'm too romantic. Always been my trouble. And I mean to say, you can't blame me, can you? Jack and Jill wasn't in it with you two. From children."

Her placid words pricked and prodded at his thoughts. "Till she married that other chap in the war. Now, that was a surprise, if you like. You could have knocked me down with a feather when she brought him home. I said — it was in this very room, Walter was here, he'll tell you — I said, 'Well, she might have done better than that. Skinny ha'porth like that,' I said, 'he wouldn't fill one leg of Jack Agass's trousers. Well,' I said, 'of course, he might have money,' but no, she said, when I asked her, not a farthing. It was a quiet wedding. You didn't come up for it, did you?"

"No. I couldn't get leave."

"Oh, well, I thought you could for these things. Anyway, she didn't stick him for long, did she; what did she leave him for?"

"I don't know. She didn't tell me."

"And then, the next thing you know, along comes the next surprise. There she is, living in a fancy flat, and someone we all know paying the rent."

"I know. I heard about it."

"And," she added bitterly, reaching for another piece of sugar, "him not the only one she's seen about with, by all accounts."

Jack rose, and said, "I got to be going. Don't want to keep you talking all the afternoon."

"Don't be silly," Mrs. Wakerell scoffed, "you don't want

to run off now. Joyce is just making tea. You've nowhere special to go, have you?"

"Not in particular."

"Well, sit down and have a rest after your dinner. You might as well make a day of it now you're here."

"You can come down The Lamb with us this evening," put in Mr. Wakerell, who up till now had shown all the signs of falling asleep, "Everyone'll be glad to see you."

Jack grinned, and sat down awkwardly. His panic was subsiding. He was glad that it had failed to drive him from this hospitable house. He felt that he had taken the first step on the road back to the old life. "Suits me." He hesitated, frowned at the backs of his hands, and after a little while spoke again. "I suppose that's all straight up?"

"All what, dear?"

"About Rosie."

"It's as true as we're sitting here. Jack, it's a judgement, I tell you, the way these things come out. Always. Didn't you know how it got out? Cyril Owers — you remember Cyril, from Number Eighteen? — working in the very estate office? He saw the lease of the flat with his own eyes. Said he'd swear to it in a court of law. Signed, 'Henry Joseph Monaghan,' bold as brass. And some people say there isn't a power at work!"

Jack sat looking at his hands.

"You're nodding off, dearie," said Mrs. Wakerell, "Why don't you have a lay down. Walter, you too. Take him in the front room. Go on, Jack, you're not shy, are you? You can take your shoes off in there and stretch out on the sofa."

In the front parlour Jack took off his jacket and shoes, unbuttoned his collar and lay down on the sofa, while his host stretched himself out in an armchair. Outside the world sparkled with the brilliance of May. Pale leaves rustled. Quick footsteps and the laughter of girls could be heard. Every sound had a glassy, fragile quality. Jack turned his back on the brightness that pressed in at the bay windows. The air was heavy from lack of ventilation, dust swirled in the shafts of sunlight, the cracked leatherette of the sofa against his cheek smelt of the sweat of generations, but this was what he had dreamed of for years, and all the beauties of sky and springtime could not tempt him from this room. He was drowsy with food and warmth, and immensely content. The pleasure of repose was familiar, but the pleasure of feeling at home was a delicious novelty of which not only the mind but even the body seemed gloriously aware. He enjoyed the approach of sleep, yet struggled against it to prolong the pleasure. As he lay, outside of time, in the dark caverns of half-awareness, he heard feminine movements and feminine voices close by — their proximity, in these domestic surroundings, a fresh delight. He opened his eyes painfully, to see the door just closing softly. He could still hear the voices coming from the hallway, Joyce's raised in remonstrance, her mother's complacent and relentless. "Well, dearie, there's one thing you may come to be grateful for. He doesn't snore." He grinned, unalarmed, and fell asleep.

Chapter 4

SOMEBODY HAD GONE BEHIND THE BAR and scrawled on the mirror in lipstick, "Welcome Home Jack Agass." Jack saw it through a dazzle of tears, for by nine o'clock he was maudlin drunk and was reaching out and shaking every hand he saw.

It was a warm evening, and the heat in the saloon bar of The Lamb was almost unbearable. It had driven many of the customers outside, where they gossiped in clusters on the pavement, lifting to every flutter of breeze faces which were still scarlet and beaded with sweat. Every time the door opened, simultaneous gusts of heat and noise burst out on them. Inside, the hardy majority congregated, seated in families along the wall, crowded beneath the revolving fans or swarming round the piano. Delegates from all these groups pushed to and from the bar, each miraculously balancing a collection of empty or freshly-filled glasses.

At the far end of the room the young blood of the street made uproarious music. In their midst were the Woodruff twins, Chick battering at the piano, Gus wrenching deafening disharmonies out of a piano-accordion. All the young men looked alike; big and well-built, with red, strong faces and abundant hair close-cropped round the base of the skull. Although none of them seemed beyond his middle-twenties, most of them moved and spoke with the authority and confidence of old soldiers. Their clothes were an answer to those who complain of lack of colour in our day — angularly-cut suits of bright blue that showed off (and embellished with Elizabethan shamelessness)

40

the magnificent proportions of shoulder and waist; sports outfits of dazzling light grey; exotic American jackets in tan or white with facings of coloured velvet; huge ties on which bolts of red and green lightning flashed across yellow sunglare or pink nymphs swam in lucent green; gay shirts of silk or creamy poplin; and splendid shoes on huge crepe soles. They always trooped about in great, rowdy gangs; they thought of themselves as the Lads of the Village, although the local middle classes (who did them an injustice, for they were a hard-working and law-abiding lot) were provoked by their animal high spirits to refer to them distastefully as 'the Lamb Street Yobs'. It was their mission, in this little community, always to be the life of the party. They went to football together every Saturday afternoon in the season, and boasted that even in a crowd of sixty thousand they could make themselves heard. They went to the pictures together in the evenings, where they were not ashamed to hail a beautiful actress with noisy approval or a particularly lush love scene with still noisier derision. Every year it was the Lads who organised a coach outing to Southend, and they could always be relied on to arrange a 'do' for the children or parties to celebrate coronations, victories or each other's weddings. On the street corner they assembled every evening as a public judging committee which pronounced aloud on the qualities of every girl who went past, and sometimes they might be seen playing Jimmy-Knacker (a violent and large-scale form of leapfrog) with as much gusto as the small boys who imitated and adored them. Their diversions, however, were entirely harmless, and it was with justice that their mothers swore that they were good boys.

The girls were confined to two basic patterns; some of them slender and painstakingly alluring, the others red-cheeked and heroically built. All of them were well dressed, and all of them displayed the same unflagging vigour. They and the Lads mingled in combative good nature like a horde of Katherines and Petruchios.

Chief among the Lads and this evening's choirmaster was the huge, red-haired Bernie Whiteflower. "Come on," he roared above the din — four years ago he had been a sergeant in the Army and he reinforced his appeal by brandishing his clenched fist as if he were rallying his platoon — "let's 'ear yer, let's 'EAR yer!" The Lads and their lasses bellowed and howled with redoubled volume; it was characteristic of the Lads that, while they could sing as harmoniously as a glee club when they were sitting on the top deck of a bus with their great knees poking out into the gangway, they considered it obligatory to caterwaul as tunelessly as possible when they were in a pub. Their elders sipped at foaming pints and went on talking solemnly, as if they could not hear the tumult; from time to time a group of them would stop talking, join absent-mindedly in a chorus or two and then resume their conversation. Bernie caught sight of Jack Agass and gave an order to the barman. "Oy!" Bernie hailed Jack with a costermonger's roar, and sent a pint off from hand to hand along the counter, "One pint of inspiration — comin' — UP!"

The drinks were lining up on the counter faster than Jack could cope with them. He was happier than he had been for years. The chatter, the shrieks of laughter, the music, the clink of glasses, the beer fumes and stale breath were more intoxicating than the liquor he was drinking. The whir of the fans beat on his confused mind. Lights burned unnoticed overhead but their beams reflected in mirrors, in massed bottles and on sweaty, glistening faces with a sickening brilliance that seemed to fuse all the heat and noise into a heavy blanket of unreality that sheltered him from the unkind world outside.

For a while he was freed from the ache of regret for his lost years and for the irrecoverable past which lay beyond them; the grinning faces of old friends appeared and vanished in the mist of sweat and tears, so many of them that for the moment he did not remember the missing ones whom the years had banished or struck down. There awoke in him a wild surge of derision at his own cowardice, four years ago, in throwing away his chance to come back to all this. Four years; he had thrown away four precious years; and all because — he thought again of his first sight of the patch of waste ground where his home had been, of the first few moments after he had heard about Rosie, and of the faces in the streets, all empty and unaware of the dead. Oh, what was the use of thinking about all that now?

"Enjoyin' yourself, boy?" Mr. Wakerell appeared at his side with a fresh glass of beer.

"Ah!" Jack wiped his hand across his forehead; it came away wet. "Feel like I do, you can get drunk without touching a drop. Straight up!"

"I know. Used to be a trick of my missus, when we were courting." Mellowed by beer, Mr. Wakerell was unexpectedly talkative, but his attitude was as shy and hangdog as ever, his voice as slow. "She wouldn't touch nothing but ginger ale in those days." He stared intently at the floor, and his words were spaced out as if he were picking them up one by one. "Nothing but ginger ale. Thirty years ago, that was. Little while back, eh? Nothing but ginger ale — and yet people always used to think she was drunk. It was just from laughing. Ah!" He made a wondering sound between tongue and teeth and withdrew for a few moments into private contemplation. "She could laugh, all right! Shriek the place down, tears pouring down her face, couldn't stop to save her life. I had to carry her home once. She was ill, just from laughing. She hadn't touched a drop." He shook his head, as if still amazed by the occurrences of thirty years ago. "Funny, she was brought up very select. Too polite to laugh out loud before she met me. I thought I'd found a quiet one there. And then, the very first time I took her out, off she went! Screaming with laughter! Frightened me out of my wits."

Jack looked across the room at Mrs. Wakerell. "I don't know about then, but she can't half mop it up now."

"Ah," Mr. Wakerell rumbled in an apologetic voice, "she soon got the taste for it. Can't blame her really. With me to put up with! Ha! Ha! One thing, she never shows it. You watch her afterwards. She'll walk home like a duchess."

"Doesn't Joycie ever come in with you?"

"Ha, no!" He laughed sadly. "Too high-class for us. I suppose it's working in that dress shop. She's one of these coffee-up-the-Corner-House girls. Well, that's the way her mother wants her."

Jack had spent a few minutes alone in the parlour with Joyce before coming out. After washing himself he had come into the room to find her reddening her lips in front of the mirror. She looked a different girl, full-bosomed but slender in a close-fitting fawn dress. Shampoo had given her fair hair a silken sheen. She was not wearing glasses; cream and powder had softened her complexion and her rouged lips were red and full. She took no notice of him, but he knew from the hostile set of her shoulders that she was aware of his presence. Abashed and delighted, he tried to think of a compliment to pay her. At last he said, "Whew! Talk about a dog's dinner!"

"Can't say the same for you," she said, without turning. "Suit's hanging off you like a busted banana skin."

"No use trying to button it up," he explained, pulling the jacket across his chest in proof, "give us a chance. Only been back a day. You wait till I been up the old Fifty Shilling."

"Wait? Me? If I had nothing more to look forward to but seeing you in a new suit I'd put my head in the oven tonight."

"Sweet kid, ain't you?"

"Sweet or sour as the fancy takes me." She turned to face him. She must have known that she had impressed him, for her attitude was more relaxed. "Only my fun, Jack. We're all glad to see you."

"Comin' up The Lamb?"

"No fear. Don't think me unsociable, but I've got better things to do than sit with all the old mums guzzling Guinnesses."

"Can't think of anything better myself. Where you going? Dancing?"

"No."

"Pictures?"

"No."

"I'll buy it."

"Who said I was selling?" Again there was the instinctive tension; again she relaxed, and this time she smiled. "In the park, if you must know. It's nice and cool, and there's a band playing, and it's all set out with tables and chairs, like the Continent. You can buy lemonade there."

"Who's the lucky chap?"

"Does your fiddle only play one tune?"

"I was only asking."

A few minutes later her friend arrived; a big, fat girl who stared at Jack until he cringed with embarrassment, and who, when she hurried out with Joyce, was obviously bursting to ask all about him.

"Funny girl," he muttered to himself, standing in the bar with his friends swarming about him.

"Wha's 'at, Jack?" said Barmy Naughton, the barman.

"Eh?" Jack became aware of his surroundings. "Only talking to myself. Must o' caught if off you, Barmy. Soon have people talking about *me*, eh?"

Barmy's eyes glowed a smile in their deep sockets, and his lips twisted, drawing the waxen skin tight over his skull. "Talk!" he said in a high, sharp voice. "Talk! You're right there. They talk. They look at yer." He broke off into a long, neighing laugh. "Don't you talk to yerself, Jack. Talk to yerself, yer barmy."

"'Ere!" Bernie Whiteflower was thumping on the counter. "'E's orf playing the First Bloody Gravedigger agin. 'Urry up with them five bitters, Barmy, an' never mind the sollyoloquy. Jack, boy, wha'r abah'r a song? I've burned me bloody throat out for your sake tonight. Time you obliged."

Jack listened joyfully to the clamour of approval. There

45

were the Wakerells smiling encouragement, the girls screaming and applauding, Chick Woodruff shouting, "What's it to be, boy? You say it, I'll play it!" He made a fuddled pretence of unwillingness. The applause increased. He had his arm — how had it happened? — round a woman's waist. She screwed moist lips against his cheek. "Elsie Cakebread!" he said, "I never see you come in." "Come on, Jack," she urged, *Lily of Laguna,* that used to be your favourite on the old charabanc, remember?"

He began to sing. The blur of white faces surrounded him. Oh, his friends, his friends! Wakerells, Braceys, Prawns, Woodruffs, Coggers, Bateses, Greens and Pennyfarthings, Elsie, Bernie, Barmy and all the others! Red faces and white faces grinning at him, mouths grotesquely open bawling at him; and, head and shoulders above them all, handsome and greyhaired, Mick Monaghan, moving among them with all the courtesy of a host in his bearing, yet aloof and watchful as a police inspector at a race meeting. Jack bellowed the chorus, glorying in the swoop and lilt of it and in the din that rolled back at him as everyone joined in. He was frantic with gratitude, brimful of wellbeing, and he poured it all out of him in the song. Elsie pressed against him, smothering him with love. The sweat was running down the back of his neck. He felt sick each time he looked up at the lights. He could have cried. He ended, "She is my Lillee-ee-ee" — prolonging the note with a glorious siren howl — "of Laguna, she is my lily and my rose."

There was more applause, and more drinks appeared on the counter in front of him. Elsie freed herself from his embrace and went back to her husband.

He lost track of the last hour. A tired, drugged feeling took possession of him. He sat down by Mrs. Wakerell, hardly able to keep his eyes open. He rested his head against her shoulder, and she made him comfortable as if he were a child. The roar and babble of voices became as meaningless and somniferous as the crash of waves and the crying of gulls on a sunny beach. He was only half aware of a voice shouting, "Time!" His hand was being shaken; people were moving past him, saying, "Goodnight!" "Goodnight!" "Goodnight!" He could only grin and mumble.

He followed the Wakerells to the door, feeling as if he were walking on water. Mick Monaghan, standing in the doorway, said, "Well, old soldier, you'll sleep tight tonight. By God you will!"

"Tight's the word," laughed Mrs. Wakerell. Jack, face to face with Monaghan, remembered the shock of rage and humiliation he had felt when they had first shaken hands earlier in the evening. There was a fleeting pang of it now. Mick said, "I'll tell Rosie you're home. She'll be putting flowers in her hair for you."

"What's it to me?" Jack thought, bitter and bewildered. He laughed idiotically and muttered, "Goo'night, Mick."

It was cool on the pavement. The twilight rang with parting shouts and the clatter of footsteps. A woman, lurching home, sang in an ugly voice and her husband could be heard hushing her, for, if drink was popular in Lamb Street, open drunkenness was not. Doors slammed. Quiet returned to the street.

Mrs. Wakerell led the way home, walking with a stately but perilous slowness. She saluted the last passers-by with a nod so slight that they might have been offended if they had not known how fearful she was of losing her balance. Her husband trudged after her, his loquacity dried up at its alcoholic source. The only sign of his condition was a slight forward lurch in his walk; this and the frown that creased his lowered face made him look like a bloodhound sniffing along the pavement. Jack, intoxicated anew by the fresh air, reeled behind them, laughing to himself.

At the front door, Mrs. Wakerell said, "Come on in, boy. You're going to stay the night, aren't you?"

Jack mumbled, "Got to go. Really got to be going."

47

"Rubbish! You couldn't walk to the corner, let alone get back to your hotel. Besides, Fred's old room's all ready for you. It won't be any trouble."

Jack followed gratefully into the house. Joyce was in the kitchen, reading a magazine. She said, "Hallo," in a disapproving voice. "I'll make you a cup of tea."

"Not for me, dear," said her mother. "It's bed for little me. Dear old, beautiful bed. Whoo! It is stuffy in here!"

"It wasn't before you came in," said Joyce. She hurried to support her mother, whose huge bulk was swaying on its narrow base. "Come on, I'll help you upstairs." She said, over her shoulder, to her father, "you give that one a hand —" she indicated Jack, who was slumped over a chair — "before he goes right off to sleep."

The two women disappeared. Jack could hear them toiling up the stairs. He let Mr. Wakerell drag him up on to his feet and lead him to the foot of the staircase. Mr. Wakerell put his foot on the first step and tugged. Jack stood as solid and still as a mule. Mr. Wakerell grunted, "Cerm — on!" and pulled again. Jack groaned, "Oh, Gawd!" and sat down on the bottom step with his head between his hands. Mr. Wakerell swayed above him, muttering to himself; then he expelled a long, hoarse, sigh, said despairingly, "I dunno!" and made his way upstairs alone, pulling himself up by the banisters.

Jack was still sitting on the stairs when Joyce came down. She said, "Another one!" Jack grinned at her. "Up you get," she said sharply. "Great baby, you are!" She stopped, put his arm round her shoulder and heaved him up on to his feet. "Come on now! And for Heaven's sake stop breathing beer all over me. I can't stand it. Up now, one, two, three, four — come on, you don't want me to pick your feet up, do you?"

She thrust him in through the door of his room, released him, then darted forward to catch him as he was on the point of falling. "Had a wonderful time, haven't you?" she said bitterly. "Grown man can't put himself to bed!"

"Lovely," cried Jack, suddenly speaking with a glassy clearness. "Lovely, lovely, lovely." He felt the words floating away from his mouth like bubbles. "Hup, they're lovely!" he shouted. "Ices, they're LOVELY!"

"Shut up! You'll have the neighbours knocking at the wall! This time of night!"

"Hoo-up, they're lovely. All alive-oh, all a lovely, lovely, live-oh!"

She flung him down on the bed. "Will you shut up?"

He sprawled backwards. "Happy, happy, happy. Happy and glorious." He sang rowdily, "Long to reign over us, happy and glorious —" He broke off and mumbled, "Happy as a, happy as a pig in —"

She smacked his face. "There! Dirty mouth! Now shut up!"

Jack said, "Ooh!" and stared at her.

He sat in stupid silence while she took off his shoes and socks. He sat up when she told him to, and let her pull off his jacket and tie.

"Now lie back," she commanded. She unbuttoned his trousers and began to pull them down. "You hold those pants up," she said, "I didn't come in here to see the poppy-show."

"Eeh," said Jack, as she tried to pull the blankets back from under him, "you're lovely. Ooh, you're lovely. Sweet and lovely! Juicy Joycie, the four-eyed beauty! Come and give us a cuddle, come on!"

"When the drink's in, the wit's out. Else I'd give you another backhander!"

"Ooh, she's soft and juicy! Come on, give us a squeeze!" He seized her wrist.

She pulled herself away and stood over him, rigid and furious. Her cheeks were burning. "Oh, you pig! Stinking, big pigs! Every one of you! You're all the same! There's only two things you think of! Well, you won't get any change out of me, I can tell you. And you can tell her too, if she asks you!"

"Her?"

49

"My lovely mother!" she cried, and rushed out of the room.

Jack stared at the door in bewilderment. At last he lay down, with his head in his arms. "Blind ol' Riley," he groaned, "What a night!" In two minutes he was asleep.

Chapter 5

JACK LAY IN BED until eleven o'clock on Sunday morning, thinking about the events of the previous night. He felt happy and victorious. At one rush, he imagined, he had crashed through the barrier of his own fears and reclaimed his place in the old life.

He knew what Joyce had meant by her last outburst. Her mother's intentions were clear. Well, he told himself, it suited him fine. When he had been young he had longed for a great passion. Somewhere inside him was a wistful memory of those desires which still tormented him from time to time and made the real business of living seem dreary and unsatisfying; but the old, wild hopes were now almost extinct, and his only conscious aspiration was to settle down. It was a home that he wanted, and the woman for whom he was looking was one who would fit into it. He had a notion that to be thirty years old was to be on the verge of old age. A week gone seemed like a last chance slipped by, and he was in a desperate hurry. He was not daunted by Joyce's attitude to him, nor by her apparent dislike of men. That only showed that she was respectable. Above all he sought respectability, both in his own future life and in whoever was going to share it. Most of the men among whom he had moved in the last ten years had had the same outlook, and the more degraded and violent their own lives had become, the more they had cherished it. He had sometimes heard, in a barrack-room conversation, some fellow soldier admitting that his wife loathed sexual intimacy and that he had to make her drunk before she would permit it. "Well," the

51

man would say defiantly, "it only goes to show she's a decent woman." And someone else would add, "That's right. If she liked it off you, she'd like it off any other sod that come along." Jack did not see marriage quite in this way, but he was inclined to think that there was something in what they said. He had known plenty of free and easy women, the companionable ones who were willing to listen to reason, the "good sports." This shy, nervous girl, who kept men at bay, appealed to him more than the lot of them. Besides, he was scared of passion. Four years ago someone had told him about Rosie, and it had been like a breath of flame in his face. For him, in future, the safe and comfortable emotions would suffice.

Therefore he was delighted when, at breakfast, Mrs. Wakerell — her placid voice betraying an undercurrent of anxiety that suggested much mental rehearsal — invited him to stay. They had been thinking of taking in a lodger, she said. Fred's room was a nice one, and Jack would be happier among friends than in a hotel or in a strange house. He accepted without giving her time to talk about the rent. Joyce, who had said "Good morning" when he had entered, poured tea and passed plates without showing any interest in the conversation. She was in hiding behind her glasses again. With her hair dull and ill-arranged and her body slack in a dressing gown, she looked as unprovoking as a draught mare. He was not deterred; she was well built and well spoken, her movements about the room were calm and decisive, she was clearly a sensible girl, and he noticed with admiration that it was she who, energetically and uncomplainingly, did most of the housework. Living with the Wakerells, he would be able to remove any bad impression that he might have made on her the previous night, and at the same time he would be able to con-solidate his position among his old friends.

These resolutions governed all his actions for the next few days. He had originally meant to spend at least a month in idleness but now, feverishly keen to "dig in" (as he put it) he decided to allow himself only a week's holiday.

He moved his belongings to his new home. He counted up his financial resources — with the remains of his Army gratuity, his savings, and the bonus from his job, he had nearly four hundred pounds — and opened a bank account, dropping self-conscious hints about his wealth to Mrs. Wakerell in order to impress her that he was a man of substance and a desirable son-in-law. He bought a blue suit, a sporty tweed jacket, a pair of chocolate slacks, and an array of shirts, ties and shoes.

He had thought of apologising to Joyce for his behaviour in the bedroom, but the task was beyond him. He made up his mind, instead, to demonstrate to her his sobriety and industriousness; for this purpose, and in order to entrench himself still more firmly in his new surroundings, he began at once his search for a job.

The clerk at the Labour Exchange quickly stripped him of the illusions which he had cultivated, leading men in the Army and training hundreds of labourers in Persia, that on his return home he would have the opportunity to better himself.

"Trade?"

"Eh? Shopfitter. I been in the Army, though —"

"Who hasn't, old man?"

"I can manage labour. I mean, I done it abroad."

"Any technical qualifications?"

"Eh? Technical? You mean? — Well, no."

"Want to work abroad again?"

"No fear!"

"No qualifications at all, except shopfitting?"

"Not really."

"Well, that's your best bet. You can't pick and choose these days, you know."

"Yes, but —"

"Look, laddie, I've spoken to thousands like you in the last few years. I'm afraid you'll have to tone your ideas down a bit, and take what you can get. I can give you one or two jobs to go after in your own line. Are you interested?"

Jack said he would come back later.

For a few days he looked at the 'Situations Vacant' columns in the newspapers. There was nothing for which he could offer himself. He lost heart quickly. He regarded himself as only an ordinary working chap; he was very self-conscious about his lack of education and his inability to speak 'clever'. He believed himself fated to spend all of his life in the station to which he was born, and his little fit of ambition soon evaporated. Driving him, too, was the fear of wasting time. "I can always look around later," he consoled himself, thus enabling himself to cling at least to a dream. On Friday he went back to the Labour Exchange. The clerk gave him an introduction card to a firm of shopfitters near King's Cross, and when he went home in the evening he was able to announce that he was starting work on Monday week.

Until he started work he got up late in the mornings, walked happily about London (how different everything looked when seen from *within* the stream of life!), enjoyed himself shopping with Mrs. Wakerell in Chapel Market, passed agreeable evenings on the street corner with Bernie and the boys, spent an evening at the pictures, another at Collins' Music Hall and another at an Irish dance, had an occasional drink and paid visits to old acquaintances.

"It's funny," he said, struggling one day to explain himself to Nancy Hogarth, to whom his first visit had been made. "I mean, the way you sort of come alive sometimes. Five days a week you walk past the pillar-box, don't even see it. Next day you go past, and you see it's red. I mean, sounds daft an' all that, but —". That was the nearest he could get to describing how beautiful life had become, and how vivid and startling an apprehension he had acquired of everything around him. Because he was happy, he heard the birds singing in the squares, although he could not remember having noticed them before; he grinned at babies in their prams, chatted with the old men who sat smoking their pipes in the park, was aware of the fresh, glinting leaves of chestnut trees in drab front gardens, and sang to himself as he pushed through crowds.

He wallowed in the friendship that was proffered to him from every hand. The news of his return had spread, and he was surprised by the number of people to whom it seemed to matter. The tobacconist called him into his shop as he went by, and told the girl behind the counter, "Here, Lil, twenty Players for this feller any time he comes in." The butcher said to Mrs. Wakerell, "I hear young Jackie Agass has come back," and slapped an extra piece of liver into her parcel. Jack came down to breakfast one morning and was given two new-laid eggs. "You're popular," Joyce said, "the milkman brought them for you." Even vendors in the market called to him, "Hi, yer! Jackie boy!" or "You're Jackie Agass, ain't you? Thought I remembered you."

It even occurred to a number of people that he would be needing a wife, and some — as was their way — offered him their help in finding one. "Time you got wed, ain't it?" said old Mr. Prawn. "Reckon so," Jack mumbled, "Look around a bit first, though." Nancy Hogarth, who counted herself as his sister, went straight to the point. "I know just the girl for you, Jack. What about it?" "Give us a chance," Jack said, "I might have ideas of my own, you know." The idea of inspecting a series of alternative prospects was attractive, but he lacked the boldness to do so, and decided to stick to Joyce.

He and Joyce maintained a civil but wary relationship. Several times during the week he asked her to go out with him, but she refused, offering him on each occasion a downcast smile and an excuse that was carefully chosen to avoid hurting his feelings.

On Saturday evening Mr. and Mrs. Wakerell went out to The Lamb. Jack said that he was going to stay at home for an hour or two. Joyce was in the house, and it was obvious from her dress that she was not thinking of going out.

"Where's your pal tonight?" Jack asked.

"She's got a date."

"Don't you ever have dates?"

"Sometimes. I didn't feel like going out tonight. This weather gives me a headache."

"I'll get you some aspirins."

"It's all right."

"No, really, it's no trouble. I thought you might, like, well — later on — if you get over it —"

"I'd just like to lie down," she said, "have a bit of peace and quiet."

Jack took the hint and left her alone. An hour later, after sitting in his room in a state of growing impatience, he came downstairs again, and said to her, "It's cool out now. Do your headache good. What about a bit of a walk?"

"No thanks, Jack."

He sat down in the armchair opposite her. She sprawled on the couch, face downwards, with her chin resting on her clenched fists, staring out of the window. She looked unhappy. They remained together in silence for a while, with the tension growing between them. At last, Jack said, "Feel any better?"

"You go on out, Jack. It's getting late." Her voice was not unkind; perhaps, against her will, she felt gratified by his male persistence.

"Don't worry about me," he said. "I'd wait all the evening if I thought — I mean."

She smiled faintly, not looking at him. "Be a pal and leave me alone."

"All right." He wandered doubtfully towards the door. He paused and exclaimed, "Look, what's the matter with me? I'm not poison, am I?"

She did not answer.

"Well, you might say something," he said, in an aggrieved voice.

"Oh, for God's sake, leave me alone," she cried.

"What's up?" he asked in despair.

"I'm fed up with it, and that's straight. Her trying to

56

push me on to you all the time, and you laughing at me."

"Me laughing at you?"

"You and that grin on your face. Certainly see the funny side of things, can't you? Grin, grin, grin!"

Jack was speechless. In a moment he would be defeated, and would flee; if he did, he was afraid that he would never be able to face her again. He said, with great savagery, "My bloody face!"

Joyce looked at him in wonderment. "Why? What's up with it?"

"I'm not laughing at you," said Jack desperately, "I never have. I mean, I never know how to look when people look at me, so I just grin. Me and my bloody grin! Hark at me! Thirty years old! You wouldn't think it, would you? Mad Jack Agass, that's me!"

Joyce sat up slowly. She said nothing, but her movements and her attitude as she faced him were soft and conciliatory. Her face was troubled. "Oh, I'm sorry Jack. I upset you, didn't I? I got fed up with myself and I took it out on you." She added, with solicitude. "You're not mad, Jack. You don't want to talk like that."

Jack took courage again. "Well, what about it, then?"

"What about what?"

"Comin' up the pictures with us. It's cool up the Odeon. Air-conditioned."

"All right," she said, "might as well."

"Here —" he was eager to say his piece before speech deserted him once more — "Here, I wish you wouldn't keep throwing your mum at me every time. I mean, I can't help liking you, can I? I don't know what it's got to do with her, throwin' her up at me every time."

Joyce laughed. "I can just see me throwing my mum at you. I'd sooner try and throw the *Queen Mary*. Wait for me, I won't be long."

Her step was light. She could not conceal her excitement as she hurried out of the room. "I don't know," said Jack to himself, "rummest bloody lot on earth, they are, and that's a fact."

Chapter 6

JACK AND JOYCE enjoyed their evening together. Jack had little to say. Joyce appeared pleased to be allowed to sit by his side in silence and, after the show, to wander along beside him lost in her own thoughts; he, in turn, was glad that she did not impose on him the agonising duty of making conversation. Thus the first sentiment that awoke between them was one of mutual gratitude.

Encouraged by this beginning, they went out together almost every night. At first, little passed between them. Jack would make a suggestion; Joyce would accept it meekly and as meekly follow him to the park. They would settle themselves side by side in deck chairs and sit for a long time without speaking, looking up at the pale evening sky, not even daring to turn their heads and look at each other. Their arms would dangle close together in the space between the chairs, and when they accidentally touched each other both he and she would flinch. Jack spent the whole of one evening trying to goad himself to hook his little finger in hers, but he could not find the courage. Nevertheless they were happy together, and each gradually became aware of the other's happiness, so that the lazy contentment each felt after the heat and work of the day, while it made them behave abstractedly and remotely towards each other, became in reality a second bond between them.

Jack had started work. He found that, even when he was apart from Joyce, there remained with him a sense of wonder at what had befallen him. From time to time, during the day's work, he would be visited by mysterious impulses of glee, that came and went without explaining themselves, and with moments of physical excitement that left him breathless. He discovered, to his astonishment, that he could face strangers without embarrassment. What was it that was changing him and opening all the world's doors to him? It was not what he had once known as love. He could look at Joyce calmly, face without dismay the prospect of not seeing her for an evening, take note of her defects as well as her merits, weigh up cold-bloodedly the arguments for and against pushing matters any further with her; it had not been like that with Rose. It was — and he was aware of it, for he knew what had ailed him in the past — the joy of relief from loneliness. For four years, ever since he had left his battalion, he had been lonely; he had been lonely with his companions in Persia, he had been lonely in card games and at drinking parties, he had been loneliest of all in the arms of women. He guessed, too, from Joyce's demeanour, that she felt the same relief, for her heavy face had become relaxed and gentle (at least, to his eyes); the wariness that he had seen in her every attitude like the defensive crouch of an animal gave way to a tenderness that made her seem almost graceful; she tackled the housework as quickly and deftly as before, but in place of the anxiety and impatience that had formerly driven her he imagined he saw a confident womanliness. Sometimes, as she looked up at him, he would see a frank and wondering expression on her face until, catching his eye, she would frown self-consciously.

In a few days their relationship underwent a new transformation. At first it was he who took heart and, labouring to find words, began to speak more freely to her; then she, flattered by his confidences, responded. Soon their tongues loosened and, as is often the case with shy people, they were chattering away to each other without mercy, each eager to pour out pent-up thoughts and feelings, each beginning every sentence with the word 'I', each greedily leaping in to take over the conversation as soon as the other paused unwillingly for breath.

Listening to her confessions, he learned a good deal about her, not so much from what she said as from the nature of the evasions, the pathetic little excuses and self-delusions to which she resorted.

"Go on," he said once, "tell us about some of your other boy-friends." Her face went rigid, her mouth was open for a second before she spoke, then she answered with a rush of words. "Oh, I've had a few. I've never thought much of them. Not the boys round here. They're a rough lot, not my type really. Maureen, my friend, she's often tried to get me to make up a foursome. Too particular, that's what she says I am. But I think, you can't be too particular, that's what I say. These chaps she goes with, no intelligence they've got. They just talk and talk and talk, and they wait for you to laugh and —" her voice rose to a comical wail — "they're so silly really. And then they get fresh. Well, I mean, if you don't make a chap respect you he knows you don't respect yourself. Liberty-takers most of them are! Then these chaps that go up the dogs and all that! I always did say, a chap that gambles is a weakling. Don't you think?" Her talk was carrying her she knew not where, like a runaway horse. She was too embarrassed to stop gabbling, and he had to save her by cutting in and desperately inventing an anecdote about how he had once gone to the dog races and learned his lesson.

He tried to discover why she was so defensive in her manner, so lacking in the natural sociability with which most of the inhabitants of the street were endowed.

"I hate that lot up on the corner," she said. "Don't you? All those boys? The way they whistle when you go past?"

"Oh, I don't know," said Jack, remembering his own young days.

"I've never had anything to do with them," she said with an almost vicious energy, "and I'm not sorry, either. I've got my mum to thank for that. She never used to let me play with just anyone, even when I was a kid. Ever so particular who I used to talk to, she was. Even after I left school. She used to ask, 'Who you going out with?' 'Is she a nice girl?' 'That wasn't Maisie Keenan I saw you with, was it?' That Maisie Keenan. Do you remember her? She got married in the war, and good riddance."

"Yes." Jack smothered a grin of knowing reminiscence. "I knew Maisie. She was a lad, all right." A nostalgic recollection came to him. "We all had bikes in my time. Proper craze, it was. We had a good time, too, mucking around in the evenings and all going out together at weekends."

"I know," there was a sudden leap of response in her voice. "I wanted one once. I cried my eyes out over it, night after night. Dad wanted to get me one. But mum said she had better things to do with her money than let me kill myself under a bus. She said she could just see herself letting me fly about in a pair of shorts showing everything off."

He taxed her with her submission to the lazy tyranny which her mother exercised in the house. Except for one occasion when she cried, "My mum won't give me credit for being grown up," she would defend her mother, or merely reply, with a tell-tale drag of hopelessness in her voice, "Oh, mum's all right." Once she added, "Besides, I won't always be living here."

At moments like this their conversations would break down and they would lapse into an embarrassed silence; for there was a limit to their confidences. As soon as either of them revealed, in some unthinking remark, the hopes which by now Jack knew they both cherished, both of them would shrink back. Neither of them knew how to go forward on to a more intimate footing.

Jack, for his part, spoke mostly of his youth in Lamb Street, which his memory served up to him as a sort of Golden Age; of the war, about which it gave him a sense of joyous relief to brag and yarn until one evening he realised, from the remote look in Joyce's eyes, that he might as well have been telling her how Drake beat the Armada; and about his new job. He was finding it hard going. For the last couple of years abroad his duties had been mainly supervisory and, muscular though he was, he came home every evening aching throughout his body at the unaccustomed toil. His employer, not yet knowing his capabilities, left him in the workshop, sawing and planing while other men went out to install the fittings. "Boy's work," he said bitterly, "and I'm older than most of them. Snotty-nosed kids, that's all they are, never done a real craftsman's job any of them. And the way they take the mickey out of me — try to, anyway — you wouldn't think they'd never heard a shot fired in anger."

Mrs. Wakerell watched their clumsy courtship with complacent interest. Sometimes Jack felt angry under her knowing scrutiny. He wanted to tell her that he knew all about her little plot, and there were even moments when he felt so humiliated that he wanted to pack his bags and run away. He was frightened, too, by the knowledge that a similar feeling of shame was at work in Joyce. However, he could not help liking Mrs. Wakerell, and he was convinced that her kindness to him was, at bottom, disinterested. Since Jack and Joyce were not deficient in the human talent for defeating circumstances by accepting them, they came at last to believe that they were outwitting Mrs. Wakerell by sharing the knowledge of her intentions. When, as they went out together, she said, "Enjoy yourselves, my dears," they would exchange guarded smiles. They considered themselves to be in alliance against her, although the conspiracy remained tacit.

Jack had been home for three weeks and had been going about with Joyce for a fortnight when he decided that it was time for the next step. Other people had begun to notice the change in Joyce. Neighbours remarked that she was looking well. Her father heard her singing to herself in her room and asked her at breakfast if she had come into a fortune. She was still obedient to her mother's incessant commands, but she had acquired the gift of infusing a hint of restrained mockery into her quiet replies. It flattered Jack's vanity to know that he was responsible for all this. It added to the feeling he gained from their constant proximity — at meals, talking to each other while she was washing her hair in the kitchen, passing each other half-dressed on the landing — that he was already half-way to being a husband. Yet once they were out of doors they were nothing more than old friends to each other. The barrier of shyness remained.

They were coming home one evening from a dance. The heat in the hall had been sweltering. They had danced stiffly and ceremoniously together. Jack had been unable to abandon himself to her embrace and had felt the same resistance in her. Other women had inflamed him in the intimacy of a dance, but she — he could not understand why — daunted him. Even walking at her side in the cool street he felt tamed and without ardour.

It was therefore quite cold-bloodedly, as a matter of tactics and as a test of his own courage that he decided that he must kiss her tonight.

They reached the house and went into the kitchen. She made tea. When they had finished she yawned demonstratively and said, "Well, I don't know about you, but I'm ready for bed." He followed her into the hall, and at the foot of the stairs he took her arm and said, "Here, what's the hurry? Let's sit in the parlour for a bit."

"Whatever for?"

"I don't know. Talk a bit."

Her face, half averted, betrayed a piteous consternation. She shook her hair, closed her mouth angrily and blinked. "On the sofa with the lights off, I suppose," she said in a grating voice.

"Well, I don't see what's wrong with that. Usual thing, ain't it?"

"Not for me it isn't." She gripped the knob of the banisters and stared at her own knuckles, a picture of panic. "Let *go* of me."

He let his hand drop. She hurried up a couple of steps, paused, said agitatedly, "G'night, Jack," and scuttled up to her room.

This repulse came as a shock to Jack, whose hopes had been raised by the soft and compliant manner in which Joyce had followed him about for the last few days. His confidence in his own judgment collapsed. He went up to his room in a bitter and despondent mood. Where was the courage which had lightened his step for the last week? Where were the speeches he had composed and silently rehearsed day after day at work? Where were the manly understanding, the boldness and the resourcefulness on which he had begun to pride himself? He reproached himself for not having persisted. One scared reply from her, and he had let go her arm and stood gaping while she escaped. Surely there was something he could have said to hold her, something graceful to flatter her, something amusing to charm her, some assurance, softly and slowly spoken, to allay her terror?

Lying in bed in a daze of self-reproach and self-pity, he stared at the ceiling, sleepless and miserable. He was unable to calm himself by rallying his thoughts and planning his next move. The inarticulacy that fettered him was not of speech alone; his thoughts, too, were inarticulate. A new situation, or a remark addressed to him, on any but the most trivial of matters, would scare up inside him a flock of unformed and contradictory ideas which hurtled about, getting in each other's way, colliding with each other, each eluding capture until he was thoroughly maddened, and fighting vainly for release with such power that his head would ache as if they were all battering at the inside of his skull. He would rather wrestle, any day, with a man twice his own size than with a problem that demanded clear and logical thinking. A hard day at the bench was less exhausting than a half-hour's brainwork.

As the night went by his bitterness against himself turned into anger against Joyce. This usually happened with him. When he had been trapped into a conversation that made excessive demands on him, he would rage against his innocent interlocutor; if a crisis caught him unawares and left him too confused to act until it was too late, he would choke with resentment against whoever had unwittingly reminded him of his own inadequacy. "The bitch," he said to himself in the darkness, "the silly little bitch! Having me on like that! Don't know her own mind! What's she afraid of? Who does she think I am, anyway, mucking me about like that?"

He went down to breakfast the next morning in a bad temper. He avoided Joyce, muttered an unintelligible reply to her timid greeting, toyed sulkily with his food like a small boy who wants to show that he is hurt, and glared at her in triumph when her mother told him that he looked pale this morning.

At work, the day seemed endless. The workshop was hot and things that did not usually worry him — the smell of dust and glue, the nagging drone of the circular saw, the sawdust which he inhaled and which settled itchily on his sweaty skin — combined to torment him. He drove his jack-plane as if he were punishing Joyce and snarled when his employer pointed out mildly that he had both blunted the blade of the plane and spoiled a good piece of wood. He was tired from lack of sleep, his thoughts were still clamant and confused, and — worst of all — he felt more of a fool every minute. He went to the cinema alone in the evening and sat impatiently through a stupid film which he had seen before. He went to bed early and had another unhappy night.

When he came face to face with Joyce the next morning she was cold and calm towards him. He said, "Good morning" in a questioning voice and she answered curtly. They both ate their breakfast in a subdued mood. He kept looking at her as if expecting her to say something; sometimes he caught her glancing at him. He tried to think of something to say, but without success. Embarrassed, he swallowed the last of his tea and rose to go out. He said, "Well, s'long." She raised her teacup to her lips, looking down into it to avoid his eyes. She tried to sip, and gasped with annoyance as a nervous jerk of her hand spilled tea. The breath in his throat felt icy cold for a second. He stared at her. Conscious of his stare, she put her cup down, still looking at it. The blood rushed to her cheeks.

He said roughly, trying to make his words sound as casual as possible, "Here, what about tonight? I'm going on the lake up Finsbury Park. Room for two in the old boat. No use wasting money. You can come if you want."

She turned pale, then blushed more fiercely than before. She raised her head as if it were too heavy. "As you like —" — there was a tiny quiver in the first few words; the rest of her reply was in the same tone of indifference as his invitation — "— I've got nothing better to do."

They spent the evening together in the park and returned in a good humour. In the hall he said, "Sittin' up for a bit?" and pointed to the parlour. His mood was as passionless and calculating as it had been two nights earlier. All his thoughts were about himself; it was his own courage that concerned him. His attitude to Joyce was that of a rider to a horse which has thrown him once. She followed him into the parlour like a victim and sat beside him on the sofa. They talked for a while in dead voices. Jack sat with his hands clasped between his knees. He asked, "Want the light on?"

She said, "No, it's all right."

He put his arms round her waist and kissed the side of her face. She drew back a little. He pressed her back, stretching his body over hers, and kissed her on the mouth. She felt as hard as a board against him, and her lips hardly moved beneath his. She clutched his shoulders, not in desire but as if fighting pain. They sprawled together for a while. He was wondering at the inertness of his own body; holding her, he felt only lethargic and content. It would be pleasant to go to sleep like this. He forced himself to think about his next move; not to rouse himself or her, but with purely experimental intent. He put his hand over a slack, soft breast. There was no response; but at least he had made the nature of their relations clear; there ought to be no fear of losing ground now. A few more tasteless kisses to stamp and seal the business, and he sat back. She leaned back against the headrest, and sighed. They were sitting apart again, and in silence.

They listened to the dance music that came from a distant radio set, and to the people who were still talking in the street. Once they laughed together at a sudden exchange of abuse that shrilled from a window opposite. Jack was wondering how to extricate himself from this silence. Alarm grew in him at the way in which he was letting his latest successes ebb away. What should he do next? Make another grab at her? — but what then? Mumble 'goodnight' and go off to bed? — but what a defeat that would be! He dared not press her too far, but he was aware that in some subtle way the night's business was unfinished, and he did not know how to finish it.

It was Joyce who, astonishingly, made the next move. He did not reflect until years later on the courage that she must have needed at this moment. She, too, must have been filled with hesitation, with shame at her own shyness, with the same fear as his that they would lose the ground they had gained and would meet in the morning constrained and apart once more; not that he ever gave her the credit she deserved — for, looking back on that moment, he thought how different things might have been if he — he! — had not gone through with it.

She picked up his hand, as if it did not belong to him, and began to examine it. He looked on as if he, too, did not recognize the hand as a part of himself. Her fingers passed gently, like a blind woman's, over his broad, rough finger-tips, lingering compassionately over a split, blackened nail. With the nail of her forefinger she

67

scratched softly at the hard skin of the palm. Timidly she lifted the hand up to her mouth; he suspected that she was surprised by the dead weight of it. She gave him a startled sidelong blink, then bent her head again and touched his knuckles with her lips.

He almost laughed. He leaned over her, and they kissed warmly. He stroked her back, feeling with relief the nervous movements beneath the fabric of her dress. Her breath touched his cheek in warm, regular jets, and the faint, chestnut taste of her mouth remained in his. At last his sense of possession was unchallenged. There was nothing to sap his self-respect; he was sure that everything was going to be all right.

After that they went, unhurriedly, to their rooms.

It became a habit for them to go into the parlour every night before bedtime, and to sit in the dark, holding hands, hugging each other, kissing occasionally and talking quietly of unimportant things.

Jack experienced a new elation which arose more from the banishment of uncertainty than from his feelings for Joyce. His vanity was restored, the critic inside him silenced. He had been in the dark, but from here onwards he knew the way. Male pride could be discerned both in his voice and in his gait. Indeed, he was so carried away by his bravado that his excited tongue brought the affair rapidly to a climax while his mind, outpaced and bewildered once more, scarcely grasped what was happening. While he was flushed and fuddled, Joyce remained calm. She did not cling to him, blush at his gaze or show any ardour in his embrace. Instead she assumed a confident and business-like concern in all his affairs. She told him off because there were holes in his socks, criticised her mother for letting his tea get cold, showed him where he could buy shirts more cheaply, praised his taste in ties, made fun of his red ears, hung plastic curtains in his bedroom, and so kept him stupid with delight.

In little more than a week he was ready to take the final plunge. He took her out of the house after tea and walked with her along Upper Street, wondering how to introduce the subject of marriage. He paused in front of a shop window. "Here —" he pointed to a white silk blouse with a lace collar and pleated breast — "that's just your style, I reckon. Just suit you, that, with a long, dark skirt, and you ought to do your hair right back on both sides, like, to go with it."

"Bit too school-teachery for me."

"No. Ladylike, that's all. Just your style."

She said that she would rather have a flowered summer frock.

"Ah," he said, "that's all right. Cool, it looks. Don't cost such a lot either. Smashin' nightdress over there. Look, that blue one. Silk, ain' it?"

"Cut low, isn't it?"

"Well?" he said boldly. The conversation came to a stop.

They went on window-shopping, growing more and more excited. Jack was as enraptured as if he were really buying her these beautiful new clothes or furnishing a home for the two of them. Soon they were both absorbed in the game, like children; but it had a double meaning for both of them.

"That's what I call classy." They were looking at a bedroom suite. "Walnut veneer," Jack said. "Look at that dressing table. See you in front of that combing your hair, eh? Talk about Rita Hayworth!"

"Go on, silly!"

"No kid! Six-foot wardrobe, too. I'd need a few more suits to fill that one up! Smashin' eh?"

"It ought to be, at sixty-eight pounds."

"That's nothing. I've got four hundred in the bank."

She blurted, "I've got a hundred pounds saved up, too."

The conversation dried up again. They walked on from shop to shop, not holding hands but swaying towards each other and bumping shoulders. They argued about the merits of radio sets, wistfully admired a refrigerator, and examined crockery.

"Look here —" Jack was deep in his own thoughts when

he heard his voice rattling away recklessly — "what about it? I mean, getting wed. Could do with a place of my own, couldn't you?" He listened to himself in wonderment. He felt numbed. "No use beating about the bush. Don't see the sense in wasting time. I mean. Sooner the better. Been thinkin' about it long enough. I reckon we get on all right together, eh?"

Joyce walked on for a few paces before she answered. "We've hardly been going together for a month."

"Month? Known you half your life, I have. That's enough, ain' it?"

"Not really we haven't. Just to say 'hallo'. And not even that for the last ten years. It's very true what they say, too often the modern girl doesn't take marriage seriously enough. It's all right for these people in the papers who get divorced five or six times —"

"Here, who's talking about getting divorced?"

"Well," she persisted, "I'm only saying. It's for a lifetime, and you ought to make sure of each other first."

"We can be engaged, can't we? I mean, it'll take a few months to find a flat. And getting some things together. Trousseau, all that caper. No harm doing things properly, I'm all for it. As long as we've got it settled."

She slipped her arm through his. "You know what I'd like, Jack? — a little house, somewhere on the outskirts. We could make a down payment and get a mortgage." She had forgotten her own objections; and evidently she regarded the matter as so clearly settled that it was not necessary to say 'yes'. She held on to Jack possessively, and outlined her plans to him with the unflagging clarity of a well-briefed lecturer. For the rest of their walk, while he was recovering from the shock of what had happened to him, he had little to do but listen.

They arrived home. Mr. Wakerell was working in the garden. Joyce called, "Hallo, dad," but did not go out to see him. "Where's mum?" she said, looking into rooms. "She must be upstairs." "Mum!" she called, scampering up the stairs. "Mum!" — on the landing. "Mum! —" Her voice was tremulous as she opened the door of her parents' bedroom. Jack heard her begin, "He's asked me!" before the door closed behind her.

He lingered in the hall. The recklessness had deserted him. From time to time he felt a twinge of fright; otherwise he felt deflated. His mind struggled to put words together and compose a lecture to him about his good fortune, about the significance of the tremendous change that had occurred in his life, about the reward which his ruthlessness in pursuit had brought him; but from beneath there came fluttering up a flock of new doubts and questions, undefined but disturbing, to disrupt the laboured progress of his thoughts. Amid the familiar confusion there stirred a vague enquiry as to who, in the chase just ended, had been the quarry. He stamped it out. A chap always felt a bit rocky after he'd shown what he was made of; he'd learned that in the war. And by God, he decided, he'd shown his mettle this time, all right.

Part 2

Chapter 1

THE FIRST EIGHT YEARS OF JACK'S LIFE were less than a memory to him; they were an oppressive background to memory, in which shadows flitted to emerge, on rare occasions, with startling clarity as figures of flesh and blood, and to disappear as suddenly, leaving only an untraceable trail of disturbed emotion.

He retained a picture of the Orphanage building, which, photographed on to a child's mind and enlarged by the imagination, he still pictured as a red brick fortress of terrifying vastness. Of its interior he could only remember a few corners: a classroom where he had sat staring with longing at the potted buttercups on the windowsill: a battered wall with a wicket chalked on it before which he had played cricket: a little dip in the playing field where he had hidden in the uncut grass to imagine himself free and alone, a hunter in the jungle, watching the ants crawl among the tall blades: the lavatory in which he had helped to beat another boy: the stained, wooden tables in the dining hall with the endless perspectives of little, cropped heads bent over plates; and a dark staircase leading down to the boiler-room, which he had always been frightened to use.

He had the impression — an unjust one, perhaps — that the whole of this part of his life had been passed in a state of fright; through the shadows at the back of his mind there tramped an endless crocodile of small boys, all dressed in plum-coloured jerseys and too-short shorts, eating, studying, going off to play or to bed in disciplined ranks like troops of little soldiers, pathetically meek when they were thus marshalled, pathetically high-spirited when they were running free, pathetically ferocious to the weak in their midst and pathetically grateful for the kindnesses that were doled out to them like chocolate bars. None of his preceptors had ever been unkind; but, with the exception of a Matron on whom he had lavished an extravagant and unrecognized love, they had all — the stern, the earnest, the tired, the offhanded and the hearty — moved about among the children like remote and forbidding giants.

He had never, at the Orphange, learned any more about himself than that he was a 'war orphan'. This information was always given to him in a tone that discouraged further questioning. To the children in the Orphanage 'the war' — that earlier war which now to Jack was no more real than any other episode in schoolbook history — was not a past event but a terrible and mysterious presence. It never left them. Most of them suspected that it was still going on. A teacher once told Jack about hospital blue, and for years afterwards, whenever Jack saw Air Force men in the streets he thought that they were wounded walking out. A friend of his named Edwin Veazey, one of the few children who knew anything about their parents, used to boast, 'My dad was gassed', and the other boys would envy him as if he had said, 'My dad plays centre-forward for the Spurs'. In those years — the early nineteen-twenties — the children still sometimes came across old magazines like the *War Illustrated* or the *Penny War Weekly;* they studied the pictures for hours at a time, spellbound with terror and admiration. They talked of 'The War' as fever-ishly as they talked of sex a few years later: it was fearful, wonderful and fantastic. Once Jack had written in an essay, 'I would like to go in the War when I grow up'; another time, after looking at a picture book, he had had a nightmare, full of star-shells and huge Germans with brutal faces and saw-edged bayonets. For years the word 'Zeppelin' terrified him. He could not remember having speculated with any intensity about his unknown parents, or having had any feelings about them. It was only years later, passing idle hours in a slit trench in the second war, that he had wondered what lonely woman and what passing soldier had conceived him in that war-weary spring of nineteen-eighteen. Why had his mother not kept him? — he asked. Perhaps — and this was the picture he let his fancy form — she was the wife of another soldier. Where was she now, and where were the men? In the summer break-through of nineteen forty-four he looked out over the tailboard of a lorry at the old cemeteries fleeting backwards, frequent as orchards, and wondered — with a touch of feeling that did not go deep enough to become pity — if his father lay beneath one of those innumerable white headstones.

His real, remembered life began on a beach in Sussex in nineteen twenty-seven; it was to the memory of the years that followed, up to the outbreak of the second war, that he fled for refuge in moments of frustration or defeat. He did not recall in detail everything that had happened ('After all', Mrs. Hogarth had once said to him, turning aside some question he had asked her about her past life, 'it'd take nigh on twenty years to remember *everything* that happened in twenty years') but his memory — that artist in all of us which selects, arranges, suppresses, falsifies and exaggerates to create the pictures that our needs commission — presented the period to him as a series of dazzling canvases to which he returned, again and again, like a man to an art gallery, to exult, to worship and to marvel that such beauty was possible.

In the summer of Jack's eighth year he was staying at the holiday home which the Orphanage maintained in Sussex. This was the best time of the year for him, not only for the joy which he felt in common with all other children at going to the seaside, but because it enabled him to study at close quarters the mysterious multitudes of human beings who inhabited the world outside the

Orphanage. At no other time did he have any dealings with the rest of the human race; the orphans lived so self-contained a life that it gave them a fierce pleasure even to exchange shouted insults at a distance with other small boys. Every morning on the beach he would wander away from the escorted group and squat on his heels near some family party, staring in a stunned silence at these representatives of a species to which, as far as he knew, he did not belong. His mind could not reach to envy: it merely recorded, in wonder, the astonishing spectacle of children whose freedom gave them a light-footedness which he had never before seen, of the way in which they flung themselves without fear or hesitation upon their parents' laps, of fathers indulging in antics of which he had never imagined that any grown-up was capable. These children lacked his outward meekness, for they often approached him without fear; they also lacked his inward ferocity, and they were not provoked when he glared at them. He had often laughed and heard laughter, but never of the kind with which the beach rang on these sunny mornings. He would pass whole hours in this way, until a parent, disconcerted, would drive him away, or until — sometimes just as he was trying to pluck up courage to accept a proffered apple — his teacher would bustle up and say, "Come away, Jack, it's rude to stare, I've told you before".

One morning he was staring at a woman and her three children when his teacher came up and took him by the hand. "Leave him be, miss," said the woman, "he's not doing any harm". He stayed. The woman gave him a sandwich, addressed him as Sunny Jim and asked him his name. His lips parted and shaped the word, but no sound came forth. "Ooh," said the woman, "the wind blew it away. You have to shout loud here or the wind blows it right out of your mouth before anyone can hear you. Listen." She mouthed a word silently. "There! Gone flying away before anyone could hear it, eh?" Jack uttered a hooting little laugh. "Now," the woman said, "try it again, quick, while the wind's dropped." Jack barked, "Jack!" as if he were answering a roll-call. He stared at her for a moment, then laughed loudly, and all the children joined in. "Well," the woman said, "this is Alf, this is Chris, and this one under the deckchair — come on out, you little puss — is Rose. Now off you go, all of you, and let me have a nap."

For the rest of his holiday he played with the family — the Hogarths, as he soon learned — every day. Mrs. Hogarth fed him, bought him ices, dried his feet when he had been paddling and took him one evening, with his teacher's permission, along with her own family to the concert on the pier. He learned that they lived in London, and that there was an older girl, Nancy, who had not come because she was fourteen and had started work in a tobacco factory. Rose told him, as if she were matching a boast of his when he said that he had no parents, that their father was dead. Jack hung about the Hogarths with passionate devotion, happy to the point of hysteria yet sick with dread at the thought that soon he must part from them. Mrs. Hogarth's affection for him became more plain every day. He learned from the children that a little brother of theirs, Tony, had died three months before. "He's gone away to daddy," said Rose, who was five years old. Chris, pale, bespectacled, bronchial and thirteen years old, explained when her back was turned, "She don't know, he's dead, she's too young. He got pneumonia." Years later Mrs. Hogarth was to open her heart to him. "I was fit to die myself that summer," she said, "I couldn't forget him, so little, and his big eyes and his cheeks on fire. Trouble is, I was afraid I'd make the kids miserable, too. It was Mick put me up to going away for a week with them. Best thing I could have done. I can't tell you what it meant when you walked up to us. Lonely little mite you were. You might say I had room for you —" she touched her breast — "here".

When the time came for the Hogarths to go home Jack begged, "Take me with you, missis," and Mrs. Hogarth, embracing him, told him, "Don't you fret, my love. It won't be many days before we see each other again." She kept her word. Every week she came to visit him at the Orphanage. She and the children sent him letters, postcards, parcels; he had toys of his own, sweets, cakes and clothes in such quantities that the Orphanage authorities had to intervene. For months Mrs. Hogarth tried to get permission to adopt him. She obtained letters of recommendation from the vicar, paid a solicitor to represent her and once brought Mick Monaghan (it was the first time Jack saw him) to speak for her before the Governing Board. Her efforts failed: a poor widow with a family of four was not considered a fit person to adopt a child. When Jack was a little older, however, he was allowed to visit the Hogarths at weekends. His whole life changed. He became more talkative, and among his fellow-orphans he would boast shamelessly about his friends and the delights he enjoyed in their home. He explored the house in Lamb Street as if it were a magic castle. He made friends among the neighbours. Every time he came Mrs. Hogarth filled the house with children and treated them to sumptuous tea parties. He learned to call her 'mum', and to squabble with the children as if he were their brother. When he was fourteen his status in the family was confirmed. The orphans, on reaching the school-leaving age, were boarded out with approved families. Mick Monaghan, who for years had been playing the squire in Lamb Street, secured him an apprenticeship with a shopfitter in Clerkenwell, and he moved in with the Hogarths.

He remembered the family party that had greeted him when, with his cardboard suitcase, he came at last to stay in that house which to him was a dazzling and beautiful shrine of laughter and — above all — of freedom. There was Chris who, at nineteen, was the educated man of the family, a clerk at thirty-two shillings a week; his girl, Estella Leone, who was as buxom and swarthy as he was thin and pale; Alf, seventeen and pugnacious, a lorry-driver's mate who shouted his way through every conversation as if he were abusing a motorist in a traffic jam; Rose, a little demon in a drill slip; the oldest girl Nancy, fat as a sack of melons, shining with laughter, and deputy mother — on this occasion she was serving them at table; and Mrs. Hogarth, facing him across the round table, her face bright with tenderness and gratification.

When he thought of Mrs. Hogarth he could not recall her as she was when he had last seen her, during the war — the lineaments of the beloved dead vanish too quickly from our minds — but he retained a mental picture of her as she was on this day, sixteen years ago, a picture which like the central figure in an old photograph grew unnaturally distinct as its background faded. He remembered her as a child sees its mother, ageless (although she was only forty-one at the time), the embodiment of womanliness yet without sex, radiant and majestic, tireless in movement, classically placid in repose; broad of lap, powerful of bosom, her arms red and strong, her dark hair swept thickly back from a full face. Her cheeks were as smooth and delicately coloured as those of a girl and, although the slight snubness of her broad nose gave her a cast of expression so ineradicably good-humoured as to make her appear an over-tolerant mother, the omniscient candour of her eyes was as effective in governing the children as it was in silencing a quarrelsome neighbour. Her voice could range from a melodious softness to the firmness of anger, and when she sported like a child with her children it became tremulous with glee, but it was never strained or shrill; her speech was clearly articulated, full of the cheerful accents of the London dialect but free from the slurred and fragmentary rhythms of modern Cockney. Whenever Jack heard laughter he compared it with her laughter; laughter was never absent from her house. Her parties — would he ever forget them? — but every meal was like a party in her house! How she loved to see her children, in their adolescent years, come stampeding in with their friends, to sing and clown and thump the piano, while she presided, smiling like a queen, at her well-stocked table!

She would open the door to a tired hawker and bring him in to dinner. Once she bribed Jack with a Banbury bun to hit a boy four years older than himself who had called him a bastard. The boy's mother came to the house, spoiling for a fight. Mrs. Hogarth confronted the woman with cold and fearless eyes, said, "Who? This little lamb —" she fondled Jack's head — "hit a boy twice his size? I don't believe it. And I must say, if a boy of mine came crying to me, I'd be ashamed to make it known," — and slammed the door. She appointed herself as guardian and comforter to Barmy Naughton, who, ever since he had been fished out of the Atlantic in the winter of nineteen-seventeen thirty hours after his ship had been torpedoed, had wandered about the district like a homeless and tormented dog. For years he was a familiar visitor to the house, slinking in whenever he felt like it, sitting silently by the fire, eating at the table in a famished but furtive way, or helping Kate Hogarth in the kitchen where, free from the agony of facing derisive eyes, he talked for hours with the disjointed volubility of a child. Kate encouraged him to take the children out for walks and compelled them to treat him with respect. In her hearing they had to address him as Uncle Dick, although long usage had already left him scarcely responsive to any other name but Barmy.

***

Kate Hogarth's name, mentioned casually in a conversation or even evoked mentally by the sight of some familiar object, always dropped into Jack's consciousness like a stone into a pool. Ripples of nostalgia, at once pleasing and painful, spread silently across the surface of his mind, countering and confusing the currents of thought. The pictures from the past would take shape, dazzling and elusive as the shifting patterns of sunlight on the surface of disturbed water, distracting him from his occupation of the moment, filling him with regret for the past and discontent with the present. He was plunged into such a mood by an encounter with Mick Monaghan a couple of weeks after his engagement.

He was walking past The Lamb one Sunday morning, about an hour before opening time, when Mick, who was standing at the private side entrance, called to him, "Ahoy, there, my lad. What about paying us a courtesy call? I've not had a chance to do more than shake your hand since you were engaged." There was little hint of the Irish in Mick's speech beyond the purity of his vowels, the relish with which he sounded each consonant and a frequent rotundity of phrase. His voice was resonant, but was more commanding than genial; together with his straight-backed tallness, his keenness of eye and his sleekly-waved, cropped-at-the-neck grey hair, it assured his success in keeping order in his own house, in presiding at the local British Legion, and in representing his neighbours as spokesman at times of crisis.

Jack followed Mick upstairs to his private parlour, and greeted Barmy Naughton, who was in the room cleaning brasses.

"What'll you drink, lad?" Mick asked. "Brown ale? All right, Barmy, you carry on with your polishing. I'll get it."

While Mick was away, Jack looked round the room. Mick had lived here alone for nearly thirty years since his wife, infuriated less by his frequent infidelities than by the unrepentant attitude which he displayed in response to her pleas, left him. A Catholic like her husband, she had always refused to divorce him. Mick employed Barmy to help in the bar and to act as a personal runner and body-servant, an old woman (who was really one of his numerous pensioners) to cook and clean, and a beefy, sluttish girl who not only came in every evening to help in the bar but was reputed to be Mick's latest comforter. The room was something of a museum of local history. Over the mantelpiece hung the D.C.M. which Mick had won on the Somme in nineteen-sixteen. In rows on the walls were photographs of annual outings, British Legion festivities, and the street's Jubilee, Coronation and victory parties. There was one frame full of faded photographs of men who had gone from Lamb Street to the first war and a similar — which included Jack's picture and which during the war had hung in the saloon bar over the Comforts Fund box — of the second war. There were letters of thanks to the people of Lamb Street from the Save the Children Fund, the Lord Mayor's Miners Fund, the Aid Russia Fund, the Salvage Organiser and the National Savings Committee.

"Takes you back, all this," said Jack, as Mick came into the room. He raised his glass. "Cheers! — Ah, it's nice and cool."

"Your health! Yes, there's a few faces there we'll never see again, eh, this side of the heavenly gates. Not that the gates will ever open for me. My sins are many, and since they're all in the feminine gender, they'll never give me rest."

"From what I hear, it hasn't occurred to you yet to give *them* a rest."

"Ah!" There was a note of pleased vanity in Mick's laugh.

"Dora, eh?" Dora was the barmaid. "Surely you don't believe an old crock of sixty has got the powder in him to bring down a high flier like that?"

"Not much you haven't! Sound bloody pleased with yourself, too, way you talk." Jack turned away and peered at photographs. There was no banter in his voice as he said, "And she's not the only one, eh?"

"I shouldn't believe too much that you hear in Lamb Street, lad." Mick, too, spoke more soberly.

"I know what's what. No green in my eye. I can put two and two together."

"I wonder!"

Jack looked at Mick. He could not stand the steady scrutiny to which the older man was subjecting him, and turned away again, conscious that Mick's eyes were still on him as he wandered along the wall. He felt that Mick was trying to make up his mind about him somehow.

"You've learned a bit, lad, these last ten years," Mick said, "but you've got a lot to learn yet."

"What you mean?" Jack was growing uncomfortable. "Talk like a bloody boss-eyed oracle, you do." Eager to change the subject, he paused in front of a photograph. "Hallo, here's Nancy's wedding group. She give you that?"

"She did."

"She give me one, too. Ol' Gran turned up for the wedding, eh? Look at her. Fierce ol' bitch, isn't she? I seen her a few times, never seen her smile that I can recall." He remembered Gran Hogarth as he spoke, the mother of Kate Hogarth's dead husband. In the old days she had been an infrequent and dreaded visitor, hobbling into the house from time to time like an old general on a tour of inspection. "Even Kate was frightened of her. We used to sit there an' stare at the old woman as if she was going to eat us. Reckon we thought she would as well. Kate used to make her welcome, put a cup of tea in front of her, ask her if she was well, but I don't know, not in her usual voice, not like — well, you know how she used to love having visitors — not like that somehow. Used to make me wonder, I can tell you, even then. The old woman glared at her once, I remember, and said, 'Don't put yourself out, Kate Hogarth, if you don't want to. It's the children I've come to see. My Victor's children. *If* you don't mind.' And Kate just looked away, not a word. Dead funny that, come to think of it. Used to give us sweets, though, the old lady did. I dunno! Still alive, too, Nancy tells me. Nance goes to see her. You know Nance, soft heart, loves the whole bloody world, she does. Living in a room up Barnsbury way. The old lady I mean. Tough old bitch, I must say, way she hangs on. More than eighty, she must be. Easy."

There was a picture of Rose, taken when she was fourteen. She looked wild and free, radiant already with a beauty that was still to bloom yet retaining the heartbreaking innocence of childhood. It was painful to look at the picture. Beside it was another photograph, of a baby in swaddling clothes, that was puzzling but vaguely familiar. Jack indicated the picture of Rose. "I should have thought you could have got a later one than that," he said thickly.

"That's the one I like best," answered Mick with tired equanimity.

"I didn't know you was so thick with the Hogarths."

"I'm thick with everybody. Here —" he indicated a photograph on the opposite wall — "this is Bernie Whiteflower's wedding. You were away at the time, weren't you?"

Jack did not move from where he stood. A wave of scalding emotion had flooded through him. For a moment he could not speak. He felt a hot prickling behind the eyes. "Kate Hogarth!" he croaked. He pointed at another photograph. "Where'd you get this one? I never seen it before." The shock had been doubly violent because for the first time he was looking as a man at the picture of the woman whom he had only seen as a boy. For the first time he saw her as she must have looked to others ten, fifteen years ago; not a mother for children but a woman for men, ripely beautiful. It seemed a sacrilege to look at her like this, to compare her with the goddess who smiled from among the mists of memory; but he could not remove his gaze.

Mick, as if understanding, let him stare for a while. At last he answered, "It's not mine, lad, it's Barmy's."

"Barmy's?"

Barmy, who had appeared to be completely oblivious to their conversation, looked up. "Yes, Barmy's! Funny, ain' it? What she wanna give Barmy a picture for, eh?" He stared down at his brasses with a trapped, glaring expression and polished furiously. "That's her! That's Kate Hogarth! Thought you knew her, eh? You knew her! —" he uttered a barking little laugh of derision. —

"Nobody knew her. I knew her! I knew her, and she knew me. God rest her dear, blessed soul, she knew me. Nobody else knew me!" He was panting. Jack stared at him.

Mick said, "That's enough, Barmy. Don't upset yourself."

Barmy muttered something inaudible.

"What's that?" Jack asked.

"He said that's not all he's got," Mick explained. "He's got a workbasket of hers. I gave it to him. It was in the wreckage of the house. I was in the Civil Defence. I found it."

"I got a letter," Barmy said.

"From Kate?"

"I got a letter. From Kate Hogarth. She writ it to me. That's another thing she did, she writ me a letter."

"When?"

Barmy did not answer.

"Show us. Go on, Barmy, show us. I — well, you know, she was like my mum."

"It's no use," said Mick, "he won't even let me near it. You'd get a knife in your throat if you tried to touch it."

"She writ it to me," Barmy muttered.

"She was a good woman to him," said Mick. "She was good to us all, God bless her."

"Ah," said Jack heavily, "I miss her."

"I dug her out. I suppose they told you that. May the Lord forgive me, I cursed Him that night."

"I reckon everyone misses her."

"Yah!" Barmy's anguished snarl startled them both. "Miss her! Think people got time to miss anyone? Them! What you think they care, that lot?"

Jack, dumbfounded, murmured, "I dunno."

"I hung myself." Barmy uttered the words in a clear, assertive voice, like a boast. Who else would have done so? — he seemed to imply.

"*Eh!*"

"I hung myself." There was no mistaking the sick pride in his voice. "She was good to me, she was. She was the only one."

"Eh?" Jack, struggling to absorb the three incredible words, spoke without thinking, to keep the others at a distance while he steadied himself. "What about Mick? He's treated you all right."

"She was the only one," repeated Barmy with terrible passion.

There was silence in the room.

When Mick spoke, his words lacked their usual resonance. They seemed to fall, like bits of dead wood in the strange silence, to the carpet. "I found him. I was just in time. Don't talk about it. It's not good for him. Get on with your work, Barmy." He resumed, self-consciously, his normal vigour of speech. "When's the wedding, lad? That's what I really wanted to talk about."

"After Christmas."

"You're taking your time, aren't you?"

"Well," said Jack, embarrassed, "it's the old lady. Mrs. Wakerell. She's a one for doing it properly. So what with her on the one hand, and me wanting to get it over before my next birthday — well, you know what I mean, thirty sounds a lot younger than thirty-one, don' it? — we split the difference and made it December. Anyway, it'll give me time to get settled, job and all that. Save up a bit. Look round for a place. Buy stuff. You know, do it in style, like."

"Well, when the time comes round you know you can count on a handsome present from Lamb Street. When Mick Monaghan passes the hat round they all dig deep. And I'll be getting you something myself that'll make 'em sit up and stare."

Jack remembered Rose and felt a flicker of the old resentment. "What for?"

"Why not? It's the least I can do for my old friends. I bought Nancy a china cabinet for her parlour. Didn't she show it to you? It cost me twenty-four pounds, and anyone else would have had to pay twice the price."

Jack felt the blood rush to his head. He wanted to

mutter thanks, but instead he heard himself blurt —
"And Rosie?"

Again the unflinching scrutiny from Mick's eyes, amused and tolerant. "I'll buy her a present, too, when she weds."

Jack subsided. "You're a cool one," he said weakly.

Mick smiled. "You're very hard on someone you think a lot of. I told you, lad, time may teach you a lot of things you don't know. Why don't you see her?"

Jack shook his head like a schoolboy.

"Why not?"

Jack shrugged his shoulders, avoiding Mick's eyes. "I said no."

"And I said, why not?"

"Oh, for crying out loud, give us a rest, can't you? Or I'll say something else I'll be sorry for." He looked up, like a boy determined to play the man. "I don't want to be bad friends with you, Mick. It's a rotten world, I know that. I been around. None o' my business what you do. Or any other party, for that matter. Leave it at that, eh?"

"All right, lad. Let's shake on it and part good friends." Jack hated these smooth, hail-fellow-well-met gestures — Mick was addicted to them — but he submitted, as always, shaking hands while he smiled foolishly and felt hangdog and defeated. "Thanks about the present and all that," he mumbled, "Joyce'll be pleased when I tell her."

"That's the spirit. And I'll tell you what, you talk over with her what you'll need, and let me know. Don't be frightened to name it. Anything up to twenty-five pounds. You'll only get the best from Mick Monaghan."

"Thanks, Mick."

"And you'll look in again, the pair of you, and let me know?"

"Yes, Mick."

"There's a fine brave lad!"

Jack wondered if there was mockery in Mick's voice. He was thirty years old, but he was crushed when people spoke to him like this, powerless to defeat their condescension. He looked desperately about him trying to think of something to say. He noticed again the picture that had puzzled him, the picture of the baby. "Here, I was going to ask you. Whose kid's that?"

"Kate's. That's Tony, the baby that died."

"Oh. Course. Should have remembered." He felt at once grateful and humiliated by his talk with Mick; and beneath that, filling him with a longing to escape and master in solitude his disordered emotions, was all the mystifying turbulence of feeling that every confrontation with the past aroused in him. "Thanks, Mick. Cheerioh!" He backed awkwardly towards the door. "All right, I can see myself out. Thanks for the drink. Cheerioh, Barmy! I'll go and tell Joyce, now, eh?" He bolted, like a boy from his schoolmaster.

Chapter 2

JACK TOLD JOYCE with enthusiasm of Mick's promised generosity, but for days after the encounter he remained in a confused and unsettled mood. There was a heat wave: people walked about like dreamers. At this time, when thought was as tiring as movement, Jack was burdened with vague but insistent problems. He was still happy — grateful for the affectionate domesticity of life with the Wakerells, grateful for his job, grateful for the surfeit of friendship which he enjoyed in Lamb Street, grateful above all for Joyce — but happiness was beginning to lose its charm, like rain after the first shower.

For years past he had, in different ways, been able to relieve boredom with violence: now he had to learn to live with no such means of escape. Work, in this heat, was an ordeal. He begged his employer to send him out on installation tasks, protesting that he was a skilled man. "In a few weeks, boy," he was told, "you've got to show us what you can do as a bench-hand before we try you as an outside fixer." He remained in the workshop, quiet but inwardly infuriated. He passed his evenings with Joyce, but courtship — indeed, all conversation — was a burden; his head ached, his body was sluggish in the oppressive heat, and he only wanted to be left in peace. Joyce, too, was suffering. She looked sallow, she wore her glasses all the time, she was too weary to brush her dry hair or to dress smartly, and she dragged gracelessly about the house in an old cotton dress; so that he could not help finding diminished satisfaction in her company. It occurred to him that for six weeks he had been living day and night within this household, scarcely ever out of Joyce's company. The monotony was becoming stifling. "You go and lay down," he said to Joyce one evening, "it's cool in your bedroom. You said so. I'm going out for a swim." She was too ill and apathetic to stop him, and he went out. He found a shady corner in an old churchyard and he sat here for hours on this and subsequent evenings, sunk in a mindless stupor or, as the air grew cooler, in languid dreams.

The subject of all these dreams was Rose. For years she had dwelt in a dark attic of his mind. He had hoped that his engagement to Joyce would double-bolt the attic door; for, although he had never ceased to be aware of Rose's presence within him, he told himself that every man — he recalled many confessions he had heard in the Army — possessed some memory like this which ached till the end of life, but that every sane man found someone else with whom to be happy.

Now Rose had broken loose. How could he have hoped to forget her when every old friend he met reminded him of her, sooner or later, with some innocent question or remark? Every mention of her name had been a wrench at the bolts. Mick's calm insistence that he should see her, and his own panic-stricken refusal, had burst open the door. Now she walked unchecked in the corridors of his mind. Wherever he was, however he tried to ignore her presence, he heard her footsteps.

It was not merely his working-class puritanism that led him to condemn Rose, nor even his disappointment at the death of his own secret hopes. The intensity of his rage against her derived, rather, from the obsession (undefined in thought) that she had betrayed her mother. Kate was enshrined in his memory as a goddess, blessed, pure and above all human failing; throughout his youth he had looked on Rose as the image, in beauty and innocence, of her adored mother. Perhaps it was this, more than his inarticulacy, or the feeling that they were brother and sister, or their disparity of temperament, that had held him back in adolescence from explicit courtship. He had been crushed by the news of what he held to be Rose's downfall so soon after her mother's death. This betrayal of his dreams was what he could not forgive.

***

She had always remained out of reach, most of all so when they were closest together physically.

"Oh," she had cried once, when they had been walking together, "I have such dreams!"

He had said, "Eh?"

That was their relationship in those days; yet they were always together. She never used, like the other girls in the street, to flirt with boys at the street corner. Sometimes she held court among her girl friends, but mostly she was content to reign over her sisters and her brothers, of whom she treated Jack as one.

Sitting in the churchyard, gloating over his hoard of dream pictures, he lingered more and more over those in which she appeared. They were all the more poignant because they revived in him emotions that had since been poisoned; the bitter accumulation of later experience, interposed in his consciousness between the present and these visions, made them all the more beatific. By turning the clock back, they enabled him to lay aside his life's load of disillusionment; and the more transient and tormenting they were, the more he sought their refuge.

Older than her by nearly three years, and not of her blood, he had always let her lead him about as if he were a younger brother. She would pull her stockings on in his presence, run into his room half-dressed to borrow a comb; once, after swimming, she had pulled her costume down to the waist and lain back on the grass, luxurious in the sunshine. Wonderstruck but abashed, he had loved her with an oafish innocence.

He could only remember one period, in all the waxing and waning of their relationship when anything might have come of it. He remembered it, tenderly and incredulously, as 'that year'. Could there really, he wondered (sitting hunched forward on a churchyard bench with his hands clasped between his knees), have been such a time in his life? 'That year' — it must have been — he reckoned backward in time — nineteen thirty-eight, when he was nineteen and Rose just turned seventeen.

It was the last full year before the war, and before the break-up of the household. That was one reason why he cherished the period so fiercely in memory. Nancy was twenty-five, monstrously fat and resigned — she implied by her aggressive cheerfulness — to spinsterhood. Chris, a year younger, was thin and pale, with hair already receding. He was active in the Labour Party and went about his political duties in all weathers, careless of his cough and answering only with a distracted frown his Estella's incessant demands that he should think a little less about the human race and a little more about her. Alf was twenty-two, driving a lorry, drinking, and a worry to his mother.

'That year', for Jack and his generation in Lamb Street, was like the brief season of the butterfly's splendour. It lived in the memory as a year of fine weather. Almost every scene was lit with mellow sunshine. Boys and girls, banded till now in two hostile tribes, cast off like a cocoon the loutish phase of adolescence, and saw each other as they had become; big, handsome lads who lounged at the corner with the relaxed assurance of manhood, and young women invested with that insolent beauty, at once bold and delicate, that reckless precipitancy of movement and seductive independence of manner that London working-class girls transitorily assume in their late 'teens. Male whistles began to express invitation instead of derision. Courting broke up long-established gangs. This youthful community was agitated by calf-love in the mass: calf-love it was, for, although they were all wise in knowledge, there was little vice among them. They were innocent in spirit if not in mind. (Of course the street, like every street, had its slut — Maisie Keenan, a handsome girl with an overblown body, red hair and a big greedy mouth, who thrived on the impatience of the lustier young men.) It was their full summer of youth, and — as if to warn them that their youth was soon to be cut short — the air that year was alive with crisis. Loudspeakers shouted through open windows into the quiet, broad streets. There was a chill touch in the sunshine, like ice in wine. Few knew what strange intoxicant quickened the blood, but all hearts beat a little faster in that year, that last full year of peace. Or so memory said.

What incredible excitements had abounded in that year! How carefree and buoyant to have lived in the shelter and security of a family, one's life enlaced down to the finest strand with others, one's problems never to be faced alone; to have swooped about the streets on bicycles, streaming off to camp every sunny weekend, leaving a trail of laughter floating on the air; to have sat in cafés till one o'clock in the morning, glorying in argument and good fellowship; to have passed one's days playing football, going to pictures, dancing, swimming, maddened and uplifted by the torrential energy of youth! All his senses had come to life. The gates had swung open to reveal the crowded and illimitable prospect of *living* that lay before him. To taste was to enjoy, for no gall of experience yet furred the palate.

It was his most treasured memory, the keenest joy in the scanty store that his life had yielded him, that he had entered upon all this side by side with Rose. The sympathy and the mutual reliance bred in them by years of puppy play had bound them together in the Spring of that year, and had enabled them to share and to sharpen in each other the first full apprehension of life. They had abandoned all their friends and wandered together, in a dual solitude, night after night. The springtime had quickened the mood that was already in them, plying them with all its mild and subtle intoxicants; the damp fresh breeze leaping upon them out of the trees with sudden sighs, the pale leaves whispering above their heads in the blue dusk, the cool rain timidly touching their faces, the sappy scent that perfumed the vast, quiet nights.

One night —

(He invoked this memory one evening when the heat-wave, gathering interminably, had reached a point where it seemed charged with climax. The air had become suffocating, and all day long everyone had been waiting, waiting; the thick stillness was like a held breath that must soon burst forth, suddenly and violently. The sky over the churchyard was of a bright saffron hue, with the outlines of buildings stamped against it black and hard. Windows glittered with a terrifying blue light. A dense coolness lay upon the city, muffling every sound. He could feel no wind, but leaves came scuttling past his feet. A few fat raindrops, not falling but flying horizontally, burst against his face. Silently the stone path became riddled with black spots. He relaxed in animal bliss as the cool rivulets ran down his skin. Perhaps it was the rain's touch which took him back to another night of rain. Never before had he been so entirely transported. He smiled as he dreamed, and the past became so real that his lips moved in a silent repetition of old conversations.)

One night, in the Spring of 'that year', he and Rose took shelter from the rain in the porch of an empty house. They were tired, for it was nearly midnight and they had been walking — neither of them had cared where — since nine o'clock.

"You haven't had much to say for yourself," she said. She had, as usual, been talking all the time and he, as usual, had been content to listen, wondering at the eagerness that never left her voice and looking furtively at her exalted, uplifted face.

He groped for words. He had nothing to say, but he

wished he could prove himself her equal. "Oh, I been thinking."

"What about?"

A pretence of cogitation occupied several seconds. Inside his head, all his thoughts fled and mocked him from beyond his reach. "Things," he said portentously.

She saw through him at once. "What things?"

Trapped and despairing, he shrugged his shoulders.

"Don't you —?" — she asked fiercely — "don't you *wonder*? Don't you want to — *do* things?"

He sought to protect himself by taking the initiative. "What things?"

"Oh," she cried, "everything!"

"What things?"

"I don't know," she wailed. "I don't know. I *wish* I knew. There's so many things to do. All these things people do. In books. On the pictures. Look what you read in the papers. How do you *start*? Don't *you* ever wonder?"

As usual, she had only mystified him, frightened him a little. "I'm all right. Learning a trade. Got something to look forward to."

"Look forward to!" she scoffed.

"Different with you. You're a girl. Out o' one job, into another." She had started work at fourteen as an usherette in a cinema, inspired by some vague ambition of becoming an actress. A year later she had become an office messenger, and had gone to evening classes until boredom had lured her back from the stuffy schoolroom to the freedom of the streets. She had worked in a shop and had been dismissed, with threats, for borrowing a beautiful dress from stock. Now she was employed in a cigarette factory. There was nothing unusual in her frequent change of occupation: most of the girls in Lamb Street went from one blind-alley job to another until they married. What distinguished Rose, and puzzled her friends, was the ambition — frustrated and inarticulate though it was — that possessed her. She looked on her present job as a temporary set-back.

"It's not just a job," she said, "it's how you feel. Don't you see what I mean? It's what you are. It's what you do with every bit of yourself. Look!" She held back her hair with both hands and displayed herself. "What am I going to do with all this?"

Embarrassment forced an ugly snigger from him, and she said bitterly, "All right, you don't have to say it!"

He said, "You can't half talk!"

She did not reply, and he spoke again. "I never meant —"

"Never mind."

The silence that followed was expressive of their relationship. All that delighted him was in her, and he looked at her, dumbly and oppressed by incomprehension. The things that enchanted her were in herself, and she leaned against the wall in wondering self-absorption. Yet — and this was the one source of intimacy between them — she seemed to need his presence. Tonight, as always, he served as a mirror in which she could interpret her own secrets. However docile and tender the looks she gave him, she never ceased to be withdrawn. Some instinct made him aware of this, awakening a tremor of bewilderment within his happiness. When he spoke he felt like an intruder; she was too attentive, as if it were not his words she was hearing but some echo of her own so far away that she had to strain to listen.

She touched his coat and said, "You're not wet." He put his arm round her waist and she leaned against him. He passed his lips across her cheek and said, "Your face is wet, though." She uttered a dark little laugh, with closed lips. It was no sudden flare of courage but a subtle and undetected flowering of their common mood that made him kiss her again. They remained in a relaxed embrace, kissing softly. They were nothing more than a unity of animal warmth, inert together, escaped from life, drained of their disparate longings. Immobile, silent, they formed a single dark bulk in the porch until the chimes of midnight awoke them from their trance.

They wandered homeward in the powdery rain. What was happening, or why, it was beyond Jack's power to understand. The death of thought had made possible a momentary, perilous contact between them; their senses fed on each other's nearness, on the silver shimmer of rain that hung round each street lamp, on the sweet scent of privet and the clean smell of black earth and wet pavement, on the mysterious shine of puddles and black roof slates in the darkness. Once they stopped under a lamppost and stood, a yard apart, half looking at each other for a long time while the rain, intensifying, soaked their clothes.

They wandered into Lamb Street, still apart and silent, smiling to themselves like a pair of happy conspirators. They passed The Lamb and began to cross the road. Footsteps burst upon them, a little cataract of sound pouring out of the darkness behind them as suddenly as if Mrs. Hogarth, who descended upon them, had shot up through the pavement. They were too overwhelmed by her instantaneous appearance to ask how she had thus materialised — it was only in retrospect that the incident provided Jack with one of those tiny mysteries in which memory abounds — and before they could recover their wits she had berated them for staying out late, swept them into the house, poured hot milk into them and packed them up to their rooms, with instructions to get their wet clothes off before they caught their deaths of pneumonia. When he came face to face with Rose in the morning he knew — against all his hopes — that the contact was broken. The imprint of the previous night was effaced from her expression. In the days that followed she showed no signs of responding to — even of understanding — the clumsy overtures to which he resorted. Soon she had found a new passion which took her away from him. The Spanish civil war was at its height. The people of Lamb Street had become aware that poor folk in Spain were fighting for their lives. Every night Chris and his comrades went round the district collecting food and money, and gifts were heaped on them with sacrificial generosity, in one of those blind and beautiful upsurges of human solidarity that sweep their class from time to time. Rose trundled a barrow joyfully. At every meal she harangued the family, her face ecstatic, about her doings. She wished, she told them ardently, she were a boy so that she could go out there and fight. Jack kept sulkily apart — he would have helped, but it felt too much like hanging at Rose's heels while she walked out with a rival — and Rose, disdainful, forgot him.

Jack did not pine. There was, in that incredible year, too powerful a stimulus working in his blood. Maisie Keenan had been pursuing him for some time. He had evaded her while Rose had been at his side but now, alone and filled with the fever of life, he began to notice, uneasily, her abundant charms.

"Been up the Blue Hall, Jack?" she asked him one day.

"Not yet."

"Lovely picture up there. Our Olive says so. I'm goin' up there tonight. Come with?"

"I can't. We're playing cricket."

"Don't tell 'em! That's Thursday night. Go on, why don't you want to come with me?"

"Who don't want to go with you?"

"You don't."

"I never said nothing o' the sort."

"Well, what about it then."

"Oh, all right."

"Ooh, lovely. Seven o'clock. Don't bring no apples. My mum's got tons."

That evening they went to the Blue Hall. Jack sat next to Maisie in the stifling heat with one arm round her waist (there was no point in taking her to the pictures unless he did this) and the other, across his lap, clutching her sweaty hand. Occasionally they unlaced themselves from each other to munch apples or lick ices. When they

100

moved together again, she rested her head on his shoulder, and once she moved his hand up so that it rested on her breast.

It was still light when they came out. The sky was lucent, and the clouds were dark but glowing from within. Maisie said, "Ooh, it's hot, isn't it?"

"Yes."

"I feel all sticky, like. Don't you?"

"A bit."

She giggled. "I dunno why. I've got hardly nothing on under my dress. Couldn't you feel, inside?"

He replied with an embarrassed grunt.

"Let's walk round a bit," she suggested, "before we go back, eh?"

"All right."

"You don't sound very keen."

"Well, what do you want me to do, cheer?"

"You needn't if you don't want to. I know plenty that would like the chance."

"There's no need to carry on. Let's walk down the Angel."

"No, this way." She steered him in the opposite direction to that which he had suggested, put her arm through his and leaned on him as they walked. They crossed a road and found themselves — to Jack it was sheer chance, but Maisie's pressure on his arm had been as firm and purposeful as if she were holding the tiller of a boat — walking into Highbury Fields.

The open spaces of London in the fine weather present a spectacle that recalls the wilder festivals of pagan antiquity. There is so much love going on, and so publicly, that late-comers have to seek far and wide before they can find a resting place. Each park becomes a vast municipal marriage-bed. This hot summer evening was no exception. Every bench was crowded with couples squirming shamelessly upon each other and the fields were littered with living black heaps as close together as unstacked sheaves in harvest time. Hundreds of other

101

people, driven out of their homes by the heat, strolled calmly about the paths or leaned over the railings chatting and smoking as if they were watching the monkeys at the Zoo.

Maisie's weight grew heavier on Jack's left arm. Her clutch grew tighter. He could feel the heat of her body through her thin dress. Her hair brushed across his face. He looked stiffly in front of him, and they walked in silence for a while. She said, in an awe-struck voice, "Ain' it awful?"

"Ain't what awful?"

"*You* know," she said confidentially, "all this."

Jack glanced furtively around him and looked to his front again. "Oh, I dunno."

Again a spell of silence.

"Hundreds of 'em," said Maisie.

"Mmmm."

"Fancy all these people doin' it!"

Silence.

"I bet you never dreamed so many people did it."

"Did what?" he said desperately.

"*You* know!" A terrifying pressure on his arm.

A little while later — "Jack?"

"Mmm?"

"I reckon there's times when you can't help it."

"Oh, I dunno."

Another pause. She whispered, "Jack, I reckon that's what's wrong with me."

"What you mean?"

"Well, *I* can't help it."

He made a vague, interrogative noise.

"Oh, Jack, I *know* I'm a bad girl. Every time I'm by myself I swear I'll never do it again. But whenever I'm with a boy I like —" another pressure on his forearm — "and he's got his arm round me —" she snuggled closer within his encircling arm — "oh, I dunno," she wailed, "they can do *just* what they like with me."

They had reached the far gate and they stood swaying

102

in a prolonged push-of-war, looking to passers-by like lovers in an ecstasy. Jack won, and they went lurching out of the gate.

"Anything they like," she repeated desperately.

" 's funny," Jack mused, and stared at the opposite side of the road as if the houses there were a novel and entirely wonderful sight.

A hundred yards further on she whispered, "Oh, Jack, you're a good chap. Tell us, what do you think I should do, I mean, well, like —"

They were safely away from the park. Jack's throat was still dry, but he felt that he could not ignore this appeal to his male wisdom. He cleared his throat. "Well, I dunno." He pondered. "Well, I dunno about girls, but I been reading a book by Lord Baden Powell. He's a big bloke in the Scouts."

She said without interest, "Oh, yes?"

"Well, like, he says, take plenty of exercise."

She said, "Oh," faintly, and began to take an interest even more passionate than that which Jack had shown in the houses they were passing.

"Cold baths every morning."

"Oh, really?"

"Well," said Jack stubbornly, "that's what he says."

They crossed a road. "He reckons," Jack resumed, speaking because he feared silence, "you ought to do things, like to take your mind off it."

She looked at him mournfully.

"Read books, like," he suggested — invaded, as he spoke, by dreadful doubt as he saw Maisie's face. He studied the shop windows. Her grip on his arm became viciously tight, and she frowned at the pavement.

At her front door they stood facing each other, both embarrassed. "Well, thanks, Jack," she said, "you ain' 'alf a clever chap."

"Oh, I dunno," he murmured modestly.

She flushed, and cried with sudden anger, "And I don't think!"

103

"Here," he said, "what's up?" He caught her arm as she turned to go indoors. "Ain't you gonna give us a kiss?"

"Sure you ain't doing me a favour?" she asked bitterly, offering her cheek without enthusiasm.

"Goo' night, Mais," he said.

She stared at him. "Goo' night, Jack. It wasn' a bad picture, was it?" Then she went indoors.

For the next few days he nagged Rose, clumsily but more persistently and more fiercely than ever before, to go out with him. She made excuses about Spain. He was nineteen years old, healthy, angered; the summer nights were hot. He took Maisie to pictures again, walked with her again across the Fields, and came home at two o'clock in the morning. After this he kept company, intermittently, with Maisie until the war. Rose, unreasonably, assumed a jilted air, and became haughty. Sarcasms flashed across the breakfast table and there were silences of a new kind between them. Thus — as if, after their lives had run almost in parallel, the gentlest of collisions had sent them flying apart — the distance between them widened.

***

Great pellets of rain, flying into his face, riddled the insubstantial walls of memory. He sat back, stung into wakefulness by the cold raindrops. The rain had washed away the heat which had weighed, enfeebling and dream-fostering, upon the city. People hurried past him, heads bowed, casting quick, puzzled glances at him as he sat on his bench. His clothes were getting wet. He went home.

Chapter 3

"COME ON," JOYCE SAID, "or we'll never get there."

"There's no rush," Jack said, "I can't see any bloody fire." It was a Saturday morning in mid-July, and he was standing waist-deep in a mob of small boys, his arms slackly extended as if he were wading out to sea. "Anyway, don't you talk! You kept me waiting long enough!"

At seven o'clock that morning he had been awakened in bed by the sound of Joyce moving about the house with bucket and broom. An hour later, at breakfast time, she had still been busy, greeting him with a smile at once shamed and pleased, and saying, "Oh, look how you've caught me," as he surveyed her dishevelled hair and smudged face. For two hours she had kept him waiting while she finished the housework, listening with passive sullenness to the commands issued by her mother (who sat, as usual, popping lumps of sugar into her mouth and presiding over a never-empty teapot) but setting about the ensuing work with an air of energetic relish. Washed and dressed at last, she had joined him on the doorstep to set out on their shopping expedition, when she had noticed that the knocker was tarnished, and with a "Tss" of impatience she had dashed indoors for cloth and polish and cleaned the knocker before starting out. She had answered his protests with a severe, "Dirty knocker, dirty wife! I won't have them talking!"

"Where you been?" Jack asked the boys, who had come thundering from nowhere into the sunlit quiet of the street.

"Pictures. Children's Club. Every Sa'day morning."

"Club, eh? What they show you? Cowboys?"

Out of the babble, a voice louder than the others. "Yuss. And Superman. An' tadpoles changin' into frogs."

Another voice. "Yuss, Jack, and the man, he comes out on the stage and we all promise to be good."

Another voice, proudly, "An' we cut up all the seats."

Jack fished in his pockets for pennies, displaying a grin of vacuous contentment. The small boys of Lamb Street, a distinct and important grouping in its community, worshipped him as a hero returned, as a man who bore the stamp of action on his hard-hewn red face, and as a philanthropist of insane generosity. He rejoiced in their clamorous adoration; it was another reminder that he was at home.

"Who'd you think you are?" Joyce asked, as he distributed pennies. "Lord Nuffield? You save your money. I'll show you where to spend it."

"What?" he scoffed. "On gypsies? You're always talking about watching the pennies, and when that gypsy comes round yesterday you give her a bob for a measly twopenny bunch of lavender."

"That's different. She'd have put a curse on us if I hadn't."

"Give us the basket," he said. They were walking towards Chapel Market.

"It's all right. You can take it when it's full." She slipped her free arm through his.

People often asked Joyce, "Well, dear, how does it feel to be engaged?" She would reply, "Oh, lovely," but the truth — which surprised her after all her expectations — was that she felt little except a faint astonishment at her own achievement; an achievement of which she looked on Jack, not without warmth and pride, as a sort of human trophy. The more actively the two of them made their preparations for marriage, the more she was excited by the prospect of the home which she needed for her own fulfilment; and the brighter this vision became, the closer

106

she clung to the man who was to be its most essential furnishing. To this grateful recognition of his function she gave the name of love.

She was one of those plain girls whom love makes beautiful. It had given her a new serenity of carriage, and had dispelled the frown of suspicion from her face. She had began to display an assiduous artfulness in the use of cosmetics of which even her mother had not thought her capable. She had relaxed her efforts a little in the enervating atmosphere of the recent heat wave, but Jack's mysterious bout of half-heartedness had startled her out of her complacency. She was as alert as a huntress once more, and felt rewarded by Jack's increased attentiveness.

They bought the local newspaper each week to study the 'Flats to Let' columns. The serious business of buying a home was still ahead, but they had already embarked upon the exciting hobby of bargain-hunting, and a stock of towels, crockery and household gadgets was beginning to accumulate in Joyce's bedroom cupboard.

Their future home was the one real link between them. She refused to share his other interests. When he talked of sport, she blinked meanly as if at the mention of a rival. When he read items from the newspaper she said, "Oh, put it away! They only write those papers to make you miserable! Lucky you can't believe a word they say! What's my horoscope today?" She was uninterested in the dreams of bettering himself to which he still clung. "You stick to what you've got," she said, "and think yourself lucky to have a steady job." "But a chap's got to try and get on," he protested. "You stay where you are," she replied, "it's safer. If you don't climb up, you can't fall down." On the other hand, she would talk joyfully for an hour about an egg-beater, and would let out a wail of annoyance if his attention strayed.

It had been one of the great days of her life when Jack had turned his bank account into a joint one. She had suggested nervously that the Post Office was good enough, but he had insisted on doing it in style. She had added her savings to his, making a total of nearly four hundred pounds, and he had arranged with his bank manager that cheques bearing either of their two signatures would be honoured. The crowning glory came when he gave Joyce a cheque book of her own. A cheque book in Lamb Street was a dazzling rarity. Joyce took it to work and showed it off more proudly than her engagement ring, and Mrs. Wakerell borrowed it to impress the neighbours with Jack's position in the world. Sometimes at nights Joyce sat on the edge of her bed looking at the cheque book as if it were a picture of her beloved.

Their shared hopes bound her to him more closely than did his awkward love-making and enabled her, in their nightly comas on the couch, to relax in his arms without feeling any of the repulsion that only a little while ago a man's touch would have induced in her. This repulsion was the result of her previous experiences. Boys had often come after Joyce in her adolescence, but they had always been the blotchy and earnest ones, never the big, audacious lads whom she secretly admired. She had let these suitors take her to films and dances, but shame, and the dreams fostered by the twopenny novelettes she read ('Some day He'll come along') had prevented her from encouraging their timid advances. Despite her mother's nagging, she had remained unmarried, acquiring a contempt for all the young men who courted her and a shrinking fear of 'real' men, as she called those at whom she looked with longing.

When she was twenty-one an episode occurred that robbed her of the last of her confidence. She had met a boy from Chapel Street at a dance, and they had gone out together several times. He was a costermonger, and what she called 'common' in his ways, but he had a reckless look, a fine laugh, broad shoulders, and he was earning good money. She worshipped him, and for the first time let herself dream of marriage. One night she hastened to meet him at the Angel. Her impatience impelled her towards the rendezvous a few minutes early, and as she approached their meeting-place she heard two men talking.

"...face like Joe Oxenbold's mare," she heard one of them say.

"Garn—!" and she halted, feeling sick as she recognized the other voice coming from the dark shop doorway. "They're all beauties in the dark. It's what's under their skirts I go for, not what keeps their — in' ears apart." There was no mistake. It was the voice of the man she was to meet. "It's these plain ones are the best. Hard up for it, they are. I can tell you, I've had a few. And grateful for it, that's the best of it —."

She had fled, and since then she had stayed at home, only going out with other girls, her face set and sulky whenever her mother lectured her about getting married. As time went by she became more lonely, and in consequence more irritable and resentful. Despair and self-pity corroded her looks and made her act pitiably whenever she came face to face with a man. She had grown so fearful of rejection that to protect herself against a fresh hurt she always hastened to be the first to rebuff. On the few occasions when she met a man she liked, she was horrified to find that she could not prevent herself from instinctively lashing out and antagonising him.

Three years of this had been like slow torture. She reminded herself of it whenever she felt downhearted at the comparison between Jack and the men of her dreams. If it had not been for the memory of it, she might have been scared away from Jack by her friend Maureen's comment, "I don't think much of him. Looks like a big lump of mutton to me," — for she was so imbued with the fear of others that she was capable of giving up someone she loved merely because the neighbours sneered at him, or even because she imagined that they might do so behind her back. However, her fear of a return to the misery of solitude overcame these spells of half-heartedness, and whenever doubt awoke in her she repressed it furiously. Her worst moments of panic were followed by moods of extravagant exultancy when she startled Jack with her eagerness.

The market, waiting for the afternoon rush, was like a placid stream disturbed in places by little pools of noise and activity between which the early shoppers drifted. Joyce, hanging on Jack's arm and steering him between clusters of people, said, "This doesn't change, does it?"

"Not really," said Jack. He looked about him as if for something that was eluding him. "I tell you what I do notice. The babies. I mean, it seems like only yesterday I went away. Not to you, like, you were a kid at school then, but it does to me. I tell you, it gives you the wind up the way time flies. Well, I mean, you look at the difference. Pasty faces the babies used to have, always something or other wrong with them. Now look at 'em — bloody little giants, I tell you, they sit up in their prams like bloody royalty going by, and they look at you with their big clear eyes as if they was laughing at you. I reckon they're born brainy, the babies nowadays."

"It's all this orange juice and cod liver oil."

"And these young mothers, they're the ones that tickle me."

"Oh, are they?"

"Gah way! You know what I mean! I mean, I don't know where they got it from. Proper high-steppers they are, heads up, push their prams as if they was made of gold, talk like ladies, wear smashin' dresses — I mean, everyone's hard up, but nobody looks poor any more. Bloody funny I call it."

"I wish you wouldn't b— so much," said Joyce, "I've told you before. You're not in the Army now. Quick!" Something had caught her attention, and she pressed Jack's arm urgently, "Let's cross the road."

Jack, always slow to react, only halted stupidly. "What's up?" Someone she loathed was bearing down on them, and it was too late to avoid him.

"Bernie Whiteflower!" Jack cried joyously "What you

doin' off work on a Saturday morning?"

"Five days a week," said Bernie, "no use knockin' up the old overtime these days. They only take it off you for income tax. Me work for the Government? That'll be the day." He grinned at Joyce, "Wotcho, popsy-dooley! Bought the ol' bed yet?"

Joyce gave him a tight-lipped little nod and looked away. She squeezed Jack's arm beseechingly, but he lingered, and the two men talked. It sickened Joyce to see them together. Jack had stepped off the pavement and stood before Bernie like a little boy, looking up at him, respectfully attentive, with a silly tentative grin on his face. Bernie towered above them both, his attitude relaxed and indulgent but indicative, like his voice, of command. She was filled with hatred for him. Come away — she tried to say silently to Jack: it was maddening that he did not receive the unspoken message that she was projecting at him with such intensity — Come away, quickly! Can't you see what a fool you look beside him? Don't you understand how hard you make it for me to love you? Oh, why can't you stand up differently? Why can't you look at him like an equal? Why don't you answer him confidently and strongly?

She could stand it no longer. "Come on," she muttered, "we can't stand all day."

"In a minute," said Jack.

"Come *on!*" It was like a little snarl, and she hauled at him so fiercely, leaning away from him with her head down, that he followed her in a sidelong shamble. "Here!" he cried. He grinned deprecatorily up at Bernie. "Women!" he mumbled, as the gap between them widened. "Be seein' you, Bern!"

"Ta-ra!" Bernie called. "Look arter yourself. Keep your 'ands on your pockets!" Joyce's only response was a brief, bitter glare over her shoulder.

"Just having a nice old jaw there," Jack said in a mild but aggrieved tone, "can't see what the rush was all about."

111

"That hooligan!" she snapped, and walked on in silence, holding his arm tightly and frowning down at the ground. She could still feel Bernie watching them. She knew, without looking round, that his stare was insolent, amused, knowing. She was frantic to get out of his sight, and hurried Jack round the corner. "Here, where we off to now? There's no shops down here." "Never mind," she said, just keep walking." After a little pause she tried to explain the impulse. "I came over a bit funny. All those people. The air's fresher here. No, I'm all right, let's just walk for a bit." She wanted to root out of herself the shame she had felt at the comparison between the two men, the terrible little seeds of contempt for Jack that so easily found soil within her and that must not be allowed to sprout.

They were walking in the roadway, in a broad, pleasant thoroughfare whose terraced pavement rose until it was six feet above their heads. On the roadward side the pavement was railed, and on the other side there were older and more ornate railings behind which lay big old houses, with long shaggy lawns and tall trees that spread clouds of foliage over gardens and pavement alike.

A babble from the pavement attracted their attention. A knot of people was gathered ahead of them. The street rang with the sound of running feet as more hastened to join the crowd. Doors were opening on the other side of the street. Coveys of shrieking children burst out of a hundred hiding places. "Here, I say —" said Jack.

A woman came running past them, her face aghast. "She'll kill herself!" she gasped.

They turned to stare after her when they heard someone else shout, "Call the fire brigade!"

"Where's the police?" said an angry voice behind them. "Never about when you want 'em."

"Come on," a man urged his wife, "or we'll miss it."

"What's up?"Jack asked him. "Dunno," said the man, and hurried on.

"Ah, look!" Joyce was standing with her head craned

back, pointing straight up as if at the sky. She spoke in a squeal of joyous wonderment. "Look, up there, — ah, poor darling!"

The pavement was crammed with people. Boys balanced on the railings. Below, in the roadway, a large crowd was already gathering.

Jack peered up into the green gloom of a big sycamore tree that grew just inside one of the front gardens and leaned across the pavement. "Can't see nothing."

"It's a kitten," Joyce explained, "oh, a poor darling tiny little pussy."

People were trying to call the cat down, prowling and meowing round the base of the tree as if they had themselves all suddenly been transformed into enormous and amorous tomcats. A huge builder's labourer was mewing in a treble key of incredible altitude. An Armoured Corps sergeant stood in a strange devotional attitude, with both arms raised above his head, rubbing his fingertips together and bellowing in a monstrous caterwaul, "Waooow, myooooo, oy, down here, this way, Waaaohw!"

Joyce and Jack heard little conversational groups forming all round them. In some, the main theme was sympathy, "Ah, poor little mite, look at it, half-dead with fright!" In others, indignation was paramount, "They ought to make people look after 'em, that's what I say, same as dogs, or children. Wouldn't like to see one of your kids up there, would you?" In others, reminiscence raged, "This is nothing. Remember when Doctor Naidoo's monkey broke loose? Five days he led 'em a dance up there on the roofs. Helped himself to everything he wanted out of the houses. I saw him one day perched up on a chimney pot waving a pair of bloomers. Who says they're not human?"

Advisers abounded. One man kept shouting, "Find out its name. You'll never get it down till you do."

A woman came running out of a house bearing a frying pan in which were a pair of kippers still sizzling. "My

113

dinner these are," she announced, holding the frying pan up seductively beneath the cat, "Hey, pussy pussy, here pussy pussy, come down and eat lovely kippers. Pussy pussy pussy pussy!"

"It's the breeze," said a man, "he can't smell 'em."

"Flap your jacket," someone shouted, "send the smell up!"

Another voice, "'E's got the breeze-up already!'"

The cat, a little ball of grey fur, glared down from thirty feet above in terror and defiance.

Some boys began to throw stones. Jack shouted, "Here, the poor little bleeder 'll fall down if you frighten it." A bald-headed man past whose ear Jack had shouted turned, glowered in mute resentment and returned to his attitude of contemplation. The boys went on throwing stones.

A fresh altercation broke out above. The householder whose garden had been invaded by the crowd was protesting volubly and calling for the police. There were shouts of, "Shut him up!" "Break his windows!" "Put his lights out!" A woman kept screaming, "Heartless brute!" and the householder retreated over his trampled flowerbeds with the bricklayer's labourer shouting after him.

A bull-terrier arrived and rushed at the tree in one frantic leap after another, barking and growling in a blood-curdling manner. A woman let out an apprehensive wail of, "Oh Gawd!" as if her only baby were at the top of the tree. The boys began to stone the dog. The dog's owner arrived and dashed in among the boys, laying about him with his leash. For yards around the crowd dissolved into an angry swirl, amid a hubbub of yells, scuffling feet and ferocious barking.

Jack said despairingly, "Here, this is a right turnout. What about the poor old cat?" Nobody took any notice. Joyce realised, with a sinking heart, that he was not the sort of man who could dominate in a crowd.

More shouting behind them. A six-ton lorry and trailer had come to a standstill in the crowd and the driver was leaning out of the cab exchanging insults with the spectators. A car pulled up behind the lorry and sounded its horn repeatedly, and the noise, already deafening, was augmented by a tremendous and prolonged chorus from the crowd of, "shu-u-u-RUP!"

A voice was still repeating, "Find out 'is name, I tell you!"

"It's Mrs. Ballard's Tibbles."

"No it's not. Tibbles 'as got a white spot on his nose."

"Well, so has this one."

"Garn, you can't see from here."

"Who can't?"

"You can't."

"Who says I can't?"

"I say you can't."

"Wanna make something of it?"

"Here!" Jack pulled his jacket off, thrust it into Joyce's arms, pushed the bald-headed man aside and scrambled up on to the pavement. "Mind out the way," he shouted, "too much bloody wind and water round here." Joyce said to herself — her weak and shaken voice had no chance of reaching him — "Your best suit!" and watched, dumbfounded, while Jack made his way into the front garden, climbed the railings and tried to get a foothold on the tree-trunk. He could not get a purchase, and the lowest branch was out of his reach. "Here," he appealed, "give us a bunk-up, someone." The bricklayer's labourer climbed up on to the railings and leaned forward against the tree. "'Ere! Ow! Stuff a duck!" he yelled as Jack scrambled up him and planted both feet on his shoulders. "Take your time, mate! No 'urry! Don't mind me, I'm only the bloody doormat, I am!" Jack got both hands round the branch and pulled himself up, to the accompaniment of a loud and sarcastic, "Hooray!" from the crowd.

Joyce was dazed with incredulity and pride. She could hardly believe that Jack had left her side, it had all happened so quickly. She could feel her heart fluttering, and she cried, "Oh, Jack! Oh, Jack!" less out of anxiety for him than to draw the crowd's attention to the fact that she was his companion. He went crashing up through the green tangle, making a lot of noise and little progress. She could see him struggling time and again to free his clothes, his face scarlet with the heat and screwed up with embarrassment each time he halted, baffled, in the crook of a branch. The crowd was divided between approbation and derision. From here and there, a cry arose of, "Go it, mate!" "Good boy!" "That branch on the right!" "No, not that one, it won't stand your weight!" A group of youths sent up a monotonous chorus of, "Git ON wiv it!" A small boy put his fingers down his throat and warbled, "Ooloolooloolooloo! I'm Tarzan the Ape Man!" Other people took up the cry, "Go on, Tarzan!" Jack sat on a branch and grinned stupidly down at them. A voice roared, "Chuck us down a coconut, Jacko!" and again, "Take yer shoes orf and 'old on wiv yer toes!" There was a perilous rustling from above as the cat retreated along its branch. Jack appealed to it with conciliatory noises and finger-tip-rubbing. He almost lost his balance, and the crowd sent up a derisive cheer.

A woman said, "Making an exhibition of himself, that's all he's doing! Fancy getting up there for a cat! Vermin, that's all they are. I'd drown the lot."

Joyce flamed with feminine fury but, obstinately ladylike, she checked herself and ejaculated a loud, "Huh!"

The woman turned on her. "Who you ha-ing at, Lady Love-a-Duck?"

Joyce answered with a demonstrative toss of the head and the withering remark, "Some people!"

"Some people are as good as some other people," the woman retorted, "some people want to put that in their pipe and smoke it!"

"Huh!"

"Don't you huh me, or I'll have your hair down, double quick, I tell you!"

"I can huh if I like."

"Not at me you can't!"

"Oh?" Joyce forgot about being a lady and became a

116

woman rampant in defence of her man. "Who's going to stop me?" she shouted, "You and whose army?"

Somebody shouted, "He's got it!" Joyce looked up, and saw Jack sitting astride the topmost branch, with the kitten squirming in his right hand. He unbuttoned his shirt and stuffed the kitten inside. She saw him grimace, and he shouted, "Here, he's christened me!" Laughter and more cheers from the crowd.

He climbed down, his descent even less impressive than the upward journey. When he was half-way down, the crowd began to thin out as those who had been hoping for broken bones drifted, disappointed, back to their houses. There was a subdued babble among the rest and a few claps, but nobody showed much inclination to give Jack a hero's welcome. The show was over. He dropped to the ground. The bricklayer helped him to his feet.

A voice, "Good boy!"

Another, "Give 'im a peanut!"

Another, "Give 'im a pennorth and sod the expense!"

Another, "Wait till your mum sees you!" His face was covered with scratches, his clothes torn, his hands filthy. He came limping back to Joyce, and she cried, "Oh, Jack, you are a sight."

He produced the kitten from inside his wet shirt. "Here he is," he said, fondling the creature, "pretty little nipper, isn't he? I reckon we might as well keep him after all that caper."

The bald-headed man turned round. "Here," he said, "that's my cat if you don't mind!" He lifted the kitten out of Jack's hands and walked away.

"Well,"Joyce gasped, "Some people!"

Jack's grin was more shamefaced than ever. He looked as if he wanted to escape from her as well as from the crowd. "Never mind!" she said. She hooked her arm through his and steered him proudly homeward, with the air of one displaying a prize exhibit, through what remained of the crowd.

Chapter 4

THE BLOCK OF FLATS on the bombed site was growing in a manner that was almost mystifying. All day long the workmen would lounge about among the heaps of bricks and cement, with little visible sign of progress to the casual passer-by; but each evening, when the site was deserted, the red walls were seen to have sprung a little higher, like some mysterious and geometrically-proportioned plant that grew of its own accord in the rich sunshine. Most people watched its growth with complacent interest, but Jack could never rid himself of a vague feeling of hurt as the traces of the old houses, the last visible memorial to his own past, were progressively obliterated.

It was a Sunday afternoon, the last day of July, and he was leaning on the lamp-post at the street corner, smoking a cigarette and staring at the site with half-seeing eyes. Back in the house Mrs. Wakerell and Joyce were busy preparing for a ceremonial visit from Joyce's brother Fred and his wife. The occasion was an important one; Mrs. Wakerell was proud of her daughter-in-law, and every effort must be made to impress her. Jack had decided to keep out of the way for as long as possible. He was frightened of Gwendoline. The first time he had met her he had made the mistake of calling her Gwen, and she had said frigidly, 'Gwendoline'. She had made him feel that she did not regard him as a particularly brilliant candidate for the honour of being received into the same family as that which she had entered, and he dreaded the coming evening.

Perhaps it was this little impulse of fear that sent him to the familiar refuge of memory; perhaps it was the sight of the young boys of the street trooping off in a happy, noisy gang to the swimming baths or of the beautiful young girls swooping round and round the block on their bicycles, making him feel young at first, then terribly old. Staring at the new red walls, he tried to reach back once again to the life that lay beneath their foundations. The past, the beautiful past, was vanishing into the mists. Every day it became more difficult to reach. When had the gap begun to open out? Not with this building — it was only the tombstone on an existing grave. Not even when the bomb had dropped. It was the war — the war — that was when his life had been sheared in two and all that he treasured had run away like an uncoupled railway wagon.

September, nineteen thirty-nine. Until then, 'the war' had meant the other war; one-legged men playing barrel organs in the street, the boozy bragging of the middle-aged men in The Lamb, two minutes of embarrassed silence every Armistice Day, and the picture of Kate Hogarth's dead husband on the parlour wall. How the children used to boast in the street! "Our dad was killed in the war, yours wasn't!" "Yours wasn't prop'ly," would come the reply. "Well," Rose — or Chris, or Alf — never Nancy — would insist, "he was as good as. He was crippled. He died four years after. Our mum used to wheel him about in a chair. She gets a pension from the King, every week." The picture on the wall; like the face of a stranger, an intruder looking in at a window, it had fastened its fixed and unrecognizing stare on them for years. Its presence had always made them uneasy. Rose, of course, had never known her father; Nancy remembered him well; the two boys pretended to, but they had been too young at the time of his death for him to be any more than a phantom in their memories. They had often pestered Kate with questions about him. "Mum, did our dad kill any Germans?" "Mum, did dad

119

win any medals?" But Kate would only answer with a 'yes' or a 'no' and a shadowed smile. What a deadly grief must have sealed her lips, Jack thought, remembering — for she had never spoken of her husband, never told the children about him during all those evenings when she fascinated them with stories by the fire, never even looked up, to the best of Jack's recollection, at the picture: he suddenly remembered the way in which she would walk past it, quietly, as if she were afraid to attract its attention. She had never even — the thought came as one of those bolts which flash from the unconscious to burst in the conscious memory — she had never even, now he came to think of it, taken the children to the cemetery with flowers for their father's grave. And it had never even occurred to the children, so remote was their father from them, so entirely a legend, to ask to go; not even Nancy, in Jack's time, had ever thought of it; not even Nancy, who remembered her father well and who was as silent about him as her mother. Jack sighed, perplexed by this new loose end traced in the threads of his memory. He must ask Nancy about that some time.

Yes, it was the war that had done it. The war, then the bomb, now this new red block growing inexorably towards the day when new people would swarm in and kill the last dying echoes with the din of new life. Day piled upon day, separating human beings from what they loved and driving them towards what they feared; one course of bricks appeared upon another, and the wall sprang up, a visible symbol of what could not be stopped.

"Jack!"

The voice came to him at last. "Ja-ack! Jackie Agass, how many more times have I got to call you?" It was Mrs. Wakerell, leaning out of the upstairs window. "You come in at once!" As usual, she addressed him as if he were a small boy. "I don't want you wearing that sweaty collar when Gwendoline comes. I've put out a starched one for you, and the new tie Joyce bought you." He went, feeling as helplessly resentful as he always did when she treated him in this way, but strangely relieved at the breaking of the spell which had lain upon him.

The visitors arrived at five o'clock. Gwendoline, a tall thin girl who seemed to think it necessary to face the world with a perpetual expression of genteel severity, marched into the parlour first, saluted Mrs. Wakerell and Joyce with perfunctory kisses, and swept the menfolk with a comprehensive and contemptuous glance. Fred cut straight across the room to his father; his subdued face was lit by a smile of astonishing eagerness and delight, which his father returned.

"Hallo father, how are you keeping?"

"In the pink, Fred." Mr. Wakerell's voice and movements seemed to have come to life, as if he had emerged from the invisible hermitage within which he usually lurked. "How are you getting along?"

"Musn't grumble."

"Mustn't grumble?" Mr. Wakerell sighed and looked at the floor, grimacing thoughtfully with his lower lip. "Yes, that's about the size of it with all of us, I suppose."

"I've brought you another book. *Wonders of the Ocean Bed*. Have you finished the other one yet?"

"*Marvels of Astronomy?* Yes, I'll give it to you before you go. Some wonderful facts in that, wonderful. It says in that book, if the sun's heat went down — er —"

"— Three per cent."

"That's right — every living thing on earth would die."

"Cheerful, ain't you?" interrupted Jack, his voice roughened by embarrassment at the crossfire of learned conversation in which he was caught.

"It's all right," said Mr. Wakerell, "there's time for you to get married. They don't reckon it'll happen for — how long was it, Fred?"

"A hundred and fifty thousand million years."

"Ah, I knew it was somewhere round about that."

"What you read all that stuff for?" Jack asked. "It don't help pick any winners."

Mr. Wakerell sank back into his chair as if retreating

into his hermit's cell. He pondered, and when he spoke again, his gruff voice seemed to be coming from a dark doorway. "Takes your mind off things." He paused. "You need something to take your mind off your work when you stand eight hours a day in a warehouse counting cardboard cartons. Twenty-seven years I've been at it: sixteen years packing 'em, and eleven years inspecting other people pack 'em. Eight hours a day, five-and-a-half days a week, fifty-one weeks a year. For twenty-seven years. Chap once said to me, it's not work, it's life-wasting. That's what he said. I reckon you have to learn to be two men if you want to hold down a job like that; one man keeping an eye on the cartons and the other — well —"

"Off to the moon, eh?" said Fred. He asked Jack innocently, "Don't you read much, then?"

Jack, lost in his own thoughts, had scarcely been listening. "Who? Me?" He made a noise that sounded like, "N'yah!"

There was another pause. Fred, wondering how to keep the conversation going, asked, "You interested in anything special?"

"Interested? Me?" Jack sounded indignant. "I work for a living, I do."

"What do you think I do? Pick petals off daisies?"

"Well, I mean," Jack scoffed, "teaching!"

Mr. Wakerell's voice rumbled up from secret places as he came to his son's defence. "It's hard work, teaching. And it's good work, too. That's more than the likes of me can say." He frowned down at the floor as if black depths opened at his feet.

Jack uttered a vague mumble of apology. He had not meant to slight Fred's profession, which he really held in awe. An 'educated boy' was like a sacred cow in Lamb Street. He had been stung by a feeling of inferiority, and by resentment at the way in which the conversation impeded his private thoughts.

"How's the job going, anyway?" Mr. Wakerell was saying.

"Oh, not too badly," said Fred. "As you say, it's satisfying. Or it would be, if we were able to do all we wanted for the kids instead of just teaching them enough to read the football scores and fill in a pools coupon. We might —" he glanced demonstratively at Jack — "get better results."

Jack took no notice. He sat with his head cocked on one side, sheltering behind a rubicund grin that made him look like a ventriloquist's dummy. The chatter of the women on one side of the room and of the men on the other combined as treble and bass, but made no more sense to him than a background music to his thoughts. September, nineteen thirty-nine: how far away it seemed now! There had been trouble in the Hogarth family that summer, but in the tranquil days at the end of August it was all over. Chris had been ill, brought down at last by the exhaustion and the exposure to all weathers which his political work had entailed: there had been a terrible quarrel, as he lay sick, between him and his wife, who after a few months of marriage had declared herself "fed up with it all." Kate had reconciled them, had made Chris promise to take a long rest from his activities for his own and his wife's sake, and had dug down, as she so often did, into the apparently bottomless depths of her savings, to give them enough money to go away for a holiday together — an enterprise which was planned for the end of September. Alf was going with a blowsy girl who played the piano at The Lamb. Kate had surprised them all by going off on her own to Broadstairs to spend — she had told them — a week with some friends of her girlhood. The children, she had pointed out, were old enough to look after themselves, and it was time — no, she did not want Nancy to come and keep her company — for her to have a bit of a change. Everybody had agreed that it was a plucky thing for a woman in her forties to do; she had thoroughly enjoyed herself, and had returned home the evening before war was declared.

"— Tea's ready," announced Joyce, who as usual had

been doing all the work. Everybody rose and Jack, feeling drugged and distant after his mental wanderings, followed reluctantly. He ate little. The noise at the tea-table annoyed him. He sat hunched over his plate, chewing like a ruminant cow and rarely looking up, returning brief and sullen replies to the remarks that were addressed to him. He could feel Gwendoline's contempt and Joyce's dismay, and his self-consciousness made him all the more surly. Tea over, he followed the others back to the parlour. He tried, for a while, to be more sociable, racking his brain for something to talk about, flashing an occasional panic-stricken glance at the clock to see how the time was passing, and wishing that Joyce, who was still in the scullery washing up, would come back to sit on the arm of his chair.

Mrs. Wakerell sat in her armchair like a female Buddha, sucking jam-pips from between her teeth and compressing her lips from time to time in a ladylike substitute for a belch. She turned from her conversation with Gwen. "Come here, Jack," she said.

Jack rose obediently and stood before her like a small boy summoned by his mother.

"Button your jacket up," she commanded. He obeyed. "There," she said to Gwendoline, "it's not a bad fit, is it?"

Gwendoline looked him frigidly up and down, like an officer inspecting a soldier on parade. "You won't let him wear that for the wedding, will you?" she rapped. "That blue is too bright. Too much padding in the shoulders. Trousers too wide in the leg. Turn-ups too big. I don't know what my family would say if they saw him like that."

Joyce had come back into the room. She was staring at Jack, waiting for him to hit back. Jack could manage only a vast, imploring grin and a feeble, "Here —!"

Joyce sank quietly on to the edge of a chair, her hands clasped in her lap. Her head was bowed. "You know a lot," she said to Gwendoline in a hostile voice. To Jack, standing helpless, it seemed that she had accepted the decision of the other two women to discuss him in his presence as if he were no more than a dummy.

"I know what's common," replied Gwendoline sharply.

Jack was in a daze of misery. He did not know at which of the women to look, and when he turned his head the muscles of his neck were stiff. He did not know how to stand, or what to do with his hands, or how to escape from where he stood.

"Don't you worry, Gwendoline dear," Mrs. Wakerell said comfortingly, "Our Jack's not common. We'll have him fitted out properly for the wedding. He's a nice, quiet feller." She beamed at Jack, and he felt a little quiver of rage inside him. He hated her when she called him "a nice, quiet feller." He, Jack Agass! — who had — he consoled himself and infuriated himself with memories of the violent adventures in which he had shared. Oh, if these women only knew the things he had done, the things he was capable of doing! They had better look out or he would show them! One day, he would show them! A nice, quiet, feller! His legs trembled. Mrs. Wakerell went on, "Eight pounds a week besides overtime. It's not every girl who can look forward to marrying that. *And* he's got a bank account, *and* nearly five hundred pounds in it, and he's given Joyce her own cheque book."

Jack waited, and he saw that Joyce, flushed and resentful, was waiting, for the customary command to "run upstairs and fetch it, there's a dear!" But Mrs. Wakerell reached instead for her handbag. "Here it is," she said complacently, rummaging and producing it. "See for yourself."

Joyce cried, "Mum!"

"It's all right, my dear. I took it from your dressing-table yesterday to show Mrs. Balmforth, and I forgot to put it back. I'm sure there's no harm in that — your own mother!"

Jack went and sat on the arm of Joyce's chair. She looked at him despairingly and laid her hot hand on his. Neither of them spoke. Mrs. Wakerell said, "Go and sit on the couch, there's a good boy, you'll ruin that armchair with your weight on it like that."

Animals obeying their trainers must feel as Jack felt when he slunk across to the couch. Gwendoline moved up with the air of a bus passenger who is being squeezed by a rude interloper, and Jack lowered his body warily into the far corner. There was a little room left between himself and Gwendoline, and he looked eagerly at Joyce, in the hope that she would come over to him. She was not looking his way. She had recovered from the mood of a moment before and was discussing interior decoration with her mother and Gwendoline: their talk was a clash of enthusiastic shrillnesses. Jack felt snubbed, resentful at her for not sharing his social inadequacy. He leaned back in his corner of the couch, his arms lying along the leathern rests, and glared at the ceiling. The more humiliating and difficult the present moment, the easier he found it to escape to the past. He lost his grip on the talk that was going on around him; people and objects became shadows, surfaces and colours moving about without meaning before his eyes. Areas of the brain and nerve centres, performing a sort of rearguard action on behalf of the rest of him, remained alert, enabling him to turn his head towards whoever spoke to him, to smile feebly when required, and to produce a series of remarks which came as meaninglessly to his own ears as the talk of the other people in the room. Thus protected, his real self fled back to nineteen thirty-nine.

***

...the evening before the declaration of war: Lamb Street is lying quiet and uneasy in the sunlight: an occasional shout echoes as disturbingly as in a church. The family takes Kate to The Lamb to celebrate her return with a few drinks before supper. The quiet has invaded the saloon bar. Mick has been out of town for days on some unspecified business. Bernie and several of his cronies

126

have already departed to their Territorial regiments. The children have been evacuated and their parents sit in the bar in despondent attitudes, sipping their beer in silence. The door bangs and the clatter of feet disturbs the anxious hush as the Hogarths walk in. Faces are upturned. Subdued 'good evenings' are exchanged. A child's smile flits across Barmy's tortured face. Kate pauses at the bar and says to him, "It's been a lonely week for you my pet, hasn't it? The both of us away? How are you, love, all merry and bright?"

Barmy: "You look happy, Kate."

Kate: "Like a young girl."

Barmy: "I don't wonder."

Kate: "My poor lamb. Do you hate me for going off like that?"

Barmy: "I'm glad you're back."

Kate: "Bless you."

The family seat themselves at a round table and Barmy brings their drinks. Jack and Alf are talking gloomily about the prospect of being conscripted. Alf suggests ways of keeping out of it. Rose breaks in passionately, calls them a pair of miseries, asks them if *they* aren't excited and ends, breathless with indignation, "Oh, if I were a man!" Alf says, "Well, you go and fight then. I'll stay behind and wear a pinnie. I ain't proud." Chris begins, in his bleating voice, to explain why this is a people's war, for which every man should volunteer. His wife shuts him up, with a gleam of angry tears in her eyes. Alf says, "When Nelson gets his eye back, I'll volunteer." Alf and Jack have, after agreeing on how to remain civilian, been driven by some mysterious alchemy of the spirit into an argument about the respective merits of the Tank Corps and the Air Force, which they carry on with schoolboy enthusiasm and violence. Barmy says to Kate, in a frightening voice, "I'd poison 'em all before I let 'em go!"

Kate: "Don't say such things."

Barmy: "I thought you knew better, Kate. I thought you

127

knew what it does to a man."

Kate: "I know what it does to a woman."

Barmy: "And you sit there smiling!"

Kate: "We've got enough troubles now, without worrying about those we've had and those to come. Now let's forget it, all of us."

Chris: "It's no use trying to shirk our responsibilities, Mum."

Kate: — all her children look up as they hear her cry in a voice that they have never heard before — "Shut up, all of you. I've had enough of it for one lifetime, I tell you! God only knows how much longer we shall be together! But I've got my children round me now, and I'm not going to think of anything else. Now, all of you, not another word about it, do you hear?" Jack, glancing at her in surprise, is too late to catch the mood: she is serene again. She says, "Aren't we a silly lot of moos?" The scene is set. Capricious memory has made its selection, posed its subjects. The family will have more good days together, for the end, which is not yet, will be gradual like a decay. More significant things will happen to Jack and around him. He will live through episodes which will seem to him at the time dramatic and unforgettable. But memory will let them all slip from its grasp. It clicks the camera, and this undistinguished tableau is imprinted on the consciousness for ever. Kate, his guardian angel, his more-than-mother, his dream of human perfection to sustain him amid all the ordures and disillusionments of life — Kate sits upright, yet placid and relaxed. Her piled black hair shines beneath the tepid lights. Her gaze is profound with secret knowledge, yet it rests on her family with contentment and repose. Her boys are all bigger than her, but they sit in attitudes of deference, and she seems to rise above them as if they were little children once again. Oh, Kate, Kate, beloved Kate...

***

And here he was, ten years later, not ten years richer but ten years emptier of heart. Here he was sitting among strangers — yes, they were strangers, like all the rest of the world — unvalued and — he was sure of it — despised. These bouts of memory were like drugs; they left him depressed, physically as well as spiritually. He felt less confidence than ever in face of the people in the room, more distaste for their company. Even Joyce, to whom he might have turned for comfort, ignored him.

"No," he heard himself saying. Mrs. Wakerell was in front of him with a bowl of fruit. "No, honest, I'm full up. Honest, full right up I am." ... Had it been that evening, in that moment, when the link with life snapped? Or had it been that other moment six months later, that other scene which he loved to run through his mind, again and again, like a reel of film? — when the five faces had sped backward past the window of his railway carriage and vanished among a crowd of white faces and waving hands? — when he had settled in his seat, jaunty, alone, with Kate's sandwiches in his pocket and Rose's parting kiss still warm on his mouth? — when his heart had been filled with the wild and stifling hopes which that kiss, unaccompanied by any spoken pledge, had aroused? — when jaunty, alone, grinning at his fellow-passengers, he had felt the first chill of terror spreading through him as the train clattered over the points and bore him out into a vast and cruel world? — when childhood and youth and all that was sweet in life vanished in a swirl of white smoke?

After all, he had assured himself in the months that followed, home was still there to go back to. Too busy to think or to feel, in his new world of marching, shouting, sweating, stabbing at sacks, shooting at dummies, he had glanced at letter after letter, not perceiving that 'home' was crumbling away. Alf called up to the Service Corps: Chris trying to join up, being rejected and informed that there was a spot on his lung, working day and night in a war factory, falling ill, working again, falling ill again, creeping back to work, falling ill again and again: Rose scribbling an occasional letter, killing with her indifference the baseless hopes her kiss had aroused, dashing off at last on a madcap impulse and joining the A.T.S.: Nancy in munitions and drafted to the North: and in the end Kate, alone in her house, writing letters to them all. Perhaps they had all looked forward, as he had, to reunion, not realising that the march of life had scattered them for ever. For ever...

The visitors were leaving. He bade them mechanical goodbyes, coming out of his shell sufficiently to notice how Gwendoline managed to impart even to her handshake — or rather, finger-squeeze — an impression of frigid superciliousness; and how reluctantly Fred — that obedient son whose marriage had been his crowning act of obedience to his mother — quit his father's side and followed his wife out of the house like a ticket-of-leave man going back to jail.

It was late in the evening. When the door had closed behind the departing guests Mr. Wakerell yawned, stretched himself and shambled off to the rear of the house, where he could be heard bolting doors and closing windows for the night. Mrs. Wakerell said to Joyce, "What a day, dear! I'm worn out, and that's a fact. You'll clear up, won't you?" — and with a blithe "goodnight" she lumbered up to bed.

Jack and Joyce, left alone in the parlour, moved about the room without speaking, gathering up cups and saucers, emptying ashtrays, straightening chairs and corners of rugs. Jack felt relieved, but tired and confused as if he had been sleeping in the sunshine. He tried to think of something amiable and conciliatory to say to Joyce, something that would enable them both to laugh away the day's ordeal; but his brain and tongue were too sluggish.

Joyce seemed to be absorbed in her own thoughts, heedless of him even when she passed close by, her face downcast and frowning; she gave vent to little flurries of furious energy, thumping and shaking at cushions as if they were naughty children and crashing cups and saucers on to the tray without regard to their fragility. At last, without looking at him, she muttered — as if she were trying to restrain with her teeth the words that some inner force was driving out of her — "You didn't have much to say for yourself."

Jack had almost reached the point of framing a coherent sentence. Joyce's remark struck into him and sent his carefully-gathered words flying like skittles. While his mind, utterly startled, tried to scrabble the words together, his bottled-up emotions forced another reply out of him, and he heard himself cry, "What about you?"

"Oh?" Joyce's voice was thick with humiliation, still unsteady with the battle between rage and restraint. "I suppose *I* sat like a dummy all day long, staring up at the ceiling with my mouth open? I suppose *I* showed the family up? I suppose *I* made my fiancée look like a fool? I suppose *I* mumbled, "Eh?" and "Yerh" and "Oomm" every time an intelligent remark was addressed to me?"

Jack, too, tried to keep his voice under control. "And I suppose *I* let myself be ordered about like a skivvy? I suppose *I* let my mum help herself out of my dressing table and flash my cheque book all over the place? Some hopes, I bet!"

"You're the one to criticise, I must say!" Joyce's voice had risen by half an octave. She went on with her work in a stifling silence. For a moment Jack, trying to hold his own feelings in check, hoped that she had regained control of herself. Then she burst out, "A fine object you are to cart about! The answer to a maiden's prayer, and I don't think!"

"Good enough for you, I can tell you! You ain't exactly a prize packet. You go and look in the mirror if you don't believe me. When I think of the lovely girls I've —" His voice shook. "Strikes me you don't know when you're lucky!"

131

"Lucky!" Her voice quavered so wildly that he grinned, and enraged her further. "I've had men after me that would make you look like two pennorth of old rope!"

"Yerh! Sing us another one!"

Joyce's voice grew shriller and more strained. "And when you find yourself in decent company you might try and act up to it."

"Meaning?"

She did not reply.

"Meaning I ought to ponce and prance about like that sister-in-law of yours, I suppose? Hold my teacup like this? —" He snatched up a cup and held it by two fingers with grotesque effeminacy. "— And stick my little finger out like this? Ooh, Fred, deah, pawss the sugah, naice weather we're heving, dewn't you think? Gah! 'Cher think I am? A bloody lapdog?"

"I'd be satisfied if you acted like a man, never mind a lapdog."

"Man? Me?" He uttered the words as bleats of incredulous dismay. "Here! —" He stood with his mouth open, breathing loudly. "Me?" He almost squealed the word. He tried to think of a fitting reply, but was able only to expel a horrified, "Gaw!" After a pause he said in a dull stubborn, voice, "Well, if you feel like chuckin' it in —"

She stared at him with wide, unfathomable eyes. There was a long moment of quiet during which he waited, terrified, for her to make her decision. At last she said, "Quiet, they'll hear us upstairs."

Jack felt deflated, unable to continue the quarrel at the same pitch as before. The two of them had vented on each other, involuntarily, their identical feelings, and now they stood like lost people on a street corner. But their quarrel still had to pass through its second stage — the dogged and sullen, the retreating, self-justifying stage.

"Well," Jack muttered, "don't you shout, then."

"I didn't shout. You did."

"Well, I never started it."

"You were the cause of it."

"Come off it! I never said a word."

"That's the trouble. You never said a word all day."

"There you go again! Can't you give it a rest?"

They both wanted to break off the action, but each wanted to fire the last shot. "And another thing," she said, "don't you talk so backhanded about my mum in future."

He sighed, entirely dejected. "Women!" he sighed. "You was looking daggers at her yourself, and then when I say a word — ah, go to bed!"

She backed towards the door, as if expecting him to say something else. He remained silent. When she had gone, he switched off the light and went out into the hall. She was standing on the stairs. "I can't go to bed like this," she said, "I won't sleep a wink. Six weeks engaged and listen to us!"

He managed a clumsy grin. "That don't do, eh? Not till we're married! Row as much as we like, then? Eh?"

"I don't know what came over us." She lifted up her head stubbornly. "But it was all your fault!" She sighed, "Oh, well, sleep it off, that's the only thing. We'll see the funny side in the morning. Good night, Jack."

"Good night."

They were both brusque, as if to speak graciously would be to yield one point too many, but they were both relieved. Nevertheless Jack was kept awake for a long time that night by the sense of lingering alarm that follows a narrow escape and he guessed from the sounds of restlessness he heard through the bedroom wall that Joyce, too, was puzzling over their quarrel.

Part 3

Chapter 1

THE TIMELESS DREAM OF SUMMER was broken early in August when — by a gigantic piece of good fortune — one of Mrs. Wakerell's cousins brought the news that she was moving in to a Council flat in November, and that Jack and Joyce were welcome to take over from her the three rooms which she at present occupied in Barnsbury, at twenty-five shillings a week.

At last Jack felt solid ground beneath his feet. His new life was no longer an astonished daydream. He and Joyce could now set a definite term to their preparations. They decided to be married at the beginning of December. They inspected the flat, drawn closer together by their proud, possessive happiness than they had ever been before, and took decisions about wallpapers, linoleum and furniture. Now they could look into shop windows and discuss where this clock could go, on which wall to hang that picture, whether these curtains would look nice in the bay window and whether there would be room for that armchair. Joyce wrote cheques under Jack's supervision (to do so, until she became used to it, filled her with an extraordinary mixture of bliss and terror) and, as their bank balance began to shrink, so the cupboard in her bedroom filled with crockery, cutlery and linen. Their first quarrel was quickly forgotten.

They were on one of their Sunday morning expeditions to Petticoat Lane, stifling in the crowds, the dusty smell and the gritty heat, when Joyce said, "Over there, Jack, on the left."

"What is?"

"What I told you about. Oh, they're lovely! Make a room beautiful, they will."

The crowds between the high black walls were like a battling of armies. People made progress by delivering themselves up to one or another of the warring surges and being ground forward, through the opposing mass, towards their destinations. Jack changed course and was borne away to the left, with Joyce struggling after him.

"This it?" To make himself heard above the din he had to turn his face up to the sky and shout, in the hope that Joyce would hear him among all the shouting of vendors and snatches of conversation around them.

"The next one. The glassware." The stalls were little islands of bright colour among the swirling black mobs. "Oh, Jack!" cried Joyce, reaching him again and clinging to his arm, "Look! Aren't they a dream?"

A huge, hoarse-voiced vendor was standing on his stall, ankle-deep in a mess of straw and brown paper amid which gleamed cut glass and brightly-coloured chinaware. He was describing, in a monstrously-magnified whisper, the merits of the utensil which he held aloft with both hands as if it were a hard-won trophy. Here was an article, he announced, known to philosophers as the Great Equalizer, to intellectuals as the Throne of Meditation, and to the vulgar as the Good Old Shoveunder. "Don't blush, ladies," he urged, "I can see you're all married, or about to be —" and indeed, it was remarkable that his entire audience consisted of young couples, each looking exactly like Jack and Joyce, each pair clinging close together and staring up at him in solemn silence — "and if you don't face the Facts of Life now, you never will." He had no hesitation, he said, in offering it for their inspection. No home was complete without one, no bride need be ashamed to include one in her trousseau, and you could give one as a wedding present in the knowledge that it would be treasured and appreciated for years to come. This model was the latest triumph of modern design, a perfect combination of beauty and utility, as supplied to the highest in the land, including His Grace the Duke of Devonshire, the Aga Khan, Mr. Ernest Bevin and Miss Margaret Lockwood. They were available in pink, blue, cream, pastel green and daffodil yellow. Note, he said — and here he broke off to command his assistant, "Pass a few round, Charlie" — note the record capacity, the broad brim for comfort, the strength of construction. He invited his audience to test them for balance. They were guaranteed, guaranteed he repeated, to take any weight. Show him, he appealed to his audience, show him the backside that was too big for one of these and he personally would hand the lady or gent a five-pound note. The proud possessor of one of these could hand it down to his children and to his children's children. No-one need fear burglars with one of these within reach. Heaven help the lodger if he came home drunk and started banging the front door down at two o'clock in the morning. "Why!" the vendor declared, in a final hoarse roar of enthusiasm, "turn it upside down and it makes a perfect air-raid shelter!"

Jack was staring at Joyce, shocked beyond words. "Here," he managed to say at last, "mean to tell me *that's* what you been thinking about?"

Joyce blinked back at him in dismay. "Oh, no," she squeaked, hesitated as she recovered from her surprise, and giggled. "Oh, no, silly! The idea! Them, I meant." She pointed at a pair of porcelain statuettes.

"Oh, them. He'll be putting them up in a minute or two. I tell you what." Jack was invaded by a sudden mood of recklessness. "I reckon we might as well get one of them jerries while we're about it."

"What! In broad daylight? Not with me you won't."

"Go away!" Jack was delighted to be able to play the man. "Who's windy? What you think I am, some old chase-me-charlie, afraid to face people?"

"Oh, Jack," she begged, at his mercy, "not now!"

He could not miss his chance to swagger before her, to assert his manhood. He fumbled in his pocket for money, ignoring her restraining clutch on his arm. "You leave it to me. I'll carry it, you won't have to. I ain't afraid. There's no-one living can put the wind up Jackie Agass, and I ain't a-kidding you."

"Jack, if you do, you can go home on your own, and *I'm* not kidding, either."

"Oh, well." He was satisfied now that he had made his demonstration. "Not worth an argument, I suppose. Some other time'll do. Surprised at you I am, girl, honest. Ah, well, takes a man, some things, I suppose."

Meanwhile the vendor, after a brisk introduction of the price question, had worked himself up into a frenzy of self-sacrifice, and in a passionate series of grand gestures, had knocked down the price to half-a-crown. Now he was reaping the reward of virtue as fast as his assistants could collect the money. "One on the right," he was directing, "gent in a trilby at the back, beautiful lady just behind you Charlie. There!" he said, as the beautiful lady took the last one, "And that's the lot. Engaged or married, madam? Engaged. I knew by the look of you. Well, God bless you, lady, and may your cup of happiness be filled to overflowing."

The salesman wiped gleaming sweat from his face, recovering his breath like an athlete between races. His assistants gathered expectantly at his feet. At last he wheezed, "Hand up them Arcadian Lovers, Charlie," and amid a great tearing-off of wrappings and flinging about of straw, the two statuettes were fully revealed. He was going, he resumed, to address himself now to those ladies and gents who were refined enough to appreciate a work of art when they saw one. To those who wanted to fill their homes with beauty. To those who wanted to bring their children up as cultured as themselves. Here, made available for the first time since the originals, by the celebrated Mr. Oscar Wilde, were bought for the nation by the National Gallery, Westminister, was a pair of genuine reproductions in porcelain of that famous pair, the Shepherd and his Sweetheart. Otherwise the

Arcadian Lovers.

There were sighs and murmurs from among the girls in the audience. Joyce's eyes were shining. She whispered, "Oh, them on the mantelpiece, and green plastic curtains, and a big bowl of flowers in the window!" Jack and the other men remained lumpish but alert.

The salesman went on to describe the merits of the statuettes, declaring that a thing of beauty was a joy for ever, and reminding his listeners of the words of the immortal Shakespeare, Breathes there a man with soul so dead, Who never to himself hath said, A little of what you fancy does you good. A man of taste himself, he regarded it as his hobby, rather than his living, to place these treasures within the reach of the general public. He was therefore not going to ask the five golden guineas you would have to pay for a pair like this in Christie's Auction Rooms, the West End of London, nor even four, nor even three, nor even two guineas, but one guinea the pair. Selling them? He was giving them away.

While he declaimed, there was a stir of feminine whispering in the crowd, all mingling in a single and distinctly supplicatory pitch. Dozens of couples were in conference. He pressed home his advantage, reminding them that he had a limited stock, and that those who were disappointed would only have themselves to blame. His assistants moved forth to the attack.

Joyce squealed, as if she were begging for love, "Oh, Jack, please, please!"

Jack, feeling more than ever the master of the situation, answered, "You wait a bit, girl. I know these geezers."

None of the statuettes had yet been sold. The men patted their girls' hands and maintained a sceptical silence.

No takers? — the vendor resumed. Ah, well, he knew how it was after Bank Holiday. Money short everywhere. We couldn't have the booze *and* the bawbees, eh? Well, he'd tell them what he'd do. He was a man of impulse, he was a man who acted first and regretted it later. "Make it an even quid. One dirty bit of paper, that was all. No? Seventeen-and-six! Fifteen shillings!"

"Jack!"

"Wait!"

"Jack! We've got to! You heard him, it's art."

"All right, girl, keep your hair on."

The girls trembled and the men, all-wise, waited. There were still no takers.

"Gawd, love us!" bellowed the salesman. "You're a soft lot, aren't you. Won't even let yourselves be done a good turn! Look here, I won't argy-bargy. Twelve-and-six. Ten bob. Me last offer. Say yes before I come to my senses. Yes, yes, yes, yes, yes — who?"

No-one.

"Who? Come along, come along — who? Going for ten bob, daylight robbery, may I drop dead if it ain't."

There was a dramatic pause. Some of the men began to stir and fumble in their pockets. The vendor did not drop dead and, as if reassured, the men relapsed into their former attitude, heads lowered, eyes vigilant. Joyce was bouncing up and down on her toes, frantic.

The vendor wiped his brow again. "All right," he said wearily, "my last offer. Three half-a-crowns. No-one at three half-a-crowns? All right, Charlie. Put 'em away, no sale."

Joyce uttered a broken-hearted sigh. A voice came from the back of the crowd. "I'll have a pair." Another voice, "Over 'ere, gov'nor." The salesman came to life. "Pass 'em out, Charlie, pass 'em out." Jack took a pair and put them in Joyce's arms. "There you are," he said, "all a matter of waiting. Got to know your way around, old girl, if you want to get on in the world, and that's a fact."

Joyce said humbly, "Yes, Jack," and hugged the statuettes to her as blissfully as if they were her own twin babies. There was a tremor of sensual delight in the fierce pressure of her arm against them. She was tasting what, to her, was the primary pleasure of marriage, beside

142

which the pleasures of the flesh were pale and doubtful. She let her weight hang heavily on Jack's arm, expressing gratitude and admiration, acknowledging her feminine dependence. Jack, as he led her away through the crowds, bragged, "Saved us a few bob there, eh? — didn't I? You trust your old Jack and you won't go far wrong." Her adoring, "Yes, Jack," was music to him. He had demonstrated his power and right to direct their joint affairs. He was uplifted by a swaggering sense of his own sapience, inflated with lordly generosity. He bought her, despite her happy protests, a gilt brooch with 'Good Luck' written on it, and they wandered off to the trolleybus terminus in Bishopsgate, she hugging her statuettes and resting her head on his shoulder, he with his arm tightly round her waist, the two of them a picture of contentment.

Now that a date for their marriage had been set, they were making a round of visits of their friends and relations to spread the news; and on the bus Jack proposed that they should make use of the time that remained before lunch to call on Alf Hogarth, whose home lay on their return journey. Joyce refused, pleading fatigue and saying that she would rather take the statuettes straight home. She suggested that Jack go on his own, and he agreed. He accompanied her to the Angel, saw her across the road, parted from her with a cheerful squeeze of the arm and a promise not to be late for dinner, and made his way back down City Road.

He turned off to the left, into Hoxton, hurrying through narrow, dirty streets that were all stamped with a squalor that was foreign to Lamb Street. It was a depressing district, a disorderly huddle of big factories, blank slimy walls and monotonous rows of little houses, all chopped in a tumbling, disorderly pattern of black against the clean sky. Here and there rose new factories, hideous cubes of ochre brick, and between them gleamed the Grand Union Canal, its dark smooth surface iridescent with pollution. The air smelt of railway grit

143

and stagnant water. He came to a huge black block of tenements, three wings of which, each floor defaced by a rusty iron balcony, looked down on a concrete courtyard, like a great jail with the roof taken off. The fourth side consisted of tall iron railings, forbiddingly spiked. Over the gate was the inscription in iron scrollwork, 'Bennett's Buildings, 1863 A.D.'

The great pool of poverty that poisoned the social fabric of London in the last century has almost vanished, but here and there, tucked away amid the growth of new life, noisome puddles can still be found: Bennett's Buildings was one of them. To Jack, whose upbringing had imbued him with the outlook of that section of the working-class whose proudest possession is the word 'respectable,' it was always unnerving to come here. The people in the 'respectable' streets hated these slums and their inhabitants as a reminder of their own origins and of the depths into which personal insecurity or some wrench of social change might one day plunge them again. A real hostility underlay the endless feuds which the children carried on. Indeed, Jack knew that it was mainly out of distaste that Joyce had refused to accompany him.

A sociable uproar of male voices could be heard through the doors of the little pub across the road, and the playground teemed with stampeding children. Most of the people whom Jack saw looked as neat as their poor clothes permitted them to be, but they all bore the impress of their surroundings. The women were more haggard or shapelessly fat than those in Lamb Street, the girls by comparison were slatternly, the men wore collarless shirts that would not have been tolerated in Lamb Street on a Sunday morning, and the children's faces were of a pallor which Jack had not seen elsewhere since his childhood. All of them, beneath their superficial vitality, betrayed the dogged weariness of people who wear out their whole lives fighting to hold their ground without the hope of gaining an inch.

He looked uncertainly at the row of staircase entrances

that faced him, narrow dark slots like the doors of tombs, each at the foot of a grim shaft of black brick. He could never remember which was Alf's. Children were gathering round him, and women with babies in their arms were hovering nearby, the babies leaning towards him out of their mothers' clutches as if they too wanted to inspect the stranger. "Who d'you want, mister?" — one of the women asked.

"Alf Hogarth, Number Ninety-Four."

"They're out."

A terrifying hubbub ensued, with one woman screeching, "They ain't," another shouting, "They are, I seen 'em over The Blue Jug," another testifying, with the clamorous support of a half-a-dozen children, that she had seen Alf and his wife come in, a small boy bleating in terror, "'E's the School Board!", a woman in the background asking loudly, "It ain't the furniture man, is it? They been watching out for 'im," and another replying, "What, on a Sunday?" Jack said, "Here! —" A woman, leaning from a balcony like a preacher from a pulpit, announced in powerful tones, "You're his brother-in-law, ain't you? I seen you with 'im up the Angel once. I arst' im after. He told me." The. assemblage seemed to be remarkably well informed on the family life of the Hogarths, for the courtyard resounded with explanations and discussions while Jack escaped and hastened up a stone staircase to his destination. At each landing someone popped out to have a look at him. One woman said, "Your name's Agass, ain't it," and promptly disappeared. Another shouted up to the next landing, "Someone for Alf Hogarth," and as he was climbing the last few steps a little boy bolted up past him, banged at Alf's front door, called through the letterbox, "The furniture man!" and scuttled away. Jack knocked at the door. There was no response. He knocked again. A man's voice bellowed from within, "— orf!" He knocked again. Again the voice, "I'm in me bath. Stick it through the letterbox." A woman's voice added, "Stick it up your

145

jumper!" Jack pushed open the letterbox with his finger and called, "That you, Alf? This is Jackie Agass."

Within, two voices shouted simultaneously: the female, "It's your Jackie!": the male, "'Old on, Jackie!" Again the woman's voice, "Well don't leave 'im standing there like a 'umpty-backed 'alfpenny. Let him in!" The door opened. Alf's florid face beamed at him in bloated good fellowship. Alf pointed at Jack, opened his mouth, threw his head back and emitted a great hooting blast of laughter. When this had subsided he said, "An' I thought you was the Never-Never! Come in, stranger." Jack followed him into an airless and foul-smelling kitchen whose disorder was mocked by the sunlight through the closed window. Poll, Alf's wife, said, "Hallo, Jackie. Pardon my neglidgee." She had rouged her lips and plastered her thin, lined face with a mask of white powder; her mop of tight black curls shone as if brilliantined; but, in spite of her reported visit to the pub, she was still slippered and barelegged, and clutched a filthy pink dressing gown across her meagre chest.

"'Ow's the world treating you, son?" she shrilled. "Cup o' tea?"

Jack said, "All right. Yes please. No sugar."

"Don't ask him," Alf shouted, "give him!" Both he and his wife seemed to be under the impression that their visitor was deaf, for, having pushed him down into a chair they stood one on each side of him and bellowed at him competitively.

There came another onslaught of noise from Alf. "What's the news? How's the Wakerells? Where's your lovey-dovey?"

Jack sat in a defensive huddle, as if beneath the impact of hurricane gusts. "All right. All okey doke. She went home get dinner ready. Sends her regards."

Poll fumbled in a zinc bath full of dirty crockery beneath the sink. Jack watched, benumbed, while she rummaged for a cup, rinsed it negligently under the tap, scratched a deposit of sugar from the inside with her

146

fingernail and filled the cup with tea.

"Here!" Jack flinched as Alf hailed his wife through an invisible megaphone. "Give him a saucer!"

"Gah way!" she screeched back. "'E's not a baby!"

"'S all right," Jack murmured, "don't trouble. I'm cushy." He sipped the tea, which was strong and well-brewed, but which seemed, in some mysterious manner, to have acquired a flavour of kippers, "All right, this." He smacked his lips loudly to indicate pleasure and went on. "Got a flat. Smashing place. Up Barnsbury. Croshers, relations they are, Mrs. Wakerell, don't think you know 'em. Moving out November. I mean them. We're moving in. Well, like, December. Week or two get place fixed up, eh?" Bowed beneath his hosts' uproarious intercourse, he could only manage a sort of telegraphic mumble.

There followed a rapid blast and counterblast over his head, in increasing volume.

Poll: "God bless yer, boy!"

Alf: "The both of you!"

Poll: "Bloody beano that'll be!"

Alf: "Right on top o' Christmas!"

Poll, in an ecstatic climax: "Two do's in a month!"

Alf nearly knocked Jack off his chair with a jovial punch between the shoulder-blades and roared, "Oohoo! Talk about a Christmas box for Joycie! Give her something she'll never forget, eh? —"

Poll went off into a deafening paroxysm of laughter, and, wiping her eyes, gasped, "To 'er dying day!"

The pair of them went off into convulsions, while Jack grinned humbly up at them. He was waiting, embarrassed, for a chance to interject a few words and change the subject, but they were too intoxicated with their joke, and between the screams and chesty barks of laughter with which they filled the room, they kept adding such elaborations as, "Saving up, boy, I bet?" and (Poll), "Got enough to fill 'er stocking with, son?" and, "Who'll put the plums in her Christmas pudden?" At last the din subsided, and Poll concluded, with a long groan of

147

pleasure, "Ooh, talk about laugh!"

Jack sniggered a dutiful little, "Herh! herh!" and hurriedly went on. "Yes, smashing flat. Three rooms. Kitchen. Use of bath. Twenty-five bob a week. All right these days, that is. Near the buses, handy for work an' all. I suppose you're looking for something else?"

Alf answered, in a boom of surprise, "What for?"

"Well, I mean, this gaff —"

"Stuck up in your old age, ain't you. Wouldn't shift out of here for a pension. Bloody buildings, it's nice and matey. Everyone mucks in. You can have a lend of anything you like, that's more that you can say in Lamb Street. None of this clean curtains lark — well, some of 'em do, but at least you got the bloody option. Think I don't remember Lamb Street? God help you if you had a dirty doorknocker down there! You come home a bit blindoh, you don't see no-one whispering behind your back. I tell you, there's a right barney here every Saturday night when the pubs close. Coppers keep out of the way, I can tell you. You got bloody friends here, you have, don't hide their business from each other either. Bailiffs come for your furniture, you've only got to whistle and there's ten strong men on the bloody staircase ready for all comers."

"Mind you," Poll cut in, "there's a lot trying to get out. Up the council day in and day out, nag, nag, nag. Not good enough for 'em, I suppose. Want their kids to be little lords and ladies."

Jack was not listening closely. A feeling of depression had come over him as he looked at Alf. He tried to catch hold of what it was that disturbed him: some memory of childhood, perhaps, that had flitted before his inner eye. How sweet and clean their life had been when they were children! How full of promise, how far removed it had been from this defeated squalor! Could this man before him — thinning hair plastered in strips like black wax across his scalp, thumbs hooked in belt scratching pleasurably with the fingers of both hands at the ugly

148

belly which sagged out below, voice coarse and gross —
could this be one of the children Kate had held in her
arms? Alf had always been something of a black sheep,
but at least in the old days he had been lithe and clean
and eager. Jack struggled to form into articulate
thoughts the realisation that was coming to him, that
time decays and defeats us. From Kate's shining kitchen
to this stale scullery: ten years. The thought crushed him.

"How's the old job going?" Alf was asking. "Bashing up
the bloody lolly?"

"Ah," Jack said, "Doing all right. Eight quid a week
plus overtime. Save a bit on that, you can. You ought to
try it, instead of pushing that old lorry around for a fiver
a week."

"That's what you think, son. It ain't the wages on my
job. It's the knocksy. The bloody pickings. You know,
what falls off the back of the old lorry, only it always falls
into our kitchen cupboard. Crate of oranges, box of butter,
jar of pickles. And all that stuff for the docks."

"No wonder the exports is going down," said Poll, "Arf
of 'em's in our bloody cupboard. Talk about export or die!"

"Well, they can bloody die for all I care," said Alf, "help
yourself out of their pockets faster than they help
theirselves out of yours, that's what I say. Sod the lot of
'em! D'you pick up much on your job?"

"Not much," Jack answered. "Pocketful of nails, length
of timber, bit of lead sometimes you can sell for a few bob.
Not a lot. Boss's too bloody sharp, anyway."

Alf grinned. "Here, talking, it reminds me when we
used to go pinching? Remember? All the kids from the
street?"

"Ah, that was a game all right."

"Our Rosie, she was the girl for that."

Musing over the spectacle that Alf presented, Jack was
taken unaware by that single, explosive word, 'Rosie'. He
had no time to throw up his painfully-constructed
defences of hostility. With Alf before him, bloated and
soiled by the years, he was suddenly pierced by an

149

anguished desire to know: *what have ten years done to her?* So suddenly that he wanted to rush away and find her, he felt himself swept by a terrible impatience to see her, to find out for himself. And from somewhere inside himself he heard a cry, so distinct that he heard it as a voice in his ears, thin but penetrating, '*I love that bloody girl!*' The words throbbed through him again and again, like a pain. He was frightened by them. He wanted to cancel them, to unthink them, to stuff them back into the dark corner from which they had burst. Above all he was astonished by the rushing, terrifying speed with which this long-repressed mood had broken loose and overwhelmed him. Meanwhile, unable to control himself and change the subject, as he would have liked to do, he was answering Alf in a gush of enthusiasm. "I'll say! First time I went I was hardly more than eight. Couldn't have been more. All the kids went up Woolworths, bloody great mob of 'em. You know the old lark —" he turned to enlighten Poll — "everyone had to bring out something, and you was a sissy if you didn't."

"Ah," said Alf, "we had good times then, didn't we?"

"Lucky none of us ever got nabbed. Wouldn't have been no joke, I can tell you. Bloody Borstal all right."

"Gah, bloody playing, that's all we was. Bloody game it was for us then. Never had the bloody sense to pinch nothing worth while, none of us."

"I wasn't half windy the first time." Jack was speaking in a dreamy, lyrical way, drunk with the words that beat inside him like the throb of bodily love. *I love that girl. I love that bloody girl.* It was not yet time to silence them: for the moment he let them fill his being. Aloud, he said, "Old Rosie says to me, 'You go on in, Jackie, like a big boy, and don't you run when you come out, or they'll come after you. You just walk out, quiet like, as if you never done nothing.' Here —" his voice became confidential. Inwardly he was wondering, in agony, *what have the years done to her?* — "I'll tell you what I done. I had a penny your mum had give me. I went in, and I stood in

150

front of the counter, and I picked up a pencil. Then I got the breeze up. I thought, well, your mum wouldn't have me round the house any more if I got caught. You know what she was for the Ten Commandments, and all that lark. Not to mention the disgrace of having a copper round the house, in Lamb Street. Well, there was me with the wind up, so I paid a penny for the pencil, and I come out, and I said I pinched it. Old Rosie give me a squeeze, and she says, 'Look what Jackie's got, everyone. Isn't he a lovely big boy?' She had a string of beads. I bet *she* never paid for 'em!"

"Not her," Alf confirmed. "What a girl! There wasn't a bloke in the street could touch her for nerve. See her ride a bike no hands, remember? Remember her running along the top of that old factory wall in Penton Street? Twenty foot high if it was an inch, and not six inches wide. Hanging on the backs of carts, in all that traffic. Scrumping apples, remember? Dickie Bannister, he says, 'But they ain't ours, Rosie.' Rosie says, 'Anything's yours if you take it. Besides,' she says, 'God didn't put 'em on that tree for Mr. Moggeridge. He put 'em there for anyone that was hungry. And I'm hungry, Dickie Bannister, if you're not.' Talk about pluck! and look at in the war what she done. Mentioned in dispatches. Bloody girl! More than what you or me ever done. Bomb on the gun site. Bang! Half the roof in, bloody ammo burning and blowing up right and left, and our Rosie under the table with another girl dying in her lap, talking down the old telephone as if she was making a date for Sunday night."

Inwardly Jack was saying, *I love that girl,* for the strange pleasure of hurting himself with the words. And now he forced himself to ask a painful question, "Ever hear what she's doing now?"

"You know as well as I do," said Alf. "Done all right for herself, she has. Can't say I bloody blame her. Mean bitch though, never comes near us. I suppose she's afraid we'll touch her for a few quid."

What have the years done to her?

151

"Estella's seen 'er," Poll began, with the delighted crow of a woman who has a choice bit of gossip to impart. "There's another one done all right for 'erself. See 'er up the dogs we do, dressed to kill. 'Ad 'er 'ead screwed on the right way, that one. Your Chris 'adn't been dead a year when she picked another one, and one with the money this time. Got a café up the Angel. Little gold mine, a place like that. You ought to see 'er now. Rings, dresses, motor-car. Up the dogs every week, race meetings, Brighton, Newmarket, Estella sees the world, I can tell you. I reckon if you asked 'er who Chris Hogarth was she'd say, 'Now let me see, I've heard the name somewhere.' "

"What about Rosie?"Jack muttered, goaded by impatience.

"That's what I'm telling you if you'll let me. Well, Estella says she's seen Rosie quite a few times — not to talk to each other, they just nod and say 'allo — she's seen 'er in one or two of them West End night clubs, an' in the posh seats at theatres, places like that. She's always been with different men and she's always been dressed like a bloody princess. And if you can't add that lot up, Jackie Agass, *you* ain't fit to go selling greens."

Jack said, "Ah." After a little while he added, "Got to be going. Dinner ready. Get rowed if I'm late."

Without warning Alf flung out his arm, pointed at Jack, threw back his head and howled, "Yah! Get rowed if he's late!" Poll, simultaneously, leaned back, flapped her arms and shrieked, "Listen to 'im! Get rowed if 'e's late!" The pair of them stood screeching and shaking with laughter. "Get rowed if he's late," panted Alf, "that's rich that is, that's a good 'un if you ever heard one." "Oh, dear, dear, dearie me," wheezed Poll. " 'Enpecked 'Erbert ain't the word for it!" As Jack, intimidated by this renewed din of mirth, sidled to the door she moaned, "Ooh, we do see life, eh? Ta-ra, sweetheart! Come again soon."

Jack walked up City Road towards the Angel, trying to master himself. He was still bewildered by the mad flurry of feeling that had overcome him in Alf's kitchen; but he had been off his guard then, bludgeoned with laughter. Now he was out in the streets, in the sunshine, and he struggled to suppress his thoughts as if he were ordering a rebellious dog down. What did it matter if he still had a soft spot for Rose? What man hadn't got something like this at the back of his mind? What if he did want to know what had become of her? Was that any reason why he should seek her out and risk — and risk —? well, never mind that! In the last few weeks he had learned how to be happy. Things were going too well for him to risk his future for the sake of a shadow from the past. He was too near his goal, a home of his own, to turn back. He said to himself, again and again, as if it were an incantation, "Joyce is the girl for me." He hastened his footsteps homeward, towards the Sunday roast.

Chapter 2

THE SUMMER DAYS SWOOPED AWAY like swallows. Jack shut Rose out of his mind. True, she continued to annoy him, like a caller to whom one refuses to answer the door and who seems determined never to stop sounding the knocker; but the sense, which the situation bred in him, of being pestered by someone he must exclude from his life, preserved him from any further flare-up of the agony of love. He worked hard and deliberately to cultivate his relationship with Joyce, and was rewarded with a surge of boisterous happiness. When he was with her he scarcely stopped talking. Since he had little to say, his chatter was mainly nonsense, but nonsense is music to lovers and Joyce thrived on it. He took her to the Palladium, spent a wonderful day with her at Brighton, carried her off on a boat trip up the river to Hampton Court, kept her in a daze of delight with dances, gifts, home-planning conferences and elephantine flattery. Joyce, under his attentions, came to full bloom.

Her eyes were alight, her carriage and behaviour animated, her laughter fresh and free from self-consciousness. When she walked with him she clung to his arm, leaned on him with her whole weight and looked up into his face with wide, enquiring eyes as if she wanted him. He, in turn, caught the spark of life from her, felt flattered and glorified by her adoration and for the first time became aware of a bodily longing for her. Thus it was that, on another Sunday morning two weeks later, Jack — turned out of the house while Joyce washed her hair and ironed her dress in preparation for an afternoon's visit to some cousins at Twickenham — found himself wandering the streets alone in a meditative mood of pleasant anticipation.

Nothing is more restorative of optimism towards life and benevolence towards the human race than a walk across London on a fine Sunday morning. The city is magically transformed.

The air seems cleaner and clearer. The streets seem broader, their pavements unblemished by scurrying waste paper. The panorama seen from each height seems wider and less dismal than on weekdays. Thousands of windows sparkle beneath the grey vistas of slate, as if even the houses are happy for a change. There is present the blessed conjunction, for one day only, of repose and enjoyed activity. The same people walk the streets as on weekdays but their faces are no longer helots' faces. They do not congest the streets, as on working days, in a roaring, sordid, compelled stampede but walk cheerfully and with dignity. They have an air of knowing — for a change — what they are doing, of knowing and caring where they are going, and of enjoying it all. No-one is in a hurry. Thousands of people are at work on allotments and ten times as many in their gardens. Flights of cyclists swoop through the streets. The football teams are clattering off to the parks in hundreds, the morning swimmers to the pools. Young couples are on their way to the railway stations carrying rucksacks on their backs and two-handled carry-cots between them from which prodigious babies bellow. From backyards comes the roar of motor-cycles being tuned for afternoon excursions. On the public athletic tracks astonishing numbers of young people, liberated from shop and factory, are sprinting, hurdling, vaulting, flying through the air in high jumps, charging doggedly at the sandpits in long jumps, proudly lifting fantastic weights and hurling discuses about. Beefy young dockers, builders, metal-workers and clerks skim in their racing shells along the barge-cluttered, factory-lined, dirty River Lea while their coaches wobble along the towpath on bicycles bawling bawdy and indefatigable exhortations at them. It is all very beautiful: a reminder that humanity still clings to its capacity for happiness.

Perhaps it was the spirit of the morning that took possession of Jack, for he was in a gay and confident mood as he trudged for two-and-a-half hours through the back streets of Islington and Stoke Newington, down to the banks of the Lea, along the river, and back homewards through Dalston and Highbury. He looked on his present life as the biggest 'bit of all right' that had ever befallen him. It was as enchanting and unreal as if he were seeing it on a cinema screen: to be 'home', to be engaged, to be surrounded by friends. Was all this really happening to Jackie Agass?

He planned his next moves. It would be a good idea to take Joyce's parents out for an evening, to a music-hall or to a West End cinema. It would increase his stock with them, win Joyce's gratitude, and above all he hoped that it would put him in command of the family relationship instead of Mrs. Wakerell. He remembered, too, Joyce's twenty-fifth birthday, which was less than a month ahead, in mid-September. He would buy her some really memorable present — say, an expensive handbag or an evening dress. He would take her out to a show with a Corner House supper to follow, and at the weekend he would take her out for a day in the country.

His thoughts lingered, particularly, on the day in the country. He had reached the point where he wanted Joyce. He had often been for months without a woman, but this time it was becoming unbearable. Certainly he could not wait until the wedding in December. He had neither the wish nor the guile to find another woman for the purpose. At home, he was intimidated by the presence of Mrs. Wakerell, and by the calm authority with which Joyce controlled him even at her most submissive moments. On the parlour sofa the idea always seemed 'a bit much'. It was not only out of physical hunger that he wanted her. It was the only way he knew to consolidate his position. It would set a final seal on their relationship, make their marriage utterly inevitable and put the possibility of any rupture between them entirely out of the question. In his code, as in hers, there was no argument about this. Besides, he told himself, he was entitled to it, wasn't he? An engaged chap! A day in the country — it was in a fiercely deliberate way that he considered it, not with the intoxication of a passionate lover — would provide the ideal time and place.

It was nearly one o'clock when he turned the corner into Lamb Street again. He passed the building site, where the brick shell was already beginning to bear some resemblance to the two-storey block of eight self-contained flats which was alluringly illustrated on a large billboard fronting the pavement. He walked on, past open windows through which a succession of front parlours could be glimpsed, some as shadowy, trinket-cluttered caves of plush and mahogany, some with airy curtains that revealed flowers and the polished whitewood of utility furniture; all of them prosperous and serene. He passed housewives in smart, brightly-coloured frocks and their menfolk in new-looking caps and freshly pressed blue suits, exchanging with all of them the gravely ceremonious courtesies that were the rule in Lamb Street, where life was full of 'good mornings,' 'good evenings,' 'much obligeds,' 'the pleasure's mines,' 'begging your pardons,' 'after you old mans,' 'sorry old chums,' and similar expressions. He exchanged greetings with the decorous group of neighbours who stood talking in the sun outside The Lamb, went in, bought his pint, and came out again with his glass in his hand to join the conversation.

Affairs of state seemed to be the subject this morning. Some of the inhabitants of the street worked hard in political parties and trade unions, and were capable of learned and skilful argument. For the most part, the

157

politics of Lamb Street were summed up by a slogan which had been painted on the blank side wall of The Lamb during the nineteen forty-five election campaign and which still had not faded. This consisted of the two words, 'DOWN WITH —' and a long smear of whitewash which hinted at sudden flight. Different people in Lamb Street could have completed the sentence in differing ways, but nobody had ever felt keen enough to do so, and the slogan faded, a reminder of one of those inconclusive fits of action into which their normal mood of baffled and dispirited indignation sometimes flared. It was not the half, but the whole of a slogan.

"Meat?" Elsie Cakebread was saying. "My week's ration for the pair of us wouldn't make one decent dinner for my feller."

"What can you expect?" said Mr. Bates. "Don't reckon there's much left for us, do you, when the bloody Cabinet's had their share?"

"They couldn't eat that much," put in Mr. Prawn, "not the Cabinet. It's not as if any of 'em did a good day's work. Besides, old Cripps don't eat meat."

"Old Bevin does," answered Mr. Bates triumphantly. "And look at the gut he's got on him. Mean to say old Cripps don't sell him his share? Stands to reason he won't waste it. That's how they make their money, these heads, they don't waste a penny. Anyway, there's the Civil Service. Stuff comes off the boat, these Whitehall chaps have to book it in. Trying to tell me they don't get a prime bit of rump put aside for the missus? And there's a lot of them, I can tell you. And then there's the Lord Mayor's banquet. Don't forget that."

Chick Woodruff said, "Old Churchill —"

Jack, who was waiting for a chance to join in, cried, "He's the kiddie!"

"What, him?" cried Mr. Prawn. "You can't deny —"

"Give old Attlee his due," interrupted Mr. Lucy, a little hunchback who collected subscriptions for the Labour Party, "He's got up as good a government as anyone could these days."

Mr. Wakerell, who had been leaning against the wall with an absent look in his eyes, turned his head and growled, "Contradiction in terms."

"What is?"

"A good government." He became aware that further explanation was expected of him, and added, with an unexpected surge of fierceness in his voice, "None of 'em'll let you alone." An affirmative chorus told him that his words had struck home. "Go on!" he insisted, glaring pugnaciously around him. "Name one of 'em that'll let you alone!"

His challenge, it appeared, was unanswerable. He uttered a darkly satisfied "Ah!" and settled back into his former dreamy attitude against the wall.

There was an impressive little pause. Mr. Prawn took courage, and began, "In Russia —"

"'Ere! —" Bernie Whiteflower was loud and peremptory as if he were summoning the attention that was his due. He towered over everyone else in the group. With his broad shoulders set proudly back beneath a yellow sports shirt whose open collar revealed his red, corded neck, with his red hair and reckless profile, he seemed joyous and heroic. "Tell you what! Next bloody election, take my tip an' vote for Newcastle United. If they licked the Arsenal last season, they can lick anything."

Miraculously the whole group shed its Sunday morning somnolence. There were indignant gasps, noises (from the younger members) of the kind known as raspberries, whistles of dissent, snarls of 'Gah way!' Chick Woodruff said angrily, "That was last season. Bloody bad luck from start to finish, that's all it was." Mr. Pennyfarthing, as deeply shocked as if he were rebuking an utterance of treason, said, "Bernie! I thought you was an Arsenal man!"

Mr. Prawn began, "In Russia —"

Bernie turned on him. "Why don't you shut up?" he bullied. "That's the trouble with your lot. Won't give no-

159

one else a chance to get a word in edgeways." Mr. Prawn subsided. He was a small man with scanty grey hair and a slack face so deeply lined that its stubbly skin seemed to hang in folds. His dark grey tweed suit of old-fashioned cut, like the celluloid collar and knitted tie that he wore, gave him the appearance of a self-improving working man of the old school. When he talked about his forty years in the Socialist movement he was listened to with inattentive tolerance, and the young people — restrained by their good-hearted parents from ribald interruption — stared at him as if he were riding up the street on a tricycle. This was not the only reason for his habitual expression of melancholy. Four years ago he had retired from his job as tram conductor, looking forward to a quiet old age with his wife, his books and his *Daily Worker*. To augment his pension he had let his three upstairs rooms. He had often pondered since on the suddenness with which a man can bring undeserved calamity crashing down on himself after a blameless, studious and hard-working lifetime — for his tenant was Bernie Whiteflower. Both Bernie and his wife were of that heroic, red-blooded, uninhibited breed whose more articulate members proclaim that 'Struggle Is Life'. They spent half their time waging war on each other: their battles, audible to the most distant of their neighbours, thundered like artillery bombardments over Mr. Prawn's head, kept his kitchen ceiling in a constant shudder, sent his most treasured ornaments reeling off the mantel-piece, seasoned his meals with falling plaster and reduced him to a state of nervous collapse. When the Whiteflowers made peace, however, there was still no peace for poor Mr. Prawn, for their abundant vitality immediately inspired them to open joint campaigns against him. He crept about in a state of constant misery, and thought with nostalgia of the tranquil days of war, when there had been no Whiteflowers above — only flying bombs. Fearful, now, of offering some new provocation, he sidled away from the group, muttered 'good morning's to his cronies and trotted off home.

Few noticed his departure, for the street outside The Lamb was alive with a little uproar of disputation, in which the prospects of the Arsenal for the coming season were thrashed out. Historical precedents (reaching back to the most remote Cup Ties) were unearthed, the life histories, characters and states of health of players were discussed, intricate computations of goal averages were entered into, diets and transfer fees were criticized, scorn was heaped on the pretensions of a succession of rival teams; there was much sapient nodding and illustrative gesticulation; there were shouts of assertion and cries of denial. Faces and voices were lit with a rare animation.

While the discussion was at its height Barmy Naughton came down the street. He walked with a long, hurrying stride, his arms swinging exaggeratedly outward, his hands flapping like dead things at the end of his arms. He seemed to be in one of his good moods, for he was singing to himself in a cracked voice and offering ingratiating smiles to everyone he passed. Usually he would mutter to himself as he walked. When he was out of temper he would snarl at every passer-by as if he were answering an insult that had been flung at him. He hesitated on the outskirts of the group, like a dog that was afraid to approach, looking all the more canine because of the enquiring way in which he cocked his head to one side. One or two people gave him kindly greetings, to which he returned eager smiles, and he sidled up closer.

Bernie Whiteflower saw him and shouted cordially, "Wotcho, Barmy boy, been out on the prowl again?"

Barmy smiled; to do so seemed to require a physical effort on his part, and an interior glow of pain shone from beneath the movements of his face. "Been for a walk." He spoke civilly and sensibly, but with a thick awkwardness as if his tongue were swollen or as if he had to force his voice up from his throat. "Got boxing kangaroos in Clissold Park. Three of 'em. Kangaroos. Hop about all

161

over the place. Talk about funny! Kangaroos. Spar up like —" he blinked with the effort of thought, and when he spoke again his voice creaked like a disused door. "Boxing kangaroos they got."

"You like the park, don't you?" Bernie asked.

"Ah!" Barmy, responding to the encouragement in Bernie's tone, invested the monosyllable with a childlike trustfulness. He stared hungrily at the pavement, racking his brain for words which would enable him to prolong this rare pleasure of being permitted by his fellows to talk normally with them. "It's all right, I tell you. Kids on the lake, laughing and screaming —"

"All right in the park, eh? I bet!" Bernie's voice took on a prodding geniality. His right eyelid flickered in a wink that was unseen by Barmy. "All the girls, eh? All them blowy summer dresses you can see right through? Lovely legs, eh? Good squint up their skirts, eh, what the old doctor saw?"

Barmy's "No!" was like a yelp of pain. He blinked more rapidly, helpless with distress as the momentary hope of friendship receded from him and it dawned on him that once more, as through all the weary years, he was being mocked. "All them kids. Hear 'em — in them little boats — laughing." He looked as if he were chasing butterflies of thought, trying to seize them and show them to the others. "Tennis — all them playing tennis — bloody kangaroos boxing."

Bernie silenced him with a raucous "GAH way!"

The group of listeners, who at first had received Barmy with passive welcome, submitted — after a transitory waver of discomfort — to Bernie's leadership. Those who felt pity for Barmy were ashamed to show it, and joined even more loudly than their neighbours in the obedient barking of laughter that broke out.

Bernie, urged on by the noise of support, uttered a loud and prolonged "W'yerh!" of derision. "Think we don't know you loonies? There may be a bit missing in the top storey, but you got plenty o' stock in the basement, eh?"

There was a chorus of laughter, ugly with self-consciousness. A tragic interflow of cruelty had been set up between Bernie and the assemblage, each evoking from the other, in successive waves, fresh surges of the malice that might otherwise have remained latent and undetected in their natures. Barmy cried, "I ain't a loonie. I can talk as good as any of you. I —" The effort was too much for him. He could not find the words to plead for a chance, to explain himself. He shrank into a bitter, defensive crouch. Jack, remembering how, in the peace and loving kindness of Kate's kitchen, Barmy had once become relaxed and articulate, a normal man, for hours at a time, said, "Here, he ain't daft," but he had not the courage to utter the words loudly enough for anyone else to hear. Barmy stood with his head bowed, his face screwed up and defiant.

Bernie drank in the laughter with distended chest and sparkling eyes. Nourished by it, his vanity drove him on to strut and trample. "Gah way, we know you're out on the batter when you go up the park. All the girls love a loonie. Dark 'orse on the quiet, our old Barmy. You think 'e's 'ard up for it, but 'e knows better. Nothing like the old slap and tickle, eh, Barmy? Come on, boy, you ain't gonna keep it secret, are you? Not from all your old friends? Tell us all about your flaming love life? 'Ere, 'at's a girl, Elsie —" Elsie Cakebread, flushed with the mood of the group and eager to make herself prominent, had slipped to Barmy's side, and was embracing him demonstratively, kissing his cold, lumpy cheek and squeezing herself up to him. "'At's a girl," Bernie shouted, "Warm 'im up! Give 'im a good ol' cuddle!"

Barmy's head was tilted back, the Adam's apple bobbing horribly in his thin neck. Muscles gathered in hard lumps at the corners of his cheeks. His mouth was open fixedly like a corpse's. Fear, hatred and desire mingled in his glare. The people grew uneasy, but the more they felt the chill of conscience the more loud and high-pitched their laughter became, the more frequent

163

their cries of encouragement to Bernie and Elsie. Jack, oppressed by a sudden and unbearable feeling of guilt and misery, laughed with the others and tried to ease himself by shouting encouragingly, "Go on, Barmy, give her a kiss she'll remember."

Barmy uttered a harsh sigh, seized Elsie's arms in a clawing grip and fastened his mouth on her face. He was shaking violently as he bent over her. Elsie began a scream of mock outrage; then, as Barmy did not release her, the note of pretence died from her voice and she made breathless, inarticulate noises of fear and protest.

"'Ere!" Bernie tore them apart. He was the embodiment of virtuous anger now, the dispenser of justice. "What you think you're doing?" He shook Barmy. "Eh?" He shook Barmy again. Now it was the awareness of his own strength that intoxicated him, and the chance to display it to others. "Come on, answer, you little rat. 'Oo d'you think you are, muckin' a decent woman about like that?" Barmy, breathing in long, shuddering gasps in his choking grip, was unable to answer, and rolled his eyes in an expression that was at once of hatred and entreaty.

The people were silent now, their mood uncertain. Jack felt released from the common spell of cruelty, and humiliation at his own cowardice invaded him. "Leave him alone." He only managed to croak the words, and no-one took any notice. He made another attempt to speak. It was not a physical fear of Bernie that throttled him, but a fear of standing out from the herdlike hesitation of which he was now part. A terrible indecision settled upon him. In a confused way the importance of this moment presented itself in his mind. He was one of those retiring people who are impelled by fits and starts of courage. There would occur in his life desperate moments of choice, when he would say to himself, 'If I wait for another moment I am lost. And if I am lost now, then I am lost for life.' Then, driven as much by terror as by resolution, he would act. There had been such a moment when he was ten years old, at a swimming lesson with his school-fellows: he had walked out on to the springboard while the other boys stood at the edge of the pool with their arms folded across their chests, waiting for him to make his first dive. There had been another such moment in the war when, at the age of twenty-four, he had taken part in an attack for the first time. He had sat waiting beneath the bank of a sunken road while the platoon commander squatted on his heels staring at a wristwatch. The officer had climbed to his feet, dusted the legs of his trousers, said, 'All right, chaps, let's go,' and walked forward through a gap in the cactus clump. The other men had begun to filter forward. Jack could remember them shambling casually through the ragged patterns of daylight between the bushes. Jack had remained, for an awful lagging moment after his neighbours had gone; then, unwillingly, he had risen and plodded after them, across the bare brown plain, towards the smoke and dull noises in the distance.

He broke free from his own cowardice. He forced himself to repeat his words with such violence that he was as surprised as the others at the shout that came from his mouth. "I said leave him alone!" Reckless — for the only way to keep up his courage was to behave recklessly — he stepped forward and gave Bernie's wrist a sudden, powerful twist that left Barmy free to lurch away.

Bernie swung round to meet Jack. His face was contorted with surprise and fury. With his left fist drawn back aggressively over his shoulder he exclaimed, "I'll bleet'n' paralyse you!"

Jack gave a cogitative sniff, and in a mild voice that concealed his inner agitation, replied, "Well, maybe you could, mate, and maybe you couldn't. You can have a try if you like, though."

Bernie lowered his fist, but remained tensed for a blow. "Gettin' tough in your old age, ain't you?"

Jack maintained his slouching, thoughtful attitude, frowning away at the bare pavement beyond Bernie.

"Well, I don't suppose I'm as tough as you, old fella. I mean, I don't reckon I'd have the nerve to chance my arm with a heavyweight like Barmy." He grimaced pensively. "I might take on that little dwarf that sells papers up the Angel. Or old Doddsy down Mintern Street in his wheelchair, the bloke that lost both his legs in an air raid. But Barmy — well, I mean to say, that takes a tough guy like you, don' it?"

Jack's intervention had acted like a magnet on the gathering, to draw forth from it a new and different mood. There were mutters and titters of approval for Jack's stand. People were surrounding Barmy and demonstratively consoling him. One of them put a pint glass of beer into his shaking hands. Elsie Cakebread was saying in a loud, defensive tone, "Well, we was only larking, me and Barmy. I never minded. I never thought Bernie 'd get hold of him like that. Could have hurt the poor chap, he could." Each person now appeared anxious to show his neighbours that he was on the side of the angels. Bernie felt the stir, lowered his hands, grinned and said to Jack, "'Ere, I'll tell you what, old son, you wanna learn to take a joke."

Jack knew that the crisis had passed. He considered himself lucky, that instead of the flare-up of rage and injured vanity which might have seized Bernie, there had been that moment of hesitation in which Bernie had tired of his sportive fit, felt the ebb of support among the crowd and realised the danger of a loss of popularity. He therefore contented himself with a conciliatory, "Well, it's all over and done with now, eh?"

Bernie clapped his arm round Barmy's shoulder, struck a pose of masterful good nature and said, "You ain't wild, are you, Barmy boy? A joke's a joke, eh? All in the day's work, ain'it? Still pals, ain't we? Drink up and I'll get you another pint."

Barmy nodded dumbly, staring into his glass. Jack said, "I reckon he's had about enough." He took Barmy's arm and led him in through the private doorway of The Lamb.

Mick called, through the hatch at the back of the bar, "What's the matter, lad?"

Jack explained.

"I thought I heard voices raised," Mick said. "Take him up to the parlour. I'll be up myself in a minute. I'm giving Dora a hand just now."

In the parlour, Jack helped Barmy into an armchair and left him to recover his wits. After a few minutes of silence, while Jack was wandering about the room looking at photographs, Barmy spoke.

"Bloody nuisance, Jack, ain' I?"

"Don't be silly, mate."

"Better out of it. That's me." Barmy's voice was tired and brittle but his speech, although disjointed, made sense. "Bloody funny —" He peered upward, as if at God "— Takes her. Leaves me. Me! Thirty years of it. Enough for anyone." His voice rose, quavering. "Too bloody much!"

"Away, boy, you'll feel better."

"Ha!" Barmy looked up desperately. "I ain't barmy, Jack."

"Of course you're not."

"No. No. I ain't." He looked about him as if he were seeking something that might help him convince Jack. "You reckon I am. Never mind what you say. Just saying it. That's all. You're just saying it. Out of — out of — Look!" he began again, his voice shaking. "I come home. Out of hospital." His eyes wandered as if he were groping for the date. As if he had given up the attempt, he pointed at Mick's medals on the wall. "Here, that lot. The last year. I was all right. I had the shakes. You know! The bloody shakes. I couldn't talk. I couldn't talk a lot. I was all right. I just — Up the hospital — Year or two, they said a year or two. Needed a rest, that's all. That's what they said." He lapsed into a long silence. "That woman!" he resumed in a sudden rage. "What she did. I could have —" His face twisted. "What she do it for? Didn't she? — All them years — I'll give her. I'll give it her one of these

167

nights." His face was ugly with pain and lust. "I'll show her!"

"Here, steady boy, she was only larking."

But Barmy had forgotten his outburst. He sat, hands in his lap, mentally groping. At last he picked up the thread of his former thoughts, staring at the floor as if he were following a path in the dark, and stumbling, too, in his speech. "I come home. End of that lot." His voice became louder again. "That bloody lot! Somebody says — barmy. Look, old Barmy. In the street. There he goes, Barmy. All the kids, run after you. Barmy!" His mouth opened and shut, but the words would not come for a second or two. "Why didn't they? — How could I? —" He paused, defeated, and said with desperate finality, "Then you're done for."

"But your family," said Jack, "— your friends?" This was a part of Barmy's story he had never heard. Barmy looked blank. "How old were you? When you come home?" Barmy opened his mouth, but the effort of calculation was too much.

"He was twenty-two." Mick had come into the room. "His mother was a widow. She had four sons. They kept themselves to themselves. You know how some folk are, respectable. The other three boys were killed in the war. Then he came home. That must have finished her. She died a couple of years after the war. He was all on his own then. Not a soul in the world to smile at him."

"Except for *her*!" Barmy's voice rang like a challenge.

"Except for her, God bless her."

"I was all right with her," Barmy said violently.

"I know," said Jack. "I remember."

"Here," said Barmy, "they talk about women! Them! That big 'un, that Bernie. Don't know what a woman is. Not a real woman. Laughing at me! That tart rubbing herself against me! Women — call them women? I could tell 'em something about women."

"Go on down and give Dora a hand in the bar," Mick said, "this isn't the time of day for us to be leaving her on her own."

"I've had —" Barmy gulped, and lost his breath. "Here!" He appealed wildly to Jack. "Rag me about women, what they think? I've —"

"Dora's waiting for you," Mick interrupted, "Go on down, boy."

Barmy gathered his breath, looked at them hesitantly and went out of the room.

"I don't know," said Jack, "I don't like to say, but the things he comes out with!"

"He gets a bit wild, that's all. I can't say I blame him."

Jack sat wondering for a moment. "You'd think they'd leave him alone. I mean —" he pondered again — "They're all right, I mean, them down there." He waved his hand at the window. "Been all right to me, I must say. What they want to muck him about like that for?"

Mick shrugged his shoulders. "The penny's got to come down tails sometimes. You know, it's not so long since your great-grand-daddy was taking the kids to Tyburn to see a hanging, or spending a happy Sunday at Bedlam having a good laugh at the loonies."

Jack pondered. "Well, I reckon I better be getting back for dinner."

"I'll walk down to the house with you. I could do with a breath of air."

"Here," Jack said as they were going downstairs, "What do you reckon? Straight up? Do you reckon he's really barmy?"

"Perhaps he is by this time. I wouldn't like to say, lad. But I do know that he needn't have been. When he came back there was nothing wrong with him that kindness couldn't have cured. But the first idiot that called him Barmy put a fence round him that nobody has ever pulled down. You heard what he was trying to tell you. Once he had the label on him he was finished. No friends. People talked to him kindly, but the way they'd talk to a dog. Find a wife? Woman go with a chap called Barmy? Not a chance. One year after another of that — it's no wonder he got worse instead of better. I suppose he had a little bit of peace here and there. With Kate, with me. But what's an hour or a day once in a while, in all that stretch of years? You try and imagine it, lad. Most of the time on his own. No company but himself. No-one to talk to but himself. All his thoughts, all his manhood, stewing and turning rank inside him. Nothing but dreams to pass the time. Is it any wonder his brainbox got addled? His mind's lost the habit of thinking. His tongue's lost the habit of talking. He's got so frightened of everybody that he hates the lot of them. You know how a dog turns savage if you neglect him. That's why he goes round glaring and muttering at everyone. His only friends are the dead folk he sees in his daydreams. You listen to him next time he goes lurching past you, and you'll hear him talking to them. I doubt if he could pull himself together now if all the saints in heaven came down to befriend him. So there you are, Jack. If that's barmy, then barmy he is."

Mrs. Wakerell came out on to the doorstep just as they arrived at the house. "Ah, there you are, Jack," she said, "I was just coming out to give you a call. How's the world treating you, Mick?"

"Admirably, my love. I wish time was as kind to me as the ladies are. You know, we haven't much longer, you and I, to add to our store of memories."

"Go on, you'll get me a bad name."

"Well, I can honestly say you're a little more beautiful every day, for by God, each time I see you there's a little more of you."

"That's a nice thing to tell a lady," said Mrs. Wakerell archly.

"My dear good lady, it's a compliment. A man who is given to the sins of the flesh should never complain at an abundance of the raw material."

"That's enough for Sunday," she said. "You go back to your barmaid and leave an honest woman alone."

Jack marvelled at this passage of words. He could not

170

imagine Mr. Wakerell ever daring to be so familiar with her. She saw his wondering smile and said, "Go on in, boy, dinner's on the table. Toodle-oo, Mick." She fluttered her fingers like a girl and closed the street door.

Chapter 3

"I T DOESN'T SEEM LIKE LONDON, does it?"Joyce said. She looked around her. "It's all so clean, and — oh, all that grass and flowers. I told Nancy last time, it must be like living in fairyland. All sunlit. If I lived here I'd be afraid it was a dream, and that I might wake up any minute and see dirty black walls again."

"Ah," said Jack, "it's like the bloody pictures or something."

"Jack, I keep on telling you. From now on you'll give me sixpence for every b— you say."

"Gawd love us, can't a bloke breathe? Bit of all right, though, ain' it?"

They walked hand in hand, like a pair of wondering children, across the grounds of the modern housing estate in Hackney where Nancy and her husband Tom Ollerenshaw lived. On their left rose blocks of buildings overlooking plots where lawns and gardens were being laid out. The flats had big sun windows and private balconies, each with a built-in flower bed projecting. On their right were rows of cottages, their frontages consisting mainly of glass and harmoniously-coloured tiles, each house with its private garden and many with neat porches. Children played everywhere, brown-skinned and clad in brief rompers.

It was the end of August. Nancy had asked them to come with her to lay flowers on Chris's grave, on the fifth anniversary of his death.

Nancy opened the door of her flat, kissed them both and whispered, "Gran Hogarth's inside. We asked her.

Tom brought her in a taxi." She added hurriedly, as they entered the parlour, "Tell her the baby loves her." Joyce answered with a close-lipped little smile of under-standing, Jack with a mystified, "Eh?"

Jack crossed to where Gran Hogarth was sitting, kissed her cheek and said, "Hallo, old dear. It's a treat to see you again."

Gran looked no different from any other of those tragic and indomitable old women one sees in the poor streets of London, lugging heavy shopping bags as they shuffle, step by step, upon the errands which they insist on performing until death is upon them. Their progress is an agony. Every couple of hundred yards they have to rest on a doorstep. Each step betrays their life's defeat, yet they never admit defeat, toiling on to the last breath against their enemies, dependence and death. She was small, dressed in black and of a deathly cleanliness. She looked at the world with pale, unseeing eyes, as if she were already burdened with thoughts of things beyond it. The lifeless, cream-coloured skin of her face was seamed with horizontal folds as straight and thin as razor-cuts, between which were scored innumerable faint wrinkles. "It's a treat you've done without long enough," she said in a faded, bitter voice. "The man with the black horses could have called for me before you'd have thought of knocking at my door."

"Ah, you know what it is, Gran. Busy an' all that. Meant to all the time."

"You could have come," she accused. "No law agen it as fur as I know. Only the law that makes the young keep away from the old." Her eyes filmed with self-pity. "Afraid of what you'll see, I expect. Still, that's the way of it. I ain't got enough breath left to waste a lot of it complaining."

Jack took refuge in a fatuous smile, shook hands with Tom, ruffled Linda Jean's curls and said, "Come and give your Uncle Jack a big kiss."

The child answered with a coy, "No." She hid her face

against her father's legs, only peeping up for a moment to bestow on Jack exactly the same shamed, teasing smile that he had seen on Joyce's face when he had pestered her for kisses. Jack uttered a high-pitched, "Ha!" of incredulous delight, and said, "See that, Tom? Not two years old? All the same, they are. Flirts from the bloody cradle."

"Ay," said Tom, "she's a smart kiddie." He had a Lancashire accent that seemed to warm the room when he spoke. "Go to your Nannybunny." He hoisted his daughter high into the air, gave her a great swing across the room that dispelled the fierce little look of unwillingness that had appeared on her face and dumped her on the old woman's lap. Gran, her face creasing up into a mass of deep wrinkles and her eyes alight with anxious pleasure as she smiled at the child in her embrace, said, "Oh, my little sweet, my honey, my little golden princess. Doesn't she love her Nanny? Isn't she the only one that loves her silly old Nannybunny?"

Linda Jean frowned, pouted, and struggled with the strength of a little serpent. She cried, "Down! Down! Dada, down!"

"There!" Joyce hurried across the room and knelt at her side. "You sit on your Nannybunny's lap like a good girl and Auntie Joycie'll get you a sweetie. There, that's a good girl. Give me my bag, Jack, there's some sweets in it." Jack, happy and startled at this new revelation of Joyce's talents, obeyed, and in a moment Linda Jean was pacified. "There!" Joyce, still kneeling, smiled up at the old woman. "Doesn't she love you? You're her favourite all right, anyone can see that."

"Ah, she knows," said Gran, "She knows I'm not such a fierce old woman as they give out. She knows, bless her! The little ones know. They look at you with the eyes God give 'em. Nigh upon eighty-one years I've trod this earth, and I've never yet seen the pair of eyes that didn't have something to hide. All but the little ones, before the sin and the bitterness gets into 'em. You think I'm a silly old party, don't you, girl? — you and your twenty-what-you-

174

may-call-it years old? You wait till you've reached my time of life, then you'll know what it is to be thankful for a bit of love. I've had little but disappointment since my wedding day. It's been all knocks, I tell you, these sixty years for me. My chap being took, then my only boy, and him crippled in the war, and worse things done to him than that, poor child. I told him, but they never listen, for they've got their own minds and they're born to suffer." She let the struggling child down. "Off you go, then," she said, "can't sit still a minute, can you? They will play. Well, I suppose I've got enough to be thankful for. I keep myself, with my pension and my annuity. I'm not obligated to a living soul for a penny. I live by myself and what's more, I look after myself. The young lady from the Council comes of a morning and cleans for me and cooks a nice dinner for me. She's a nice young woman, too, she looks well brought up and she's not snobby neither. She always stays for a nice chat. Then Nancy comes, bless her. Oh, I've got me friends. There's precious few can say that at my time, when everyone's gone from them."

Joyce squeezed her hand and said, "Well, I'd like to be another of them, Gran, dear."

Tom said, "We can't wait much longer for Alf. I'll take baby in to the neighbours — they're going to mind her for the afternoon — and then I'll go for a taxi. If him and Poll's not here by the time I get back they've had it."

He went out with Linda Jean. Nancy said, "I'll just hang some of the baby's washing out to air before we go. It's a pity to waste this sunshine." She brought a basket from the kitchen. Jack said, "Here, give us," and took it from her. He followed her out on to the balcony, leaving Joyce talking with Gran.

"We've got a little surprise for you," Nancy said as she began to hang up the washing.

"Eh? What sort?"

"A surprise. You know, open your mouth and shut your eyes and see what God brings you."

"What, now?"

175

"Oh, Jack, Jack, Jackass, not now. And it's not something to eat. You wait and see, and before the afternoon's out you'll know all about it. You'll both come back to tea afterwards, won't you? Good. I got some shrimps off the barrow-man this morning. It ought to be a nice little party. Bring back old times." She finished her task and stooped to put the basket beneath a chair. Unexpectedly, she turned on him. "Happy, Jack?"

He answered at once with an alarmed, "Yes." Then, doubtfully, "Well, I don't know. I suppose so."

She sat down on the chair. For all her bulk, the movement was graceful, as if her body had no weight. She laid her hands in her lap, the palms downward, one hand on top of the other. The gesture reminded him painfully of her mother. "You are, Jack. Don't let yourself have any doubts about it. You are happy, and you stick to that." She smiled. Nested in the fat of her face, in the candid eyes and the flawless skin over her cheekbones, he saw her mother's beauty. He felt humble and loving before her, like a small boy again. "Falling in love," she said, "I don't know anything about that. They say it's not always a pleasant experience. But happiness is nothing like that. It doesn't happen to you. You have to work for it, and you have to keep trying. It's like —" she inclined her head towards the flowers on the parapet: the most beautiful of girls could not have made the gesture more gently or graciously — "it's like a garden, I suppose. Nothing may come up for a while. It does in the long run if you don't lose heart. Look at me and Tom —"

He looked at her, and at Tom who was returning along the path below, both of them pink, elephantine, double-chinned. If they had been strangers seen on a bus he would have whispered some gross jest about them to Joyce.

"— we're not the most romantic of couples, are we? We started going together when I was up in Oldham. I was in lodgings, and terribly lonely. Tom had a lot of friends, they all liked him, they said he was always ready for a

176

laugh, but he only had the crowd of them, no one person among them, you know how it is. When he first asked me to go to pictures I felt so ashamed. I mean, he's not exactly a girl's dream man, and I knew that people — even our friends — would have a quiet laugh when they saw us walking out together. It never occurred to me that Tom might feel the same sort of shame about me. And so it went on, and we got more and more used to each other — more and more dependent on each other, you might say — till Tom popped the question. When we went to the registry office I wanted to die. I felt I was throwing away all my dreams. I looked at him, and I thought, 'Oh, Lord, to spend the rest of my life with that!' And then I saw exactly the same look in his eyes. I felt so sorry for him, Jack, dear. I wanted to take hold of him and comfort him. And then he squeezed my hand and he said, 'There, lass, I'll do what I can for you,' and I knew that he pitied me, too. We've spent every day of our lives since making things as good for each other as we could. And it's been so beautiful, every day of it. You'll have to ask someone clever if you want to know whether that's love, but I know that neither of us would change for anyone else, and now the baby — oh, Jack, she's going to be what both of us have always dreamed of being." She sighed, and looked down at her folded hands.

Jack felt embarrassed and inadequate. He said, "Ah, I reckon you're about right, Nance. When you talk like that you remind me of your Mum." It had been there in her voice the same placid gentleness, the same sad wisdom.

Suddenly encouraged, he blurted, "Here, Nance. I know what I wanted to ask you. It just occurred to me the other week, we never been to see your dad's grave, even when we were kids."

"My dad?" Nancy, startled, echoed his words to give her mind time to absorb them.

"Your dad. I can still see his picture on the wall, looking down on us, can't you? Yet we never —"

Nancy looked into the parlour, with a light of what

seemed like anxiety in her eyes. She closed the french windows, shutting off the murmur of voices from within. "We used to go," she said. "I used to go with mum. You know, quietly, no fuss. I still go sometimes, with Gran."

"Quietly? That's a bit queer, ain't it?"

"Why? There was no point in taking the whole family. You were all very small then."

"I know, but it wasn't like her, to let them forget their dad."

"Their dad?" Nancy smiled, with compressed lips. "It wasn't like her to be a hypocrite."

"Hypocrite?" The word offended him.

"Trailing the kids about and doing the loving widow act. She did enough, Jack. She kept the grave tidy. She paid her respects. You see —" she hesitated "— well, they weren't the happiest of couples."

He said, stupidly because of the shock, "Who weren't?"

"My mother and father."

The words, evenly uttered, penetrated his consciousness as quietly and rapidly as four drops of some corrosive liquid. For a moment he felt that the whole fabric of moral certainty on which he based his life was endangered by this scar that burned and spread. He wanted to ask more questions, but he was afraid. The idea that Kate, the perfect Kate, the dream Kate against whom he measured everything in the world, might lack perfection in her relations with any other human being — it was an impossibility, a sacrilege. He hesitated wretchedly.

Nancy sighed. "Well, let the dead rest quiet. Talking won't serve them. Alf didn't answer my letter, but I was hoping he'd come."

From inside the flat they heard sounds of movement. Tom was helping Gran to the door.

"Oh," Jack said bitterly, "he loved his brother all right. But what's a bloody graveside get-together compared with the beginning of the football season?"

Tom called out that the taxi was waiting at the gate,

and they followed him downstairs.

At the gate of the cemetery they bought big bunches of chrysanthemums, bronze, white and yellow. Jack walked on, flanked by Nancy and Joyce. Tom followed, with Gran leaning on his arm and smashing at the gravel with the point of her walking-stick.

Talking quietly, but with the extraordinary levity that afflicts peoples in such surroundings, they followed a path through a clutter of monuments that was as ugly and overcrowded as any city street.

They turned a bend in the path. Jack said, "That's it, over there." A woman, her back to them, stooped at the foot of the grave. She straightened up. A red splash of flowers remained on the brown mound at her feet. Jack recognized from behind the queenly set of head and shoulders. Joyce was chattering at him, but he could no longer make out what she was saying. His feet were so heavy that he could hardly lift them. There was a pain across the top of his chest, beneath the collarbone. He was conscious of not a single thought or emotion, only a numbed thickness in his head. The command centre of his body was out of action but his legs, like dogged soldiers, bore him on.

Hearing their footsteps, the woman turned to meet them just as Nancy said, "Rose, my darling. I'm so glad you've come."

Jack and Rose were face to face. He could see nothing of her but her frank and smiling scrutiny, which cowed him. He lowered his head. He forced his mouth to move, mumbling gluily, " 'lo, Rose. Beenlongtime."

Rose said, in a soft, kindly voice, "Hallo, Jack. I've been wanting and wanting to see you."

He could not absorb the sight of her, let alone assess her. She had always been one of those people who seem firmer, clearer-cut against the daylight, than anyone around them, who impress themselves on the vision with the impact of metal stamps. Now, to Jack, the impact had been too great: she was like someone seen in a doorway

179

from a dark interior, only a shape black-rimmed between him and the light. He could not seize on a single detail. Around her, the sunlight seemed to break up into countless points of brilliance.

People were talking. He heard Nancy's gurgling laugh, and her voice, "I promised him a surprise!" Joyce was speaking in tones of delighted astonishment. The voices in the sunlight were as confusing as water splashing and flashing in sunlight. He mumbled, "This is Joyce."

Rose laughed. "Silly, you don't think I've forgotten Joyce. I wish I had a pound for every pennorth of fish and chips we shared when we were kids."

Joyce added excitedly, "And you never liked vinegar and I did!"

They were laughing. Jack was outside the laughter. He was as remote from all this as the dreamer from his dream. He felt no hatred for Rose, no love, only a paralysed fright and the sense of a great weight upon him.

The old woman had been standing in silence, gripping her stick with both hands and grinding the tip in the gravel. Her dead, grating voice startled them all. "You're at your brother's grave."

The grave had been a forgotten background to their happiness. In abashed silence they turned to look at it. Nobody knew what to say. Joyce and Nancy laid their chrysanthemums by the side of the cluster of red roses.

Jack stood side by side with Rose. He was afraid to look at her. So far he had received absolutely no impression of her. A terrible self-consciousness had taken hold of him, so that he felt every movement or attitude of his to be a foolish and unsuccessful pose for her benefit. He dared a furtive peep at her. Her cheeks were fuller, her skin was of the same misty pallor as of old. Her clothes set her apart from the women he saw in workaday streets: a long skirt that made her look more tall and slender than anyone else in the group, a jacket that fell in loose, flaring folds from shoulder to waist like a short cape, a hat (to

180

Jack a strange sight on a woman) and long cream gloves. She turned her candid gaze on him and smiled, and he jerked his head away ridiculously. He stared at the grave and longed for deliverance from his embarrassment.

Joyce said, "It's a lovely grave." The headstone was of plain white marble, inscribed with Chris's name and the dates of his birth and death: no rhymes and no gilt. The brown mound was surrounded by a low white wall of marble, and there was a bank of little flowers, blue and white, at its foot. "It must have cost no end. Who paid for it? Chris's wife?"

"Her!" Jack said bitterly, "She was in another man's lap before she'd paid the undertaker. I reckon she chose her mourning clothes to go courting in."

His own words aroused in him a mournful feeling of defeat and desolation. This was how the past had petered out. The laughing children, the happy household, the flashing lightness of youth — all these were innocence, and innocence had died. One life had led to this grave, before which none of them had felt any recognition; another to Alf's beer-bloated face; another — he sneaked a second sidelong glance at Rose's smart clothes, and thought with sickness of some man's thick, nicotine-stained fingers creeping over her body to exact the price of them. All life, after childhood, ran downhill. More painful than articulate thoughts, these fragments of comprehension struggled for release within him, and failing, died, leaving him puzzled and upset.

"Mum saw to the grave," Nancy said quietly.

"She must have been a wonderful woman," Joyce said. "I don't know how she managed it, on her money. I mean, the way she was able to take the children on holiday every year, and keep them in clothes, and help Chris when he was ill, and everything like that. She must have had a magic purse."

Gran uttered a bitter cackle. They looked at her in surprise. She stood crouched over her stick, looking past the grave with an abstracted glare. Her head was shaking.

181

Jack, who was still groping after his own fugitive half-thoughts, said, "It was his politics that done for Chris."

"Day and night," Nancy said, "he never would listen. All his politics and his war work. It was wet clothes and snatched meals and not enough sleep for him all the time, ill as he was. I begrudge it when I see him forgotten and all the clever ones up the top getting the praise."

"Why begrudge it?" Rose said. "There ought to be more like Chris."

"Why begrudge it?" Jack answered. "Because he begrudged it, at the end, that's why. Know the last time I saw Chris? I was on leave, in, — ooh, it must have been in forty-two, sometime. I gets off a bus in Old Street, all loaded up with clobber, pack, rifle, the whole bloody performance, you know — I'm walking past a block of buildings to the trolley stop when I hear a voice up on a landing. 'Hallo,' says I, 'I know that voice.' I look up. You know those buildings. Falling to bits. Iron landings. Smell 'em a mile off. And there's this voice up on the landing, all hoarse like, nagging, that nasty husky cough every other minute. 'Don't give me your excuses,' the chap's saying, 'I'm sick of listening to 'em. Think you're clever the way you play me up?' Nearly in tears the bloke is, by the sound of it, although he's bullying away for all he's worth. 'I'll have that rent off you,' he says, 'if I have to make you pawn every stick you possess. I told you, don't start that hard luck stuff again. I'll lose my job over you and your rent if I'm not careful, and I'm bloody sure I'd sooner see you in tears than my own wife and child.' I can hear a woman crying her eyes out and saying, 'Have a heart, can't you? What you want to come here for shouting at us and making my life a misery?' 'Making *your* life a misery,' the bloke bloody nigh screams, 'it's you who's doing that to mine, all of you, all the lot of you, you're all as bad as each other. The way you play me up. I'll have it out on you, by God I will.' And he comes down the stairs, shouting and coughing and grumbling, and he comes out into the street, and sure enough it's Chris. You

182

should have seen him. Thin. Yellow. Face like a bloody skull. All stooping, like — a nasty, cringy sort of stoop. Shabby. I tell you, it broke my bloody heart. I wished I could have cleared off without him seeing me. Well, it's too late. He gives me a scared sort of look, then his face lights up, and he says, 'Hallo, Jackie boy.' Well, we stand there talking for a bit, ordinary things, like, as you might with anyone, then I come right out with it. 'Look here, Chris,' I says, 'what's all this lark in aid of?' He says, 'What lark?' 'This rent collecting lark,' I says. 'It ain't exactly a bloody picnic by the sound of it.' He laughs, gets all mixed up coughing, and then he says, 'Too bloody true, boy. It's the bane of my life.' 'Well, then,' I says, 'what you do it for?' 'I'm in a bad way,' he says, 'they've turned me off war work because of my lungs. I can't get anything else. Every time I cough it's a dead giveaway. I see the doctor every week, on the panel, and I get my sick benefit, but that doesn't go far, not with my Estella, she's a lady, she is, she's not the kind to count pennies. Well, to be frank, Jack, since I haven't got long, I thought I'd put a bit aside for her and the child while I could, so I took this on.' 'What about mum?' I ask him, 'she'd help you, wouldn't she?' 'I'm fed up with sponging on her,' he says, 'I've got my pride.' 'Well,' I says, 'what about your Labour lot? You've done enough for them in your time.' 'Them,' he says, 'here,' he says, 'that's the bloody working-class, that lot up there —' and he points up at the flats — 'the swine,' he says, 'driving me to my grave, they are.' From what I heard, he'd been doing his bit to drive them to theirs, but I don't suppose that occurred to him, poor devil. 'I'd sell the lot of them for the price of a good dinner,' he says, 'I've got a right to, I tell you, after all I've been through.' And that's what poor old Chris thought about his life, at the end of it."

Nobody spoke for a while. Nancy wiped her eyes with her handkerchief. Rose said, "It makes no difference. He failed, but he did put up a fight." Nancy sighed, and said, "Well, you'll all come back to tea now, won't you?"

Their feet scraped in the gravel as they collected themselves uncertainly, preparing for the departure.

Gran looked up, with a darting movement of her head. "Not with her," she said suddenly, "not with her I won't.."

Jack exclaimed, "Here —"

"You keep quiet. You know nothing. I've stood it long enough. I've stood here with my mouth shut out of respect for the dead. Why didn't she have the decency to keep away? It was an insult to this one, yes, and to my own poor boy."

Rose began, "Please, Gran —"

"Don't you Gran me. I'm no Gran of yours."

Jack muttered to Joyce, "Oh, crumbs, what an afternoon it's turned out." The day's tranquillity was gone. One shock, one mystification was following another.

"Broken spine," the old woman said, "it was a broken heart my poor son died of, not a broken spine. He lay there on his deathbed and he didn't say a word. Oh, no, he didn't say a thing. You needn't worry. He couldn't, poor child, dying there in torture. But he looked at me with his poor eyes, and his mother knew what was killing him. Yes, I knew as sure as if I had the proof for a court of law. Her!" she hissed. "Her and her mother! Not with her I'm not going. That's flat. Not if you bring a pair of brewer's horses to drag me."

Jack whispered to Nancy, "Here, what's this all about?" She did not answer. Everything was happening around Jack as if he were not there. Nancy was crying. Tom was soothing her. Joyce was standing apart, displayed a frightened stare. Jack realised that Rose was speaking to him; he did not know what she was saying, nor what reply it was that he heard himself mumbling. Rose said to Nancy, "It's all right, Nance, it's nothing to cry about, darling. I should have come on my own some other time. It's best if I go now. Don't you worry about me. You go off home to tea."

Jack looked around. She was gone. It was incredible.

184

The rest of them were standing there, in a dream, and she was gone. He could not convince himself, with any certainty, that she had been there at all.

Tea, at the flat, was a miserable affair. Gran sat crouched in her armchair in a sullen, defiant silence. Tom and Nancy were too busy, too attentive, too cheerful in their commonplace talk, to succeed in anything but underlining the failure of the expedition. Joyce maintained that painful pretence of deafness and blindness common to all who find themselves the involuntary witnesses of other people's family quarrels. Jack was still sunk in mystification. Once, catching Nancy alone for a moment, he said, "Here, Nance. I don't catch on. What's old Gran got her rag out about? All that rigmarole. I mean, I know Rose ain't what she ought to be, but —"

"It's not that."

"Well, what then?"

"Jack, I feel so tired, and I've got a headache. Please, dear." Jack muttered, "Sorry, Nancy," with the resentful voice of a small boy who has been rebuffed.

When he rose to leave he felt worn out. He was incapable of coherent thought, and still numbed emotionally.

As they walked to the bus stop, Joyce, freed from the restraining presence of others, chattered mercilessly. "I can't see what business it is of the old woman's the way Rose lives. I can understand her not liking the idea of her son's daughter carrying on like that, but what all that's got to do with driving him to his grave I can't imagine. Rose was hardly four years old when he died, was she? It doesn't make sense."

He mumbled knowingly, "It wasn't that."

"What then?"

He shrugged his shoulders. When he spoke, it was to answer his own questions as well as hers. "Ah, you know these old folk. They get weak in the head. They get everything muddled up, what happened last week and

185

what happened twenty years ago. That's all it is. You don't want to take any notice."

His answer seemed to satisfy Joyce more than it satisfied his own doubts. After all, she was not deeply interested. She shot off on a new tack, full of admiration for Rose — for her poise, her speech, her complexion, her clothes. She seemed to have caught in her own cheeks the glow of Rose's warmth. Under its melting influence she had forgotten to adopt the stern attitude of disapproval she usually displayed to the errant of her sex. She was too flattered and excited to be critical.

Jack realised that now, only an hour after the encounter, he had not retained a single impression of Rose. Had she changed? He could not remember. What did she look like? There was no picture in his mind. Instead, he felt as if he were recovering from a blow on the head. Joyce's maddening chatter was the only proof that the whole episode was not merely a freak of his imagination.

"She asked us to come and see her," Joyce said.

"Who did?"

"Rose, of course."

"Did she? When?"

"Before she went, silly. You remember, you said, maybe."

"Did I? I don't remember."

"Are you kidding? What's come over you? Shall we?"

"Shall we what?"

"Jack, you dummy, wake up! Shall we go and see her?"

"No."

"Why not?"

His voice shook. "Because I said so." He steadied himself. "Here, Joycie, be a pal. I feel bloody tired. I got a headache."

Half-sulky, half repentant, she said, "Sorry, Jack." Silence soon became too much for her, and all the way home she overwhelmed him with admiring talk about Rose.

Chapter 4

SIX MONTHS AGO Joyce had dreaded the approach of her twenty-fifth birthday: the end of another year unmarried. Now that her future was settled, she was able to enjoy a birthday as she had done in her childhood and 'teens. The week had been a happy one. On Thursday morning, the fifteenth of September, she had lain in bed with her eyes shut pretending to sleep while footsteps creaked in the room. Alone, she had sat up, feeling not only the old wild, childish thrill as she reached for the parcels, but an added sense of pleasure in the knowledge that she was still capable of feeling the thrill. A pair of bedroom slippers from her father ('Mum bought them for him,' she decided), an imitation pearl necklace from her mother, a pair of nylon stockings from her friend Maureen — they had all spent more on her than usual this year, in tribute to her betrothed state — and a handbag from Jack. Jack's note, 'To the future Mrs. Agass, with love and kisses,' had provoked from her a critical grimace, not only because she despised his large and clumsy handwriting, but because she did not like to be reminded of her future surname. There had been kisses all round at breakfast and several birthday cards arriving by the first post; three days later they still decorated the parlour mantelpiece. In the evening Jack had taken her to the Palladium and to supper afterwards. Yesterday afternoon there had been a big family tea, and today — Sunday — Jack was taking her on their long-discussed trip to the country.

Joyce sat, prim and erect, on a roadside bench, gripping

her handbag in her lap with both hands, while Jack spoke with a passer-by. She watched him with the complacent approval of a mother who sees in her child's behaviour the proof of her own good management. Jack came back to her. "It's not far now," he said, "you leave it to me."

"Oh, dear," she said, as they walked away along the unpaved road, "my poor tootsies! Lucky I dressed for a long walk."

The Surrey hills, sweeping away into the autumn mist, were crested with clumps of trees; their flanks were girdled with serpentine rows of houses. Here and there pale patches of grassland still showed.

"I thought Surrey was the country," Joyce said.

"It used to be." Jack sounded perplexed. "Perhaps we should have gone a bit further out. We used to come here a lot."

"Who's 'we'?"

"Oh, you know, all the 'Erbs, on our bikes."

"Didn't you know any better places to bring me?"

"Well, where is there?"

Joyce was unable to answer. Where, indeed, was this mysterious place called 'the country?' Few people in Lamb Street could have answered. London stretched away, in all directions, a brick maze without discoverable exits. One could walk all day and not come to the end of it. One could ride to the end of any bus line or bump about for hours in a tram and still be surrounded by houses. True, it was possible to go to a railway station and be whisked away to Southend, Margate or Brighton. It was true that fields, cows, woods and streams could be glimpsed on such journeys, behind the billboards and the swooping telegraph wires. It was true that some of one's friends, the cyclists, the ramblers, the adventurers, seemed to be able to find their way out to it and come home brown and bluebell-laden. But Joyce, for all her quick intelligence and shopgirl's worldliness, had never explored outside the imprisoning city. Indeed, she only knew her own corner of her own borough, and a square mile or two of the West End. "Never mind," she said, "it's nice walking, for a change, and the air is definitely fresher, isn't it?"

Jack sniffed loudly and said, "Mmm. Not half. You can tell the difference right away."

"Well, let's find somewhere we can eat our lunch. We don't want to carry it around all day, do we?"

"You leave it to me."

She was content to stroll at his side. His presence did not intrude into her consciousness. She remembered a couple they had passed a half-hour ago, the girl sagging raptly against the man, the pair of them obviously lost to all but each other. Well, she supposed that was all right for some people. She preferred to ignore the mysterious sadness the sight of them had left in the background of her emotions, and to walk aloofly, reminding herself with a glance of Jack's presence from time to time but otherwise busy with her own dreams and plans, enjoying the unexciting but still novel surroundings and the mild autumn sunshine.

"Joyce." His voice disturbed her thoughts. "About what I was saying in the train. Can't we hurry it up a bit?"

"I thought we'd settled that. We've had it out half-a-dozen times this last week or two. I don't know what's come over you."

"Look, it's like I said. Why wait till December? We could get married in a couple of weeks."

"Oh, how can we?" She could not help being curt, going over it all again, "We've got to wait for the flat. There's things to buy. What's the hurry? Everything's going all right."

"We could still wait for the flat. But we could share a room in your house in the meantime. At least we'd have each other."

"We've got each other."

"Ah, Joycie, you know what I mean."

"I know what you mean all right. You men! Marriage only means one thing to you. You've got no time to think

189

about a nice home, and giving people a good impression. Well, it doesn't to me, and you can jolly well wait and like it, see?"

"Well, there's a nice thing to say! Trying to tell me you don't look forward to — wah, you know!"

"Perhaps I do and perhaps I don't. I'm the same as the next woman. Anyway, my dear, you wait till the time comes, and you'll find out soon enough then."

"I don't know," Jack groaned. "You want to have kids, don't you?"

"Of course I do. What's that got to do with it?"

"Here —" Jack looked at her in alarm. "You mean to say you don't know —? Here, it's me that works the oracle, old girl, not the bloody stork, you know."

She laughed and laid her hand on his arm. "I know, dear. And Columbus discovered America in ten-sixty-six. So what?"

She uttered a triumphant little sound as Jack relapsed into a puzzled silence, and squeezed his arm consolingly. She had long ago discovered that she could always subdue him with a little repartee. She enjoyed seeing him blinking dazedly at her; it made her feel superior, subtle, a possessor of the ancient womanly power; but instinct also prevented her from pushing him too far, and she would always relent and soothe him. "It's been such a lovely week, Jack. I told Maureen about the seats we had at the Palladium, right in the front. She was green with envy, I could see."

"I bet she was. Took a lot of trouble to get them seats. You got to know how to talk to 'em."

"I know, dear."

He led her into a field. "Here we are, what did I tell you?"

There were houses behind one side of the field, and another row was being built opposite, the wooden frames gleaming white in the sunlight. Heaps of fresh red bricks were stacked in the field along the hedge.

"It's all right if you look that way." Jack pointed

downhill. "Look, you can see right across to them hills. Fields and fields."

"It's lovely," she said. In any case, she could see little without her glasses. Jack spread his coat and they sat down in the long grass. "It's all right here, Jack," she said, "I like it like this. The country's all right, but I get frightened when there's too much of it. It makes you so lonely."

"I know. It's the sky that puts the wind up me. Here, I'll tell you something. You know the time in the war when I was most windy? It wasn't overseas. It was one evening, Salisbury way. I was walking back to camp on my own. It was getting dark. The road ran along the edge of a valley, and there was hills all round. There I was like a little flea crawling round the edge of a great big bowl. It got all darker and darker. Proper mysterious, I can tell you. The valley filled up with shadows. All the trees went black. And the sky, it was — ooh, it was — well, I tell you, it was too bloody big. No end to it. All mauvy, like. You reckoned you were looking up about a million miles. Then them bloody big black clouds started piling up behind the hills. You couldn't hear a sound. Not a bloody sound. Do you know, I didn't half shiver. I felt as if I was the only one left on earth. Whoo, I says, time I got out of this. And I run all the way back to camp. Two mile. All the bloody way. Well, I mean, that shows you what the country's like, don' it?"

They finished their lunch and lay back. Jack put his arm beneath her shoulders. He drew close and kissed her. She returned his kisses lazily, pressing her parted lips softly against the side of his face nearest to her. Once she leaned over him to kiss his mouth and his other cheek. She felt warm, tender and trustful. A moment later she knocked his hand away from her body.

He put his hands behind his head, fingers linked, and stared up at the sky. His chest heaved in brief, private grunts of laughter. She was assailed with misgivings. Ought she yield to him? She was bemused by the

191

sunshine and by the scent of the hot grass beneath them. Enervating impulses moved about her body. Perhaps she might lose him if she continued to repel him. There was no mistaking his mood for days past; his stifling embraces; his painful grip on her arm; the urgency of his footsteps at her heels; the edge to his voice. It was frightening and flattering. For some seconds she lay in a dreamy sweetness, awaiting him. Fear, a coldness, returned. She remembered all the solemn advice she had heard from her mother and her girl friend. She heard another dark grunt from the man at her side. Oh, what ridiculous animals they were! She asked, "Are you laughing at me?"

"No." There was another little quiver of laughter. "Something I remembered."

"Secret?"

A second's hesitation. "No. It's something happened with Rosie once. We went to Kew Gardens once. We were laying on the grass like this, and all of a sudden she says, 'Oh, Jack, if there's one thing I love it's a lark.'"

"Well?"

"Well —" another reminiscent splutter — "I reckon I got the wrong idea." He pointed at a bird wheeling above them. "She meant one of them things."

A note in his voice had caught her interest. "Did you go there often?"

"Oh, on and off. She loved it. She was the girl for the country. Knew all about it, she did. I don't know where she picked it up. Any tree you like, she could tell you right off. Oak tree. Elm tree." — He was trying to think of another. — "Beech tree. Bloody marvellous. Takes some doing, that. She didn't half used to get excited down there. Face all —" he was twisting his lips about in the effort to find the words — "well, you know, her eyes all — whoo, you know! She used to stretch herself out in the sun, you'd think some geezer was kissing her, the look on her face." His voice foundered. "She was a girl all right."

She let him recover before she asked, "Jack, you were a

192

bit gone on Rose, weren't you?"

"Me?" A prolonged, "N'yah!"

She pondered. "Jack, how did you feel when you saw her again the other week?"

"Me?" A stupid laugh. "Can't say. Never really noticed her, I reckon. Why?"

"Jack." She forced herself to speak calmly, in her precise, shopgirl's voice. "Why are you so keen to get married all of a sudden? Just lately?"

"Me? Can't help being sweet on you, can I?" He turned on her and pinned her down by the shoulders. "Oh, Joycie!" He stifled her with kisses. Her body felt leaden and muscleless, inert upon the earth, but her arms clung to him as if they must never let him go.

"Jack!" Turning her head, she had kept her senses sufficiently to see movement at a distant window. Propriety, which never slumbered in her, rose against passion. "Jack —" she struggled free of him — "there's people watching us."

He squinted angrily at her, took a disbelieving look at the houses and sighed. "Dunno what you trouble to wear glasses for. You can see an excuse a mile off."

"Let's find somewhere else." She still felt too stifled to talk coherently.

They rose, sluggish and heavy-eyed, brushed grass from each other and walked away, arms closely round each other's waists.

They spent the rest of the afternoon searching for a secluded place. Every time they headed for a clump of trees they were driven off by a glimpse of villa turrets or a gleam of windows. Whenever they hopefully rounded a bend in the road another string of houses faced them on the opposing slopes, like a row of beaters hemming them in. They became hot, dusty and dispirited. Jack cracked stubborn, feeble jokes. Joyce looked up with distaste at his red, sweat-beaded face. They loosened their grip on each other, held sticky hands for a while, then walked apart.

As the mood guttered out in both of them, Joyce

193

wondered angrily how she had ever succumbed to it. How had that wild idea about Rose ever entered her head? Why had it made her give way, instantaneously, to a wild, jealous panic of surrender? Why! — she reminded herself — Jack had not even noticed what Rose was wearing. He had not even heard what she had said to him or remembered his own offhand reply. He had not said a word about her since the encounter. He had never shown any desire to accept her invitation to see her again, although he was usually enthusiastic about visiting old acquaintances. What a foolish idea! As if her old slow Jack could harbour secret passions! And did his kisses feel like those of a man who has room in his thoughts for another woman? Joyce remembered her mother's advice, "When a feller loses his head about you, you keep yours, and you've got him, my girl, you've got him just where you want him." What a fool she'd almost made of herself! Well, a miss was as good as a mile. She peeped into her mirror and said, "You haven't half messed me up." She had to be careful of her looks: her nose left unpowdered in the heat, a smear of lipstick, a wave of her dry bleached hair out of place, and she would look a real sight, Plain Jane again, lonely Joyce Wakerell. "Let's sit down on this bench and I'll tidy myself up before we go back to the train."

In the train they sat opposite each other, slumped back with their heads leaning against the windows, eyeing each other as if they wanted to find out each other's thoughts and conceal their own. Joyce did not know whether she had escaped the crisis or merely postponed it. She could see that Jack, equally uncertain, was wondering whether to accept defeat or to make another attempt. She could not even decide what she wanted to happen, for, although her cautious self had been aroused to stand guard over her, another part of her had been awakened for the first time by the hint of more profound satisfactions than she had ever known. She was left mentally indecisive and physically weak.

They returned to an empty house. They moved about

their rooms, washing themselves and changing their clothes, Joyce humming and Jack whistling, each expressing a spirit of vague defiance towards the other. Joyce prepared supper. When they had eaten they went into the parlour. Joyce, her actions as oppressed and helpless as if she were in a trance, drew the curtains and sat by Jack's side in the gloom.

They sprawled for an hour, not moving, in each other's arms. Lovers of another class are able to use words as a means of communication. Jack and Joyce had not the gift of words. Their only communion was in this prolonged and passive embrace, when their bodies learned to know each other. A heavy sigh from Jack in the shadows, unexplained, a private little laugh from Joyce; these were the only clues, to be thought over later but never discussed, that each could find to the other's secret personality.

Joyce was lying back, passionately content once more, with her mouth fastened over Jack's, noticing the single rhythm of their breathing, as if it were she who was filling and emptying his lungs. They did not speak. In these moments of extreme intimacy each was liberated from the other, enabled to escape from the other into a private world of dream. To Joyce, the animate weight on her arms lost its identity. Jack was forgotten, and with him all the impulses of half-heartedness, shame and contempt that at some other times she could not help feeling towards him. It was no particular man whom she was clasping; merely a man, whom she could invest with any identity that pleased her. The room had become dark but she could still see Jack clearly, for the darkness was transparent, a glassy indoor twilight in which every object in the room was violently outlined. His face, near to her, looked sharp and strong. The lamplight through the gap in the curtains caught the smooth shine over his cheekbones and made his eyes glitter in the dark, endowing him with an appearance of strength and ferocity that he did not possess by daylight.

195

The flow of reverie that lulled her was disturbed. His weight on her seemed to have increased. His breathing was out of time with hers. Unformulated questions struggled in her mind. The face close to hers was hostile. Panic clawed icily at her insides and was gone. There were pulse-beats all over her body. She wanted to weep wildly, to stroke his head, to die. She was a human sacrifice to the stranger who held her.

Yet even now she could not prevent herself from recording other sensations. The uneven springs of the sofa nudged her back as if in derision. His hair, gleaming with its varnish of brilliantine, would not rumple and stuck out in ridiculous black spikes that sprang stiffly beneath her touch. She was offended by the sickly scent of the brilliantine and by the odour of kitchen soap that clung to his skin. She could even see, while her spirit was stifling in his embrace, white specks of dandruff on his shirt collar.

What impulse of protest seized her body, or where it came from, she never knew. She repulsed him with a force that was not naturally hers, and felt as if someone else had wrenched him, against her will, from her arms. A second later she was overcome with regret. She could feel her heart thumping. She wanted to pull him down upon her and put an end to her misery. She longed for him to overwhelm her with male rage.

He said, in a broken voice, "Well, that's that, eh?"

She was silent. He said, "End of a perfect day."

She had the sensation of weeping inwardly. She searched her mind for words of remorse. She wanted to beg his forgiveness. There were no words. She shrugged her shoulders.

"I only wanted my rights," he muttered.

She tried to tell him, with an imploring look, that she was his for the taking. His face was averted. He said sullenly, "I suppose you're afraid."

She made a harsh sound in her throat, swallowed, and whispered, "Why afraid?"

196

He had not understood. He added, "Of getting lumbered, eh?"

"Lumbered?" Her voice, interrupted by the hint of a sob, was almost inaudible. Her hands refused to move towards him. "Oh, no."

He looked at her. The expectant brightness that returned to her eyes in the darkness, the tentative move of her shoulders towards him, told him nothing. She saw only uncomprehension in his eyes. He said, smothered, "I suppose you're right. It just took me, that's all. You know." He hovered, embarrassed. "Been hard day, all that walking. Get to bed early, I reckon, eh? Tired. Best thing." He said goodnight and kissed her. The kiss left no taste. She did not stir. She could not even summon the flood of tears that might relieve her grief and tell him what her lips could not. She heard his puzzled and shuffling step and the soft click of the door closing behind him. She sat for a little while with bowed head, wrenching her fingers together in her lap. Then she cast herself face downward on the cushions, shaken by tearless, unrelieving sobs: at her cowardice, at the uncontrollable transience of her emotions, and at the realisation that she — a woman of twenty-five — didn't know what to do for the best.

Chapter 5

JACK WALKED INTO THE WORKSHOP next morning too depressed to notice the unnatural solemnity of the "Good-morning' with which his workmates addressed him in chorus, or the fidgeting gravity with which they watched him go to his bench. He returned an empty "Mornin' " and reached to take his overalls from their peg. He pulled; there was resistance; before his mind had awakened he pulled again, impatiently, and there was the sound of tearing. He stopped and found that the legs of the overalls had been tacked to the wall.

The others were restraining their laughter until he should break into loud and bitter complaint. Denying them the satisfaction he sighed and said, as if to himself, "Ah, well, some people got their goolies where their brains ought to be."

Foiled, they tried to save face with a clamour of affability. "Lovely weekend," said Sam. He was five years younger than Jack, small and squat with an oversize face that was topped by a mop of dirty yellow hair and covered with numerous red knobbles of which his nose was the largest. "Talk about summer everlasting! I reckon we'll get an 'ell of a winter to make up for it."

The two boys, Leo and the fifteen-year-old Tich, broke into deafening and simultaneous judgments on the latest achievements of the Arsenal and the Harringay Racers.

Sam asked Jack, " 'Ad it in, this weekend?" His tone was one of polite enquiry: the question was one he might address, out of courtesy, to any friend.

"I did," said Leo ferociously. Leo was seventeen. "Smashin' cob. Parliament Hill Fields. Wanted half-a-crown. I pinned her bloody ears back."

"Here," Sam said to Jack, "what's up with you, tosh? You've gorn as red as a monkey's arse."

"Mind your own," Jack grunted, pulling his overalls on.

"Well I was only asking a civil question."

"All right, nob. Have a heart. The joke's over. I want to think."

Sam moved away to his bench, showing his willingness to desist. Leo said, "He's takin' up Yogo. I seen it on the tele. He's gonna stand on his head an' attain Nirvana."

"All right, Leo," Sam said, "leave the bloke alone and give us 'and with this shelving, or you'll be the one that gets stood on his head."

Leo was lanky, with a predatory stoop. People who heard him for the first time were startled at the depth of his cracked, malicious voice. His black hair was plastered down and his face was of an extreme pallor which gave a frightening hint not of weakness but of a sort of fungoid hardihood. His eyes, close-set, small and brilliant, were horribly knowing. He twisted his mouth into an enormous sidelong snarl, said, "Smarrerwitchoo," struck a fighting attitude, added, "Take on the pair of yer. Alan Ladd. John Garfield. That's me. See me wi' my ol' muscle expander every morning! I'll slay yer! Give yer the ol' one-two!"— and went obediently back to his work.

Tich, who stood scarcely bench-high, and who looked like a rosy-cheeked little cherub in frayed long trousers, helped to pull the dust sheets from the mahogany counter which it was Jack's task to finish. It was a beautiful piece of work, designed for one corner of a tobacconist's shop. Jack, whose work on it had been a labour of love, looked on it as a poem of flawless curves and imperceptible joints. Whenever he had an object like this to make, something for which he was personally responsible, his work would cease to be a resented drudgery, the days would fly past, he would quit unwillingly in the evenings

199

or even readily consent to put in overtime. His pride in it was tinged with a heaviness of heart, for after today, when he had finished smoothing it off, the polishers would come for it. His beloved child would have gone out into the world and he would have to join Sam and Leo in the detestable task of turning out innumerable yards of shelving and cutting it up into required lengths.

He began working on the counter, enjoying the even, experienced rhythm into which his body lapsed, the pleasant stress on his muscles and the relief of focusing his mind wholly on a single, uncomplicated object. At work, with the flight of time accelerated, and the warm air cosily laden with the smells of sawdust and boiling glue, he was able to rock all the unneeded part of himself to sleep. The burden of yesterday's failure slipped from him. He forgot the loss of painfully-acquired confidence with which the repulse had left him, the recriminations he had heaped on himself for his inability to master Joyce, and the despondency he had felt at what he took to be the proof of her coldness. Even the name of Rose, which for the last two weeks had been sounding like a bell through the confusion of his thoughts, grew faint.

The morning slipped by. He was surprised to realise, when Tich came round for the tea money, that the time for the mid-morning break was at hand. Leo's voice, as ceaseless and irritant as the nagging of a circular saw, had been droning in the background of his consciousness; now he became aware of it.

"Wotcha gonna do when you lose your job, mate? Sell bootlaces or push a barrel organ?"

"Eh? You talking to me?"

"I ain't talking to Gandhi, mate."

"What you talking about, lose my job?"

"Slack times, mate." Leo's face was twisted into an expression of ferocious relish. "Read the papers, mate. Prices goin' up. Less money to spend. Less shops to fit. Less jobs for us. Bash! Crash! Fini la guerre! Give 'im 'is cards!"

"Give who his cards?"

"You, mate, you. Look in the mirror and say howdo to a mug."

"Me? Why me?"

"Last on, first orf. That's logic, ain' it? We've all been here longer than you. You'll be the first to go."

"Go 'way! You're dreaming!"

"Oho, I'm dreaming, he says. You ask the guv'nor how he's fixed for orders. Here —" he called the attention of the others with a derisive gesture at Jack — "who's dreaming round here? Who's getting wed with his head in the clouds? Me or ol' Jack Fishcakes?"

Sam hooted with laughter and shouted, "Give 'im 'is cards!"

Tich, from the door, squeaked, "Give 'im 'is cards!"

"If you had the sense to read a proper newspaper," Leo went on mercilessly, "'stead of readin' up the rapes in the ol' *Pictorial,* you'd have some idea what was going on. Budgets. Scares. Slumps. Speeches. All sorts. A proper muckup, I can tell you."

"Well," Jack said — miserably, for, although he had been able throughout the dreamy heat of the summer to ignore the world in the rush of his own life, the unread headlines had gathered about his consciousness like black bogeymen prying for admission, "I don't see what *you* got to laugh about."

The others roared and screeched with laughter. They had started without any particular malice. It was their custom, from day to day, to relieve the tedium of work by baiting one or another in their midst. If Jack had responded with spirit they would have left him alone, perhaps turned on Tich. But his lethargic resentment only provoked them further. Moreover, the subject that had now arisen was one on which their inner fears were as deep as his. They could, by hounding him, create in themselves the transient illusion that they were exempt. They yelled in chorus, "Give 'im 'is cards!"

Tich came in with four cups of tea on a tray. He served

the others and brought the remaining cup to Jack. Jack took the cup. He stared at his workmates, who were standing in subdued attitudes, in one of those strange, sudden silences that seem pregnant with uproar. Oppressed by a wondering half-suspicion, he poured the contents of the cup down his throat in a single long swallow. "Here!" he exclaimed, "Sugar boat gone down or something? Tastes like bloody leather, this tea. Here —" he tasted the bitterness in his mouth and looked down into his cup — "what you? —"

The explosion came. "Oohoo!" Sam danced about, flinging out his arms in ecstasy. "He's done it! He's drunk it!" Tich sat on the floor with his arms pressed across his waist, doubled up with mirth, shrieking, "He's drunk it! Oh, Leo, he's drunk it! All at one go!"

"Here, I say —"

"Get your running pumps ready." It was Leo, leering with triumph. "You got a gut full of Epsom salts, mate."

He felt a leap of fury: at them, and at himself for being stupid and confused instead of confounding them with some unexpected act of retaliation. He restrained himself: he was ashamed of the depths of rage and resentment he might reveal if he lost control. He sighed harshly and turned away from them.

Throughout the rest of the morning, and after a silent, sullen lunch-hour, he toiled at the counter. The accumulated unhappiness in his life had not been dispelled by his happy summer, but had settled deep within him like a heavy sediment. Stirred up by the trifling events of the morning, this sediment rose to cloud his thoughts. Waves of anger overcame him; against his workmates; against the world which, he persuaded himself, they represented; against himself; and against Joyce. His movements became self-conscious and needle pains of fatigue stabbed his back and shoulders. Under the stress of anger his thoughts became childish. Who did Joyce think she was, denying him, teasing him, laughing at him? Oh, yes, he knew that she laughed at him! It wasn't as if she was such a catch. He had pretended not to hear when the 'Erbs on the street corner had called, "Flossie Four-Eyes!" after her; but he had heard, and had felt ashamed. All the time, he heard inside him, 'Rose, Rose, Rose, Rose!' He could have got something better than Joyce. There was Rose, asking after him, sending him messages through Mick and Nancy, inviting him to see her. He'd been square with Joyce. All these months without a woman. It was as much as a chap could bear. Here he was, working at King's Cross within a few minutes' walk of Rose's flat, coming here to work every day for months, and never once (thus he represented his weakness to himself as strength) had he gone to see her. 'Oh, Rose, Rose, Rose!'

And these others, bloody civvies, never suffered in their lives, jeering at him, taking advantage of his patience. He wanted to fight, or to run away; to go berserk, or to bury his head in a warm lap. His workmates, like banderilleros plying their darts, assailed him each time he looked up with the cry, "Give 'im 'is cards!" Now there were all these things Leo had thrown up at him, the things in the newspapers, the besieging calamities he had always stubbornly ignored or shrugged away; the incomprehensible doings of coldfaced strangers, faraway and utterly outside his control, that might (but how, how, how?) blot out even that tiny gleam of hope for a secure and settled life towards which, in war and peace, he had spent his whole adult life trudging. "Give 'im 'is cards," his workmates jeered, "Give 'im 'is cards!"

"That's what you think." It was late afternoon, and he could stand their goading no longer. Feeling shamed by his silence, the evidence of his obtuseness, he had been trying for some time to think of a suitable remark. Now he produced it. "Even if someone does have to go — which I don't believe — it won't be me. For one thing, I'm the best tradesman here. For another —" he looked around him in ponderous triumph — "I'm a bloody ex-service-man."

203

Sam said, "What's 'at got to do with it?"

"Bloody ex-chump," Leo jeered. "You never knew no better, that's all. There's plenty had the brains to keep out. Not ol' Jack Fishcakes, though."

"Why, you little —" Jack swung his hand at Leo. Leo ducked and punched Jack on the nose. Jack went after him. "I'll slaughter you," he gasped, "cheeky little bastard you are. I'll smear the bloody floor with you. I'll show you what bloody for. I was fighting for you when you was eating bloody bread and drip in the infants' school." Leo retreated, crouching pugnaciously behind his clenched fists, pulling fearsome faces, ducking and prancing about as if in a demonstration of shadow-boxing. "Come on, hit me! Come on, give yer a dollar if you can hit me! Whoa, come on, you can do better than that. Middle-age spread, that's your trouble." He hit Jack. "Senile decay." He hit Jack again. "Monkey glands, that's what you want." He hit Jack again and pranced easily out of reach. Jack halted, scarlet and breathless.

Leo began to sing, "Old soldiers neVAH die, neVAH die, neVAH die." Sam and Tich joined in. "They only fa-a-a-ade — ay-way."

Jack turned on Tich and sent him sprawling across the floor with a mighty clout. Tich began to blubber loudly. Jack stood over the boy, appalled. Then he glared at Leo and Sam and strode out of the workshop into the street.

He walked up to the main road. At this point, between King's Cross Station and Caledonian Road, the foot of Pentonville Road forms a bottleneck through which a continuous torrent of traffic pours. Buses on half-a-dozen routes, taxis shooting to and from the station, private cars, heavy goods wagons, swing in and out of the eight thoroughfares which converge in this vicinity, in a chaos which the traffic police control to their own seeming satisfaction but which leaves pedestrians bewildered and, when scurrying across the road, in constant peril of their lives.

He went into a teashop and sat at a table near the

window. He looked out through the plate glass windows, at the snarling, charging herds of traffic and at the hurrying crowds whose white, hostile faces stared in at him. The hideous mingling of noises — voices, pneumatic drills, roar of wheels and engines, freezing scream of gears, clattering crockery, vibrating rumble from the Underground — became unbearable. He sought refuge in memory. The noise lost significance in his ears. His eyes emptied as he looked, beyond the narrow, black-walled street, into the past. He was back in Sicily. He looked out, over a parapet, at an olive grove, at a stretch of vineyards, at a wide sunlit landscape. The sky was vast and blue. Hills rose in the distance, and the great blue shadow of Etna, snowcapped. He was crawling along a shallow ditch. He rejoiced at the burning touch of the sun on his skin. He could hear his heart thumping and feel an icy exhilaration in his blood. His hand pushed through white dust, warm and powder-soft. He was crawling along the ditch, and the sweat was trickling coldly on his body. He dared not lift his head. The buzz of a mosquito was loud in the shimmering silence. A mine exploded in the distance. He crawled on. He lay still, and the exhilaration, fear-fed, raced through his veins as voices came from nearby: German voices, muffled by the heat and by the dust-blanketed earth, German voices from the trench past which he was crawling. He moved one hand silently forward, then a leg, then a lift of his body, then the other arm and the other leg; silently, inch by inch. The voices were relaxed, unsuspecting. He crawled on. The voices grew faint behind him. There was a shadowy bulk above him: his objective. He eased himself up out of the ditch and, lying full length on the ground, picked blackberries from the lower part of the hedge which he had crawled half a mile in broad daylight, through the enemy positions, to reach. His steel helmet lay upside-down by his side and he filled it. When he had filled it he picked more berries, eating as much as he could, till his chin and fingers were purple-stained. Then the long crawl back, pushing the laden helmet in front of him, past the Germans, across the plain, into the vineyards and, with a crouched, scuttling run, back to the olive grove. He was full of laughter and exultation, drunk with the vanity and madness of youth. He passed the helmet round among the platoon. The men ate berries and passed insulting, admiring remarks. He was Mad Jack Agass. Twenty-four years old. The men around him were his friends. They would follow him anywhere. Among them, he was never inarticulate, his mind was never sluggish. He always had a quick answer. They roared at his jokes. He was a man who knew how to dare.

When he walked out of the teashop, his dream ended, he was shivering in spite of the sunshine. He stood on the edge of the pavement, wondering what held him there. Unformulated thought, as painful as a thorn in his mind, groped for the memory of having dared.

He shut his eyes tightly and stepped off the kerb. Eyes closed, he walked out across the road. The din in his ears became deafening. Shadows flitted terrifyingly against his eyelids. He heard snatches of shouting, angry and startled. He resisted the impulse to open his eyes. He was in a vast, lucent darkness, daring. He wanted to grope in front of him but he kept his hands at his sides. Engines roared close by like wild beasts. Exhaust fumes fanned his face in hot, animal breaths. He was stumbling through a jungle in the dark, the quarry of everything that prowled. He had never realised before that it took twenty years to cross a road. Out of his fear the old feeling began to blossom, icy and glorious, the joy of daring. He stumbled on the far kerb and opened his eyes. He was on the pavement once more, safe; sweating and breathing hard.

Someone stepped forward and spoke to him. The face was familiar. He tried to focus. His reason returned, and he realised what he had done. Fear clutched him, in retrospect. His legs were weak and he trembled more violently than before. He recognized the face. He was dumbfounded at its appearance, and doubly ashamed.

Rose said, "I've been watching you for the last few minutes. You'd better come home with me."

He could not speak.

She said, "I was in the bus queue. I saw you come out of Lyons. Can you walk? It's not far."

He was still shuddering, white-faced and speechless.

She asked, "Are you ill, Jack?"

He pressed his clenched fist against his stomach as if covering a bullet-hole. His eyes wandered, and he moved his lips, trying to speak. "Oh Gawd," he moaned at last, "them Epsom salts!"

Part 4

Chapter 1

UNTIL HE WAS COMFORTABLY ESTABLISHED in an armchair in her flat, Rose did not trouble Jack with questions. Crushed within himself by shame and confusion, he had scarcely dared to look at her. Now he sat, legs crossed, leaning over the side of the chair with a glass of brandy in his hand, watching her sheepishly as she paced up and down the room.

"Another drink?" Her own glass was already empty.

He shook his head and managed to say, "No, thank you."

"Feeling better?" She did not trouble to look at him as she moved about, restless and severe, with her arms clasped across her chest, frowning down at her shoes as if unsure of what she wanted from this encounter.

"I'm all right."

She swung suddenly to face him. "Jack, what on earth were you up to, in the street, there?"

He shrugged his shoulders and looked down at the rug. "Dunno. Come over a bit funny I suppose."

She studied him with concern. "Has it happened before?"

He shook his head. The action was absent-minded, for he was comparing her with her mother. She had the same fullness of cheek as Kate, and the same pastel colouring; but she was taller; her hair was darker, with a blue-black gleam, and less luxuriant; her eyes were as wide and clear as Kate's, but lit with points of intentness which robbed them of Kate's expression of wondering frankness; her face, not composed and placid like her mother's, was

211

marked with a keenness that added to its vitality but detracted from its beauty.

"What was it? You had your eyes shut, didn't you? Did you know what you were doing? Or was it some sort of a faint?" He did not answer. She said, "Here, let me fill your glass again."

They drank. When she walked, it was with Joyce that he compared her. Joyce walked with the short, rapid, toe-tapping step of a Cockney girl. Rose, even indoors, walked erectly and with her head back, with a long stride from, the hip, firm yet light. Her movements were lithe and impatient. She wandered again to the other end of the room, as if she were not really interested in him. She pottered over some books, and when she spoke again it was to change the subject. She asked about the Wakerells, his job, the preparations for his marriage. His reticence had created a constraint between them. Her voice was over-bright, his was dull and careful.

He was not stirred by her nearness. It had been the same in his youth. Most of his outbursts of hope and anguish had been in her absence. As soon as she had appeared, his emotions had taken flight to hide like animals in their caves. He tried to force his numbed mind to provide him with something to say. "Suppose you're doin' all right, eh?"

"Me? I'm—" she paused, as if making a calculation, and with an ardent little intake of breath went on, "oh, I'm happy." After the drinks her manner had softened. Her eyes were brighter, and a faint flush had crept into the misty pallor of her cheeks. She sank on to her knees on a settee near him, and leaned over the armrest towards him, her hands clasped. "Aren't you?"

Some strange emotion wrenched at him, and in a moment of miraculous relief he realised that his inarticulacy had vanished. He blurted the word, "I —". All his troubles were crowding into his mouth, waiting to pour out. But she was not interested in hearing an answer to her question. She spoke again, and his confidence evaporated in a long, loud breath.

"I used to be a mad little idiot, didn't I?" She was alive now with the joy of talking about herself. Her eyes shone with remembrance; he could not see in them any hint that he was visible to her; he felt baulked and, for the first time in this encounter, angry. "I was always, I was always looking for something, and I never had the faintest idea what it was. My mother used to tell me that it was a man. She had all that — she also had all that —" Rose pressed her hand against her breast — "all that life hurting inside her, and she never knew of anything except a man that a woman could give it to."

Jack, still smarting at her withdrawal of offered comfort, and at the contempt for him which, as in the old days, he had felt in her self-absorption, was hardly listening. He was too busy trying to grasp his own thoughts and prepare them for speech before they again deserted him. Those fragments of her talk which penetrated him only mystified him.

"And now that I know what I was looking for," she said, "I feel sad sometimes because she's gone, and I can't tell her all about it."

Jack looked up at her, his face heavy with bitterness. "What? About this?"

"This?" She acknowledged his presence with a startled blink. When she looked at him steadfastly again the dreamy ardour in her eyes had been replaced by a mournful and understanding scrutiny. "Oh!" She uttered a laugh that was nothing more than a broken exhalation.

"Nice little love nest, eh?"

"I hadn't exactly thought of it that way." She spoke with a humiliating, low-toned tenderness as if showing patience to a child. "If I had, I might have furnished it a bit differently."

The flat, in fact, was not what he had expected. It consisted of one living room, with a bathroom and a kitchenette. There was a divan against one wall of the living room, warm but plain curtains on the windows, a couple of woolly rugs on the polished floor, a small settee, on which Rose sprawled, at an angle near the fireplace, and a comfortable but ill-matched assortment of chairs and small tables. A large and well-filled bookcase stood against the opposite wall. On the mantelpiece were a doll, a plain alarm clock with a lot of papers stuffed behind it, two little wooden peasant figures painted in bright colours, and a photograph of Mick Monaghan. Wherever he looked in the room there were littered magazines and unemptied ashtrays.

"You're a cheeky customer you are, and no mistake."

"Well." Her laughter subsided in a sigh. "So your mind's made up? You've heard all about me? The good neighbours of Lamb Street have told you the worst. Weren't you surprised?"

"No."

"Why?"

He said miserably, "I never could understand you, Rosie."

"Didn't you want to find out more?"

"No."

"Why not?"

His look, for a moment, was imploring. He mumbled. "None o' my bloody business."

"Didn't you want to come and see me? Didn't you ever think of —" her compressed little smile was not for him — "pleading with me to mend my ways?"

His voice was a cry of protest, but the words that he uttered were, "Do what you like for all I bloody care."

"And now that we're face to face, haven't you anything to say? Isn't there anything more you want to know? Here I am, Rosie Hogarth, the girl you grew up with. And you were so fond of me, you thought so much of me, you had so much confidence in me, that it's quite clear to you, without a shadow of doubt, that I'm a prostitute."

He cried, "Well, ain't you?"

She opened her mouth to reply, then smiled again. "You tell me first."

"Why?"

"Oh, I have a certain curiosity about the way your mind works. And a little pride, too."

"Pride?"

"Yes. I like the people I like to think well of me. About the others, to be frank, I don't give a damn."

"Well?"

"I want to find out whether you're one of the people I like."

Jack felt bewildered. He looked desperately about him and said tormentedly, "You can't half talk."

The telephone bell rang. Rose picked up the receiver. "Oh, hallo. Peter?... Of course I recognized the voice. I'm famous for it... Mmm?... Well, it's useful... For me, yes... All right, dear, the usual place. One o'clock, for lunch... No, come back here, otherwise someone is sure to see us... Mmm?... They always do. Take it from me. I've had plenty of experience. Where are you speaking from?... Oh, Peter, I told you not to 'phone from there... All right, I believe you, never again, there's no need to be so fervent. Oh, and Peter —" she looked across the room at Jack, her eyes alight with mischief — "I'm sure you can manage more than a fiver this week... Mmm?... Well, I always do put things brutally, don't I? I hope you won't feel too sulky if I tell you that others are managing more... Yes, I know these are hard times, darling. That's why I'm asking for more... Well, don't let it worry you. Just see what you can do... Bye-bye. Bless you."

She smiled at Jack, who was sitting with his head bowed. "That sounded bad, didn't it?"

He rose to his feet, and made inconclusive little movements, looking everywhere but at her, with a slack-lipped, despairing expression.

She said, "You're hovering. That's the want-to-get-away-look, isn't it?"

"I better be going." His voice was gruff.

"So you don't want an answer to your question."

"Answer?" A spasm of grief distorted his face, and his

voice cracked absurdly as he pointed to the telephone and said, "What about that?"

"I'm not going to explain that," she said evenly. "Your question called for a 'yes' or a 'no'. You can have one or the other, no more. You're the one who's on trial, Jack, not me."

"Me? I don't know what you're talking about. You're barmy." He hesitated, and exclaimed, "Words! You're like the rest of 'em. Talk, talk. Think they can stuff a chap up with anything."

They stood on opposite sides of the room, in silence. Rose said, "Oh, well."

"Oh, well."

"So that's that."

"Looks like it."

There was another silence. "You're sure you're feeling all right?"

"Oh, fine. Lucky I bumped into you."

"Yes. If you're not well, or something, you ought to see a doctor."

"Nah. Nothing wrong with me. "Well, I —" he gaped at the door.

"Another drink for the road?"

"No thanks."

She opened the door. "It's been nice, Jack."

He mumbled, "Ah," and edged past her, "S'long."

"Bye-bye."

She began to close the door, saying after him, "Come again sometime."

He called back, from the head of the staircase, "OK." To himself he said, with great bitterness, as he went downstairs, "Some hopes!"

As if she shared his disillusionment she shut the door, and the sound came to him loudly enough to seem final.

Chapter 2

"**W**ELL," Jack said as he walked away from Rose's flat, "that's that!" As was his habit, he actually spoke the words softly to himself. "Glad I've got that one out of my system." For a few days it seemed as if his words were true.

He went about in a strange mood of emptiness. Life had become tasteless, without pleasure and without that other poignant flavouring, unhappiness. All emotion had become as remote from him as the words and actions of the people around him, who all seemed to be separated from him by a window of invisible glass.

It was this lethargic indifference which prevented him from actively noticing a remarkable change which had taken place in Joyce's behaviour. After she had repulsed him on the night of their country excursion, he had expected that her attitude to him would become tinged with suspicion, disapproval and fear. On the contrary, she had all at once begun to manifest a clinging, quivering ardour that baffled him. She prolonged their kisses, pressed her body against his at every opportunity, cast long, glistening looks of entreaty at him, and when walking with him she clutched his arm desperately to her side with both hands instead of strolling comfortably arm-in-arm. She put extra blankets on his bed when he did not need them, and plagued him with her solicitousness at meals, offering him extra helpings and titbits from her plate with such eager persistence that he could not help muttering protests. Usually these had no effect on her. Like a mother, she would sweep them aside with loving, scornful laughter and continue undeterred. Once or twice, however, when she had stung him into making some savage comment, he was bewildered by the gleam of tears in her eyes, by her hot, pleading handclasps, or by the muffled incoherence of her speech.

Even if he had noticed the transformation in her, he would not have been able to interpret it. For one thing, she knew nothing of his meeting with Rose, so that this sudden emotional siege could not have been inspired by fear of a rival. For another, he now believed her to be unshakeably respectably, in other words, incurably frigid; a belief which ought, according to his standards, have delighted him but which instead increased his misgivings. If he had been asked for an explanation of her passionate attentions, he would have mumbled that she was trying to fob him off with 'baby stuff,' to keep him contented until their wedding day by feeding him with tit-bits of affection.

Nevertheless she persisted with her wooing, and succeeded — it was inevitable that his starved senses should be aroused by her kittenish provocations — in melting his numbed emotions into life; not to love, however, but to distaste. He regained his awareness of the surrounding world like a man aroused from sleep; he remained dazed and vulnerable. Her attentions, when he noticed them, only irritated him. A mysterious impatience, like a spring being wound up inside him, made him feel more tense every day. He found some relief in furious outbursts of energy at work, but longed ceaselessly for a form of easement from which he only restrained himself with the greatest of difficulty — a mighty explosion of unmotivated bad temper.

These new impulses threatened disaster to his plans, and he tried to suppress them. He once again begged Joyce to hasten their wedding, but she pointed out, with maddening coyness, that they could not be married in less than two months. There was the dressmaker, there were the decorators — he cut short her explanations and fled, feeling more than ever frustrated.

To make matters worse, she had become so used to his presence in the house that she no longer took care always to look her best in front of him. With a pitiful confidence she shuffled about in slippers and dressing-gown, her hair disarrayed and her skin blotchy, as if he were already her husband. It was this mistake of hers which finally nullified any effect her wooing might have had.

Only an hour after their discussion about the wedding, while Jack was sitting in the parlour reminding himself what a splendid girl she was, she came scurrying into the room, turned her face up to him with a trustful and pathetic smile, sniffed loudly and said, "Blow my nose, dear, my hands are all wet." A few days before he would have obeyed without thought, but now disgust overcame him at her clumsiness and ugliness. The image of another was alive in his mind, mockingly inviting comparison. A twinge of pity prompted him to put his handkerchief to her nose, and she thanked him with a coarse, innocent giggle.

The next day, at work, he fell into a daydream. It was about his meeting with Rose. He did not conduct himself in the dream as he had in the real encounter. Nor did he find the tongue to tell Rose that he had worshipped her for years. Instead he treated her with violence and contempt, as he imagined a man of the world would treat a whore. He insulted her, attacked her, loved her brutally, exacting murmurs of wonderment and an abandoned response, pulled out a bulging wallet that showed her what a successful man he had become, and flung a bundle of notes at her feet. When he left her she was sobbing with adoration, pleading with him to forgive her for never having discovered in the past the kind of man he really was, and begging him to come back soon.

The dream provided a little oasis of revenge and satisfaction in the desert of his days, but the memory of it made his real life all the more desolate, and he resorted to it again and again, inventing different versions.

Sometimes it was his strength that astounded her, sometimes his bitter eloquence. This recurring fantasy was not connected with any conscious desire to see her again; but, inevitably, the repeated invocation of his first encounter with her led to a second series of dreams which were based on the idea of another accidental meeting. This miraculous second chance took many forms. He would jump on to a passing bus and find her in the next seat; walk past her block of flats and meet her coming down the steps; call at Nancy's place and find her playing with the baby; dive into the river to save an unknown woman and discover that it was her. And in each dream he seized the fleeting chance, acted recklessly and successfully, and enjoyed his triumph.

Still unaware of any conscious intent, he became so dominated in his daily life by these dreams that expressed his real will, that he began to look out for Rose wherever he went. He was determined not to seek her out, but he had become the victim of an unacknowledged conviction that fate, which must have had some unfathomable purpose in bringing them together once, would transform his life at this eleventh hour by bringing them together again. He watched for her in the streets. Sometimes he thought he had glimpsed her and followed some hurrying woman, sick with eagerness, until he was undeceived. An evening at the cinema would be ruined by the fantastic notion that she was sitting behind him in the darkness. One evening, at home with the Wakerells, the obsession grew on him that she was spending that evening with Nancy. He made foolish excuses, hurried to Nancy's place, trembled as he rang the bell, uttered more unintelligible excuses to Nancy and pushed into the flat, overwhelmed with expectation. Of course, Rose was not there; but he was as crushed by her absence as if she had failed to keep a promised rendezvous.

All this was so ridiculous in the light of conscious consideration that he refused to admit to himself that it was happening; yet it went on governing his life. It was only natural that, after hoping for fate to bring them together, he went on to do what he could to lend fate a hand. Every working day — refusing ever to acknowledge that the action was intentional — he strolled in his lunch hour — past Rose's block of flats. Sometimes he found his way there in the evening and loitered among the deserted lawns in the square, watching the doorway. Once he saw her coming out, accompanied by a man whose tallness, well-dressed appearance and smooth deference of manner filled Jack with shame at his own loutishness.

After this he kept away from Russell Square for three days, during which he lived in a state of stunned misery, imagining the man making love to Rose, crushed by the thought of all the other sleek and prosperous men that she must know, and seeing himself as he thought that Rose must see him beside these men, dumb, pitiful and poor.

On the evening of the fourth day he was again drawn by the obscure compulsion that dominated him, to resume his patrol opposite her street door. This time he found himself, as helpless as in a dream, walking up the steps, climbing the staircase and ringing her doorbell. There was no reply. He rang again, still wondering how his legs had come to carry him to this spot. There was silence from behind the closed door. He was weak with terror: he longed for the door to open, and at the same time he prayed that it would not. He resisted the temptation to rush off and rang a third time. He waited for five minutes, then walked away, dazed by the conflict of disappointment and relief. His legs were shaking.

On his way home he managed to regain his wits, and realised to what a condition he had been reduced. He derided himself, and swore that he would put an end to this nonsense. In the days that followed he struggled to master himself, and succeeded in keeping away from Russell Square. He could not rid himself of the conflicting feelings which had been driving him, but he was able to bring them into a state of perilous equilibrium which left him, free but apprehensive, in a fit state to carry on his normal life with the Wakerells.

One evening he and Joyce took their cheque books and bank paying-in book and went into the parlour to ascertain the state of their finances.

"Three hundred and eighty-four quid I paid in," muttered Jack, "and ninety-one quid of yours. That makes —" he scribbled a reckoning on a scrap of paper — "four hundred and seventy-five quid. Now, give me that cheque book." He thumbed through the stubs. "Blimey, we've got through a bit. Quite a few o' these you've signed, eh?"

"I've always let you know. I've bought curtains, crockery, cutlery, sheets — oh, there's three cupboards full of the stuff, and a lot in the back room. It's as well to buy now. They say all the prices are going up. It's as good as money in the bank, anyway. It's all for our home."

"That's all right, duck. Now let's see." He copied a list of figures from the cheque stubs, muttering and pulling studious faces. "Whoof!" he grimaced. "Hundred and sixty-one quid. Goes quick enough on the q.t., don' it?"

"A hundred and sixty-one?" she echoed incredulously. "Whatever have we spent all that on?"

"Twenty quid I drew to live on before I started work. Seventeen for a new best suit. Ten more for shirts and shoes and whatnot. Here we are, June the eighteenth, another five quid for the same, five quid on June the twenty-fourth for my sports jacket and slacks. That's forty quid, and twenty makes sixty, just for a bloody outfit. Then, subs for myself, three fives and a ten —"

"Subs?" she queried in a nervous voice.

"Taking you out, and all that, and your birthday present. No use being stingy when you're courting, is it?"

She frowned. "You never told me."

"Told you! Here, whose bloody money is it?"

She blinked at him in alarm, and opened her mouth to answer. He felt ashamed, and before she could speak, he said gruffly, "All right, all right, I never meant nothing. I won't do it in future without telling you."

"Telling me?"

"Well, I mean, asking you."

"And another thing, I think it's time we started to economise. You know what they say, look after the pennies."

"Oh, Gawd, naggin' a-bloody-gain."

"Well it's my home we're talking about," she said, with a sudden gleam of firmness in her eyes, "and I'll be the one that has to manage on the wages, so we might as well start now. It'll be no use my tramping round the shops trying to save a few pence on a pair of socks if we're going to throw pounds away before we start."

"You leave the worrying to me," he muttered. "I'm the one who's wearing the bloody pants round here." He could not face her determined look, and busied himself with calculations again. "Anyway, that makes eighty-five. And all the rest —" more muttering — "seventy-six quid you and your mum spent on pots and sheets and all that other carry-on. You got to be a bloody millionaire to get married these days, I reckon."

"Never mind, there's plenty left."

"There won't be for bloody long, I can tell you. Wait till we start furnishing. There's the bedroom suite. That's forty-six pounds —"

"Nineteen-and-fourpence."

"And the dining-room suite. Thirty-four pounds."

"Sixteen and twopence."

"Oh, you and your sixteen and twopences. I'm going to have a fine old time with you, I can see. Sweep up the crumbs every night for bloody bread pudding, an' stand on your bloody head all day to save shoe leather. Two armchairs, table and four chairs for the kitchen. Fourteen quid. Twenty quid for a radio. Here, I've said it before and I'll say it again. We can't pay all this lot out at once. Do far better to get it on the never-never, few quid a week, I mean, you don't miss it."

"No."

"That's what everybody does, ain't it?"

"No."

"They do, you know."

"Well, we're not. For one thing, we save sixteen pounds all round, paying outright. For another thing, I don't want to be in anybody's debt so long as we've got the money. When we walk into that home, it's going to be our own, every tiny little bit of it. There isn't another girl in Lamb Street that's ever been able to say that on her wedding day. There's enough girls in this street got married in front of me, had their little laugh at me on the quiet. Now it's going to be my turn to laugh." She was very firm and serene, and somehow he could not argue.

"Well, anyway," he said, "the money'll be there when we want it."

"I should hope so. Now, take off the cost of the wedding, and my dress, and the honeymoon, and we'll see what we've got left in the kitty."

"I reckon on twenty quid for the do, what with the church, and beer, and a car for the day, and whatnot. Can't grumble at that. This honeymoon lark, though, it's gonna knock us back twenty-five quid easy, for the week. Bloody queer idea, I call it, in December."

"It's not the time, it's the principle of the thing." She had put on her glasses. Their blind glimmer, and the stubborn set of her mouth, made her appear for a moment almost malignantly defiant.

"You and your principles! A minute ago it was 'look after the pennies'. Now where's all your economy, and common sense, and being practical, poncin' up an' down the front at Eastbourne for a week in the freezing cold?"

She moved her head, and her glasses flashed angrily. "Jack Agass, we've been over this a dozen times. I hope you're not going back on your word."

"I ain't going back on nothing, ducks. You want it, you'll get it. That's me. Nothing too good for my Joycie. You got me a bit mogadored, that's all, first blowing one way, then the other."

She took off her glasses, moved her head voluptuously and smiled secretively at the floor. "It's got nothing to do with economy, or showing up the other girls, or anything like that."

"What then?"

"Oh, you wouldn't understand."

"Yes I would. Honest. No sense in being shy. Not with me. Is there, girl?"

She shrugged her shoulders. "I don't know. It's what I've always dreamed of. Things like that, you can't think about money."

"What? You mean, falling in love ?"

She uttered a little laugh of denial that contradicted her, "I suppose so." After a pause she said, "It's what I said. You can't explain to a man."

He let her brood. She said, "Well, there's just that one day. It's like a dream. You're wearing that wonderful white dress —"

"Another twenty quid," he murmured.

She did not seem to hear him. "— clouds and clouds of tulle, and lovely flowers, and all those thousands of sequins all white and yet they flash every colour when you stand in the light, and you walk down the aisle, and everyone's looking at you, and it's not like the way they usually look at you, no-one's laughing at you, no-one's saying bitchy things about you, no-one's hating you. You can hear them all murmuring and crying, and you feel like crying yourself." The words were gushing up out of her, and she seemed to be listening to them in wonderment. She was unable to stop herself even long enough to catch her breath. "It's all a dream. It's a funny kind of dream, because you've dreamed about it for thousands and thousands of nights, for years and years, ever since you were a tiny little girl. And now it's really happening. For once it's not a dream. And yet it is a dream, more than ever. It used to seem more real when you lay in bed imagining it. And then you go off on a honeymoon. A honeymoon! In December, when everyone

225

else is at work. Like on the pictures. You're a real lady, new clothes, no work, nothing to worry about, everyone's nice to you, they treat you like a princess, and all the time you can remember the way people looked after you when you drove off in a car to the station, all shouting and calling out nice things, and all the girls still talking about your wedding dress, saying to each other what a dream you looked." She gulped, became aware of Jack, and went on in a dogged voice as if she were determined to go through with it. "And then you come back to your home, and it's all your own. You can do what you like there. You're It. You're someone. Fancy being someone! I mean, you're not just someone who works for somebody, or somebody's lodger, you're not just Mrs. Wakerell's youngest, you're someone. And everybody talks to you differently after that." She pondered, working out the train of thought to its conclusion. "Well, I mean, all your life after that you've got something to look back on."

At any other time Jack might have been impressed. Such an unexpected torrent of words falling from Joyce's lips might have given him his first bewildered glimpse of the woman who dwelt, stifled, within the heavy and unresponsive body he was accustomed to fondle. He was, however, shut up within his own preoccupations. He said, "Like to hear yourself talk, don't you?"

Joyce had got over the embarrassment of hearing herself speak from the heart, and she sat back, her face soft and elated with achievement, listening with slightly parted lips and warm, remote eyes to the inward echo of her own voice. Then she laughed. It was a soft and broken laughter, whose import other women had taught him to recognize, a simultaneous exhalation of concupiscence and faint mockery. He believed firmly in the existence of two kinds of women, and it was a fixed idea to him that Joyce was not 'that kind'. She was his chosen household vassal and brood mare, the one person in the world upon whose meekness, dependence and acknowledged inferiority he could always nourish his self-respect.

226

Therefore he ignored the stirring of his instincts and refused to recognize the overtones of her laughter. "That's right, duck," he said, "have a good laugh. That's one thing that don't cost nothing. Not yet, anyway."

"Oh, you," she said in tender derision, "You men don't know what time it is. Don't you feel just a little bit excited?"

"Eh? What for?"

She took his hand and placed it over her left breast. "Here." She pressed the flat of her hand down on his. "Feel my heart. Can't you feel it going thump, thump, thump? Don't you ever feel like that when you think?" He was not thinking of her heartbeats, but of the fleshy firmness of her breast. His legs began to tremble and he drew his hand away hastily.

"Proper teaser you are. Get more than you bargain for, muck about with me like that."

"Will I?" She smiled at him again.

"Yes. I know you." He put his hands in his trousers pockets and pressed the fingertips into his thighs to check the quivering of his muscles. "First of all it's chase me Charlie, then all of a sudden it's keep off the grass."

"Is it?" She was still smiling.

"Yes." He saw only mockery in her attitude. To make another grab at her, to find himself mistaken and again to be repulsed, was a blow to his self-respect which he dared not risk. He strove to master his resentment and, hoping to mollify her, he added, " 'S all right. That's what I like about you."

Her smile died, though the smiling set of her lips remained "Is it?"

He said, trying to inject a tone of sincerity into the lie, "You bet. Had enough of the other kind, I have. There's some dirty bitches around, I can tell you. Seen a bit of the world, I have. You wouldn't know, thank God. I know a good girl when I see one. So don't think I don't appreciate it, because I do. See?"

"That's plain enough." She sat down limply. After a few

227

moments she brightened up and flashed a determined little smile at him.

"Jack," she said, "am I pretty?"

"Eh? Course you are. Why?"

"You've never told me."

"Yes I have. Lots of times."

"No you haven't. We've sat in here in the dark, and, you know, all that sort of thing. But you've never once, not in all those six months, said — oh, you know, all those lovely things they do say."

"Eh? Don't be daft. I ain't Charles bleeding Boyer, am I?" He was beginning to feel irritated. A quiet room, a woman — what did she think he was made of, rousing him like this?

"Have I got a good figure?" She pulled her dress back to show the outlines of her body and pivoted seductively to and fro.

He frowned, clenching his teeth. "Pack it up, Joyce. I'm telling you."

She continued to show herself off, smiling at him. "Isn't it quiet in the house, with Mum and Dad out?"

He could not stand her presence any longer. "I'm goin' out," he muttered, "buy some fags." He had to get away, to cool off. She couldn't know, surely, what effect her behaviour was having, on him? — not a respectable girl like Joyce? Oh, these respectable girls! No wonder a man had to turn to — well, to women like — well, like Rose! Trying to retain the semblance of composure, he said, at the door, "Well, there's one thing. After all that reckoning, we'll still have a hundred and thirty quid in the bank. When we're wed, I mean, and everything's paid."

She said, all the vibrancy strangely gone from her voice, "That's wonderful," and sat down. Her hands were in her lap, and her smile, emptied suddenly of its warmth, betrayed only despairing appeal.

He closed the door on her and hurried into the street. He walked through the chilly dusk, trembling with anger and frustration. Why didn't she leave him alone? It was only eight weeks to the wedding, and if she wanted him to hold out that long — and what else could she want after she had already repulsed him? — she ought to leave him alone. But eight weeks, eight weeks! He thought of Rose, the divan behind her, in the shadowed lamplit warmth of her room. The chill of the evening penetrated his clothes and he shivered, thinking of the warmth of her room. He walked faster and faster, bumped into people, felt the jarring shock of them but did not see them. He thought of Rose as warmth, as release, and rest. He was no longer the conqueror of his earlier dreams; he wanted to run to her like a child and yield himself up to her.

He went into a telephone booth, fumbled for pennies and dropped them into the slot. His fingers felt powerless, and the effort of using them was agonising. He dialled Rose's number. He heard the purr of the bell. He could hardly breathe. He was convinced that there would be no reply. For a terrible second he hoped, crazy with fear, that she would not reply. There was a click and he heard her voice, very soft.

The shock was like a blow. His teeth were chattering. He croaked a senseless jumble of words. "Who is that?" she asked. Her voice was strange on the telephone; higher and thinner than he remembered it. "It's Jack," he said jerkily, "Jack, it's Jack." Her voice came again, still interrogative. He said, unnaturally loud, "Jack Agass, Jackie Agass." A pause. He took a deep breath and steadied the receiver against his ear. He shouted, "How are you?" He felt stupid, and did not know what to say next. "Hallo, Jack," she said, "I'm fine. How are you?" Her voice was puzzled. "I'm fine," he shouted. She said, "Don't speak so loudly, Jack. Your voice is deafening." He sniggered. "Look," he said, "when can I see you?" "Oh." Another pause. He was sick with suspense; then her voice came over the line, "Is that you breathing I can hear on the line? Is there anything wrong? You haven't had another one of those turns?" "No, I'm all right. Look, I want to come round and see you." "Of course." The puzzled tone was still in her voice. She spoke again, "Is it about anything special? Can't we talk now? Or it is just going to be a social visit?" Maddened by the way the talk was drawing out, he cried, "Don't you want me to come? It's all right with me if you don't." "Don't be silly, Jack, come whenever you like." "Now?" "I'm sorry. I'm going out in a few minutes. I shan't be back till late." "Tomorrow, dinner-time?" "I'm fixed up tomorrow evening." "Dinner-time, Rosie, midday. I'll come from work." "Thursday evening would be better. I shall be in from seven onwards." He wondered how he could bear to wait two days. "All right," he said, "Thursday. I'll come." "Are you sure there's nothing wrong?" "I'm all right, I told you." "You don't sound like it. Thursday, then. It'll be nice, won't it? Bye-bye." He said, "S'long," hung up the receiver and left the booth. Everything in the street seemed unreal. How could he wait, through two endless days, till Thursday?

Chapter 3

O NE EVENING A FORTNIGHT LATER Rose was standing
in a shop doorway in Oxford Circus, waiting for
Jack. She loved the West End streets at this time
of the evening, the shop windows like great cubes of
yellow light, each containing its own pattern of beautiful
shapes and colours, and each shedding a pallid glare
upon the dark, thronged pavements. She looked with
admiration at a fur coat in a window on her left, and
imagined it, black, glossy and graceful, on her own back.
She had a taste for luxuries; most of her friends chaffed
her about it and told her it ill became the rebellious
opinions she expressed; she remained serenely
indifferent to them and went on longing for lovely things.

By arriving early she had broken a long-standing rule
of hers; always to let the man get there first. She was not
an advocate of chronic lateness as a means of impressing
men; the tactics of coyness and ostentatious femininity
disgusted her and conflicted with the energy and
efficiency she displayed in all her doings and demanded
of her associates. But her life involved her in many
dealings, whose purpose she took seriously, with men. It
was important to her that she should always keep the
upper hand in these affairs; and to do so, to seize and
maintain the initiative, she was not above the use of art.
To let the man get there first, even if only by a few
minutes, and then to sweep down on him out of the
crowd, often ensured, if she continued skilfully enough,
that he remained morally under her thumb for the rest of
the evening.

As the crowds streamed past her she thought of the events of the last fortnight and wondered why she had not only neglected her rule this evening but why she had troubled to meet Jack at all. She was tired. Her round of engagements had been particularly merciless for the last few weeks. She was a young woman of immense energy. Her energy had, if anything, increased since her girlhood, although it was no longer the torrential, unpredictable ardour that had endowed her in early youth with a wild charm, but was controlled and deliberate, so that her friends regarded her as hard and tireless. Nevertheless she was tired. Her character forbade her ever to admit it, but sometimes she spent an evening lying exhausted across her bed, and this was what her body had craved to do before she had come out tonight.

Was it boredom that had brought her? She could rarely endure a blank evening. She dreaded being alone. When she was alone for a few hours she suffered from an ennui in which there arose speculations and misgivings that called the whole of her present life into question. That was why she would put up with almost any company rather than remain alone.

Was it nostalgia? She was ashamed of sentiment, even in her secret thoughts — she refused, for instance, to keep souvenirs although it hurt her to destroy them — but she could not help looking back with tenderness, from time to time, at her girlhood; and Jack, like an apparition from the past, brought with him sweet and painful memories of her own adolescence.

Was it loneliness? She had a multitude of acquaintances, but there was no-one to whom she could open her heart, except Mick and Nancy.

But even if she were to admit to loneliness, which she dared not do, a man of Jack's type had nothing to offer her. She was fastidious concerning the character and behaviour of her intimates. One man had amused her by telling her that she was a snob; another had pleased her by calling her aristocratic. It was not people's social standing that interested her. She looked for certitude, for assurance, in their behaviour. "I like people," she had once said, "who walk about as if they belong in the world and as if it belongs to them; not people who act as if they belong to nothing and nothing belongs to them." When she uttered the condemnatory part of this pronouncement, it was Lamb Street that she had in mind. She could not bear the childlike incapacity which seemed to her to stamp the people she had left behind in Lamb Street. It had been a hard fight to root it out of herself; and she was always afraid that she might still betray signs of it; hence she hated it all the more. This alone would have kept her away from the street, once she had escaped (for this was how she thought of her departure), although more practical reasons existed.

It was not only boredom, however, or nostalgia, or the fact that her anger with Jack had faded into an amused pity, that had brought her here. It was clear that he was in some kind of distress, and she wanted to help him if she could. In the old days she had always played the part of the senior, although she was the younger of the two; in recent years she had become the confidante and counsellor of a considerable number of men; she liked to think that it was charity that inspired her new relationship with Jack, but in reality her vanity, which was always demanding fresh nourishment from men, played just as large a part.

Since his telephone call, when her curiosity had overcome her annoyance and led her to see him again, they had met twice. He had given plenty of evidence of his unrest, but he had not revealed its cause. She had asked him why he was spending so much time away from Joyce. "Oh, she's all right," he had answered in the strained, defiant voice in which he always spoke to her, "All her time shopping and whatnot these days, round the dressmaker with her mum and all that lark. No time for me. I thought you'd like to be a pal and keep us company, you know, like, just for a bit."

Their two evenings together had not been pleasant for her. They were unlike anything she had previously experienced with men, and left her feeling strained and provoked. They were so crazy and inconsequential as to seem dreamlike, yet the more puzzled she became the more she wanted to follow them through to their outcome, just as, however agitating and disagreeable a dream, interrupted at night, might have been, she always tried to go back to sleep and see how it would turn out.

On the first evening he had sat morosely at her flat, saying little, drinking a lot of her brandy and casting occasional furtive looks at her, until in embarrassment she had suggested going out. "Of course," he had mumbled, "all for a good time, ain't you? Come on, then, I won't let you down." They had gone to a dinner dance, and he had spent a lot of money, repeatedly showing her his wallet in a way that perplexed her, and saying, to her annoyance, "'S all right, girl. Plenty more where that comes from." The second time, he had taken her to a third-rate night club where, in spite of his efforts to appear at home, he had shown himself clearly to be ill at ease and in unfamiliar surroundings, spending even more money than before on the most offensive imitation of champagne that she had ever tasted. She had protested at his prodigality, and he had shouted back at her with horrible gaiety, "Don't you worry! Jackie Agass may live in Islington, but he's got as much bloody rhino as any other bastard. And don't you forget!"

She could not help knowing that he wanted her. His fierce, quick glances, his sullen silences, his brutal grip on her arm as he steered her through doorways, and the way in which he lagged at her heels as they walked in the streets, gave her a feeling of being dogged. This was the one thing which, like most women, she could not bear. She might submit, however little she thought of a man, to outright importunities, out of appetite, pity, good humour or even sheer weariness of spirit; but when a man did nothing but haunt her it awoke a contempt in her which she could never overcome. Moreover, she had no idea that Jack was in love with her, and thought that it was from contempt for her that his desire sprang. He apparently imagined that (to use the language of Lamb Street) she was 'easy'. He was 'after a bit' to pass the time while his Joyce was occupied elsewhere. In the two evenings Rose and Jack had spent together, there had not been a single moment of real intimacy. Rose had not found a chance to speak about herself, and in any case, the more she saw of Jack the less inclined she felt to do so. She would not be sorry to get him off her hands; after their first evening she had given him the slip at her doorway; after their second she had taken a taxi home and left him in the street; she supposed she would do the same tonight. However, she could not help pitying him, and she had sent him — partly to soothe any hurt she had inflicted on his feelings, partly to bring matters to a head — an affectionate and sympathetic note suggesting this appointment. She had excused her hurried departure on the last occasion ('I was in such a hurry to grab the taxi before it got away'), she had thanked him for a lovely evening, and she had suggested that it was time for 'a real heart-to-heart'. The phrase, like the ponderous jocularity of the rest of the note, was selected to please him, but she shuddered as she wrote it. Before she finally dismissed him she wanted to satisfy her generosity, her curiosity and her vanity by getting to the bottom of his troubles.

"Who's gonna buy you that one?" Jack was at her elbow, looking with her at the fur coat in the shop window.

"Hallo." She smiled without turning. "It's a dear, isn't it. I might get it for a Christmas present yet, if I drop a hint in the right place."

"I bet!" Jack's voice thickened. "I tell you this, whoever he is, he ain't the only one got the money to burn if he's treated right."

She looked at him askance. "Oh, well, it'll do to dream about in the meantime." She turned away from the window. "Let's go somewhere quiet tonight, Jack. We've never really had a chance to hear the sound of our own voices, have we?"

Fright twitched across his face, and in a voice drained of strength he said, "If you like, Rosie."

She took him to an Italian restaurant in Frith Street, led him to a table and ordered food and wine. He sat dumbly, looking down at his fists clenched side by side on the table, He did not take his raincoat off until she told him to. "How's the job?" she asked. "Still going strong?"

"Nah," he said without looking up, "Goin' on short time. Next month. Reckons he'll keep us all on, though, the old fella. The boss I mean."

"Is that what's worrying you?"

"Nah." He started on his ravioli, still refusing to look at her.

She tried more questions, but each time he answered her briefly and remained hunched over his plate. She contented herself for a while with letting him eat, urging him to drink and refilling his glass as soon as he emptied it.

"I like this food," she said, "don't you?"

"Ah." He looked up at last. "Had it before. In Italy. They don' 'alf eat there. Bloody sight to watch, I can tell you. Thin little girl, bloody great plate of spaghetti, pasta they call it, twice her size it looks. See her whop it inside her. Wallop, all gorn, *and* she wipes the plate. And that's only a start. Bloody appetizer. There you are, hanging over the back of your chair ready to bust, and there she is waiting to start the real meal. Gaw, talk about women!"

"You sound as if you could."

"What?"

"Talk about women."

"Me?" He made a reminiscent little sucking noise with his tongue. "Here, this wine's all right, ain't it? Used to drink pints of it. The ol' vino. Shaved in it once. We was hard up for water, dug in 'undred yards from a wine cellar we was. Bloody great barrels. Hundreds of 'em. Can y' imagine?" He was flushed now with wine and warmth. "Ah, some right tarts there was over there. Never even had to ask 'em. Opens her front door one of 'em does, points to her skirt and says, "Buono!" Walks right in, me and my mate. She didn't 'alf give us what for. Glad to get out, the pair of us, and I ain't ashamed to say it. Well, I mean, not to you. Catch me talking like this to Joycie. Ooh, some hopes! Throw two bloody fits and end up on the clothes line, she would. Different with you, though, ain't it? I know a sport when I see one."

His expression had relaxed, and he rattled on, with the pathetic uplifted smile of a small boy bragging. She assumed her favourite pose, aloof but receptive. She had learned that the best way to assert her mastery over men was to remain silent and let them talk. They submitted to her because, once they had lost control of their tongues and spewed up all their confidences without receiving any in return, they felt themselves morally in bond to her. It was this self-control — with which she had overcome her girlhood habit of pouring out all her self in talk — that gave her some of her physical attraction. When she was still or silent she seemed to blaze all the more with contained energy. She made a man feel that he was the only one who could discern it behind the amused, sympathetic scrutiny with which she provoked him to keep on talking; while he spoke his curiosity grew, and forced him to talk still more, in the hope of discovering her mysterious inner self and of provoking the volcanic outburst of which, however subdued, she always seemed on the verge.

She scarcely paid attention to what Jack was saying. It was sufficient that he was talking, more and more recklessly. In a little while, when his mind had altogether lost its power to check his eager, betraying tongue, she would strike with a sudden question. In the meantime she kept her liquid and sympathetic eyes on him. If he imagined that her steadfast dilated gaze was for him, or that he was the cause of the little light of brightness and

237

pleasure that danced in her eyes (and he probably did, for the note of excited hope grew louder and louder in his voice) he was wrong, for what in reality attracted her fascinated stare and absorbed all her thoughts was her own image in the mirror behind him.

She was delighted with herself. What she saw in the mirror filled her with love, and her eyes were like a lover's. She sat upright, but tranquil and relaxed, her head tilted slightly back, her lips parted. She admired the harmonies of her face, soft and full, yet appearing small within the compact casque of black hair; the hint of audacity conveyed by her bright eyes, her small mouth and the saucy curve of her chin; the soft and sensuous texture of her skin, whose matt pallor was mottled from beneath by the faintest violet bloom, and which set off all the more vividly the jet gleam of her hair and the bright red flower of her lips.

She was settled in her favourite pose. Life for her was a series of poses; not the exaggerated and laughable postures clumsily copied from the princesses of the cinema screen, to which, in one stage of her childhood, her confused ambitions had driven her; but a series of attitudes, the very attitudes which caused her acquaintances to refer to her as 'natural', 'unaffected', and 'spontaneous', but all of which were premeditated. She had learned how to simulate, in silence, profundities of thought and feeling that were in reality beyond her; she had in stock 'spontaneities' of speech, movement and gesture to meet every situation; her trump card was always the contemplative, which could be infinitely varied but was always effective. The essence of her struggle to establish herself in a wider and more satisfying world than that of Lamb Street had been the effort to harness her ardour (which might, as with many other working girls, have driven her hither and thither, witless and credulous, perhaps to disaster) and to turn it from her master into her servant. She was, too, still subconsciously not 'at home' in the wider world, and however successful she was in winning admiration she still remained secretly self-conscious, unable to relax her watch over herself. She had, in fact, in the struggle to take advantage of her character, changed it. True spontaneity had vanished with her first youth. Now, as long as she was awake she was an actress; so successful an actress that no-one had ever suspected her of artifice and she was often pointed to as one of those delightful people, natural and unspoilt, who are at home wherever they go and carry their passionate love of life with them like a torch. Tonight, with poor simple Jack, an uncritical ambassador from Lamb Street, as her only audience, her vigilance could relax, her confidence could expand. She sparkled.

It was time to attack. "Jack," she said, laying her hand on the back of his. He stopped in mid-sentence, the breath caught in his throat. "Jack, never mind all that. Tell me what's really been troubling you these last few weeks."

His face, like a child's, betrayed each transient vibration of feeling — determination, irresolution, appeal — as he struggled to speak. He said huskily, "Marry me."

It was Rose's turn to be taken aback. Too unprepared to rise above the commonplace, she said, "But what about Joyce?"

"Oh, sod her! She won't let me have my rights, she'll have to take the consequences. Talk about frozen cod! Hands orf, that's all she knows."

"And that's why you want to marry me?"

He cried out, with a violence that surprised her, "Oh, no!"

"Well, that's what it sounds like." She tried to keep her voice sympathetic, to remain the wise, assured confessor, but a sarcasm which she could not restrain brought her down to his level. "After all, the idea's come to you very suddenly, and very late in the day. You didn't exactly rush to throw yourself at my feet when you came home."

"Well I — How could I? All them years — I've dreamed and bloody dreamed — Not in your street, me, that's what

239

I've always thought." He wailed, in a ridiculous voice, "Why do you always put the wind up me?"

She seized the chance to assume the maternal role again. "I'm sure I don't dear. You've just been carried away a bit, that's all. I saw you that day in the street — remember? — before you saw me, and I'm sure it wasn't because of me you were acting strangely then. I think it's all been a bit too much for you, dear, all that you've been through and perhaps what you've come back to. All the strangeness of settling down again, and the strain and suspense of waiting to marry, and then seeing me again, and having a few drinks, and getting a bit excited, and letting your imagination play tricks with you. There's nothing wrong with you that a nice sweet girl like Joyce can't cure, if only you're patient for a little while longer. That's all it is, Jack, pet. It's only natural." She smiled and squeezed the back of his hand. "It's very sweet of you. But you and I are not for each other. You've got your life to lead, and I have mine."

"Ah," he protested harshly, "all that guff. I don't want that. Soft soap. Poor old Jack. Give him a pat and send him home to bed, eh?" His voice rose. "I know you. I know just what you are, and I know just how much you're worth. I'd have a dog's life with you. I'd be all right with Joycie, I know that, never mind what I said before. She's all right, she is. I know, you don't have to tell me. Think I bloody care? Bloody laugh it is, sitting here, thought of her makes me sick, but you —!" His face was contorted with the effort of speaking. "I never come here to ask you what I did. Me marry you? I'd ha' died laughing if anyone'd told me that an hour ago. Get you on your bloody back, that's all I wanted. All these bloody months without it! More than a bloke can stand, my age. She's the girl to see you right, I said to myself, Rosie's the girl. Just in her line, it is. And then I sit here, and I look at you, and I remember, all these bloody years — An' out it comes, 'Marry me,' couldn't stop it if I tried. And Rosie, I mean it, that's the bloody joke. I'd do anything for you,

240

Rosie. I'd eat dirt. I'd do bloody murder for you. I don't care what you are. Oh, I'd marry you all right."

"Thank you," she said with bitterness. She made another effort to remain gentle. "My life's not what you think it is, Jack."

"What then?"

She hesitated. "I'm afraid that's more than I can tell you. Just now, at any rate. All I can say is that if my mother was alive she wouldn't be ashamed of me. Won't you take my word for it?"

"I told you, I don't care. If you was peddling your pratt up the bloody Angel I'd still want you. I love you. Ain't that enough?"

"If you loved me, you'd believe me."

"I believe you. Tell me you're the Queen of Sheba. Go on, tell me! I'll believe you. I swear I will. I'll believe anything. I'll do anything you want me to. Rosie, I've got money. That's what's worrying you, ain't it, the money? I've got money in the bank, and a bloody cheque book, too. It's all yours, you can have the bloody lot, every penny of it. Here, look! —" He pulled out his cheque book. "Write your own cheque. It's yours for the asking!"

"Jack!" She laughed, but anger rang through the note of incredulity.

"Go-on! I ain't sprucing! Here!—" He scribbled, and tore out a cheque. "There y'are, I've signed it for you. Filled in the name, Rose Hogarth — all you got to do is put in the amount."

She sighed, and pushed the cheque back towards him. "I could be very angry with you, Jack, but there's no point in it, is there?"

He folded the cheque and slipped it into her handbag. She let it stay there: better to tear it up later than continue this ridiculous haggling. "There y'are," he said, "No bluff, I mean it. It's there when you want it. Rosie love, stick to me and you won't go short, I swear you won't!"

She called the waiter and ordered brandies. "There,"

she said when the drinks came, "you drink that up and pull yourself together. It's strange how we can't talk to each other any more — not to reach each other, that is. That's the pity of growing up. While you were talking I was thinking how useless it was. You can't trust me, you simply couldn't. And though I suppose I could make you see me differently if I took you into my confidence, I feel from what I've seen of you that I can't trust you either. It's not our thoughts that don't trust each other, but our natures."

"I don't know what you're talking about."

"No, I suppose not. Anyway, you take my advice. Whatever your troubles are, you stick to Joyce and you'll get over them. I don't know what misunderstanding there's been between you, but surely if you could speak to me you can speak to her. It's worth trying, isn't it?"

He gave no sign of having heard her. The flush in his face had deepened, there was a gleam of sweat on his brow, and his lips quivered faintly as he looked vacantly past her.

"Isn't it, Jack?" she persisted.

His eyes flickered at her, then moved away again. "What's the use," he said, almost inaudibly. "Next few days, I'll think up all the things I ought to told you. Now, here you are in front of me, can't do it." He tapped his forehead with his knuckles. "Nothing there. Laugh, ain't it?" His tongue appeared between his lips for a second. "It's all right for them that's got the words. Say anything, they can." His voice trailed off, and he gave himself up entirely to his stare at the other end of the room.

"Another brandy?" He shook his head. She paid the bill, expecting him to protest, but he remained huddled on his chair, apparently bereft of all initiative. He rose when she rose, and followed her out to the street. She stopped a taxi, opened the door, and turned, ready to dismiss him with a parting admonition, a bright and friendly farewell. He pushed past her into the cab, sat in the far corner and glowered at her from the shadow. "See you home."

He remained silent throughout the journey, huddled as far away from her as he could get, brooding to himself but watching her intently all the time. Their destination reached, he let her pay off the cabbie, gripped her arm before she could say anything, and accompanied her up the stairs.

She decided to speak to him at the door of her flat, but there he forestalled her again, pushing her against the wall, and holding her so tightly by both arms that the hard quivering of his hands passed into her. Mute, his eyes glaring, he tried to force his mouth against hers. Even while she held her body rigidly back from him and averted her face, indecision seized her. She gave her mouth to him, lifelessly. She wanted to be rid of him. He had no interest for her, and she was sick of being hounded, then mauled. But, to her hatred of the squalid little struggle which threatened, there was added a feeling of concern for him. He was ill, and frantic. She could not bear to let him loose upon the streets in this state. She imagined him being knocked down at the first crossing. It was only a trifling mercy for which he was begging. Afterwards she could pack him off, slaked and happy, to his Joyce. Stifled, she managed to say, "Let's go inside."

His expression, as he followed her into the flat, was bitter and inflamed. He wandered about the room, his movements fierce and restless, saying nothing. But when he was at her bedside he appeared hesitant. She had to take his hand and speak to him kindly. Making love, he was violent, artless and self-absorbed, his burning face averted, his occasional inarticulate endearments muttered as if to himself. Rose let her body make its own responses to him, but its ardours were local, dying in the unimpassioned flesh long before they could reach her thoughts or emotions. She too, remained silent, except for a few vague comforting sounds. Impatience crawled in her. Her mind, detached, was occupied with self-criticism and with plans for his final dismissal.

Later he lay, raised on one elbow, at her side. He looked crestfallen and uncertain. He wiped his hand over his face, from forehead to mouth, and said, with a propitiatory smile, "D'you love us?"

Her answering smile was cool but deliberately uncomprehending. "Just to be nice, I'll say 'yes'."

"Just to be nice?"

"Well — we're friends, aren't we? We've had a pleasant evening, and we've both been kind to each other. We're both old enough to know that these things don't go any farther than that. We shall go our own ways, like grown-ups, and leave it at that. Mm?"

"Don't you want to see us again?"

"Why not, dear? — one day. You, and Joyce too, after you're married. I don't think we ought to see each other before then, though. And we certainly can't carry on like this."

"Why not?"

"Because it's not right."

"Not right! Listen who's talking!" He sat up. "I'll chuck Joyce. I said so."

She shook her head. She was used to men, but his nearness now, great-shouldered, clumsy, red and sheepish of face, embarrassed her. "Dress yourself. You can't stay here all night, or the Wakerells will be wondering where you've got to."

"Oh, to hell with the Wakerells." He rose, however, and began to dress. The sight increased her embarrassment. "I don't want Joyce," he exclaimed, "I want you. I always have."

"No you haven't. I've known you a long time, Jack, dear, and I know when a man loves me, and I've never seen a spark of it in you."

"What? Look, years and bloody years — I ain't clever, I —"

"We're both together in a bedroom, and you're still all full of me, and you think you've loved me since the day you were born. I know, I've felt like that myself. Too

244

often. The more you give away to it, the bigger the bump you'll come down with afterwards. You take my word for it."

"Bloody expert advice she's giving me now!"

"Jack, let's part happily, or everything will be wasted, and we'll spoil our memories of each other. You feel nice, and easy, and happy now, and all that bad time you've been having is wiped out. You've got all your good times with Joyce to look forward to. Go away in that mood. You'll forget me in the morning."

"It's all right for you! Love 'em and leave 'em. Bang the bloody cash register and take on the next one. You're a one to sit there telling me about love! Never 'ad someone workin' on your bloody tripes with a cold chisel. Don't know what it means —"

"Don't shout Jack!"

"Think everyone's the same as you! Don't care what's on the bed so long as it's warm. ' 'Ad a sample off me, now go and get the goods from Joyce.' That's what I call cool, that is —"

"Oh, for heaven's sake!" She jumped to her feet, slipped on her dressing gown and tied the girdle violently. She was humiliated at having been driven into this vulgar quarrel, naked, face to face with a half-dressed man, like some cheap prostitute with a client. She was sick with disappointment at herself for having become the slave of events. "Go away, will you, please. I don't know what I've done to deserve all this, and I'm sick and tired and disgusted, and I want to be left alone."

"What's the matter!" Fury made him loud and vicious. "Expecting someone else?"

She was too dejected to have any more consideration for him. "Maybe. Now go away."

"I should ha' guessed. Simple Simon, that's me, Charlie Cheesecake, Dopey Joe! Rosie loves me — ah-way! — too bloody blind with joy to use my loaf. Rosie only loves the cash customers. Charity boy, that's me. Orphanage bloody brat. Give him a toy for Christmas, good deed for

245

the year, now shove off, sonnie. Give him a cuddle buckshee and sling him out."

She was near to weeping. "Oh, go away!"

"Well, you ain't dealing with a charity boy no more. Here's a feller can pay his way with the next man. Don't let no bastard spit in my eye, I can tell you. Here!" He threw a handful of notes down on the bed.

All her control was gone. She picked up the notes, threw them back at him and screamed, "You wretched little beast! Get out, and take your filthy money with you. And don't let me see you again. My stomach won't stand it."

"Gah way!" He pushed the money back towards her with his foot. His raucous laughter made her feel dizzy. "I know the old proud stunt. 'Wouldn't touch your money!' Not much you won't. Leave it on the floor till I've gone, then pick it up and put it in with all the rest you've earned on your bloody back. Well, there it is, you're welcome to it."

She was overwhelmed with shame, not at his words but at the memory of her own voice a few moments ago, shrill and stripped of all the modulations it had so carefully acquired. She pressed her lips together to contain her anger, picked up the money, strode to the gas fire and held the notes to it. She could feel Jack's stare on her as she crouched, trembling, her cheeks hot with blood, her eyes blazing. She dropped the ashes in the grate and hissed, "Now get — out!"

He did not move. He watched her with the look of a beast uncertain whether to spring or to take flight.

She turned her back on him, hurried to the window, pulled back the curtains and flung the window open. She leaned out and breathed deeply. He was still watching her. Ignoring him, she crossed to the bathroom, and went in, leaving the door open so that he could see her turning on the taps and emptying bath salts recklessly into the water. She heard the front door bang, and the scutter of his footsteps as he ran downstairs.

Chapter 4

JOYCE HAD FOR WEEKS BEEN TRYING, in her immature and artless way, to overwhelm Jack with her love, to atone for having rebuffed him, to bind him beyond the possibility of escape in the silken cords of her womanhood. Perhaps she was puzzled at his apparent lack of response, but she did not dream that she had achieved a result opposite to that which she had intended — she had driven him to another woman. However, she need not be pitied, for in the long run, and also without her knowledge, her efforts acted on Jack in his private crisis and saved him from disaster.

When he left Rose he was capable of anything. He might have fled from London, for there was a part of him that was utterly humiliated. He might have turned back and done murder, for there was also the stuff in him from which explosions of passion are ignited. He did neither of these things, because there was also in him the capacity to make the most of what shreds of satisfaction he possessed; and Joyce's attentions, however little he had consciously noticed them, had accumulated in a kind of reservoir of memory from which he was able to draw, when he most needed it, the assurance that there was someone on earth who wanted him, someone who valued him at his full worth and in whose presence he could feel big instead of little. In short there was Joyce, and he hastened back to her.

Twenty-four hours after he had met Rose in Oxford Circus he sat down to supper with Joyce.

When he had left Rose's flat, he had walked blindly for

hours, his limbs driven by an undefined violence of emotion. He was conscious of nothing but the desire to run as far as he could from the scene of his humiliation, and he walked northwards, impelled vaguely by the idea of reaching the Great North Road and catching a lorry out of town. He let his mind play with the notion in a dark, melodramatic way, without any firm intent, while his thoughts recalled to him, in a stream of self-pity, all the defeats and disenchantments he had suffered since his return. He wanted to run away not only from Rose, but from all these difficulties. When he had walked for two hours and tired his emotions out, he took a taxi home, went to bed and slept soundly.

He awoke refreshed the next morning, and all day at work relieved his love for Rose and his anger against her in an intensity of rage that had previously been quite outside the range of his emotions. Rose was the blackest, the foulest, the most hideous creature on earth. She had subjected him to the most unbearable tortures, the most cruel injustices, that any man had ever undergone. He had sometimes read, in a spirit of unsympathetic ribaldry, the reports which abounded in the Sunday papers of crimes of passion committed in poor homes, and he had muttered, "Must ha' been daft," or, looking at a photograph, "Little runt like that, wouldn't think he had it in him." Now he understood what had driven them, and fed himself on dreams of violence. However, if the rages of real life are as towering as those of literature, there is one saving difference about them — they usually fizzle out. At the end of the day's work, Jack not only forgot the fury which had been consuming him for hours, but even felt better for having worked it off. He was ravenously hungry.

It was not love with which he healed his wounds that evening, but self-importance. He swelled with pleasure at the quick look of welcome he received from Joyce as he walked in. He gloated over her servility at the supper table. He smothered in an effusion of vainglorious thoughts the unpleasant memory of yesterday's humiliation.

Perhaps he was merely intoxicated emotionally; he looked it, flushed and fierce, unnaturally loud and jolly, trying to show off his manliness. Perhaps he wanted to repair his vanity by proving the strength of Joyce's devotion: or perhaps, obscurely, it relieved his hurt to trample on her. Whatever the reason, his behaviour was beyond his control. He knew that he ought to give thanks for his deliverance and safeguard his position by being grateful, conciliatory and gentle. Instead he tyrannized wildly. Inwardly he had the helpless, whirling feeling of a man swept along on a torrent. Outwardly he grew more and more boisterous.

Joyce, who was clearly caught off her guard by his sudden change of temper, did not know how to cope with it. She played up to his mood, joyfully obeyed his commands, and laughed when he poked clumsy fun at her. But she must have felt the strain in him, for sometimes she reddened even as she laughed, and sometimes she would flash a furtive, apprehensive glance at him when she thought he was not looking. When she had finished washing up after supper (without any help from her mother, who was upstairs 'giving her poor feet a rest') she said, "I've got something to show you," and slipped out of the room.

Jack waited, pretending to glance at the paper, but in reality studying Mr. Wakerell, who was hunched over a book in his high-backed wooden armchair. Since supper Joyce's father had appeared oblivious of everything that had happened in the room. Reading, to him, was a physical rather than an intellectual exercise. As he sat reading, he could be seen struggling to form words, with a glow of triumph shining and fading in his face like the light of a revolving beacon. Yet his eyes were empty of understanding, for once he had conquered each row of words he forgot them. He did not read in order to think, but to attain an inner stillness, an absence of thought, which to him, in an unpleasant world, was half the art of

249

living. He gave the same impression when he was working in the garden. He was not a good gardener; not one of those little townsmen who produce prize roses. He would potter about behind the house, on a blighted little plot of black earth which looked more like the deposited grime of generations than the original soil, scratching with a blunt old rake, negligently treading a few seeds into the ground or slopping water around him. He was not interested in results; he only wanted to while away a little of his living time. In the same way he would wander off in summer-time, to the park, and stand in hour-long trances in front of the flower beds, as if his body's only function was to absorb the pale violet beauty of the lupins, the clear bright colours of the tulips, the unbelievable blue intensity of the cornflowers and the soft, pure comforting yellow, with a moist and tender gleam on it, of kingcups in the grass. It seemed that no hurt could reach him in his retreat; none of the terrors of the great world; none of the drudgery of his work; none of the disappointments of his married life. He was so far away that other people's words took a long time to reach him. Years of habitude had led to a state of affairs in the household in which, as tonight, he seemed unaware of the rest of the family while they behaved as if he were not there.

Joyce came back into the room. "There," she said, showing herself off, "look what I've bought." She was wearing a hat. Her bodily attitude, and the gentle, expectant glow of appeal in her face suggested that she was hoping to touch a new spring of feeling in him.

Jack was seared with relief that he, who had been so contemptuously cast out last night, could command this eager and attractive girl. The hat suited her, a tightly-fitting black cap with a white osprey spray on the right-hand side. The impulse to please her struggled in his mind, but he could only utter a jeering laugh. "Who d'you think you are? The Lord Chief Bloody Justice?"

She answered with a silly, uncertain laugh. "What

d'you mean, Jack?"

"Slow on the uptake, ain't you? Bloody black cap. 'The prisoner will rise and face the bar.' Whoops-a-daisy! Away with the mixer!"

"Double Dutch to me, Jack." Her smile was pleading and childishly pathetic. "Haven't you got anything else to say?"

"What d'you want me to say?"

"Something nice would be a change."

"What?" He was trying, inwardly, to think of some compliment, but the insults continued to spurt out. "With that bunch of feathers sprouting out? It's like a turkey's arse on your head."

"Oh, Jack!" He heard tears, as well as laughter, in her thick cry of protest. His mind strove to form a sentence: slowly there began to form a clumsy phrase of endearment.

He heard her saying, "Don't you want me to be smart when I walk out with you? I thought you'd be proud of me. It's just like a certain person wears."

"What certain person?"

She looked coy. "*You* know."

"No, I don't know."

"Rosie Hogarth. Don't you remember, that day?"

The conciliatory phrase flew to pieces in his head. He uttered a shaken, "Ha!" Anger swept compunction away, and he began to bait her without mercy, feeling increasingly miserable but deriving a mysterious satisfaction from the sight of her laughing hysterically with him and growing more and more flushed, alarmed and muddled behind her gaping smile. She bandied foolish quips with him, trying to make his mood harmless by entering into it. She was trying desperately to understand and calm him. The more spiteful he became, the more she laughed, and the more strained and shrill her laughter sounded.

At last, when he had uttered some particularly vicious sally, she looked up at him with her face wide open in a foolish smile and, without warning, burst into tears.

The suddenness of it knocked all the breath out of him. Fear and remorse flooded into him. He stood over her, helpless.

"Here." The deep voice, gentle and unconcerned, startled him. Joyce, too, paused in her weeping and looked up in surprise. Mr. Wakerell had lowered his book and was looking at them, with a mild and meditative expression. "I knew what I meant to ask you. What about coming up Collins' with us next week? My treat. There's all the old-timers on the bill. I was thinking of Saturday night."

Jack could not speak for a moment. The innocence of Mr. Wakerell's gaze, the stupid solemnity of his heavy face, as he waited for a reply without the least indication that anything untoward had been happening, suddenly seemed fantastically funny. Jack sniggered, and Joyce laughed painfully with him. They looked together at Mr. Wakerell and then at each other, as if in joint recognition of his ridiculousness, and both burst out laughing again.

Joyce said, "Oh, dad, you are a scream!"

Mr. Wakerell continued to wait calmly.

Jack managed to control himself, and said, "All right. Smashin' idea. Only let me get the tickets."

"You can get them if you like. It'll save me going up there. Only I'll pay for them. I don't want any arguments." Mr. Wakerell lifted his book up again and shut himself off from them as effectively as if he had performed a vanishing trick.

Jack was left with a weak, melted feeling. Mr. Wakerell's absurd intervention had saved him and brought him to rest. Somehow he and Joyce were re-united. Joyce rose and said, "Oh, well."

"Where you going?"

She smiled wanly. "To put this silly thing away."

He was about to call her back, but he checked himself and let her go. He waited contentedly, and when she came back he was very genial with her. The evening ended happily for both of them.

This episode let the tension out of him. He was able to relax. He felt that he had ridden the storm and come out into calm waters, within sight of his anchorage. He kept close to Joyce, finding safety and comfort in her presence. His peace was founded on tiredness and disillusionment, but he welcomed this, for it left him without the desire to make any more dangerous forays into the world beyond the front door.

He felt benign towards everyone, and although he did not want to see Rose again — the thought of it terrified him — he wondered how to make his peace with her. It seemed wrong, in this new, calm life, to have any enemies, least of all the girl who was associated with some of the most precious memories of his youth; and besides, he could not avoid feeling a painful, obscure gratitude for her embraces. He made several attempts to write, but could not complete a letter. Finally he decided to ask Nancy to act as his messenger. He would only tell her that he had quarrelled with Rose, and that he now wanted to ask Rose to let bygones be bygones. With this in mind he went up to Nancy's flat one evening, but she was out. Her husband explained that Gran Hogarth was ill, and was waiting to go into hospital. In the meantime Nancy was looking after her, cheerfully travelling back and forth every day to run two homes at once. Jack promised to call again.

His new mood also led him to another good deed. He was on his way to Collins' Music Hall to book the tickets, when he saw Barmy Naughton on the opposite pavement. Jack was often oppressed by the thought of Barmy's loneliness, and he was delighted when he thought of inviting Barmy to join the theatre party. Barmy accepted, with a painfully happy smile, and Jack went on to get the tickets.

To his surprise this led to a flare-up with Joyce. Subservient though she was, she wanted no interlopers in their private world. When Jack told her what he had done, she grimaced with displeasure.

"What's up, girl? I thought you liked to do a good turn."

"There's a limit. We don't have to cart loonies round with us."

"He ain't a loonie. He's a bloody good friend of mine."

"Well," Joyce said, "he's no friend of mine, so don't sit him next to me, or I'll have the creeps." She avoided any further argument, but when he tried, later, to arouse her sympathy for Barmy, she shut her face up stubbornly and refused to answer. The visit to the theatre took place on the last Saturday night in October.

The first part of the show consisted of cheap and boring turns. The huge, draughty hall was astir with fidgeting. Laughter and conversation floated down from the gallery, where the younger couples sat. The packed audience on the ground floor included innumerable family parties, within each of which refreshments were continually being unwrapped and exchanged, children were being audibly dissuaded from mischief, and babes in arms were giving voice to their woes. There were many old folk present, whose poor pinched lives on the old age pension could be guessed not only from their shabby clothes and from the care with which the menfolk scraped together their little spills of tobacco, but from the rapt and obstinate enjoyment their uplifted faces showed at even the most untalented performance — as if, against all odds, they were determined to wring enjoyment from the one bright evening they could afford in the whole week. There could be felt, in the audience as a whole, a current of kinship and tolerant sympathy for the performers. Some of the worst turns drew the loudest applause. When a pathetic little troupe of chorus girls, who all looked as if they had come straight from a hard week's work in the laundry, pranced off the stage, a woman in front of Jack turned round and said to him, "Ah, poor dears, they do work hard, don't they?" A red-nosed comic in a check suit provoked the remark from Mrs. Wakerell that "he ought to be in bed with that chest of his," and when a man nearby shouted, "Lahsy!", someone else retorted, "He's doing his best," and there was a violent outburst of clapping from roundabout as the comedian, looking relieved and surprised, took his parting bow.

After the interval the old-timers appeared. Some of them were only the ghosts of their former selves. Others, aged as they were, showed themselves as capable as ever of filling the hall with their magical gusto. Each of them was greeted as an old friend, with people shouting delightedly, "Wotcher, Georgie boy!" or "Good ol' Lil!", or calling for favourite songs, or passing to their neighbours such remarks as, "He's looking well, bless him! And seventy if he's a day!"

Jack and Joyce were not greatly impressed by these artists, and wondered why their elders had always made such a fuss about them; but they joined in the familiar choruses with pleasure. Mr. and Mrs. Wakerell were having a wonderful time, and Barmy was gazing at the stage with an unsmiling stare of such fixity that he did not hear when Jack spoke to him. Joyce whispered, "Look, he's trembling," and Jack replied softly, "Leave him alone." The old folk looked as if they were in another world, especially the women. However old a woman is, there are certain moments when she is touched by a spontaneous emotion, and a miracle happens. For a little while the lineaments of her girlhood reappear from beneath the sagging wrinkled surface of her face. Her eyes become tender and ardent. Jack and Joyce could discern, though without understanding, the beauty and innocence that shone forth from a score of aged faces around them; they were moved, and nudged each other gently, without saying anything.

There was an old man near them. He was square and solid, with a massive, grey-fringed bald head, a red face and a predatory nose. He sat hunched with his head cocked to one side and a hand cupped to one ear. His eyes were looking away into strange distances as if it were not the voice of the singer on the stage that he was straining to catch, but that of his own vanished youth, audible to no-one but him, echoing and receding, faintly and tantalisingly, from far away.

The older people made no attempt to sing loudly. They sang softly and timidly, seeming afraid to disturb the faint voices of memory that they heard within them; and their singing was drowned by the roaring choruses that came, unnostalgic and cruelly strong, from the boys and girls in the gallery.

The air was astir with emotion; with happiness and grief, love, regret, disappointment. Each of us becomes another being at each stage of life; that being dies, but haunts us to the grave, so that we are each followed through life by a train of ghosts, and all the ghosts are ourselves. These were the ghosts that stirred in the theatre, whispering in the ears of the middle-aged and the old.

There was a prolonged ovation at the end of the show, and the people swarmed out of the theatre, some of them excited and talkative, some still quiet and preoccupied. Mrs. Wakerell said, "Ah, well, that was a real treat. I could just do with some supper now." Barmy remained in his seat, staring at the safety curtain. Jack took him by the arm and said, "Show's over, old son." Barmy looked up as if at a stranger, then muttered, with a faint smile of recognition, "I reckon so," and rose to follow the others down the aisle.

On the way home Jack, in the midst of an excited conversation, noticed that Barmy was trailing behind, wandering along with his hands in the pockets of his dirty raincoat and his lips moving silently.

Jack dropped back and fell in step with him. "What's up, nob?"

Barmy shrugged his shoulders.

"Didn't you enjoy the show?"

Barmy nodded feebly but his expression did not brighten.

"Well cheer up, tosh, you ain't dead yet."

Barmy whispered, "Wish I was."

"Here, that ain't the way to talk on a Saturday night."

Barmy did not answer. The others had slowed their pace, and they were all walking together again.

Jack put his arms round Barmy's shoulder. "Here, come on, boy, snap out of it. You can smile if you try. What's on your mind? I don't get it. Smashing show, good seats, a nice drop of wet in the interval — what more do you want?"

"All that in there," Barmy blurted, "I used to — with her — I used to go, we used to have a real good time. Only," he turned to Jack and clutched his arm, "I was alive then. Here, I'll tell you. I couldn't feel nothing tonight. Dead, I am. You could stick pins in me. I couldn't feel 'em. Walking the earth dead, I am. All in their graves, the only ones that wanted me. Me — that's where I ought to be. One day nothing. Next day nothing. Next day nothing. Next day nothing. Here," he shouted, his face working desperately, "three hundred and sixty-five days in a year. Know that? I ain't daft. I know! Three hundred and sixty-five. That's only one year. I've had — millions of years, I've had. I tell you, I've had about enough!"

"Oh, for God's sake,"Joyce said, "put his head in a bag, someone! The life of the party, an' I don't think! I told you what to expect."

"Quiet," Jack muttered, "you'll upset him."

"What about us?" she insisted. "I thought this was supposed to be our night out? You want to think of your own, you do, before you break your heart over strangers."

Jack said, "He'll be all right." He spoke to Barmy again. "Look, boy, I know, you've had a rough time. But you've got friends. You've got Mick, and you've got us."

Barmy leaned towards him, peering into his face. "Here, her — you know what she said? A loving heart. Can't live without you find one, she said. A loving heart. That was her. She was the only one. Never mind Mick. Never mind you. She was the only one. Her, and the kids,

257

and that kitchen." His voice rose. "All them kids. They're gone. All of 'em. Little Nance, and Alf, and Rosie, and Jackie."

"Here, come off it," Jack said, "here I am! They're all about, all of 'em."

Barmy's high-pitched voice grated on. "All them lovely kids, they're all gone. All right that was, playing with the kids. You can't beat it. Lovely kids they was. Used to hold my hand. Never shouted after me, none of 'em. 'Ba-army!' 'Ba-army!' That's what the kids scream after me now. Go near one of 'em, woman comes out. 'You leave my child alone, Barmy Naughton, or I'll call the police.' Menace, I am —"

"Gah way!" Jack consoled, "You'll be all right now. Wait till I'm settled down. You'll have a home to come to, just like you used to. You'll always be welcome. Play with my kids you can, and welcome, any time. That'll make a difference, won' it?"

Barmy blinked at him piteously. "Can I? Honest?"

"Of course you can."

Barmy suddenly swerved across Jack's path, laid his hand on Joyce's arm and said eagerly, "Can I, Joycie? Can I come and play with your kiddies?"

"My kiddies? — Well of all the nerve!" Jack was pleading with her, in grimaces, over Barmy's shoulder, shaping with his lips the words, "Be nice to him. It's only for now. Get him quiet." She said to Barmy, "Now you go back and talk to Jack, go on."

"Oh, go on, Joycie," Barmy pleaded, "can I come in your kitchen every day? Wash up? Little stool by the gas stove, nice and warm there it was."

"Look here," she exclaimed to Jack, "he's your precious pal. Get him off my arm. Let him ruin your evening, not mine. It's, all very well playing up to him like this, you'll never hear the last of it. He'll be round every day on the strength of this, you see if he won't, and when I complain, you'll say, 'Well, we promised him, Joycie, didn't we?' Well, I'm not promising anything and I'm not wet-nursing anybody, and," she turned to Barmy, carried away by anger, "you're the last one I ever want crawling across my doorstep, and don't you forget it."

"Oh, you mean bitch!" Jack cried. "Haven't you got any kindness in you?"

"Yes," she answered defiantly, "plenty, and it's all for you. When there's any left over, I'll let you know."

Barmy was walking rapidly away into the crowds. Jack hesitated. "Look, I've got to — Look, Joycie, I never meant that just now. I've got to get hold of him, though, state he's in. I'll take him back to Mick's place. I'll see you at home later." He went in pursuit of Barmy.

Barmy plunged on through the crowds, leaning forward as if he were butting against a gale. The young couples who thronged the pavements in the gay glare of the shop lights, hastening to dances and restaurants, pouring out of the cinemas or strolling to their assignations in the parks, bumped into him without noticing him, or turned to laugh at him and then forget him in their happiness. He ignored Jack, who hurried at his heels pleading with him.

He turned into a narrow side street, hastening along beneath the high blank wall of a cinema. As he turned a bend, with Jack still following, the clamour and excitement and the pearly dazzle of lights were left behind, rolling up behind the walls in a faint red-tinged glare and a muffled roar of pleasure; so that now Jack could hear what he was saying to himself.

"Oh, that was a lovely show. Old Florrie Forde wasn't arf grand..."

"But she wasn't in the show," Jack protested, unheard.

"...You're all right, Kate, you are. You're a blessed sweet angel to me. I'd cut my throat in a day without you. Nobody else in the world has got eyes for me. They all look where I am, as if I wasn't there. Everybody in the world. All them people, millions of 'em, hurry about, here and there, I ain't there, not for them. Katie, what have I done to them? I can enjoy life. I do, with you. I can talk. I

259

can when I'm with you, can't I, Katie love? I can talk like anyone else, can't I? You know I can talk properly, don't you? Here, Kate, they got them synchronised pictures up the Olympia. Let's go there. It's only down Shoreditch. It ain't far. You hear the chap sing. You see him on the pictures and you can hear him singing. Bloke told me about it. Bloody marvel it is. Talking pictures. Kate, take us, sweetheart, take us for a treat. Here, Kate, I had an idea. I'll take Rosie to school every day if you like. Kid her age oughtn't to cross that big road all by herself, all that traffic, four times a day. Here, know what she said to me yesterday? In the kitchen, she said to me, 'When I'm a big girl, guess who I'm going to marry?' 'Who?' I says. 'The Prince of Wales,' she says. So I says, 'When's the happy day?' And she says, 'When I'm ten.' And then she says, 'And you can be my page-boy.' Laugh? She's a wonder, she is!"

Jack seized Barmy by the arm and pushed him up against the wall. "Here, what's up, ol' lad? Here, come on boy, it's me, it's Jackie."

Barmy stood there trembling. At last he said, "What you want?"

"You come on home, boy, come on, there's a good chap."

Barmy walked on, at a slower pace than before. Jack kept at his side. "I know when I ain't wanted," Barmy said.

"Don t be daft. You don't want to take no notice of what women say when they're in a temper."

"I ain't wanted and I know it. You don't want to waste time on me, Jackie. Bloody old nuisance. Old rags and lumber. In the way. There was only one wanted me, that was her."

"Steady boy. You ain't the only one that loved her. We all miss her."

"Not like I do. She was good to me."

"She was good to all of us." They had reached the side door of The Lamb.

"Not like she was to me. You don't know. Nobody ever

know. I never let on. She says, 'I trust you, pet,' she says, 'I trust you, my love. A still tongue means a wise head.' I never let on to anyone. 'Not in the house,' she says, 'it's a sin in the house. Up the church, in the porch,' she says, 'it's dark and quiet, we can't be seen, and there's never a soul goes by at night. The Almighty won't mind,' she says, 'some might, but not Him. When I've put the kids to bed,' she says, 'I'll be there with you.' "

"You get to bed, lad. We've had a lovely evening. You cheer up and smile, and we'll go again soon."

"Many a time we went there. Late at night. It was lovely and quiet."

"All right, boy. You got a key? Get up to bed now."

"You don't believe me, do you?"

"Course I do. Open the door now."

"Nah, you don't believe me. Who would? You don't believe any woman'd put her arms round Barmy, do you?"

"Course I do." Barmy's assertion had aroused in Jack a sudden frantic eagerness to get away. His brain, as if struggling not to absorb what he had heard, span clouds of irrelevant and unrelated ideas. He felt as if his ears had just been boxed. He was trying at once to account for what he had heard, to pretend he had not heard it, and to avoid hearing any more. "G'night, boy."

"Wait!" Barmy's voice was harsh and angry. "You wait here. I'll show you! I ain't fit to be loved, am I? Barmy Naughton, who'd touch him? Fancy the queen of 'em all picking him of all people! Makes you die of laughing, don' it? You wait here, I'll show you something!"

Jack heard his own voice, hollow with unbelief. "Kate? Her, with a man? She was a good woman, she was."

"Too true she was a good woman!"

"But her — She — She was our mum, she was."

"She writ me a letter. You wait here."

He waited in a daze, wanting to run away, till Barmy had returned from within the house.

"Here." Barmy handed him the letter. "God forgive us,

I swore I'd never show this to no-one."

Jack took the letter between deadened fingertips. It was dirty and splitting at the folds. It was headed, Broadstairs, August 22nd, 1939.

"That summer," he muttered, "a week before the war. When she went on holiday."

'My dearest lamb, (he read silently), How do you feel being all on your own, and a man of responsibility for a week? Just think, you are master of a pub, not to mention me relying on you to keep an eye on the youngsters. You see, dear, we trust you more than anyone. Everything is wonderful here, the weather is blazing hot, the sea is so blue and sparkling, it's years since I've seen it like this. It makes me like a young girl again, I buy ice cream cornets, and laugh like anything, I feel so light on my feet I want to run down to the sea on tiptoes, but alas, that's one thing I'm past. When I lay back in a deckchair I shut my eyes and feel the sun, and all my cares fly away. I think, well, I have had my troubles, who hasn't? — but they're all behind me now. My sweet children are growing up, bless them, and everything — I have made up my mind — everything is going to be beautiful from now on, for it's about time...

' "The week before the war," Jack said softly. ... 'And that is true for you, too, my dear. I shall never desert you. My home will always be open to you, there will always be a chair at my table, and we will always squeeze up to make room for you at the fire. Yes, and when you need me that badly, there will always be a kiss and a cuddle for you. Why not? It's not shameful, my poor pet, God made us so that we can't live without it, and we all need a loving heart to turn to, don't we? But people have wicked tongues, and I treasure my children's good name more than anything else in the world. But I know I can rely on you. You are a clever, clever dear, and you know that a still tongue means a wise head...'

Jack looked up for a moment, and sighed. All his notions about life were crashing down like the streets of a city when the earth trembles. New questions and ideas were flashing across his mind. He could not grasp a single one of them, but he already felt tantalised by the new pages of knowledge that waited, as yet beyond the range of his eyes, to be read. Beneath the shock and confusion there lurked no anger or disappointment nor even, to his surprise, disgust that Barmy had been the man, but a strange sweet hurt, as if his spirit grieved because she was dust in the grave and it was too late for him to look at her again, with new and wondering eyes.

'...So don't fret, dear (the letter ended), a week is not a long time to be alone. Don't forget, dear, keep an eye on the youngsters for me, and tell Milkie I'm sorry I missed him before I went, I'll pay him next week. With love, Kate.'

When Jack had finished reading he folded the letter, gave it back to Barmy, said, "Good night, boy, God bless," in a quiet, heavy voice, and walked slowly home.

Chapter 5

NANCY HAD POSTED A CARD TO JACK, to reach him on Monday morning. "We've got Gran into hospital. She'll be better looked after there. I'm visiting, Tuesday, three o'clock. Come if you can get time off."

Jack arrived at her flat early on Tuesday afternoon. "I've just put baby down to sleep," she said. "I won't wake her up, but you can have a peep. The woman next door is coming in to watch her while we're away. Sit down and I'll get you something to eat."

Jack refused, but agreed not to say 'no' to a cup of tea. He asked about Gran's condition, which was not alarming, answered Nancy's enquiries about the Wakerells, told her that he had been able to come because he was now on short time (it felt, he said, like being on holiday to walk the streets on a weekday afternoon) and mentioned that he had been wanting to see her for the last couple of weeks. The conventional exchanges exhausted, he fell into a brief silence, sipped his tea, and asked, "Heard from Rosie lately?"

"No. I suppose she's been busy. Why?"

"I been seeing her. Did you know?"

"No, dear. Oh, I am glad. How is she?"

"She's all right." There followed a grunt which Nancy took for a laugh. "Suppose so, anyway. We didn't exactly part on speaking terms."

"Mmm?" Nancy's mouth was full of cake. A moment later she uttered an incredulous laugh and said, "Whatever are you talking about? Do you mean you had a row? What on earth have you two got to quarrel over?"

264

"Oh, I dunno." He leaned back and let his head lie against the crossbar of his chair. "She's a hellcat, your sister, ain't she?"

"A hellcat? — Jack, are you delirious or am I dreaming?"

He continued to study the ceiling. "Blowed if I know! Maybe she ain't, I don't know. I've had a few shocks these last few days, women this and women that. Never know where you are with them, I can tell you."

"Yes, but what's it all about? I always used to think you were so fond of her."

He sat up. "You can say that again. I was crazy about her. I worshipped the ground she walked on. And I ain't kidding, either. Ever since we were kids. Never guessed that, did you?"

Nancy pondered, looking troubled. "Not like that. Brother and sister, yes, but — do you really mean like *that*, to? —" she looked helpless — "like when people marry each other?"

"I'll say! Day and bloody night!"

"Mum said so once. I told her not to be silly. She said, 'There's a packet of grief waiting for that poor boy one of these days.' I said rubbish — you were tarting around with that Maisie Keenan just then. She said, 'I know him, he's all eyes and no tongue, and that kind can wait till doomsday before our Rosie notices them.' Well I mean, Jack, after that time you never showed the slightest sign of interest in Rosie, and certainly, by the way you acted when you came home, nobody would have guessed. What's been happening between you two?"

"Oh, nothing much." He rose from his chair. "Forget it. Hadn't we better be going?"

"There's plenty of time. You sit down."

He walked to the window, where he turned to face her. "Look, I'll give it to you straight. I've been having a rare old tear-up with that girl. I couldn't get her out of my mind. I started going out with her, a few weeks ago. One thing led to another — you know how it is. Specially with a girl like that. I spent a bloody fortune on her. Took me home, she did, give me the bloody works, all right. Then wallop, out on my bloody ear'ole, and bang went the door."

She sighed. "I don't know! The things people get up to! It's all beyond me. I've got my little home, and that's all I know. There's only one thing I do know, and that's not to judge. She's a strange girl, our Rose. I would never set up to understand her. But she's never done anything wrong, not that I know of. I can't imagine what led her to give you encouragement — if she did encourage you. And you, Jack! What about poor Joyce?"

"That's what she said. Not a stitch on, and she sat there talking about Joyce. She said, 'You go back to Joyce, and kiss and be happy.' Can you beat it?"

"Well, there's wrong been done, and I'm sorry to hear it. It frightens me, Jack, what I see and hear, the things other people do. It almost makes me glad that me and Tom are such a couple of Jumbos." She smiled sadly. "But if it's done with, it's done with, and thank the Lord for that. It's Joyce you must think of, from now on."

"That's all right, love. I know a good girl when I see one. I wouldn't give her up for a bloody pension. No —" he hesitated — "What I was thinking about — Well, next time you see Rose, you tell her, forget it. From me, I mean. Tell her, no hard feelings. I can't make her out, and that's a fact, but I wouldn't like her and me to go on having the needle for each other, not after all these years. The life she leads, anyway, I don't suppose I should have expected anything better from her."

"Jack, don't start on that! I've told you, there's nothing wrong with Rose or with the life she leads."

"The facts speak for themselves, don't they?"

"No, they don't. There's a few things you ought to know, and if she'd let me, I'd tell you. But she won't, and it's up to her."

"I don't know,"Jack groaned. "Bloody mysteries you make!"

266

"Never mind that now. Jack, why don't you go yourself, and make up with her, and have a proper talk with her."

"Have a heart, Nance, how can I?"

"Why not?"

He made inarticulate noises.

"Well," she said, "Write to her, dear."

"I've tried. Look, you go, Nance. You could put it better than me. Proper Joe Muggins I am. I never know what I'm going to say next."

"All right, dear. You can put your mind at rest. I couldn't bear to think there was any ill feeling between you two. Anyway, I must confess I'm all in a muddle after what you've told me. I should like to hear what Rose has to say about it. I'll see her, Jack, as soon as I can." She considered. "I'll tell you what, this very night. Tom won't mind staying in with the baby. I shan't sleep easy till I've seen her, so I might as well get it over and done with."

The doorbell rang. "That's Mrs. Elmore," she said, "come to mind the baby. We can go now. All right, Jack, dear, don't you worry. After I've seen Rose and I'm clear in my own mind, we'll have another talk. It breaks my heart, all this silly business about Rose, and it's time it was settled once and for all."

***

At the hospital, Nancy noticed that Jack appeared depressed as they made their way through the echoing, yellow-walled corridors. His face was pinched by a vague fear as he looked at the trolleys and glimpsed through open doors the murmuring doctors, the mysterious rows of bottles on dispensary shelves and the wan, too-cheerful faces of patients. The set of his nostrils suggested that he was sniffing for the sweetness of corruption that underlay the sharp clean smell of antiseptics. Nancy's serenity was undisturbed. Her step was as quick and eager as on any other visit that she was glad to make. He caught her glance and said, "Put the wind up me, these places do."

"Oh, dear," she laughed, "Tom's just the same. Like little boys, you are."

Gran did not see them when they entered her ward. She was sitting up in bed, propped up by pillows, listening to a young woman in a hospital dressing-gown who sat beside her.

Nancy said, "Hallo, my darling. You do look nice and comfy," and kissed Gran's cheek.

Gran turned her head toward Nancy. "What's the matter with me, Nance?" She spoke in a frightened, husky whisper. "They won't tell me. The lady doctor comes in the morning, and when I ask her she just laughs and says, 'Don't you bother yourself, mother, you'll soon be all right,' and the nurses, they all say the same thing, too."

"And why shouldn't they?" Nancy said. "They've got nothing to hide, dear. You're just in here for a nice rest, and to be properly looked after. We'll soon have you home again."

"They look after you in here, all right," the young woman said. "We had chicken today, as much as we wanted, and trifle afterwards. You can have a Guinness every day if you want it, or orange juice. They come round with it on a tray and you can have whichever you like. Talk about Christmas! It's wonderful."

The young woman's voice had brought a spark of recognition into Gran's eyes. "This is Mrs. Roberts," she whispered, "she's a nice young lady. She sits and talks to me."

"Cheer her up," said Mrs. Roberts, "it don't do to lie on your back and brood, does it? It never does anywhere, let alone here. It's a real pleasure for me in here, I can tell you. Never had a time like it for years. No shopping, no washing up, being waited on hand and foot, all those beautiful things to eat you can never afford outside."

"She's in here for a operation," Gran broke in, "what do they call it, dear?"

"Malignant growth," Mrs. Roberts said cheerfully, "it's

a real whopper. They showed me the X-Rays. Isn't it lovely and bright in here? There's a wireless for every bed, and the nurses are ever so pleasant. They can't do too much for you. Isn't it a lovely day? Look at them flowers a lady visitor brought yesterday. You wouldn't think it was November, would you? Ah, well, I'll love you and leave you, and get back to my knitting. I'm sure you'd rather be on your own-e-oh."

Gran settled back against her pillows, looking straight in front of her with a faint grin of irony and disbelief, while Nancy chatted reassuringly and Jack, who had seated himself near the foot of the bed after uttering an uneasy greeting, unpacked the parcel of eggs, chocolate and butter which Nancy had made up out of her family's rations. Gran's cheeks had caved in, robbing her face of its lifelong set of grim obstinacy. She looked as if, in the struggle to sustain her waning strength, she had consumed all the flesh from her face, leaving only a skull clothed in waxy skin. Her hair, no longer piled in a firm white bun, straggled in white wisps of surprising sparsity, exposing the hideous newborn pinkness of her scalp. Her sunken eyes gleamed from wet sockets, giving her the appearance of some inanimate refuge through whose windows life glared, at bay, watching with a mixture of defiance and horrified fascination the approach of the executioner. Faint traces of expression crossed her face while she listened to Nancy, as if, half-hearing, she were trying to simulate undistracted attention, but the fear of death glared from beneath them all. She puckered her face up into a transparent smile and whispered, "How is the little one? Does she ask after me?"

"She's expecting you at her birthday party. Isn't it wonderful how time flies? — only another month and she'll be two. Oh, she doesn't stop worrying me! 'Where's Nanny, where's our Nanny-bunny?' that's all — on my word of honour — that's all we can get out of her. How she chatters away! When I think of all those months we were

269

trying to teach her words, we were beginning to get worried about her, and she just sat and stared up at us. And now all of a sudden she rattles away as if she'd been storing it all up. It's like a miracle, Gran dear, you wait till you hear her."

Gran uttered a laugh that was like a querulous little cry. "That's the way with them. That's the way it is with the little ones. There you are with a helpless babe, a tiny white bundle of woollies and a tiny pink face, and before you know where you are there's a young lady dancing about you." She broke off, exhausted by the moment of animation, and lay listening to her own breathing, long and harsh. "I have to make myself breathe. It don't hurt, but it's like working a bellows. It's hard." On each expiring breath she moaned, "It's hard."

Nancy patted the back of Gran's hand. "Don't you excite yourself. You just lay back and listen. That's right, you close your eyes, I don't mind. There," she crooned, as if to a baby, "quiet, quiet. Isn't that nice? You lay nice and quiet, and I'll talk. She's just learned about cats. They've got a kitten next door. It's called Fluffy. She knows the name, she goes about all day looking under the sofa and calling out, 'Fluffy, Fluffy.' And do you know, she's started eating fish, so that she can give Fluffy the bones. She used to scream the house down before when I tried to give her fish."

Gran opened her eyes. "You wrap her up," she crowed. "You wrap her up warm. It's dangerous, this time of the year."

"Of course I will, darling. You know I always do just what you say. We'll wrap her up ever so carefully. She's got a wonderful new woolly two-piece for the winter."

"You wrap her up." Gran's voice, broken by her quick breathing, was becoming feverish. "Letting her run about half-naked all the summer. That didn't do her no good. Didn't listen to me then, did you? Oh, no! I never knew nothing then, did I? The silly old woman! It's wicked — wicked ideas you young ones have got. Rub her in with

270

camphorated oil. Never mind what they tell you, these nurses, these clinics. They've not brought young ones up themselves. Rub her in warm. You watch her. Or you'll lose her!" Gran struggled to sit up, her breath rattling in her throat. "You'll lose her!"

Nancy pressed her gently back by the shoulder, but Gran seized her wrist and pulled herself up, panting, into a sitting position. "Nancy!" Her eyes were glaring with the effort. "Take me out of here! They don't know what's good for me. They wash me all over, every morning. I tell 'em, it'll be the death of me I say, but they don't listen. Nobody listens here. I'm cold here, Nance. I'm deathly cold all the time." Her face betrayed the same uncomprehending fear that makes a baby look so piteous when it is in pain. She beckoned Nancy closer, and her whisper became confidentially hoarse. "Nance, there's germs here. Lady over in that bed told me. Germs —" her voice shook — "you never used to hear about 'em years ago. That's what they've done for us with all their inventions, filled the place up with germs. They've got 'em in here, all over. They get in you when you breathe, and they get down to your heart, and you're done for. Makes you afraid to breathe, it do. Lady in here died the other day, only sixty-nine she was. They reckon that was germs."

Jack looked embarrassed, but Nancy laughed heartily. "Oh, you are a silly old thing. You are a silly old, silly old thing. If I didn't laugh at you I'd lose patience with you. Here I come to invite you to a birthday party, and Jack's come to remind you about the wedding — that's next month, too, isn't it, Jack? — and you sit there telling us all about germs. Why, there's less germs here than there are in my flat. They put stuff in the air to kill them. You ask the lady doctor, she'll tell you. Now, what are you going to give Linda for a present? She's been worrying me to tell her. I said you were going to get better and come home and bake a cake."

Gran relaxed and lay still, her eyes closed, till her

breathing had become more regular. "You don't know what's for the best," she murmured. "Some says do this, and some says do that. You don't know what to do not to peg out. Nance, I don't want to peg out. I want to see that kiddie grow up. My life has been a bitter one, Nance. I've lived on all these years in the hope of getting some goodness out of it, but never a taste have I had. I want to stay here till that kiddie's old enough to remember me. I want to see her pretty and happy. If I go now, there'll not be a soul left on earth after a few years that ever knew I was here. That's what makes me cold, Nance, being forgotten. If I lived to a hundred I could see her wed. Nance, there's plenty that lives to a hundred, ain't there?"

"Of course there are, dear. And you'll be one more. Here, I'll break you off a nice piece of chocolate and you can suck it."

Having silenced Gran, Nancy went on chatting about family affairs, while the old woman sucked noisily and regathered her strength. Brown threads of chocolate began to dribble from the corners of Gran's mouth. Jack frowned squeamishly and looked away. Nancy took out a handkerchief and, without altering the serene tenor of her talk, wiped Gran's chin like a baby's.

"Yes —" Gran had finished the chocolate, and she took up her plaint, speaking now comfortably, almost boastfully — "I've had a hard time of it, I have. Live too easy, you young ones. You should have been young in my time, kep' house on fourteen shilling a week like me. When it was coming in. Many a time it wasn't, in a freezing winter, when my chap was out of work. Tramp in the snow with a thin shawl and broken shoes. Five in the morning till twelve at night breaking my back over other people's washing. Lining up in the wet for meal tickets. Begging a pair of breeches from the school for my little barefoot boy. Running up the Guardians for 'undredweight of coal. That's hard when you're proud like me. That's what it was like in my time." She rested, gazing dimly at the past. "Year in, year out, your life goes away in the steam, over stove and boiler. There's precious little youth and beauty left in you after that. Yes," she croaked, "and it got worse after my chap pegged out."

"Oh, I don' know," Jack said, "he left you all right, didn't he? I mean, I know it's only a few bob a week, your annuity, but it's something."

"Him," she said, "he didn't leave me enough to buy a box of matches. Never saved a penny in his life. It wasn't his fault. He was one of them that never had the luck. It was my Victor saw to me. He had a bit saved up, and he left it all to me when he died. Yes —" her voice rose — "that's one thing *she* never got, his money, what there was of it."

Nancy saw the look of startled attention that had appeared on Jack's face. "We'll have to being going now, Gran," she said. "You won't get better quickly if you wear yourself out talking. You try and go off to sleep, now, for a bit. I'll come back on Thursday, and we'll have another talk."

Gran went on as if she had not heard. "Ah!" — there was a pathetic, malicious chuckle — "that Kate, she never even knew there was a will till the vicar come in and said my Victor had give it him. Then he read it. Ah, I laughed then. I laughed all right. In her face I laughed. 'All my savings in the Post Office I leave to my dear mother, Georgina Susan Hogarth, who never spared herself for me.'" She sat there listening. Her face didn't move. Calm as you like, a little smile, haughty as if she was the Queen of England. Shame? Not her? She lay panting, watching while Nancy rose and gathered her things. Jack had not moved from his chair. "He left her without a penny. Nothing but the furniture and the pension. Not that she cared. The slut! She was provided for! Ah, he wouldn't tell me when he was alive. I said to him once, I said, 'Victor, my love, you can tell me. You can tell your own mother.' He was too proud. He was like me, proud. Paralysed from the waist down, and creeping up him till it killed him. Him father those last two children?

273

How could he? But he was ashamed, poor sweet, he was ashamed to tell his own mother. He said, 'Go away, mother. You mind your affairs and I'll mind mine.' But at the last, it was me he thought of, not her. He as good as told me. In his will, he as good as told me." She closed her eyes, utterly exhausted, and they listened to her raucous breathing. "Don't go, Nance. Give us a drop of water. Drop of warm water. For me throat." Nancy gave her a drink and sat down reluctantly to wait till she had recovered. Gran opened her eyes and drew a long breath. "I always hated her. The first time I set eyes on her I knew the kind she was. Eighteen when he brought her home the first time. Ah, she was pretty all right. A cheek full of roses. A bosom that nearly bust her bodice. He was so proud. A young man with a beauty to show off. He held her arm as if she might run away. It was the way she smiled at me. A girl comes home with your son, she ought to smile afraid. Not that one. Bold, she smiles, straight at me. 'I'm not afraid of you,' she says with her eyes. Ah, I hated her from that moment and she knew it. She wasn't the kind to give up her joys, and serve a man, and slave and scrape in his kitchen like a respectable woman." Her voice quavered and weakened, and tears of self-pity collected in the corners of her eyes. "The Lord sent a judgement on her when He dropped that bomb. She took my boy away. She made him unhappy. She left me alone. I lived my life out alone in a room, without my boy. Sixty years of suffering, and not a day's happiness for a reward. Nance, I can't be taken, not now, afore a little pleasure comes my way."

Nancy soothed Gran, made her comfortable again, kissed her and repeated her promise to return soon. She roused Jack, who was brooding as if he had forgotten them both, and led him out of the ward. She knew that he would be full of questions and she was wondering, with some alarm, how she could evade them, at least until she had seen Rose.

On the way out she paused at Mrs. Roberts' bed and

said, "Well, bye-bye, dear, we're off now. I'll bring you some flowers when I come on Thursday. And I do wish you better."

"Bye-bye, duck," Mrs. Roberts said, "I'll keep an eye on the old lady." She held up the socks that she was knitting. "They're coming on lovely, aren't they? They're for my chap. I thought I'd get 'em finished while I can. After all, you never know, do you?"

They walked to the bus stop in silence. Jack was the first to speak. "Thank God for the fresh air! She looks as if she'd been in the grave a month already. I can't stand 'em when they're like that. I know it's wicked, but I can't. I don't want to go near 'em."

"We all come to it, dear. We should go to people when they need us, not just when we need them."

"But don't it make you sick?"

"Sick, dear? Where's your heart?"

"That's your mother talking. You're her all right. You're the only one that is."

Nancy laughed. "I'm half of her." She was afraid to say any more, and she was surprised when Jack said it for her.

"Yes, and I know who's the other half." She had not thought him capable of this. She was surprised, too, at his calmness. For the first time she found herself regarding him as a fellow-adult. "You thought I'd be all over you with questions," he said, "didn't you, Nance, when we come out of there?" His face, harassed and reflective, was lit by a vague smile. "All that business she was going on about."

"She's wandering, poor thing. She doesn't know what she's saying any more."

"Turn it up, Nance. I ain't so green as I'm cabbage-looking. Not quite, anyway. You going to tell us all about it, Nance?"

"When I've seen Rosie. Do us a favour, Jack, and leave us alone till then. I'm not so clever. I don't know what to say, not till I've thought."

275

"All right, love." Again she was surprised at his gentleness. He spoke again. "Here, tell us one thing. Does Barmy come into the story?"

"Barmy?" She stared in bewilderment.

He studied her expression, then grinned. "All right, skip it, Nance. Just an idea come to me. Here, she is done for, isn't she, the old lady?"

"Yes, I'm afraid her time has come."

"You don't sound upset. You with your soft heart, I thought you'd cry buckets over it."

"What for?" Nancy asked calmly. "The young may die but the old must. That's the last thing to cry over."

"You're a funny one, all right."

She took him home for tea, and did not detain him when he offered to leave early. "Don't forget about Rosie," he said at the door. "Tell her to forget the whole thing. You know, I mean, no hard feelings and all that."

"Don't you worry, dear. Look, you come to tea on Thursday. I'll tell you how Gran's getting on, and then we'll have that talk."

"Roll on Thursday! So long sweetheart."

Chapter 6

WHEN NANCY HAD WASHED UP the tea things, seen to the baby, finished her ironing, run out to telephone and make sure that Rose would be at home, banked up the fire, cooked Tom's dinner, served it and apologised for leaving him alone for the evening, she forced her aching feet into her outdoor shoes, sighed, "Poor old me! Always on the go! I could just do with an evening by the fire," and went out.

After a few minutes of chat she put the question directly to Rose, "What have you been up to with Jackie Agass?"

Rose gave her version of the affair, in an angry, defensive tone that was unfamiliar to Nancy. "I couldn't help it," she concluded, "he came worrying me. I put up with him. I don't know why. Old times' sake, I suppose. He seemed all at sea. I thought I'd help him. He had the usual queer ideas about me. He insulted me right and left. I can't imagine why I swallowed it. I even let him nag me into bed. That's shocked you, hasn't it, my poor innocent?"

"It's all in a lifetime."

"Why, why, why?" Rose said intensely, pressing the knuckles of her clenched fists together, "Why did I ever tolerate him? That's what I can't forgive myself. I've felt dirty and humiliated ever since." She went to the side table and poured a brandy for herself. "I won't offer you brandy. I know you don't like it. The kettle's boiling, there'll be tea in a minute. He couldn't touch me with his insults, but somehow he got right through my skin. Look at the way I acted. That's the devil of it! Losing my temper, like any little Lamb Street girl."

"Well, that's what you are, aren't you?"

"Oh, am I?" Rose cried. Her voice softened. "I've been wondering about myself ever since. All my confidence —" She broke off and exclaimed suddenly, "I *need* confidence!"

"Don't be too hard on him."

"Hard on him! I never want to see him again! Or any of those other stupid people!"

"You always set up to be all for them."

"Oh! —" Flushed and tense, she seemed to be blazing inwardly. "What did he send you for?"

"To clear things up. He thought it best not to come himself. Perhaps he was right."

"Oh, he was right!" Rose refilled her glass.

"You're drinking a lot, dear."

"Don't worry. I'm not on the bottle. It steadies me. It muddles other people's behaviour, it helps me control mine."

"He won't give you any more trouble, dear. All he wants is to settle down in peace with his Joycie. He says, let bygones be bygones."

"Thanks very much!" Rose's movements, in girlhood, had been like those of a bird in a cage, at once violent, delicate and unpredictable. At twenty-seven, she usually carried herself like a woman who was aware of her bodily resources and knew how to use them; sometimes languid and negligent, with the lazy grace of an animal; sometimes, moving about a room or walking in the street, stepping with long quick strides, straight to an objective. Occasionally Nancy had seen her display strange, contradictory touches of nervousness, fidgeting with the edge of a curtain, toying with the pages of a book. Now she was walking up and down, arms folded, looking down at her feet without ever facing Nancy's gaze, and adjusting her step to the pattern of the carpet. "Here's your tea," she said, as if glad of the diversion.

"Well, he means it, dear, and I think he's quite right.

Whatever's happened, it would be a sin for you and him to be enemies."

"He's not my enemy," Rose said vehemently, "I'm particular who I have for my enemies. And it's a little too late to kiss and make up."

"Why, dear? Surely it can't mean much to you to let me tell him everything's all right."

"Listen, Nancy. He humiliated me. It's all very well for him to toddle off back to his girl, and live happily ever after, and make grand, generous, careless gestures of peace towards me. You should have seen him when he was here. Did he tell you? He offered me everything. Everything!" She was play-acting derisively. "All his money. Everything he had. If I'd only be good to him. Well, he's had what he wanted, and now — well, I've taken him at his word, too."

"What do you mean?"

"Oh, he'll find out."

"Rose, you're not going to do something spiteful to that boy."

"I'm not *going* to do anything; and I'm never spiteful. I've just — well, he'll know soon enough. And when he does, tell him, then's the time to declare his peaceful intentions." She laughed. "If he wants to send me any goodwill messages then, I shall receive them with pleasure and return them with interest. And now, if you don't object, I'll have another drink. Oh, men," she exclaimed, "I wish we could do without them. I swore I'd never let one of them get the better of me again! And now, of all of them, it has to be this worm, this stupid ignorant lout, that does it, and without knowing it! Oh, it maddens me! It makes me sick with myself!"

She finished her brandy, stared down into the glass with compressed lips, and laughed. "Do you know what a man once told me? He said, when I'd had a couple of drinks, I was flashing and glacial and maddeningly attractive. Luckily he never saw me when I'd had half-a-dozen. I always give them the slip before then." Her voice

279

was higher in pitch and more liquid than usual, and she spoke with an unnatural clarity. Her eyes smiled secretively as she looked everywhere about the room except at Nancy. The flush over her cheekbones had deepened and the liquor seemed to have generated within her a ferment of excitement. "I don't like to babble. Not to men. I'd rather let them do it. I did enough of it when I was a girl, letting everyone see what a fool I was. Still, I can talk to you, Nancy, let off steam. Heart to heart, as they say in the women's weeklies. What angers me most of all is that that silly stupid lout, and others, it seems, should imagine that I had a weakness for men. Men, Nancy! I didn't look at a boy when I was a kid. I used to dash about with my brothers, and with Jack. But it never occurred to me to look at any others, and I never missed them. I think that even then I valued myself too much to throw myself away on someone else. Do you know, when I joined the Army — how old was I? Oh, nearly twenty — I was startled, I swear, Nancy, I was startled out of my wits when the men started running after me. I felt as if I'd been jerked out of a daydream. And what a collection they were! Clumsy great pudding-faced louts staring after me, sooty scrawny little boilermen making passes at me in the cookhouse, skinny long Romeos with greasy hair lolloping after me in the streets. Wherever I went I was leered at, whispered at, pawed at — oh, I loathed them, but for the first time in my life I couldn't help becoming conscious of them. It dawned on me for the first time that there really were two sexes in the world, and even if the men I saw didn't excite me, I must admit the idea did. And then I began to feel silly just going about with girls, although I was really quite happy with them. Even among my girl friends I began to feel at a disadvantage. I suppose I'd already learned, even if only through holding men off, that I could do what I liked with them, and it annoyed me when other girls, the silliest little sluts, were condescending towards me because they had men and I hadn't. And all of a sudden I wanted to be married. I was crazy with curiosity. I wanted a man as a sort of badge that I was grown up. And, poor me, who should come along and catch me in that state but Keith? Oh, what a ninny he was! And I married him! God!" She leaned over and refilled Nancy's teacup. "Well, after all, he was the first of his kind I'd ever met. Slim, good-looking in that weak intellectual way, smooth fair hair, and that pleasant, relaxed way of talking I'd never heard before. And he was educated. That excited me. He was nice to me, and I felt flattered. He didn't hound me or humiliate me with his attentions, and he made me feel very important. I used to purr with pride when he sat on a cushion at my feet. And then there was all that poetry he was always on about. That was new to me, and I got terribly excited about it. And he was full of politics, like Chris only much more extreme, and that, oh, that seemed to be what I'd been waiting for. It made the world ten times as big, and twenty times as exciting. Revolution! My chance to be Joan of Arc! — You know! I suppose I thought that it was from him that all the excitement came, instead of from these things he happened to bring my way. Anyway, God forgive me, I married him."

She stopped to light a cigarette and to wait for comment. Nancy, listening gravely, hands in lap, was not disposed to speak. Rose left her chair and adopted a proud pose by the mantelpiece. She glanced in the mirror and gave her own image a glowing, lingering smile of recognition. When she spoke again her eyes were rapt and admiring, those of a listener. "I was just about to ask you, Nance, what on earth you saw in marriage. Then I realised, I have no right to talk about marriage, really. Oh, we had two years of it, but we were in different units, we lived our own lives, and we only saw each other weekends and for a week every three months. And yet, if we'd lived together, that wouldn't have saved our marriage. It would have broken it all the sooner. I'm sure of that. I liked it at first. I liked it, and I was disappointed, both at once. I enjoyed love, and having someone's

281

company like that, and that madcap way for the first few weeks you make fools of yourselves all over the place, day and night, and you only laugh all the more if people see you. I liked walking into public places with him, and feeling, 'I'm the real thing now, a married woman.' I liked going back to camp, and being pestered with questions by the girls, and just smiling to myself and refusing to answer them. And yet it was a let-down. When you've imagined that love was going to be a sort of white-hot blaze, like the sun or something, the real thing is liable to be unimpressive. And" — she laughed, and took another quick peep at the mirror — "for all my disdain beforehand, whenever I had a taste of it, I wanted to go on for ever. He didn't, poor thing. So there it was. Not at all bad, at first, but nothing more. He was very childish. He liked to be petted. He was vain. He enjoyed little sulks and being mooed over to make him better. He told me all his troubles, from the cradle up, as if my function on earth was to be a sort of human cure for all his complexes and whatnot. He didn't know it, but for all his weakness and shyness he was horribly conceited. All he cared for was the sound of his own voice. I can't stand that. Can you?"

Nancy smiled at the floor.

"Yet at first," Rose swept on, "I even enjoyed mothering him. You know, I like to feel strong, and sort of in charge, and I did with him. And it did me good in other ways. I bloomed, as they say in books. Everyone told me how well I looked. When I was back in camp, away from him, I felt more capable than I ever had before. I was tremendously confident in a new way. There was nothing and there was nobody that could make me nervous. I was more popular and I knew it. I could brush men aside like flies. I was bubbling, bubbling with energy, all the time, as if I always had just those first couple of drinks thrilling away inside me. I got promoted, and I got more and more satisfaction out of my work. Now here's the funny thing. I suppose it was marriage had done that. Yet each time I went on leave and met him, I had less and less patience with him. It was on my own that I enjoyed being a married woman, not with him. It was through him that I learned my own capabilities, but learning them made me despise him. I began to lead an inner life of my own again. I had thoughts without revealing them to him, I plunged into activities in which he had no part, I troubled less and less to coddle him, and the more contempt I came to feel for him the less I tried to hide it. I suppose he couldn't help noticing — there were so many times when I was short with him, when I didn't trouble to answer his questions, when I was sarcastic — and he started to get horribly querulous and exacting, like a child. Oh, I couldn't stand that! The more he tried to make me pity him by acting that way, the more I regretted having married him. Then he tried to start quarrels. Only it didn't work because I wouldn't quarrel back. I'd just stare at him, as if I was wondering, then I'd look him up and down, from head to toe, letting him know I saw right through him, then I'd lose interest and turn away without a word, while he raved and cried and pleaded and I don't know what else.

"I remember, after one of these scenes, it — oh, it must have been well on in nineteen forty-four. I went back to camp, and I dumped my kit, and I went for a walk round the guns. I was in a heavy ack-ack battery by that time. And it came to me that night, I don't suppose I'd ever completely admitted it up till then, that I was sick and tired of this dreary marriage. You know, I was standing there, right under a three-seven gun, the crew were huddled around dozing, the whole site was flooded with moonlight, and suddenly I had one of those moments of *seeing* we all have from time to time. I can still remember the black shape of the gun, and the crew squatting around, not moving, their heads bowed — it was like a war memorial. Then I looked up at the sky. It had never seemed so immense, and so mysterious, and so full of moonlight. And I thought, 'There are millions of people asleep all around us, in our care. And if anything comes crawling across the sky to harm them, I' — she laid her hand on her breast — 'can reach up into the sky to protect them, I can find a target that's no bigger than a pin's head in all that space, I can guide a shell to hit it. Here am I, courageous and intelligent, and I don't need him or anyone else.' Well, I soon had my chance to get shot of him. He started going with another woman. Of course, I found out. I think he meant me to. I think he wanted to show me that he was a male, you know, to be competed for, and won back. I suppose he expected me to be surprised, and upset, and jealous. And then, poor wretch, I suppose he wanted from the other girl what he couldn't get from me, to be mothered when he felt little and adored when he felt big. Anyway, if I'd cared for him I wouldn't have broken with him over a thing like that, but I despised the pair of them. I felt that it was beneath my dignity to compete with such a woman for such a man. She was welcome to him. I seized the chance, and flabbergasted him by suing for divorce. He came and pleaded, he said it was me he loved, that I must forgive him, that these slips weren't important, that I mustn't take it to heart — as if I had! I couldn't have cared less! — but I just stared at him without saying a word, and walked away when he'd finished. And I got the divorce.

"Well, after that I said, 'Now for some peace and quiet. I shan't play the fool again in a hurry.' Do you know how long I kept away from them? Three months, that's all. A girl like me, who looks down on all the men she's met, do you know what she dreams of? Not of doing without them, she of all people can't do that. And certainly not of some vague, goody-goody equal partnership and all that rot. No, she dreams that somewhere there's a man so much bigger than her that she can gladly grovel at his feet. And I thought I'd found him. He was everything a silly girl could dream of, bomber pilot, big, handsome, every woman who saw him crazy about him, and me mad with pride because he'd picked on me. I felt as if he'd crowned me Queen. He used to take me out in his car, seventy miles an hour was about the usual speed. I used to love sitting there with the wind battering at my face, fancying that death was flashing past us at every bend of those twisty country lanes, watching him at the wheel calm and almost sleepy with confidence. He was extravagant with money in a reckless, unselfconscious way. He absolutely overwhelmed me with attentions, flowers, wonderful things he'd say in a strong, caressing kind of voice I'd never heard before, yet all so beautifully careless. If men only knew how loathsome they are when they're deferential! Not him, though, he always left such a wonderful impression that he didn't give a damn. Making love — oh, I can still hardly bear to talk about it! I hadn't known there was as much violence in the universe as I discovered inside myself, or as much humility. And in that, he was always my master, he was always so effortlessly in control of me. But most of all what attracted me was this tremendous indifference I spoke about just now, to what everyone, me included, thought of his actions. I worshipped him. With him I was meek, obedient, loving. I hung on his arm, I gloried in the little things he did for me in front of other people, I went to him like a tamed animal. I never made any demands on him. I never spoke about marriage. At that time I don't think I ever had a single thought about the future, or about the past either, for that matter. When I first heard of other women that he went with, I had a bit of a cry, then I laughed, and I even ended up by feeling rather proud of him. I was quite willing to allow them to him. You see, I was unshakeably sure that I ranked above them. It was, well, self-obvious that between them and him it couldn't possibly be like it was between me and him. Oh, I tried it on with him! I tried to be haughty with him, and I quarrelled — which made as little impression on him as my husband's tantrums had made on me — and I walked out on him every so often. But I always went back. I gloried in being humbled. I'd curl up to him like a kitten, with a wonderful feeling, not of forgiveness, that didn't come into it, but that *I* was being forgiven.

"This happened several times, but the strange thing was that it wasn't one of these quarrels that ended it. In fact, we'd just been reconciled. We'd laughed together, and he'd told me — oh, he could be very amusing! — what a bitch the other girl was, and all about her antics in bed. He went into a lot of detail, and I laughed like mad. And when we parted, we made a date for the next week in London. I came up to town and he didn't keep it. I wandered about, I had a few drinks, I got horribly wretched, I had a sudden idea that he'd been killed and rushed to 'phone his squadron, but they said, no, he'd gone up to town. I had some more drinks and promised myself a tremendous row with him. Then I thought of what a wonderful reconciliation we'd have. Oh, I was in a terrible state! I decided the best thing was to go home and cool off, but I couldn't. I started going the rounds of all the places he'd taken me to. I didn't care what sort of an ex-hibition I made of myself. And I walked into one — some stupid club — and there he was sitting at a table with this other girl. For a moment I thought I was going to rush up to them. Then she laughed. And it was exactly the same way I'd laughed when he was telling me about her. After that I couldn't face him. I was convinced that he was telling her jokes about me. I felt like killing myself. I drank a lot more. Then I flopped into a taxi and told the man to take me to Lamb Street. I wanted to go to mum and put my head in her lap and cry my eyes out. It's funny, while the taxi was taking me there, I knew, underneath all my rage and misery, that I'd go back to him. Yes, I'd have gone back to him, Nance. I couldn't have kept away. But when the taxi turned into Lamb Street, there were a lot of people talking on the pavements, and there were policemen, and where there should have been houses on our side of the street there was only the sky, and jagged bits of wall sticking up, and it was all roped off and — it was that night, Nancy. Our mum was dead. I sat down on the kerb and I had hysterics. Me, Nancy, of all people! I sat there and I screamed that God had punished me. And then Mick came along, and picked me up, and took me back to The Lamb, and put me to bed, and I lay there for a week, pretty well out of my mind." She stubbed her cigarette. "And I never went back to that man."

Rose sat still when she had finished, in an intent attitude, as if still affected by a play she had been watching. "Well," she said, "Don't sit there looking as if you're sorry for me."

"I'm not. I think I envy you."

"Oh, Nancy, don't be silly. You're the one to be envied."

"I'd sooner be you than me." Nancy sat up straight. "Oh, listen to me. I am stupid. I've got nothing to grumble about," she said with determination. She looked vaguely at Rose for a few moments, then she said, "Rosie dear, look, I'd like to tell him."

"Tell him what?"

"About you. And about our mum."

"Why?"

"Oh, there you go, hard as nails again. I thought you'd talked all your bitterness away."

Rose's face contracted in a stubborn pout. "No!"

"Rosie, please! Why bear malice?"

"Because I'm me."

"We could trust him."

"I say, no. He'd tell his girl, she'd tell her mother, and her mother would tell the whole street. No, no, no, no! Our mum didn't keep her secrets for us to advertise them. And as for myself, I'm not a free agent, and you know it."

"But he's like our brother."

"Not mine!"

Nancy shrugged her shoulders. "All right, dear. I won't argue if it's no use."

Rose put an arm round her sister's shoulders. "Come again, dear. I feel so good when you're here. It's the only time I can relax."

"You come round to us. This Sunday. Make a day of it."

Rose made a tired gesture. "I don't know. I'm so busy. There's one thing after another. I'd love to, though. It's so nice with you, and Tom, and playing with the baby. It's like another world. I'll try to come one Sunday another week, dear. I'll let you know beforehand." She accompanied Nancy down to the street, put her, despite her objections, into a cab, held her in a long parting embrace, and gave the driver a ten-shilling note for his fare.

Chapter 7

"GIRLS!" THE PROPRIETRESS of Madame Sophie's Salon stood at the foot of a dingy staircase and screamed, "Come down and look at the bride!" The Salon, where Joyce worked, was in a side street off Tottenham Court Road. Geographically, at least, her mother's description of her as 'a West End saleslady' was therefore accurate. Madame Sophie and Joyce looked after the shop. In the workroom above, Maureen reigned as 'forelady' over half-a-dozen pallid young girls. A Maltese family of seven occupied the second floor. Of the two rooms on the top floor, one was tenanted by an elderly waiter who rarely appeared during the girls' working hours, the other by a genial middle-aged prostitute whom everybody called Black Bess, and who usually, when she rose at three in the afternoon, came downstairs for a chat and a cup of tea with the girls before beginning her comings and goings.

The girls ceased the shrill, jerky chant in which they had been informing the world that "If a man could do continually, what he only does spasmodically, A man could be, indubitably, A wonderful, wonderful thing." A noise broke loose upon the stairway as if a flock of escaped parrots had caused a panic among a troupe of drunken tap-dancers and Madame Sophie, who had returned to the fitting-room, said complacently, "Ah, here they come."

It was the day after Jack's visit to the hospital. Joyce was in the tiny fitting-room behind the shop, having the third and penultimate fitting of her wedding dress. She stood in the electric glare before a tall mirror while Maureen assembled strips of white satin and puffs of tulle, pinning them about her until they took on the shape of the wedding dress.

The girls pushed into the room and crowded the doorway, uttering oohs and aahs of ecstasy. Joyce bridled with pride, turning back her hands and looking at the extended fingertips. One of the girls ran upstairs calling, "Bess! Bess! Maddalena! Come down and see the bride!"

"Oh!" Madame Sophie struck her breast with both fists. "A beauty! A duchess! So lovely! Such a figure! Pull your belly in, young lady." She beamed at the girls. "An artist our Maureen is, on my life! A nice broad flounce there, and no-one will see the belly!" Madame Sophie, swarthy, frizzy-haired and adorned with many bangles, looked like a fat old white-slaver, but although she was a merciless business woman she was a kindly employer, and had given Maureen time off to work on the dress.

Maureen, who loved making dresses more than anything else in life, spent not only part of her daily time but most of her evenings working on the dress. It was like a dream materialised to her. Its forty yards of tulle were covered with flower patterns of mother-of-pearl sequins — "Fourteen thousand," she muttered through a mouthful of pins, "and don't ask me how I know, 'cause I sewed 'em all on by hand, every one of 'em. Stop fidgeting!" Her whole family watched with pride the progress of the dress. Every evening she talked to them passionately about it for hours. She had bought her boyfriend an enormous jigsaw puzzle to keep him occupied till the dress was finished. It was less for Joyce's sake than for her own that she looked forward to the wedding day. Her work of art would be on exhibition, and she had already invited a large contingent of her friends to the church to see it.

Maddalena, a shrivelled little Maltese woman, wriggled in through the crush, clutching her latest baby to her. Bess followed, ushering two more of Maddalena's young. "There y'are," she said to them, "look at the pretty lady! Ain't she pretty? Now then, keep your jammy hands off, or you won't get your pennies from Auntie Bess." She smiled at Joyce. "Bless you, girl! You know what I wish you!" Maddalena screwed up her face and began to cry, rocking her baby violently against her breast. "Gawd!" she blubbered. "Like a poor-a leetle lamb! *Jesu- Giusepp'-e-Mari'!* He lucky the bugger he get a girl like that, ain' 'e?" A fifteen-year-old workgirl began to sniffle in sympathy. "I always cry when I see brides," she sobbed, "I can't help it!" "Lucky's the word, all right," Bess declared. She looked commandingly about her and boomed into the wailing and chattering that filled the little room, "Look what they get for seven-and-sixpence! And they don't appreciate it, none of 'em!"

"Lucky?" Madame Sophie screamed. "I should say so! Look at that backside! Look at that bosom! A bargain he's getting! Two for the price of one!"

"I'm not fat,"Joyce protested.

"Fat?" Sophie screeched. "Who says fat? Did I say fat? Did anybody hear me say fat? Is a swan fat? Is a firm red apple fat? Is a nice horse fat? Handsome, you are! Handsome!"

"Don't you fret, girl," Bess added loudly, "They like a nice arse. Mine's money in the bank to me."

Joyce looked down modestly and murmured, in friendly disapproval, "Oh, you are vulgar, Bess!" Maureen went on working absorbedly, taking no notice of the commotion. "Keep still!" She smacked Joyce's hand. "Leave it alone! You can touch it when it's yours."

"Ooh," one of the girls moaned, "you do look lovely. I bet I've seen more brides than anyone. I've seen hundreds. Every week I go to see the brides. Miles I go sometimes. Two or three in a day, more than once. And you're the prettiest." She giggled. "I bet you ain' 'alf excited. You excited, Joycie?"

"Course not," Joyce answered, looking haughty. She was madly excited. She was flushed and fuddled by the heat of the room. The gross praises of Bess and Sophie shocked and inflamed her. Her senses fed on the noisy adulation of the workgirls crowded around her, on the sight of Maddalena's face worshippingly upturned, and on her awareness of Maureen kneeling at her feet. She posed proudly and felt supreme.

"What's he like?" a new girl squealed. The others, who had seen Jack's photograph, broke out into a shrill babble of praise. Joy befogged Joyce's mind and pressed down on her chest like a great weight. The thrilling inside her was so unbearable that she wondered how she would be able to live through the even greater excitement of her wedding day. "Is he like Gregory Peck?" the new girl asked.

"No," Joyce said, "he's more the Spencer Tracy type." She had spoken without thinking. The words were a flash of revelation to her. Of course, that was it! The Spencer Tracy type, stocky and reliable! They always went back to Spencer Tracy after the better-looking ones had been found wanting! How stupid she had been, always to look at him with a sinking heart! Now that she could see him as Spencer Tracy, all his deficiencies were magically transformed into merits. He was tough, he was silent, he was heroic! Her voice burst forth, "Oh, he's wonderful! He was ever so brave in the war. He got all medals. They wanted him to be a captain, but he wouldn't leave his pals. He knows ever so much. He's ever so clever. He can't half kiss" — she tried to swallow what felt like a chip of ice in her throat — "oh, you know, an' all that. It makes you feel all, you know, oh" — she paused for breath again, and plunged on recklessly — "like all funny when he kisses you. You want to faint." She believed it. "And he doesn't say a lot. He just, like, he just whispers all lovely things. And his hair's all wavy and thick, and he's so strong, he's got great huge shoulders. He could make a fortune boxing, only I won't let him. I said, 'No,' and he said, 'All right, my love, your word will always be my law.' He bought me this dress. I mean, what girl ever has a wedding dress like this? He's got hundreds of pounds in the bank. Throws it about like water, he does. Of course, he can, he earns such a lot. He's in a big firm, shopfitters, all men under him. He's the boss's right-hand man, he runs the place really. Oh, I mean, if you knew what he earned every week! Only I mustn't tell you. He'd be cross."

She had withdrawn into herself. The gasps and broken cries of delight that filled the room when she stopped speaking, and the chatter that followed, meant nothing to her; and she had no eyes for anything but her own image in the mirror. Was this really Joyce Wakerell, this proud body smoothly sheathed in gleaming satin, veiled in clouds of gossamer tulle? In the last few weeks, as her marriage had crept nearer, a silent, secret madness had been born in her. Some mysterious climax of transformation had reversed her attitude to life. Bodily love, which she had thought of a year ago as the price of marriage, now appeared as its principal reward. She was more frightened than ever, but fright and eagerness had dissolved inseparably into the single beautiful torment that filled her day and night. She had tried to signal her feelings to Jack, and she felt dismayed and confused by his failure to respond. She knew that he wanted her, for had he not — she shivered at her own cowardice in having refused — previously entreated her to yield? She could only conclude that it was because he was a respectable chap. She was beside herself with curiosity about what lay ahead. She knew little about it, and she spent hours with Maureen whispering in frightened and eager surmise.

Madame Sophie shepherded the girls back to their work. Maddalena followed with her smaller flock. Bess said, "Ah, well, duty calls," and went off on her beat.

When Sophie returned, Joyce said, "Oh, it's no use, Soph, I can't stay any more today. Let me go home early. Please, dear! I'm so excited, I'm afraid I'll be sick."

Sophie agreed and Joyce hurried home, humming a song to herself. She wondered, on the way, if waiting was as hard for Jack as it was for her. She could not tell from his behaviour. He was affectionate but strangely docile and contented. She made a little grimace with her lower lip as she compared him with the picture she had painted to the girls. He was ceremoniously attentive to her, but he seemed lately to be living within himself, more quiet and thoughtful than she had thought it in his character to be. Perhaps it was the strain; or the weather. Perhaps she had offended him last weekend by shouting at Barmy. But she had apologised, and he had said that he understood. Brrr! That Barmy! Never mind! Good old Jack! She thought of his big shoulders and his ruddy, hard-hewn face. He respected her. Ah, well, he wouldn't have to respect her when they were married, and then it would be all right!

Jack would be home late this evening, for he was away on an outside job at Barnet, doing his first full day's work of the week. She decided to surprise him by changing into one of her weekend dresses. He would come home tired and grimy, and she would be waiting for him, at her best. She would give him his supper, produce a bottle of his favourite brown ale, warm his towel and have his slippers ready. She would light a fire in the parlour and they would go there afterward, to sprawl on the sofa, warm and lazy in the glow. If she embraced him he must surely feel all that was throbbing in her. She felt as if fingernails were scratching at her insides. She wanted to run and skip in the streets, to lock her fingertips round a lamp-post and swing at arms' length. She squealed aloud with exaltation, and people looked at her. Self-conscious, she composed her face and walked home with prim, rapid steps.

When she entered the house her mother said, "You're early. What's up? Aren't you well?"

"I'm O.K.," Joyce answered gaily, "I had the most wonderful, glorious fitting. Oh, mum, the dress is the most marvellous thing on earth! You must come next time. The girls went mad. And I didn't feel like doing any more, so Sophie let me off."

"Good, you'll have time to wring out the washing. Here, where are you off to?"

Joyce, whirling out through the door like a dancer going offstage, paused and half-sang, "Put the bath on. No wringing today." She ran thunderously upstairs.

"What's come over the girl?" Mrs. Wakerell muttered. "First time she's ever said no to me in her life." She followed to the door and shouted, "There's a letter come. In a big envelope. I put it on the front room table. It's addressed to Jackie."

"I suppose it's from the bank. He asked them for a statement of the account," Joyce called, as she leaned over the bath. She was astonished at the ease with which she had refused to obey an order of her mother's, rapturous at the discovery that her own individuality was strong enough to burst out of its chrysalis. Life was a wonderful sunlight in which to soar freely. She surrendered herself to the enervating warmth of the bath, sliding into a lucent world of overheated dream, released from her body yet voluptuously aware of it as the soft weight of the water pressed upon her flesh and, answering her languid movements, caressed her flanks with underwater eddies.

When she emerged from the bath she felt as if her own hands and eyes were those of her lover. She wiped steam from the mirror and looked with pride at herself. It gave her pleasure to touch herself, to feel the rough bite of the towel, to shimmy into her dress, to roll her stockings up her legs, and to comb her hair. Her joy increased, and with it an icy fright at her joy that only made the joy itself more piquant. She finished her lingering labours with cream, powder, scent and lipstick, and surveyed the results with satisfaction.

She returned to the kitchen. Her mother said, "What's all this in aid off? Going in for a beauty contest?"

Joyce laughed, poured a cup of tea for herself and entered into a detailed account of what had taken place at the fitting. When she had finished, she said, "I'll tell you what I'll do. I'll dust the front room for you. It won't make me untidy, and I'm using the room tonight, anyway."

She went into the front room, noticed the big buff envelope on the table, put her duster down and tore at the thick manila paper. She extracted a bundle of papers, and glanced respectfully at the heading, with the name of the bank and a coat of arms impressively printed in blue, above the words, "In account with JOHN AGASS, ESQ." She felt flattered at handling so official and important-looking a document. She looked down the columns of figures, frowning and biting her lower lip as she failed to make sense of them, lost interest and stuffed the papers back into the envelope.

As she did so, a bundle of used cheques slid from between the folded sheets and scattered to the floor. She stooped to pick them up, looking idly at them. One of them caught her eye. She straightened her back and stood looking at the cheque for a long time. Her face became blank and impassive, as it always was when she was struggling to think. Her heart began to beat violently, and she could feel the lower part of her face quivering. She put the cheque into the pocket of her apron, took out her handkerchief and wiped her nose carefully. She folded her arms and stood for a long time by the table, her breathing long and powerful, her face heavy and unrevealing except for the nervous flickering of her eyes and the lights of purpose and recollection that flared and disappeared in them, damped down by thought.

She went upstairs, her step heavy and deliberative, entered Jack's bedroom and searched through the drawers of his dressing-table. She scrutinised every piece of paper that she found, opened his cheque book and turned over the stubs. She sat at the dressing-table for a while, sucking her lips. Then she strode downstairs, put on an overall, swept past her astonished mother into the scullery and began to work the mangle thunderously.

Mrs. Wakerell stood in the doorway staring at her daughter. Joyce, her head bowed, her lowered lids giving her a blind, stubborn expression, ignored her mother's questions and drove the big wheel of the mangle round and round. The intermittent rumble answered for her, a roar of challenge, keeping her mother's voice from her. Joyce looked up to find that she was alone. There was a liquid glitter in her eyes which she wiped away with the back of her hand. She went on with her work, forcing thick wads of sodden clothing between the rollers as if punishing them, grunting with anger and effort as she threw her whole weight upon the wheel handle. She turned the wheel with tireless vigour, seeming to generate strength in herself instead of expending it. The wheel slowed. The rumbling ceased. Joyce leaned forward in thought, resting her chin on the knuckles of her two hands grasping the handle. She took the overall off, wiped her hands and went back to the parlour. As she passed through the kitchen her mother asked, "What was the letter? Anything important?" Joyce spoke for the first time. "For Jack. It's nothing."

She wandered about the room, dusting the furniture. She noticed in the mirror that her hair and make-up were spoiled, and tidied herself. Then, leaving the door open, she sat by the table and waited.

Her father came in from work. She twitched a smile of recognition in answer to his greeting, but did not speak or move. She sat as still as a spider in the web, giving no sign of her feelings except for her carefully-controlled breathing. Twenty minutes later Jack came in.

"Hallo, duck," he said, "Here, you do look a treat! Are you courting?"

She permitted herself a slight smile.

"What you sitting in there for, in the cold?"

She glanced over her shoulder. She had forgotten to light the fire. She did not feel cold. She indicated the letter, and said quietly, "This came for you."

He came into the room and kissed her lightly on the cheek. She could not help lifting her face slightly to his kiss; otherwise she remained still, her hands in her lap.

"You're freezing cold, girl. Your cheek's like marble."

The kiss, the unaffected warmth in his voice, the solicitude, were all new things in him, part of the relaxed happiness with which he had shone in the last few days. He had lost his fidgety tension. He seemed to move about the house with a new sense of belonging, of achievement. He would look at her with calm, unanxious eyes, and in a room full of other people he would smile at her for no apparent reason, so that she had to smile back, feeling like the sharer of some mischievous secret. She had not understood this new turn in his behaviour, but she had accepted it, for she had the gift of accepting everything as it came and treating it as natural and inevitable. Now, however, it made her go cold with grief. It clashed with all that she had just discovered, with all her seething thoughts, and made her confusion worse. She had thought she knew him: she had summed him up as a man without the wit to deceive. He had seemed so natural. He seemed so natural now. She looked at him with wide, shadowed eyes, and shivered for a moment.

"Look, you're shivering all over." He rested his arm along her shoulders. "Sitting there day-dreaming, like a tit in a trance! Come on, love! Your mum's got the supper on. Can't you smell those onions?"

She was completely lost. She had no idea where she was, or what to do. This was worse than a bad dream. There was the man standing over her, happy and appealing, and there was the monster in her mind. How could they be the same person? In the fog of her mind, she could not find a policy, but she stumbled on principles that she must cling to. She did not know why, for she was incapable of ordered thought, but she knew that she must cling to them to the death. She must not crumple. She must not surrender. She must not go to her mother. She must not quarrel. She asked quietly, "Aren't you going to look at this?"

"Oh." His glance did not even linger on the envelope. "From the bank. What's with the onions? Sausages?"

"Pork sausages. Let's look at it now."

"Well, come in the kitchen and get warm."

"No." The sudden snapping in her voice made him look at her. She steadied herself. "In here."

He pulled the papers out of the envelope. "Want to count up the Agass millions, eh? All right, let's have a look at it."

She must not quarrel. She did not know why, but as she fought her cold anger, she knew that she must not quarrel. She did not know what was going to happen in the next few minutes, but instinct told her that to remain calm was to cast him down. Each time he spoke to her she did not know what she was going to reply until she opened her mouth; but she gripped her anger tight and let instinct guide her. "Can you see what the balance is?"

"Ah." His mouth was open. He was looking at the bank sheet with puzzled but innocent eyes. She could not doubt their innocence, and this struck a sudden doubt into her anger. He had been so natural these last few days, so eager, so happy to be at her side! Was she right to strike him down? What was she destroying? Doubt, unresolved, only increased the stifling, chilled anger.

"I thought we had more than that," she said calmly. "A hundred and ninety-four. I thought we had twice that much."

"We have. Three hundred quid at least," he said in a vague, pondering voice, looking irresolutely up and down the sheet. He folded it to put it away. "Some mistake, I reckon. They do make mistakes. The money's all right, anyway. You can count on that. Come on inside. I'm starving."

"Count it up."

"Oh, it'll wait. I'll go round to the bank in the morning, they'll put it right. What's up with you, Joycie, sitting there like the Rock of Ages?"

"Count up the cheques."

"Here!" He tried to be jovially commanding. "When I say move, move! You have got the wind up, girl! Money's all right in the bank. It don't melt."

"Doesn't it?"

He sighed, and began to count through the cheques. "Mistake, all right."

She took the slip of paper from her pocket and handed it to him. "Add this one in."

He looked at it for a long time. He raised his eyes and looked, brooding, at her.

"One hundred pounds," she said evenly. "Made out to Rose Hogarth. That brings the total out right, doesn't it?"

"You've got it all worked out, haven't you?" he muttered. "Jury's brought in the verdict already, eh?"

She did not answer. The mental tension was becoming unbearable in her, but she was surprised to find that with it came a bodily lassitude that helped her to maintain her placid, threatening pose.

"Bitch," he muttered. "The rotten bitch!"

The beginnings of scorn glowed in her eyes, deceptively like a smile. "Seen her often?"

He shook his head, and spoke through a throat full of phlegm. "You don't understand."

"No?" Her voice was low, and she knew that to him it sounded amused.

"No you don't!"

"Don't shout!" She waited.

He made a few little hunted movements about the room. "I seen her a few times. It's all over. You don't understand. It's — Oh, you don't, that's all!"

"If you're going to cry, here's my hankie."

"Oh, for God's sake! Don't come that lark with me! I know what you want to say — say it!"

She kept herself quiet. A vengeful happiness filled her. It had no relation to her previous emotions, or to her intentions. It was simply an exultation that she — Joyce Wakerell! — was able to play this part. She could have wished for an audience. She felt supreme, imperial. She felt as if there *were* an audience. She was willing to throw her whole life away to enjoy the unexpected, undreamed-of ecstasy of acting this moment out. Someone — a man — was squirming before her. She was filled with wonder at herself. She was not crying! She was not raving at him! She had not run to her mother! She was not lost for words! All her hopes had collapsed, and she could behave like this! "There's nothing for me to say. Suppose you tell *me.*"

"I —" He paced away, then back to her, and smote his left fist against his thigh. "I never give her this. I don't know how she got it. She's done me. I never thought she'd — Oh, I should have expected it! Tart like that, she's used to robbing fellers blind."

"Then we can go to the police."

"Police? Why?"

"Because you never gave it to her."

"Police? Joycie, leave us alone. You don't know how I'm feeling. I never knew people were like this."

The anguish in his face did not touch her. "You break my heart."

"I can't — Look, I can't go to the police. I give it to her. I mean, I did and I didn't. It was a blank cheque. I forgot all about it. I — Oh, there's nothing I can do about it. I can't explain now. Give us an hour. I feel as if the bloody world was coming to bits. I mean, after, I'll tell you all about it, afterwards I will."

She sat as if she had not heard him. She knew that her calm, stubborn appearance was not only maddening him but was shattering his entire understanding of her. She was a woman, and it was her best weapon, this bovine obduracy. "Tell me," she said, "tell me about this other money you drew out without my knowing. All those fivers I found the stubs for in your cheque book. Did you spend them on her? Did you get your money's-worth?"

"Oh!" It was a cry of despair. He clenched his fists helplessly. "You don't know! You don't know!"

"I suppose I'm jumping to conclusions?"

"Yes, you are!"

"I told you not to shout. And you didn't get your money's-worth?"

"No, I didn't!"

"Now this —" She produced another piece of paper from her pocket. "This letter is interesting. 'My dear Jack, I was in such a hurry to grab that taxi the other night before it got away, that I didn't have time to thank you properly for a lovely evening. Night clubs and champagne! What a man of the world our Jackie Agass has become! Lamb Street ought to know! The dinner-dance was nice, too. Now, Jack, let's face it. We haven't really had that heart-to-heart, have we? Don't let's put it off any more. Let's have a nice quiet evening next time and put our cards on the table. I know where we can go, where no-one will disturb us. Ring me, and we'll fix it. All my love, Rose.'"

"Where'd you get that?"

"Where do you think?"

"Been in my room spying, eh?"

She smiled. "And you tell me you didn't get your money's-worth? Yet you thought this was worth keeping. There must be some sweet memories attached to it. Jackie Agass, man of the world. "Night clubs and champagne... the dinner-dance was nice, too." You never took me to any of those places. She must have something that I haven't got. Or perhaps she's just freer with it. Oh, well, I hope you enjoyed yourself —" her voice flamed momentarily — "on our money."

"Your money's safe! Hundred quid was all you put in. You can have it any time you like."

"Thank you for nothing. And what about our home?"

"Our home?"

"The money for our home. Remember? It used to mean something to you."

"I'll make it up, Joycie. Look, I can't argue with you now. I know it looks bad, but let me get my head clear —

please! — and then let me try to tell you."

"There's only one thing I want you to do, and that's to get out."

"Get out?"

She was still able to speak slowly and quietly. "Mr. Echo today, aren't you? Pack your bags and get out. As soon as you like. You're no use to me any more."

"You're daft!"

"Thank you. Now get out."

"Joycie, you can't do this! You're not in your right mind. Not now, you can't. Joyce, I've been through a lot. You don't know a thing about it. But it's all right now. I've never felt so good as I did these last few days. Everything had started to be all right between us. I felt it. You must have felt it, too. We were just starting —" He looked down at her heavy, indifferent face, and his voice died away.

She remained silent.

"Are you prepared to make a fool of yourself?" His voice was harsh and loud with bitterness. "In front of all the neighbours? In front of all your friends? Breaking it off at this time of day? You'll have some explaining to do, won't you? And another thing, you might have to wait a bit, you know, before you get another chance. If you get another chance!"

She lifted up her head as if it were very heavy, and looked at him with unfamiliar, glittering eyes. "That's my business. I've made a fool of myself already. Grovelling to you. 'Yes, dear. No, dear. Don't you like this hat, dear? Then I won't wear it.' I'll tell you something you didn't know, Jack Agass. I've got pride. You didn't know that. As far as I can see, no-one has ever known it. But I have, and I'd rather keep it than keep you." She lowered her head. "Now go away."

"Not likely! Wild horses wouldn't get me out of this house. I'm fed up with it! I've never had a life of my own, not a proper one. All these years, wandering about like some old moggy in the back-yards. I'm not having any more of that. There's only four weeks between me and a home of my own, and I'm not letting that go down the pan now, not for you or no-one." She did not speak. He made a last attempt to strike a response from her. "You see what your mum says. Go on! You ask your Mum. See what she tells you to do."

"Ha!" For a moment she thought her hysteria was going to burst out of her; then she was under control again. She said, in an even, grating voice, "I know her advice. A girl should marry any man that'll have her. She'd marry me off to a hunchbacked pansy with a glass eye, she would, and expect me to thank her. You're leavings," she said vengefully, "you're somebody's leavings, and I don't want you. Go away."

There was a long pause.

"Well, I don't know,"Jack sighed. "I feel too done up to carry on with this kind of a shindy. It's a waste of breath arguing with you now. You'll change your mind. We'll talk later."

"Do me a favour and don't try."

"I've got a lot more to say to you, my girl. You're all wet if you think I'm giving up that easy."

She made a pout of indifference. "Suit yourself. I can't throw you out. But you'll find me deaf, dumb and blind from now on."

"You're daft," Jack said despondently. "I'm going to wash now. I'll talk to you when you're in your right mind."

She maintained her attitude of disdainful serenity until he had gone. When the door closed, there was a last mad flare of triumph in her. Then, in a flash, the illusion of victory vanished, and the unseeing anger died. Her mood had turned instantaneously into its opposite, a crushing sense of defeat and loneliness. She relaxed. Her body had been slack and tired all the time, yet it was aching with strain. She went out quietly into the hall, fearful that her mother might be lying in wait to find out what had been happening. She had managed to carry off her scene with Jack, but she knew that it was beyond her to face another minute of coherent conversation. All that had happened was beyond her understanding, and now she was lost. She ran up to her room, locked herself in, collapsed on to the bed and went off into a quiet fit of hysterics.

Part 5

Chapter 1

IT WAS SATURDAY AFTERNOON, and Lamb Street was quiet. A couple of hours earlier all its menfolk had departed, accompanied by some of the younger women and a horde of small boys who, even though it was November the Fifth — Guy Fawkes' Day — had abandoned the heap of timber they were assembling on the building site for the evening's bonfire and had joined in the pilgrimage. From every street in the borough contingents had set forth at the same time, every side turning contributing its trickle to the flow of people that streamed along Upper Street, thickened into black tides as it poured through Highbury and, reinforced by thousands of men and women coming from other directions, surged in a great crowd at the approaches to the Arsenal Football Stadium.

It was more than a mere desire for diversion that brought these masses of people together. They were bound by a fervour, a spirit of community almost religious in its intensity; it showed in their faces as they smiled at each other, stranger to stranger, and in their voices as they exchanged comments; as it must have shown itself in the faces and voices of ancient Greeks thronging to their festive Games or to the ritual performances at their vast theatres. These people lived in little groups, some recognizing no constant loyalty outside the household, few having any ties outside the street. The outside world meant nothing to them except when, on some occasion, a wider allegiance stirred them; the General Strike, when their class called to them and they responded, whether they agreed with the strike or not, and regardless of the cost to themselves; or the war when, with invasion threatening, they became aware of their country and rose nobly to its defence. At all other times they distrusted and feared everyone in the world but their own personal friends. They hated no-one in particular, but they were prepared, with a little persuasion, to hate Irishmen, Welshmen, Jews, Germans, Russians, Americans, people who talked in any other accent than their own, people who lived in more prosperous districts and people who lived in poorer districts. Their need for a larger unity, but one not too large to understand, was fulfilled by their football team. A common interest in it bound together a hundred thousand people. Within the borough, a man could strike up a conversation about it with any passer-by; their faces would light up, their voices would become eager, and in a few minutes they would be like old friends. There was an excitement in the clatter of feet all walking in the same direction, in the sight of the vast, packed stadium, in feeling the surge of all these thousands of friends against one's shoulders, in the appearance of the eleven splendid young men — the sons and champions of the whole community — and in joining in the inspiring, unifying roar that greeted their feats. Every man in Islington felt bigger and better when the Arsenal won a game.

Mr. Wakerell and Jack had gone to the match. Mrs. Wakerell, in the meantime, was preparing for a weekly ritual that was almost as important as the game: Saturday afternoon tea. She banked up the kitchen fire, laid a clean tablecloth, put fresh flowers in the vase and set out a large cream cake and a plate of pastries. Kippers lay in the pan on the gas stove, to be fried as soon as the men came in.

Joyce helped her, but she did not speak to her mother, pushing to and fro past her with face averted. Joyce's whole appearance had changed in the last three days. Throughout that time she had been ill with rage and misery; violently, physically ill. Her head throbbed incessantly with pain and confusion. She had fits of dizziness, and there were times when she could not see

310

clearly. She vomited after meals, felt tired all the time, and when people spoke to her their voices seemed to come from far away. Grief had made her ugly. Her eyes were red, her skin, turned dark and muddy in hue, was blotched and greasy. The lustre had gone from her hair, which looked coarse and obviously bleached, with dark streaks at the roots. She wore her glasses, blinking malignantly through them at everyone who approached her, and she moved about with a neglectful, self-pitying lassitude that made her look clumsy and gross.

She had not been to work since her quarrel with Jack. Maureen had called and had been sent packing with a few muttered and false excuses. Joyce had spent most of the time in her room, lying across her bed. When she came downstairs she behaved like an animal at bay, snarling and shrinking back whenever anyone spoke to her. Jack had tried repeatedly to approach her. Each time she had shut her eyes, pressed her lips together and turned her back on him. He had pleaded across the table, told her a long story about himself and Rose, begged her to think of the future, pointed out that the money she had entrusted to him was still in the bank for her to draw if she wanted it, urged her to 'be a sport', followed her up to her room and even pushed a letter (which she had torn up) under her door. He had put his case to her parents and Mrs. Wakerell, after reviling him, had promised him her support. This had taken the form of following Joyce about the house with such arguments as, "If you play your cards right, my girl, you'll never have any more trouble with him. Break his spirit, that's what I say. Now's the time to do it," or, "What about all that stuff in your cupboard? It's worth a fortune. As long as you've got it, you've got him where you want him," or, "Don't be a little fool! What right have you got to be so particular?" Joyce had faced each verbal assault in a rigid posture of defiance, her head tilted back, her face pinched and unmoving, with only an occasional flash of dissent in her eyes to show that her mother's words were reaching her.

311

Mr. Wakerell had tried, in a quiet, shamefaced way, to talk to her. Joyce liked him, but she had never been able to penetrate his shyness nor he to break out of it to her. She would listen, her expression patient, and sometimes she would glance up quickly as if about to speak; but the moment would pass unfulfilled; she would turn away and her father would break off, abashed, and retire behind his seed catalogue.

Behind the mask of obstinacy which Joyce wore, lay the real cause of her suffering, the confusion with which she was filled. She was frightened by what she had done. She was appalled at the thought of losing a chance of marriage. She wanted, as much as Jack did, to be settled and to have her own home. In the past week her passions, long dormant, had been inflamed, all her dreams had been let loose. She had been close to independence, had seen herself free of her mother at last, standing on her own feet, a 'somebody', a woman to be respected. She had let everybody see it; she had betrayed herself, with her elation, her boasts, her frantic attentions to her lover. How could she avoid disgrace, and secure the prize so nearly won?

But how, on the other hand, could she make it up with Jack? She was tormented by a violence of character which no-one had ever suspected. It had always hurt her to be treated as a dull, obedient nonentity, her secret self insulted by even the most well-meaning gestures of those around her. She had always nursed her pride as a secret possession, throughout the years of servitude to her mother, throughout her humiliations with men. Now that she had publicly asserted her pride she could not betray it. It had brought her to life. She wanted to make peace, but the more Jack and her mother pressed her, the more she dreaded doing anything that might appear as bowing the knee to them.

To be happy, to be a real woman, she needed Jack. But to be happy, to be a real woman with Jack, she needed to secure some recognition of her pride. This purpose lived only in her emotions. She had not been able to define it in the form of thought, and when she muttered, aware of it only as an expression of anger, "I'll show him!" she did not know what she wanted to show him, or how.

Imprisoned within her clumsy and inarticulate bodily self, she was tortured by this seemingly insoluble conflict. Once again she became aware how undeveloped she was, both mentally and emotionally. Her anger and illness were fed still more by shame at her inability to cope with a crisis. It was uncertainty that made her shut herself up in her room, shrink from everyone else, and work herself up, for hour after hour, into rages and fantasies that sometimes drove her thoughts beyond the frontiers of reason. She told herself, 'I can't go on like this', but, seeing no way to save herself or even to relieve the explosive gathering of emotion in her, she continued to drift.

Today the dull pain had flared up into a new fury. There had been some hope for her in the thought that Jack was suffering as she was, even though she did not know how to reach out to him. But this afternoon he had brightened up and gone to the football match with her father. How could he have done such a thing? The outside world no longer existed for her, and she could not understand why it should exist for him. If it did, surely it proved that he still did not take her seriously, that he regarded her present mood as nothing but petty tantrums, and that if she made any gesture to him he would only accept it as the surrender of an inferior, a submission that would condemn her to lifelong indignity. She felt trapped.

Jack and Mr. Wakerell were in high spirits when they came in. They greeted the womenfolk noisily and were both too happy to pay attention to Joyce's hostile stare. "What a game!" Jack said. "Eleventh on the trot they've won this season. Hoo! No stoppin' 'em now!"

They took their places at the table. Jack smote his hands together. "Kippers and cream cake! That's the

313

kiddie! I'm just in the mood for a blowout. Here" — he addressed Joyce, refusing to recognize her indifference — "you ought ha' been there, Joycie. What a finish? One each and three minutes to go. Quiet? I tell you, I'd ha' died of fright if a bloody sparrow 'ad sneezed. Then all of a sudden there's a bundle round the goal mouth and —wallop! — old McPherson heads the ball in. Talk about noise! Sixty thousand people tearin' their tonsils out and jiggin' about as if it was raining pound notes. Then the final whistle blows. Phew, right in the nick of time that winning goal, I can tell you."

"Lovely grub!" Mr. Wakerell rumbled, referring to the game, not to the meal.

Joyce sat upright, staring down into her teacup.

Jack was still grinning. "Here, come on, girl. Your tongue'll go mouldy if you don't give it an airing. What about calling it evens and coming out with us tonight? Ah, come on, we can watch the bonfire, have a bit of a lark over there, then we can go up the pictures for the last house." There was no reply. "Ah, come on, give us a smile. They ain't rationed, you know."

Joyce looked up, her eyes dilated in an alarmed, wondering expression. She stared at Jack for some seconds and he, stubbornly maintaining his grin, stared back. She lowered her eyelids, and her face contracted again. Jack pulled a face expressive of defeat, and concentrated on the bones of his kipper. They went on with the meal in silence. Jack offered her the pepper cruet. She ignored him. A moment later he said, "Vinegar?" She gave no sign that she had heard.

Her mother screamed, "Say something, you little bitch!"

Joyce blinked, as if at a spasm of pain, recovered herself and continued to sit upright. A slight tremor became visible beneath the neckline of her dress.

"You think too much of yourself," Mrs. Wakerell shrilled, "you're not too old to get my hand across your face, you know!"

Joyce looked quickly about her. Her mother's bulk was

between her and the door. She sat trembling, staring straight in front of her with an obstinate, suffering look.

Jack muttered, "Leave her alone." Mrs. Wakerell, invaded by a maudlin rage, did not heed him, and moaned, "I'm sure I don't deserve a daughter like this."

Joyce said softly, "Shut up!"

"Listen to the way she talks to her own mother! After all the years I've slaved for her!"

Joyce's voice was more intense but no louder than before. "For God's sake, shut up. I'm warning you!"

"She treats me as if I was dirt beneath her feet. She — Joycie!"

Joyce sprang to her feet, seized the edge of the tablecloth and swept it across the table in a single violent flurry. Mrs. Wakerell's scream, the exclamations of the men and the backward crash of their chairs mingled with the noise of breaking china as knives, forks, food, crockery and flowers swept to the floor. Joyce cried, "*Now* shut up!" and stood shaking from head to foot with the edge of the cloth still in her paralysed grasp. She stared at the wreckage in astonishment until, understanding what she had done, she raised her head and faced the others in agonised defiance. She was full of tears but could not cry. She was terrified but unable to flee.

Mrs. Wakerell uttered a prolonged, high wail of hysteria, advanced on Joyce and began to slap her face hard, using the front and back of her hand in alternate blows. She whimpered and wept as she did so, spitting insults at Joyce in a hurt, childlike voice. Joyce remained rigid, her head tilted back, taking the slaps as if she could not feel them.

Mr. Wakerell pulled his wife away and pushed her into a chair, saying, "Here, that's enough! You're worse than she is." Mrs. Wakerell subsided into a loud and tearful monologue of self-pity.

Jack was looking at Joyce with a gentle, questioning expression that surprised her. He said, "All right, Joycie. I'm sorry. This is all my fault. I know when I'm licked. I'll clear out, you won't have to worry any more."

"You keep your mouth shut, boy." Both Jack and Joyce, lost for a moment in a strange colloquy of the eyes which neither of them could understand, were startled by Mr. Wakerell's intervention. In his deep, ox-like voice, he went on, "You go and change your trousers. Talk afterwards. You're sopping wet with tea."

Jack continued to study Joyce. He appeared puzzled by the faint emanation of appeal that her bodily attitude suggested. Then the look of resignation came into his face again, and he grimaced. "I'm not worried about a drop o' tea spilled over me." He uttered a shaky laugh. "I knew you had it in for me, Joycie, but I didn't dream you hated me. Not like this." Joyce, looking piteous, make a little protesting movement of the hands, but did not speak. Mr. Wakerell was watching them both while, with his handkerchief, he at once comforted his wife and muffled her complaints.

"Well," Jack said, "I'm all right, anyway. If I'm not wanted here I know where I am welcome. Back in the bloody Army. At least I'll know where I am there. I won't go mucking things up for myself and everyone else. I'll have bloody mates I can count on, and a bloody job to get on with."

"Don't be a fool," Mr. Wakerell said, "You'll sign your life away while you're out of your wits."

There was a knock at the street door.

"Funny when you come to think of it," Jack said, "I suppose they'll shove me off to Malaya or somewhere, chase some poor sod round the jungle that never done me no harm. Well, I feel like sticking a bayonet up someone's jacksey. Someone's bad luck, that's all. All right —" There had been another knock — "I'll go."

Joyce and her father watched in silence while he went out. They heard him speaking at the street door. Voices were raised, then Jack slammed the door, came back alone into the hall and went up to his room.

Mr. Wakerell said, "You know, you've done it all wrong,

316

girl."

Joyce looked imploringly at him and murmured, "I know." She drew her breath and forced out the words, "Good riddance to bad rubbish! Him and his football!" Her voice broke. "All he thinks of."

Mrs. Wakerell had recovered sufficiently to begin railing at her daughter again. Mr. Wakerell said, "Be quiet, Liz. You go and fill the kettle again, get some more tea on." He pushed her into the scullery. "Go on, do as I tell you."

He said to Joyce, "You're a funny kid, aren't you? You're like me. That's why she doesn't understand you. You live inside yourself. You can't say what you want to, so you go and say the opposite."

Joyce muttered, "Clever all of a sudden."

"Not all of a sudden. Not so clever, either, for that matter. Or I'd have known what to say before now. But I didn't, no more than you did. You ought to understand that, Joycie."

She refused to meet his eyes.

"And here we are, strangers, after all these years. When I do try and get a word in edgeways, I suppose you think I'm interfering."

She shook her head violently, still not looking at him. He rested his hand on her arm, and she did not shrink from it. "There," he said, "you just stay still and listen. That boy's all right, take my word for it. I had a long talk with him, coming back from the match. I knew it was there, all bottled up. He kept on wanting to speak, but I left him alone, and then on the way back it all come out with a rush. I tell you, he's broken-hearted. He reckons he's just about done for. Ever since he come back, everything's been strange, he felt out of it, and in the end he blew up. That's all it was with this woman. It'll be the finish of him if he gives up and runs off now. He'll be a drifter for the rest of his life."

Joyce let her arm press a little closer to his hand, but she whispered, "Sorry for himself, that's all."

"And what about you? I saw the way you were looking at him before. You're eating yourself up with pride and misery. There's the pair of you suffering, and for what reason I don't know." He slipped his hand down to her wrist and grasped it. "Come on, Joycie. Come with me."

She pulled her arm away. "Oh, what's the use? If you'd all left me in peace instead of pushing me around I might have been able to think what to do."

He took her hand again. "Perhaps you're right. We haven't been much help. But never mind that now. Come on upstairs with me."

"What for?"

"You'll find out. Come with me." She resisted, but did not pull her hand away. "You think I don't know you," he said. "We've never said a word that mattered to each other in all our lives, have we? But I'm not such a fool as I look, Joycie. I know why you did that." He indicated the wreckage on the floor. "You were at your wits' end. If you'd been sure of yourself — I mean, if you'd really wanted nothing else but to see the back of him, you'd never have had to do it. We're a funny lot. When we can't sort it out in words we go and bust something up for fear of getting busted up ourselves. I smashed a chair up myself once." He smiled sombrely. "With my bare hands. That's shook you, eh? The last one to do his nut, your dozy old dad, eh? I've had my troubles, though. More like yours than you think. I found out something once that sent me crackers for a bit. Never mind what it was, it wouldn't do you any good to know. I rampaged around in this kitchen, ready to do murder I was. Then I picked up a chair and pulled it to bits. I ripped it apart and stamped on the bits till there wasn't enough left to plug a rathole with. And then I sat down, I was all weak and shaking, sweating like a pig I was, and I took a good deep breath and I thought, 'That's better. Now I must think it all out.' And I decided, live and let live. Anything for a quiet life. None of us is a prize packet. We expect others to put up with us, so it stands to reason we've got to put up with them, for

318

all their faults. I've managed to make the best of it ever since. Now you come on upstairs to his room and see what we can do about it."

She shook her head, fiercely but with longing.

"You won't regret it, girl."

"Oh, no. I can't. I'd rather die than face him now."

"Come on, love. You're a coward if you let your pride frighten you. Come on, I'll come with you."

"And give us another lecture?"

"I shan't come in. I'll put you in through that door and shut it from the outside."

She clutched his hand and looked up at him like a child. "But what'll I say?"

"It's my guess you won't say anything. The state you two are in, the pair of you, you'll be surprised what'll happen as soon as you take a good look at each other. I shall probably hear a lot of boo-hooing through the door, and then I'll know it's all right." He smiled. "It's marvellous what a tonic a good cry can be."

She made a helpless, repentant gesture towards the mess on the floor.

"Never mind that," he said. "Your mother can clear that up. It'll do her good."

She replied with a pallid, painful smile. She wanted to make some demonstration of love and nascent understanding, but she could not.

They heard Jack's footsteps coming down the stairs. The street door banged.

"He's gone out," she wailed. Without initiative, she clung to him and waited, like a child, for his instructions.

"I suppose he's gone to the bonfire. Put your coat on."

"But we can't just hang about after him."

"We'll see what we'll see. A breath of air'll do you good, anyway. You just tidy your face up and get dressed. Come along, love."

She obeyed gratefully.

Chapter 2

THE OUTWARD ASPECT OF LAMB STREET changed with the seasons. In spring and summer there was a touch of the fairground about it. Doors were left open. The characteristic noises of each household issued forth to mingle in a cheerful background to the common life. Old folk sat in front of their doors, and the babies were put out in their prams to enjoy the long hours of sunlight. People gathered to gossip or came out to watch street entertainers. Children swarmed at their play. Boys and girls in their early 'teens, every one with a bicycle, congregated at the corner and set off from time to time on reckless, bell-jangling races round the block. Their elder brothers kicked footballs about, crouched in gambling schools (with sentries posted against the police), boxed playfully, or joined with the girls to flirt or sing.

As the year drew to its end, darkness and bad weather drove the people indoors. After dusk, groups of lads huddled in shop doorways at the corners, conspiring quietly. A few pairs of lovers, whose courtships were not approved by their families, haunted the dark building site. Sometimes a group of kerchiefed girls, going out for the evening, would clatter arm-in-arm through the gloom, singing in chorus. Every afternoon the rattle of a barrow announced the arrival of the vegetable man, defying the drizzle or the dreary mist with his cheerful shout of, "LOVerly ripe tomatoes", but looking so miserable as he plodded along that often a housewife brought him out a cup of tea or made an unnecessary purchase out of pity. Otherwise the street was quiet.

Warmth glowed behind drawn curtains. Light and the muffled noises of life tempted through the ornately-patterned frosted glass windows of The Lamb. People hurried towards these refuges, let themselves in with an eager banging of doors, and left the dark, dismal pavements deserted.

Families, crowding round their fires, took little interest in what went on elsewhere. It was only occasionally that, when some domestic friction had worn through the bonds of respectability, a household would so far forget itself as to divide in civil war, and the neighbours on each side would switch off their radio sets and listen delightedly to the commotion. There had been little excitement this autumn, except for an outbreak between Mr. Prawn and his sub-tenant Bernie Whiteflower. Mr. Prawn, unable to make ends meet on his pension, had tried to put Bernie's rent up by half-a-crown, explaining his reasons in a long and flowery letter which included quotations about the cost of living from *The Economist* and *The Daily Worker*. Bernie had rushed into the street with the letter, and gathered his neighbours about him in an impromptu protest meeting, pointing to the unfortunate Mr. Prawn (who was watching in terror from his window) and shouting, "Gah! Calls hisself a Socialist! Bleed'n' capitalist, that's all he is!" Bernie had thereupon declared, and had since maintained, a rent strike, and Mr. Prawn had lived henceforth shut up in his kitchen, too upset to demand his rent, and only scurrying out from time to time to do his shopping, pursued by shouts from the upstairs window of, 'Bloodsucker!' 'Parasite!' 'Shylock!'

The more quiet the season, however, the more eager the people were for an excuse to flock out of their houses, and by seven o'clock on Guy Fawkes' Night the dark street was astir with activity. There had been rain during the day, and many families watched from the shelter of their doorways. The youngsters braved the damp chill wind and the muddy puddles on the building site to

321

gather round the bonfire.

The wood was wet. Dark figures hurried to and fro across the road with fresh combustibles. The screaming and scampering of children rose above the general murmur. Whenever a new piece of timber was flung on to the reluctant fire a great burst of sparks would shoot up into the night; but the sparks would die, leaving the darkness deeper than before, and the bonfire remained a black, smoking heap, with only a feeble smoulder of red at its heart. Occasionally a rocket would rush up over the rooftops, or the flash and detonation of a 'Little Demon' would make the girls shriek with mock fright, but most people were keeping their fireworks until the fun was more obviously under way.

Barmy Naughton wandered in the crowd with a paper bag full of fireworks under his arm. He had looked forward to this event for weeks. Mick had bought him the fireworks, and had given him the evening off, taking on another barman in his place. For weeks there had gathered in him all that agonising and immense happiness which unhappy people enjoy in their rare moments of relief. It had reached a pitch that was almost beyond endurance. Now, in a few seconds, this swelling store of emotion had been transmuted back into a misery more terrifying than he had ever undergone and, still growing upon itself, had become entirely unbearable.

A half-hour ago he had hurried to the Wakerells' house to call for his one friend, Jack. Barmy was as frightened of the crowd as a maltreated animal. Among people, his loneliness was the greater, unless he had a friend, a protector, who could lift the burden of fear from him and through whose presence he could enter into the common spirit. But Jack, his last friend, had opened the door on him angrily; had listened impatiently to his eager babble; had said, "Be a good chap, leave us alone now, run away, go on"; and when he had protested, Jack had shouted, "For cryin' out loud, blow! Go on, beat it! You're more trouble than you're worth, and I'm bloody fed up with you!" Jack had slammed the door in his face, and the slam of the door had killed the last seeds of hope in Barmy. It was the door of life that had finally shut upon him. For the first time his despair was absolute; as freezing and inescapable as if the earth had spat him out into space, condemning him to fall for ever through an infinite star-sprinkled darkness. The crowd had become a collection of unrecognizable beings. He shambled past people, and their smiles and greetings could not reach him.

He could see Jack now, standing on the other side of the fire, hands in the pockets of his raincoat, talking to Elsie Cakebread and looking about him as if seeking someone. Whenever Jack's head turned his way Barmy skulked out of sight. More people were coming across the road. Joyce Wakerell and her father were standing on the edge of the pavement with Mr. and Mrs. Cogger. A rowdy procession of children arrived with a guy, which they carried on a crude litter made of an old kitchen chair and two poles. They set it down near the fire and put finishing touches to the effigy. One brought an old trilby hat to perch on its head; another a pipe to stick in its mouth. Elsie Cakebread rushed forward and arranged a Roman Candle between the legs of its trousers in a way that provoked shouts of laughter. Her husband called, "Trust my Else to make the sparks fly," to which she replied at the top of her voice, "You keep quiet! I've never had no fireworks out of you!"

The clamour in the street increased. The crowd grew. Voices, movement, the intermittent glare of the fire as the flames began to take hold, the more and more frequent explosions of fireworks and fountains of coloured fire, generated an atmosphere of carnival. Attracted by the noise, a large contingent came pouring out of The Lamb, where they had been putting in an hour's preparatory drinking. With Bernie Whiteflower at their head and Gus Woodruff alongside playing his piano-accordion, they came down the street bawling a local ballad —

One Sunday over the Lea,
My feller he done it on me.
He done it once, he done it twice,
And then he had the cheek to say it was nice —

while the girls in the procession whooped and linked arms in a high-kicking dance. Gloom and quiet were gone from the street; the evening was now under way.

Barmy lingered on the fringes of the group that surrounded the guy. Children swarmed round him, shouting greetings and pawing at the parcel of fireworks he carried. Barmy clutched the parcel defensively to his breast, slapped at the outstretched hands and snarled at the children. They drew back, intimidated by his glaring eyes and by the unexpected hostility of his manner. A small boy shouted, 'Mingy bleeder, won't give us no fireworks,' and charged at Barmy's legs. Others followed, and in a moment Barmy was struggling in their midst. Horrified parents dragged their children away, slapping them and asking loudly where their manners were. Some of Barmy's fireworks had been snatched away; others were trampled in the mud. Mr. Bates, who had just informed his son that he would have the skin off his backside if he didn't behave, picked up a few that looked as if they might still be usable and offered them to Barmy, saying, "'Ere y'are, boy. You know what kids are. You don't want to take no notice." Barmy glowered at him and slunk away without a word, hiding under his jacket the torn bag and the few fireworks that remained to him. A boy began to chant, "Barmy Naughton is no good, chop him up for firewood," and others took up the cry. Barmy stumbled away among the knots of people near the fire, pursued by a handful of children who kept up their chant.

A rowdy debate was in progress about the naming of the guy. Bernie Whiteflower suggested, with much support from those round him, that it should represent an acid-bath murderer whose trial was a favourite topic of conversation at the time. Someone else shouted, "Old

324

Attlee," and was answered with a cry from the darkness of, "What about old Churchill?" Boris Karloff, Sidney Stanley, Joe Stalin, the rent collector, Frank Sinatra, Jack Doyle and Old Mother Riley were nominated, with yells of, "'Ear, 'ear," and "Git aht of it" creating a background of babble in which each successive suggestion was drowned. Bernie and Gus hoisted the guy up by its poles and carried it towards the bonfire. Mr. Bates's boy, who had appeared again in the forefront of the crowd, called, "'Ere, wait a minute," ran alongside and stood a large square of white cardboard in the guy's lap. People crowded in to see what was written on it. Bernie and Gus deposited the guy on the summit of the bonfire, and as they drew back someone emptied a can of paraffin across the smouldering mound. A white sheet of flame flashed up into the air, and in its light there could be read, daubed in thick charcoal strokes, the name BARMY.

Elsie Cakebread screeched, "It's Barmy," and the information passed back, in a confusion of voices, into the gloom of the street. Among most of the people who were wandering about or standing in little groups there was no response. Their vague murmuring and chattering continued at the same pitch as before. Someone said, "Ah, leave him alone," and there were mutters of assent in the darkness. Along the street the rhythm of strolling footsteps continued, punctuated by the intermittent bang and flash of fireworks. In the small but dense crowd of younger people around the bonfire a different atmosphere prevailed. Excited by the heat and the leaping glare of the flames they howled, "Good ol' Barmy!" "Take a bow, Barmy!" "Burn, you bastard!" "Warm enough, Barmy?" An inner fringe of small boys, their ferocity increasing as the flames climbed and crackled, chanted, "Barmy Naughton is no good, chop him up for firewood."

Barmy, standing with his back to the fire, felt hemmed in by the faces crowding out of the night. All the faces, red in the flickering glare, were grinning, their open mouths baying malice at him. Beyond them was a shadowy darkness in which he could neither see nor hear any sign of a friendly, living world. He shrieked, with the terror-driven force of a child left alone in the dark, "Jack! Jack! Jackie!" No friendly face appeared in the circle around him. Over his own voice their shouting came to him, "Get your chestnuts roasted, Barmy!" "Guy, guy, stick him up on high!" "Why don't you get up there wiv 'im, Barmy?" "Burn, you bastard, burn!" The flames were beginning to catch at the guy's clothing. Barmy cried, "You're killing him! Let him live! Leave him alone!" Laughter swept back at him. He faced the fire, his head lowered, his arm across in front of his eyes. More laughter. He leaped through the flames at the base of the fire, fell forward on to the burning timbers and began to claw his way up towards the guy. The laughter stopped and a high-pitched outcry of alarm surged back through the crowd. People rushed forward and stopped helplessly at the foot of the fire. Barmy, bellowing with pain, was dragging at the feet of the guy. His clothes were catching fire. The onlookers caught a terrifying glimpse of his blackened, death's-head face, with the eyes full of firelight shining out of it. Bernie Whiteflower roared, "Come on!" and plunged into the fire. Jack Agass, who had been pushing his way through the crowd in response to Barmy's appeal, flung aside a wailing woman who blocked his path and went crashing in after Bernie. Some of the younger men took heart and began to pull burning timbers away, while other people shouted useless suggestions and others scurried about calling for water, for the police, for the fire brigade. Others came running to see what the hubbub was about. Barmy, grinning with pain and hatred at the crowd, screamed something unintelligible; then the charred wood gave way beneath his feet and his body crashed waist-deep into the heart of the fire. A last terrible cry died suddenly, as a great gout of sparks shot up into the sky and burning fragments showered down upon Jack and Bernie. All this had happened in the space of perhaps four seconds.

Jack, scrambling over red-hot timbers, felt the scorching buffet of a flame and half-leaped, half-toppled back, clutching at Bernie Whiteflower's leg as he fell. He was sprawling in the mud at the foot of the bonfire, aware of little but the pain in his hands and the fact that Bernie's weight had become inert. He shouted for aid and dragged Bernie clear. Others helped him to roll Bernie over on the wet ground and to beat out the glowing, smouldering patches in Bernie's clothes. Jack sat up. Bernie lay moaning with his hands over his face. Jack muttered, "Where's Barmy?" His nostrils were full of the smell of burning hair and cloth. The pain in his hands had increased, and his legs also hurt. He felt dazed and unable to make a complete picture of all that was happening as people hurried to and fro, blazing planks were flung aside, voices screamed, chattered and shouted, bells clanged, an ambulance came lurching on to the site, a fire engine drew up in the kerb, helmeted men raced past with hoses, a jet of water roared past his ears, a great cloud of steam, full of floating ash, rolled over him and vanished, the glare died and the darkness thickened. People swarmed round him in the gloom. He felt the tug of a knife as the legs of his trousers were slit open. Some cool and easing substance was being applied to his burned skin. A voice filtered into his dizzy brain, "You've come off light, my lad, there's not much wrong with you —" and in what sounded like an aside, "— It's only his hands and calves. His face isn't touched. How's the other one?" He tried to grasp what was happening, but the effort only brought a new wave of giddiness. Firemen were crashing through the smoking, dark remnants of the bonfire, dragging something forth. There was a revolting smell in the air. He could hear men whispering and women whimpering, and one voice saying, "Oh, my God!" He mumbled again, "Where's Barmy?" Nobody answered. A policeman was bending over him. "Can you stand up, old son?" He tried to raise himself, and felt sick. He heard a calm feminine voice, "Leave him alone a minute." A cool hand rested on the back of his neck, and another held a mug of water to his lips. Bernie Whiteflower was being carried past on a stretcher. Jack sipped at the water and vomited. The hand at the back of his neck pressed his head forward till it was between his knees. "That's right, Jackie dear, bring it up." The voice was Joyce's. He felt relieved, and turned his face up like a child's while she wiped his mouth with her handkerchief. His memory had not yet begun to function, and there seemed nothing remarkable about her presence. He heard her voice again, "He doesn't want any stretchers. He can walk. Come on, dear, ups-a-daisy." He rose obediently, swayed and put his arm round Joyce's shoulders. The ambulance, with Bernie aboard, went clanging away. Joyce said — her voice still seemed distant — "We'll follow on in the police car." He moved his lips and at last managed to express, a coherent thought. "Where?" "To the hospital," she replied. He said, "Don' wanna go no hospital. I'm all right." She steadied him as he sagged against her. "There! It's just to make sure. They won't keep you in." People pressed close. Their voices came to him without meaning. Joyce helped him into the car. A policeman shut the door and climbed in at the front next to the driver. A blur of faces moved backwards past the windows. He sighed, and leaned back against the cushions.

Joyce sat at his side without speaking. Jack looked at her. His mind had cleared, and he wondered what significance to attach to her presence. He wanted to ask her but did not dare. His breathing quickened, and the brief grunt which he uttered at each exhalation betrayed his pain. Joyce said, "Lean on me, you'll feel better."

He looked at her again. Her face was composed, her expression prim. He put his head on her shoulder and closed his eyes. She put her arm round him. He felt warm and comfortable in her embrace. The pain remained, but it seemed to have become detached from his real self. He was not conscious of the car, or of the policemen sitting in front, or of the journey; only of the pressure of her arm

328

and the noise of his own heavy breathing.

They reached the hospital, and Joyce accompanied him into the casualty department. His hands were bandaged, and some minor burns were treated on his legs below the knees. A doctor suggested that he should stay the night and go home in the morning. Before he could answer, Joyce said quickly, "No, he'd rather go home now, if you don't mind. I'll take him." The doctor agreed, handed Joyce some sedative tablets and told Jack when to come back for fresh dressings. A nurse brought tea. Jack and Joyce each took a cup. As Jack sipped, he glanced guiltily at Joyce. She returned a candid, serene look as if she did not see any meaning in his regard. He tried an ingratiating smile. A slight severity crept into her expression. She said calmly, "Are you feeling better?" He nodded, and asked, "Where's Barmy?" "We'll find out," she said. "Don't worry now."

Mick Monaghan came into the room. "Ah, here you are," he said. "They tell me you're fine and dandy. I came in the ambulance with Bernie and his missus. I've just been upstairs in the ward with them."

Jack asked, "Is he bad?"

"It caught his face and body a bit, but he's in no danger. He'll be out in a week or two."

"Where's Barmy?"

Mick's eyes, lit by brilliant points of anger so that they seemed almost to be smiling, studied Jack for a few seconds. "I'll give you one guess."

Jack shivered. "Oh, Gawd!"

Joyce said sharply, "Leave him alone, Mick, he's had enough for one night."

"He's a big boy now," Mick said. "He's been through more than this in his time, haven't you, soldier?"

Jack nodded. "Poor old Barmy! What an end!"

"Oh, I don't know." Both Jack and Joyce were surprised by the savage levity in Mick's voice. "He'd probably call it cushy. Well, don't look so shocked! It was no worse than he suffered every day of his life, near enough, for the last thirty years. And through the same lot, too." He laughed, and went on more loudly and harshly. "I bet they buy him a hell of a fine wreath! You know, when I first saw what had happened, I was fit to shoot the lot of 'em. 'Bastards,' I thought, 'You've done for him at last.' And then I thought, 'Well, maybe they've done the poor devil a favour. He's out of their reach now. Perhaps he even knew what he was doing.' Funny, isn't it? I'd have stopped him if I could. So would you. But he wouldn't have thanked us for it. Ah —" He made an impatient movement of his head. "Why be soft? He's well out of it. And may the Lord have more mercy on his soul than the blasted human race ever did!"

Jack and Joyce finished their tea without speaking. Mick said, "I've got a taxi waiting. I'll take you home."

None of them spoke on the return journey. Joyce sat apart from Jack, placid and upright, with her hands in her lap. Lamb Street was quiet, with groups of people standing about talking softly. As they stepped out of the cab neighbours hurried towards them, but Mick and Joyce helped Jack quietly into the house and shut the door behind them.

Mr. and Mrs. Wakerell, who had been waiting on the doorstep, hovered around them in the hall. "Thank God you're back," Mrs. Wakerell quavered, "I wanted to follow on, but this one —" she indicated her husband — "wouldn't let me. Are you all right, Jackie dear?"

"Leave him alone," Joyce said. "He's all right. Have you lit the fire in his room? All right, never mind, I'll do it. No, don't you come up. You make a cup of tea for Mick. Could you eat a bit, Jack? Try, I know you feel sick, but it'll do you good. All right, just a cup of hot milk then. Dad, you bring up some sticks and coal."

Mick and Joyce went upstairs with Jack. Jack sat on his bed, with his bandaged hands against his chest, while Mick undressed him. Joyce took the fuel from her father, sent him out of the room and busied herself lighting the fire. "There," she said, "now we're all cosy. Thanks, Mick, you've been a dear."

"I'll be off now," Mick said, "I'll look in tomorrow morning, and see how he is."

Jack lay in bed. He wanted to sleep, but he wanted still more to be alone with Joyce, to settle the questions that were tormenting him. He said, "Goodnight, Mick. Thanks a lot." A thought, unexpected and startling, emerged from some recess of his mind. He sat up. "Here, Mick."

Mick paused at the door. "What is it boy?"

Jack hesitated. He did not know what to say or whether, even, to speak his thoughts at all. "Never mind," he said, "some other time. No, wait a minute. About Barmy."

"Well?"

"Well, there's something —" His courage failed him again. "Look, are you going to tell Rose?"

"Rose? I suppose she'll hear about it in time. No reason why not. Why, what's it got to do with her especially?"

Joyce had straightened up in front of the fire and was listening in an apprehensive, attentive pose. Jack glanced about him in panic, first at her, then at Mick. "Well, I mean — Look, you're thick with her?"

"Yes, you might say I was thick with her."

"I suppose she's told you a lot about herself."

The points of light were gleaming in Mick's eyes again. "Yes, she's told me a good deal about herself. Why?"

"And then, you knew Kate. Look, Barmy —" Jack paused. "He was her father, wasn't he?"

Joyce stood as if afraid to move. Mick was as still as a statue. "Was he?" he said at last. "And why would you be thinking that?"

"Well, Kate's husband — he wasn't the father, I know that. And Kate and Barmy — well, I know that, too."

"You do, do you?" There was a strange force in Mick's harsh voice that touched Jack with fright. "And what do you know about Kate and Barmy?"

Under Mick's burning, intent gaze, Jack felt doubt growing, but he plunged on, "They were — you know! I

331

mean, like — Barmy told me. And it was in that letter."

"Ah, yes." Mick bowed his head, as if brooding, and his voice became heavy. "That letter."

"I mean, I'm not even sure if Rose knows or not. I couldn't see how she did, at first. Or she'd have done something for him. Then I thought, well, she's a right proper bitch, I've learned that for myself. I reckon she could even turn her back on her own father, rather than have him round her neck."

"So that's your opinion of Rose, is it?"

"Yes it is. After what she done to me."

"What did she do to you?"

"She got hold of a blank cheque of mine. With my signature on it. Filled it in for a hundred quid." Jack hesitated. "I'd been going about with her. Only two or three times. There was nothing to it. Then I stopped seeing her. I thought it was all over. Didn't know about the cheque till she'd cashed it." He burst out, "She's not what you'd call particular, is she? Pals with you, pals with me, pals with any chap got the money as far as I can see. I've heard a few things about her mother, too, that make me wonder."

Mick's face darkened, and he lowered his head like a bull, but he said nothing.

"So there you are," Jack ended weakly.

Mick looked terrible. "Are you speaking the truth?"

"On my Bible oath I am."

"Well," Mick said, breaking a painful silence. "You can rest easy. Barmy wasn't her father."

"Are you sure?"

"Yes, I'm sure."

"But how do you know?"

Mick had opened the door. He paused again, and said, "Because I am."

He lingered for a moment, as if to continue. "You go to sleep, damn your eyes," he said, and went out of the room.

Chapter 3

A S SOON AS THE DOOR CLOSED Joyce abandoned her frozen posture and came to sit by the bed. "And now, what was all that about?"

Jack was still sitting up. He shrugged his shoulders. "I don't know. It's got me beat, I tell you, Joycie. My brain's going round and round like a bloody old gramophone record. Only I'm blowed if I know what it's playing. Kate and Mick! Our Kate! I can't — why, she was a bloody angel!"

"She was an old trot, by the sound of it."

"Joycie!" He leaned back. "Oh, I don't know! It don't sound like the same woman."

"Well, it was. The facts speak, don't they?"

"Oh!" Lying back, he pressed his face wearily against the pillow. "I wish I could make head or tail of it. I could bloody cry! You wouldn't talk like that if you knew."

"Knew what? I fancy it's my right to know, after these last few weeks."

"Oh!" He shut his eyes. "Don't start on that now! I wish I could tell you. I don't know where to begin. I tell you, Joycie, I'm in the dark myself. Old Nance was going to tell me. I thought I knew them. Kate, Rosie, I thought they were like my own family. It's as if all my life has only been a bloody dream. You open your eyes, and everything's different, and you don't know where you are."

"Well, you'd better find out. Or I might not be there when you do wake up. Just for a start, what's all this about Kate and Barmy?"

"Ah, nothing much."

She looked at him sternly. "All right, have it your own way. If you won't trust me you can start looking for someone that suits you better."

He sat up in alarm. "Here, hold on, girl! Well, they — you know! — they had a sort of carry-on."

"Those two? Ugh!"

Jack's heart sank. He dared not argue.

"And Mick as well," she went on, "according to him. You can see where the daughter got it from. Nice lot you've been brought up with, I must say."

"Oh," he protested miserably, "you don't understand."

"Don't I? Then here's your chance to educate me."

He pondered, wondering how to defend what he had cherished without antagonising Joyce. "It was a good home. I don't care what you say." He laid his bandaged hand on her arm. "Tell you the truth, I don't understand, either. What's good and what's bad? I mean, you can't say."

"I can."

"Well," he said in an obstinate undertone, "you know more than I do."

Her look was scornful. "Then you'd better learn if you want to cut any ice with me."

"How d'you mean?"

"Work it out for yourself, genius."

She left him to his thoughts. Her unrelenting attitude had increased his mental confusion, but to his surprise he discovered that he was more comforted than dismayed by her demand for unconditional surrender. The sight of her sitting by his side, upright and vigilant as a school-mistress, confirmed the flash of recognition he had felt earlier in the day, when she had staggered him with her blind outburst of violence. For the first time he saw in her a superior strength,which offered shelter to him from a bewildering world. He saw anew the stupid, chattering, heavy-fleshed girl who had hung obediently on his arm. For the first time he felt in her presence those impulses of mystification, fear and respect that what he called 'real' women had sometimes aroused in him; she was not to be patronised; she was no animated household furnishing to be bought with a marriage licence; but an independent, self-willed being, full of the passion and promise he had vainly sought in others, to be courted with care and anxiety lest he might lose her. Today he had seen the womanly flame in her. He said, "It is all right, isn't it?"

"What is?"

"Us two."

She pouted, and let a few seconds elapse before she said, "I'll get you your hot milk. It's time you got some sleep. You've talked too much already. I shouldn't have left you." She spoke gently, but the hand that she laid on his forehead was cool, with no hint of fondness in its touch. "Your skin's as hot as fire. It's what they call the reaction. Ah!" The door had opened, and Mrs. Wakerell appeared with a tray. "I wondered where you'd got to with that milk."

Mrs. Wakerell bustled into the room with the air of one about to take command. "And how's the hero?" she trilled.

"Hero?" It was Joyce who answered. "Don't give him ideas. Just because he burned his hands on the bonfire."

"There's a way to talk! You should have heard everyone while we were waiting for you to come back! They were all saying what a fine boy our Jackie was."

Jack said, "I seem to remember it was ol' Bernie done the most, and got the worst of it, too."

"Ah," said Mrs. Wakerell, smiling broadly upon him and speaking in a horribly honeyed coo, "But you're the one we're interested in." She inclined her head archly towards her daughter. "Aren't we, Joycie?"

"Speak for yourself."

"Well, hark at her!" Mrs. Wakerell gave Joyce a hurt incredulous look. "Haven't you two made it up yet?"

"Never you mind. You'll find out in God's good time."

335

"You're a saucy one these days, and no mistake." Mrs. Wakerell spun her great bulk round to face Jack and threw up her hands in a gossip's gesture of relish. "What do you think about poor Barmy Naughton? Terrible! They say he must have suffered agonies." Her voice rose greedily. "Mr. Cogger saw him when the firemen lifted him out. He says it was the most horrible sight he's ever seen. Says he'll never forget it to his dying day. The body was all shrunk, like a dwarf. And in that short while! Isn't it a marvel? And he says you couldn't tell clothes from skin, just all black and rough, like blistered paint."

"Shut up, mother!"

"And no face you could see, and no hair on the head. Just a shrivelled little black lump. And the smell! Well, I was fifty yards off, and I felt sick!"

"Mother, I told you to shut up. Haven't you got any sense? Can't you see he's all on edge still, and feverish? Do you want to give him nightmares? Out you go, now, and let him sleep."

"Well!" Mrs. Wakerell let herself be ushered to the door, looking annoyed and bewildered at her inability to disobey her daughter. "I'm sure I don't need advice from you before I say a few kind words to an invalid. You're getting above yourself." She made a last stand in the doorway. "Miss High-and-Mighty, you are! You weren't so high-and-mighty an hour or two ago." She craned her head to call to Jack, past Joyce. "You should have seen her, Jackie! Charlie Green come running past us, he was shouting, 'Get the p'lice, Jackie Agass 'as burned 'isself to death!' My Joycie here, she lets out a scream like a pig with its throat cut. White as a sheet she goes. She runs off, her dad behind her, she's crying, 'Oh, Jackie, Jackie, where are you?' People get in the way, she says, 'Where's my Jackie? Where is he?' Tears streaming down her face. And then she sees you, sitting on the ground there — don't you shut the door on me, my girl, till I've had my say — and she catches hold of her father's arm, fit to fall down in a faint she is, and she says out loud, 'Oh, thank the blessed Lord Almighty!' He wipes her eyes and she gets her breath back, then she says, 'Why doesn't someone give him a cup of water?' And someone passes her one, and she walks up to you and gives it to you as if she'd never shed a tear in her life."

With a last push Joyce managed to shut the door on her mother. She stood with her head bowed, her face scarlet. She said, "Your milk's getting cold." She crushed the sedative tablets in a spoon and emptied the powder into the milk. "Here —" Her attitude was shamed and surly "— Drink this up and go to sleep."

Jack was smiling up at her.

"What you grinning at?"

"You."

"Drink your milk."

"How can I?" He held up his hands. "Can't hold the glass."

She put the glass to his lips. "There, drink! And don't dribble." Her voice was brusque. "What a big baby you are! Biggest baby I've ever seen!"

He sipped, fixing a steadfast grin upon her and watching the embarrassment gather in her hot face. He took his time. She snapped, "Hurry up!" He went on grinning at her and sipping slowly. At last she turned her head, to look directly and furiously at him. She said, in a strained, high voice, "Well?"

"Well?"

She held his gaze for several seconds. Her face remained pinched, angry and flushed. "Well, so you've discovered I'm not made of stone. Have a good laugh at that if you like!"

"Who's laughing? Give us a kiss."

"Oh, go away." She went to put his empty glass on the mantelpiece. "Go to sleep now. I can't stay up all night."

"Come on, give us a kiss and I'll go to sleep."

She crossed the room again and seated herself in the wickerwork armchair by the window. "Big baby! You ought to be ashamed of yourself."

"Ah, come on, girl!"

She did not answer. She stretched her legs, lay back and shut her eyes. Jack listened to her breathing, long and fierce, and remained silent so that she might have time to relax emotionally. The sedative was working, and he felt sleep gathering in him. "Why don't you go to bed?" he asked.

She opened her eyes and turned her head. Her colour was normal again; her lips were still compressed; but her face moved in a slight smile, faintly friendly, faintly triumphant. "When you're asleep," she replied. "Leave me alone, now. I'm thinking."

Jack closed his eyes contentedly and fell asleep.

He slept till eleven o'clock the next morning and woke up feeling radiant. It was only the throbbing of his bandaged hands that reminded him of the events of the night before. He was buoyant with relief and well-being. A vague puzzlement awoke in him when he recalled, after a few minutes, Mick's parting words; but, although he asked himself many questions, he was unable to feel deeply concerned. Nor was he able to muster up an appropriately heavy grief at Barmy's death; despite all the efforts of his conscience, Barmy kept vanishing from his thoughts.

He heard noises at the street door from time to time, the trampling of footsteps in the hall and the murmur of voices in the parlour below.

Joyce came in. Usually on Sunday mornings she shuffled about in her dressing gown, unwashed and unkempt. This morning she wore a smart beige frock, her hair was neat and gleaming, and she did not wear her glasses. "You awake?" she asked, in a vigorous, unemotional voice. "Did you sleep all right? How are your hands? Half the street's been calling to ask about you. Sit up and I'll bring your breakfast."

She returned in a few minutes with a tray. "Here you are, two eggs and two rashers. That's my ration you're getting, so look grateful." Jack waited, like a baby, to be fed. "None of that nonsense," she commanded, "you're not as helpless as all that. Your fingers aren't bandaged. You can use a knife and fork. Get weaving!" While Jack ate, she pulled the curtains apart, opened the windows wide and tidied the room. "There! The worst thing out is a stuffy room in the morning. More tea?"

She brought a bowl and a jug of hot water. "You don't want to wash in the scullery this morning. Can you get up all right?" He climbed stiffly out of bed. "You can shave yourself. Then I'll wash your face. Save you getting your bandage wet. Just suit you, won't it, mummy's pet, having your face washed for you?" She washed him and rubbed the towel mercilessly over his face.

Through the folds of the towel he spoke for the first time since he had greeted her on her entry. "Here, I haven't had that kiss yet."

"Wipe your ears out."

"Don't gi' me that nursemaid lark." He put his bandaged paws round her waist and hugged her to him. "Come on."

She returned his embrace, but she only offered a cool cheek to his mouth, like a mother humouring a child. "Satisfied?"

"Are you kidding?"

"Well, you'll have to be for now. Here's the comb. Your hair's sticking up like the Mad Professor's."

He pulled at his hair with the comb. "All merry and bright again, eh?"

"I haven't been in mourning that I know of."

"Nah, I mean — us like this again. It's all right, ain' it?"

Her voice remained firm, but there was a hint of teasing in it. "You don't see me swooning for joy."

"Don't give a bloke much encouragement, do you?"

"I've given you my eggs and bacon, and that's more than you deserve."

"Joycie, can I put the banns up next week?"

"It's a free country, isn't it?" Her eyebrows were raised in disdain, but under the lashes amusement glimmered in her eyes.

"Ah, don't muck about."

"Then don't ask silly questions, with only four weeks to go."

"All right, girl. Nod's as good as a wink, eh? Look, Joycie, now that you are listening, for a change, I'll say it again — it never meant nothing, between me and Rose. I mean, I can't explain exactly what it was, but it was all over and done with before you found out. It is finished, honest it is."

"It had better be."

"I never give her that money. I'd forgot all about the cheque. She took advantage."

"Well, no-one else ever will. I promise you that. Not while I'm breathing."

"I'll never see her again, I swear."

"Say you don't know."

"What you mean?"

"You might see her sooner than you think."

"Who says?"

"I do. She happens to be in the parlour now, having a cup of tea. Mick's brought her."

Jack put the brush and comb down. "Oh, Gawd! Here, I can't see her. I don't want to. Tell her to buzz off."

"I've told her you're coming downstairs. So get your clothes on."

"But I don't —"

"Yes, you do. There's a bit more explaining to be done round here before I'm satisfied."

"Will you come down with us?"

"Too true I will." She sat on the edge of the bed and watched placidly while he dressed. "Ready? By the right, quick march!" She followed him downstairs.

Jack led the way into the parlour, said, "Good morning," to Mick, turned an unhappy grin on Rose and greeted her with a vague ah-ha-ing sound in the roof of his mouth.

Rose sat in the armchair by the fireplace, holding her handbag on her lap, leaning forward slightly, her expression composed and disdainful as if, whatever might follow, she had no intention of becoming interested. When she looked at Joyce it was with a faint, patronising smile. Joyce in return, studied Rose in a calm, unafraid manner, her face as blank of either friendship or hostility as if she were gazing through a shop window. Rose leaned back, put her handbag down on the floor and allowed herself to sink into a languid pose, with her head resting to one side and one hand dangling over the armrest of the chair. Joyce sat down beside Jack, watching him sidelong like an animal's keeper. Jack uttered a preparatory grunt, but Mick spoke first.

"How are you feeling this morning?"

"All right." A hollowness in Jack's voice showed that his thoughts and his speech were following separate tracks.

"You're looking better. I rang the hospital. Bernie's had a quiet night." He smiled grimly. "That's more than I've had. Do you feel well enough to stand a bit of straight talking?"

Joyce said, "He does."

"Good! It's my belief that the time has come for it. This young lady thinks so too."

Rose directed a frown of contradiction at him. "Or perhaps I should admit," he added, "that we had a difference of opinion on the subject. Quite a long one. It lasted from eleven o'clock last night till two o'clock this morning. However, I made it clear that I was going to hold this little conference whether or no, and my daughter decided that she might as well come along — to hold, as you might say, a watching brief on her own behalf. You'll see why in a little while. First of all, let's get one thing out of the way." He handed Jack a slip of paper.

Jack looked at it, saw that it was a cheque for a hundred pounds and said to Rose, "I don't want your bloody money."

Rose glanced idly at him and turned her head towards her father again.

Mick said, "It's not her bloody money. It's mine. Look at

341

the signature."

Joyce interjected, "I'll have that." She took the cheque from Jack, folded it and held it in her lap, between her fingertips. "Thank you, Mick." She did not favour Jack with even a glance of explanation, and Jack made no motion of protest.

"You might like to know," Mick said, "that it wasn't for her own benefit that she helped herself to your money."

"Does it matter?" Rose murmured.

"Although whether you'll think any better of her when you know where it did go, I can't say." Mick rose, walked to the window, looked out at the street for a few moments and turned suddenly to face them. "Jack, I'll be frank with you. I don't care a hang what sort of shenanigans you get mixed up in. I don't give a damn what you know or what you don't know. But there's one thing I do care about — and that's Kate. That woman loved you as a son. I want you to know her as I know her, and to remember her as I do. I'll not have you talking about her the way you did last night. That's why I've come here this morning." He walked towards Jack and looked down at him like a prosecutor. "Jack, I wonder how much you know about people? How you judge them? Or whether you're able to judge them at all? I wonder if you've learned that the only way to judge people is by balancing what they give against what they take? Kate gave a thousand times more than she took. You've good cause to know that, of all people, and to be grateful for it." He had returned to the window, and looked out as he talked. "I'll tell you about Kate. And I won't leave anything out. You'd have less chance of understanding if I did. I wasn't the first man she went with besides her husband. Not by a long chalk. She married him in nineteen-twelve. They weren't a good match. He was a quiet, stay-at-home chap, didn't notice she was there most of the time. She — well, you can imagine what she was like at twenty. And there she was, stuck in his kitchen, day and night. No more sing-songs up The Lamb, no more dancing, no more evenings up in the gallery at Collins', no more swings and roundabouts on Hampstead Heath — he didn't care tuppence for 'em, and he didn't see why she should. She had his mother glaring at her all the time like an old witch. Scrubbing and slaving, and three kids in a row. That was her life with him.

"Mind you, she looked after him all right. She was faithful. She was fond of him. She kept his house spotless. She was as meek and mild as he could wish. She got downhearted sometimes, she'd long for a bit of life, but she wouldn't let herself brood over it, not while there was housework to keep her occupied. In nineteen-fifteen he joined up, and the loneliness, even with the kids, just about finished her. She stuck it for a year; then she went off the deep end. He was in France, she was on war work, so his mother couldn't keep an eye on her. I came into her life, as they say, in 'seventeen — on a ten-day leave — but I wasn't the only one, and she made no bones about it. We never took each other seriously. It was just what she called a lark. And that's how it was with her — till he came home in nineteen-eighteen, with his legs paralysed.

"She could have tried to shove him off into a hospital, or a home, or one of those places. She wouldn't. She knew he only had a few years, and she said he had a right to spend them in his own home. After he came back she didn't look at another man. She nursed him like a baby. She pushed him about in his wheelchair. She was sweet and loving to him. She spent half her time slaving for him and the kids, and the other half out charring to bring in a bit of extra money. Day and night she was at it. She was wearing herself out. She said to me once, 'I deserve it, Mick, God forgive me! It's the least I can do.' For a year she was like that. She was cleaning for me at The Lamb. She wouldn't let me come near her. She went like stone if I tried to touch her. It says something if I tell you that even I gave up trying. Then, one evening, she'd been dusting my parlour, I was doing my accounts at the desk, taking no notice of her, and she said, 'Goodnight, Mick.'

"Goodnight," says I, not even turning round. I went on writing. Something seemed wrong, I couldn't tell what it was. Then I realised, I hadn't heard her go. I turned round. There she was sitting on the edge of the sofa, looking at me, a little bit scared, a little bit defiant. I stood up. She said, 'That's the way it is, Mick,' and she came across the room to me.

"A year later Tony was born, the boy, the one that died the year Kate first saw you. Nobody knew what was going on, except her husband, and he — it was a funny thing with him — he turned a blind eye to it. He used to talk to her as kindly as ever. When she put her coat on of an evening and said she was going to slip out for a bit, he'd just give her a sad sort of smile and go back to his reading.

"Me? I've had a few in my time, but there's not one of them I've ever lost my head over — except for her. I went mad over that woman. I worshipped her. I wanted to rave when she was out of my sight. I begged her to leave him. I offered her money, everything she could wish for. She used to shut her mouth, and shake her head, and not say a word. And she went on looking after him. Well, that was the way we carried on. I couldn't look at another woman. She had no eyes for any other man. We'd both found the one we wanted. And still she wouldn't leave him.

"Then he began to change. I think it was the pain. He was suffering agonies. He knew he hadn't long, and his mind began to go. You know, they get full of despair, jealousy, self-pity. They think they're being ill-treated if they're not coddled day and night. They imagine everyone's trying to hurry them into their graves. You try to pity them, but it gets harder and harder to keep your patience. She stood for it. She never answered back. He used to get in a frenzy, drive himself mad trying to provoke her. She'd just stand there like a statue. He used to order her about — get this, get that, no, not this, take this back, take that back, hurry up, shut up, clear out. He'd sit brooding in his chair for hours, glaring at her, thinking up every dirty, humiliating demand he could try her with. She used to obey him without a word. He'd wet himself, like a baby, in his chair, just to see her kneeling and cleaning up. The worse his health got, the worse he tormented her. He'd jeer at her, call her all the filthiest names he could think of. He'd hit her when she came near enough, catch hold of her and pinch her and twist her arms. If I tried to say anything when I saw the bruises she'd put her hand over my mouth. I wanted to murder him. She begged me to pity him. She said, 'Think what he's suffering,' and there were tears in her eyes. And they talk about the holy saints!

"He was always threatening to show her up in front of the neighbours, but he never did. I suppose he was ashamed to admit he wasn't a man any more. He used to swear he'd divorce her. I wish to God he had! He needed her too much to let her go — or perhaps he wanted to go on punishing her. She said he loved her right up to the end. She said that was why he tortured her. Maybe — I don't know! Anyway, even when Rose was born in nineteen twenty-two, he didn't do anything about it. He died a little over a year later."

Jack fidgeted, and was glad that he did not have to meet Mick's eyes. "What about the children? Didn't they catch on?"

The languid insolence had gone out of Rose's attitude while her father was talking. She looked sombre and subdued. She said quietly, "Nancy knew."

"Nancy was the only one that ever knew," Mick said. "He used to leave Kate alone when the boys were there. I don't know why. She said he was afraid of losing their sympathy by letting them see him ill-treat her. Anyway, they were very young and they were out in the street most of the time. Nancy wasn't. She lived in the kitchen with her mother. Poor kiddie, she was fat as a little pig even at that time. She was very shy and sensitive, and she was afraid to play in the street. She got over it later, but at that age she lived in Kate's arms. She must have been terrified by what she heard, but she couldn't have understood very much of it. It wasn't till later on — oh, three or four years after, when she was about fourteen — that Kate told her everything. They were very close together, those two. More like sisters than mother and daughter. It was a great comfort to Kate, having someone she could talk to like that, and have a bit of a cry with on the quiet, sometimes."

"And Rose," Jack said. He looked at her. "I suppose you knew, too, later on." Rose shook her head.

"Rose never knew a thing," Mick said. "I wanted her to. I used to tell Kate, 'She's my only daughter, and I want her to know it.' 'No,' Kate used to say, 'I've brought them up as his children, and I've taught them to respect his memory. I'm not going to undo that.' Do you know when Rose found out? The night her mother died. She collapsed in the street when she heard the news, and I took her back to The Lamb, and that night I told her." He smiled briefly at his daughter. "Not that it did me much good. I wanted her to come and live with me, but she wouldn't hear of it. 'I shall live my own life,' she said. So I've had to content myself with renting a flat for her and giving her an allowance, and having a friendly evening with her now and again. Well, that's something, I suppose. At least she knows who I am."

Joyce was the only one who was not visibly under the spell of Mick's story. She asked, in an unrelenting voice, "Why didn't you and Kate get married?"

"I'm a married man, Joyce, and a Catholic. My wife left me many years ago — not without reason, to do her justice. And for a lifetime since, she's had the pleasure of combining religion and revenge. I asked her a hundred times but she wouldn't divorce me. I went to lawyers galore, but they couldn't help. I offered her well nigh every penny I had. She wouldn't listen.

"And without we were married, Kate wouldn't come to live with me. She wouldn't hear of taking money from me, except for the kids when she wanted to buy them

346

some clothes or take them away on a holiday. She wouldn't even give up scrubbing floors for a living till the boys were old enough to leave school and start bringing home wages. Later on she let me treat her a bit more generously: I gave her a present now and again. I helped her out when she was short. In nineteen thirty-nine we went away for a holiday together, for the first time. But she wouldn't take a regular allowance from me. She wouldn't let me buy her a nice little house. She wouldn't move in with me. It was the kids she was thinking of. 'Say the word, Mick,' she said, "and I'll walk naked in the Lord Mayor's Show. But I'm not going to let my children see their mother living in sin. And I'm not going to give the neighbours a chance to sneer at them because of me. I'd rather leave my children a good name than anything else in the world.' So for twenty years we went on seeing each other on the quiet, like a couple of criminals. That woman was made to share a home with a chap like me. She'd have been set free to live. She'd have had all the good times she was born for. But she turned her back on it, because she wanted to bring her children up respectable. Funny, isn't it? You wouldn't think a woman like that would have feared convention. But there you are!"

Jack was silent. A host of fragmentary and hitherto unexplained memories were coming together in his mind like jigsaw pieces: Mick coming to the Orphanage with Kate: Mick arranging for Jack's adoption: Mick securing Jack an apprenticeship: the photograph of the child Tony on Mick's mantelpiece: Kate on holiday in nineteen thirty-nine and Mick "out of town on business": Kate penniless but always finding money for the children's pleasures and necessities, for Chris's illness and for Chris's grave: Kate's mysterious appearance, late on one remembered Spring night, in the street near the side door of The Lamb: Gran Hogarth's outbursts and Nancy's silences. All these and a hundred other clues to the past had been there in his memory, but his memory had

347

preferred to ignore them, and to content itself with the shimmering illusions he had demanded from it as a refuge from the harsh present. He looked at Rose with a shamed smile. "And I thought you was his fancy bit!"

"No." There was no indulgence in her voice. "And I'm nobody else's fancy bit, either."

Joyce uttered a low, "Ha!" Rose gave her a negligent glance. Joyce glared back.

"Well, I don't know," Jack said, with a stupid laugh. "I can believe anything now. After today I reckon black's white, an' the Orient's a cert for Wembley."

They waited for Rose to speak, but she remained silent, looking at her father.

"She thinks you can't be trusted," Mick said. "I say you can. Am I right? Will you promise that nothing that's said in here this morning will go any further?"

Jack stared. "Suits me." Mick looked interrogatively at Joyce. She nodded scornfully.

"My daughter," Mick said, "is a revolutionary." He rolled the V with savage exaggeration. "A what?" Jack exclaimed.

"A revolutionary. A Red. An enemy of the state. Or should I say —" his smile to Rose was embittered "— a saviour of the people?"

Rose smiled faintly. Joyce laughed and said, "I'm not surprised."

"Well, I'll be —!" Jack's voice cracked into a bleat of incredulity. "What for?"

Rose sat smiling and tapping the points of her shoes together. "Don't start her off on that," Mick said. "She's told me often enough, and if she tells me a hundred times more I'll still think she's crazy."

"Anyway!" Jack was grimacing with the effort to understand. "What's all the hush-hush about? Old Prawn's a Bolshie, and a few others round here, and they don't hide it."

"That's different," Rose said. "My work is confidential. I can't talk about it."

"You'd better," Mick said, "or he'll think you're after burning down Buckingham Palace."

Rose frowned down at her shoes and went on tapping them together. "Very well!" She looked up. "Many of our people work for the Government. Scientists. Senior Civil Servants. If they're found out they lose their jobs. They have to remain undercover members. They can't belong to Party branches, where we know that police agents are active. We can't even bring them together in groups of their own. It would only need one spy or informer among them and they'd all be identified. So I keep in touch with each of them, separately. I meet them, discuss their problems with them, put them in touch with others where it's essential, help them to plan their work, and above all — since they're mostly well off — I collect all the money I can from them for the Party funds. Some of them make very big sacrifices. That's all there is to it. There's nothing illegal about it. I don't ask them to tell me anything they shouldn't. But if I became known for what I am, the police would only have to shadow me and I'd lead them to every one of our people in turn."

"Well, strike a light!" Jack muttered. "So that's why you're always going about with chaps. And asking them for money."

"I'm glad the penny's dropped."

"You mean —?" Jack was still struggling to understand. "You ain't —?"

"I don't live like a nun, if that's what you mean —"

Joyce whispered very audibly to Jack, "I don't doubt that."

"— and I've no intention of sobbing out the sad story of my life to you. But if you're wondering whether I'm a gold-digging glamour girl, the answer is no."

Jack became belligerent. "Then what about my money?"

"Oh, that?" She seemed quite unconcerned. "You've had it back. Aren't you satisfied?"

"No, I'm not."

349

"Well, you'll have to be, won't you?"

Mick seated himself on the arm of a chair and lit a cigarette. The flare of the match reflected in his eyes, giving them a momentary flare of fierce intentness. "Can't you guess? My noble daughter did a noble deed. Or so her comrades would say. A fine example of revolutionary firmness and initiative. Have I got the lingo right? She was told to raise four hundred pounds in a hurry. For the Good Cause. She went round to all her — what is it you call them, contacts? — and she beat the daylight out of them. How much did you tell me you'd got from them? A hundred and ninety pounds? Nice work! She tipped her own bank balance into the kitty, and sold a wristwatch I'd given her for a birthday present. No false sentiment about my daughter, you see. And she was still a hundred pounds short. Then — hard luck on you — she came across your blank cheque in her handbag. Ah, an inspiration! What more could a resourceful revolutionary want? No flinching! No silly softness! No cowardice. No bourgeois scruples! What is it they're always telling you? Be hard! Be decisive! Be audacious! So she fills it in and cashes it."

Rose stood up and smoothed her costume down. "I can't stay here all day. Well?" She addressed Jack. "What are you looking at me like that for?" Her voice was cool and amused. "I did nothing I hadn't a right to. You gave me it. I used it. What's wrong with that? Did you want a voice in the way I spent it? Was I supposed to sleep with you a certain number of times in return? You didn't say so. I can't remember any agreement being made." She turned to her father. "Are you ready?"

"You're a hard one," Jack said. "Haven't you got any shame?"

"On the contrary." She spoke without defiance. Her expression was candid and pitying. "I feel very proud of my contribution. I have no doubt that I'm in the right. I know that whatever I do is for the good of all of you. It doesn't disturb me in the least if I'm misunderstood sometimes. Why should it? Parents are misunderstood by their children."

"It's no use," Mick said. "Right and wrong don't mean the same to her as they do to us. Anyway, Jack, I'm trusting you to keep your mouth shut. It's best that nothing should get out. The more people know about Rose, the more they'll ask about me. And the more they know about me, the more they'll know about Kate. God knows, I don't think she had anything to hide, but she thought different, and we've got to respect her wishes. It's her memory we've got to protect. All right?"

"All right, Mick."

Joyce opened the door. "Well, if you must go."

Rose flashed a gay and guileless smile at Jack. "Yes, we must run. No ill feelings, Jack?"

Jack flushed, checked an impulse to glance at Joyce and mumbled, "No ill feelings."

There was an interchange of farewells. Joyce looked calmly past Rose and said, "Bye-bye, Mick."

Jack sat in a daze while Joyce ushered the visitors out. He felt no hostility for Rose. Her words and behaviour had drained him of all emotion and removed her far beyond his understanding. Even when she had been sitting face-to-face with him, she had not aroused any intensity of feeling in him. It was the first time that this had been the case. Where was the girl, ardent, impulsive, yet as fresh as petals, whose spirit was as elusive as a butterfly's dance? The cast of the face was the same, the profile was the same, the eyes were as brilliant. Whoever had known the girl would recognize the woman. But the brightness in the eyes was of a changed quality. It was not a radiance that softened but an intensity that made the surrounding features seem firmer and more determined. The tenderness and promise of unmoulded youth were lost. He was sad, for he also remembered himself as he had been, his body slimmer and without the lumpy muscles with which years of work and war had thickened it, his forehead unlined, his hair thicker, more

351

lustrous and more rebellious, the skin of his face less florid and youthfully soft, without its present enamelled hardness. He even recalled, in painful glimpses, how he had looked at her, his face uplifted and shining with a daft and pathetic innocence. And Chris had been alive, and Alf had been handsome, and Kate had been alive. The mysterious agony of change, of irredeemable time, weighed upon him.

Rose was still beautiful in his eyes, but now she had no more impact upon him than a lovely image on a cinema screen. She was no longer clad in illusion. The magic of remembered youth had been stripped from her. She was no longer the faery being, always just beyond his reach, whom he had gazed after as the embodiment of all the poetry that real life lacked. She had gone out of his world, taking his own youth with her, and he did not gaze after her.

Joyce came back into the room. "Let's have some fresh air in the room."

Her violent and determined movements as she dragged the window open brought a flash of memory to him, poignant but ridiculous, of Rose making the same gesture against him in her bedroom, and he smiled vaguely.

"Her sort of people," Joyce said, "they make me sick to the stomach."

He looked at her in wonderment, but he did not protest.

Chapter 4

"ONCE UPON A TIME —" Mick had taken Rose back to The Lamb, and they were sitting in the parlour. "Once upon a time I was courting an Irish girl, a parlourmaid. That was, oh, forty years ago. The gentry were still living hereabouts, and a young fellow like me spent half his nights creeping down their basement steps. I remember one day she stood at the other end of the kitchen, with her back to me, cutting bread. 'D'ye love me, Mick?' she asked, without turning round. I swore a terrible oath that I did. 'D'ye really love me?' she asked again, and she looked over her shoulder with one of those melting smiles. 'To me dyin' day,' I said. 'You don't, you devil,' she shouted all of a sudden, turnin' on me with a face black and furious, her eyes glaring jealousy, 'You're lyin' to me and I hate you!' And — crash! — she threw the breadboard at me. And before I'd finished ducking, she was across the room with her arms round my neck, and smothering my face with kisses."

"Very interesting," said Rose. "And why this particular tale at this particular time?"

"Oh, I don't know. Just being matey."

"You look about as matey as a tiger. You didn't have a word to say walking up the street. The veins were standing up on your temples like flex."

"All right, I'm talking my temper away. Listen, you pride yourself on having a mind of your own. Are you sure you know your own mind any more than that skivvy did?"

"Quite sure. Why?"

"You've had crazes before. Different jobs. Different

353

men. What makes you so sure you won't blaze up tomorrow with some new lunacy you don't even dream of today ?"

"Lunacy?" She put her cigarette down in an ashtray and faced him didactically. "The trouble with you, Mick, is that you're like most fathers. You still think I'm fifteen years old. You can only see me as I was, and you can't understand what I've become. It hurts you because I'm not the little apple of your eye any more, but myself, a separate person, growing away from you. I suppose it hurts all parents when they realise it. But after all, why don't you face facts, and give me credit for having some grown-up motives for taking the course I have? Why don't you credit me with having developed a bit of purpose and intelligence. Because I have, you know."

"That's all I need from you, a lecture. 'Fathers Must Face the Facts of Life.' You don't have to tell me you've changed. It's the way you've changed I don't like." A darker hue gathered beneath the weathered ruddiness of his face. "I wish I'd had the rearing of you!"

"Mick!" She was gentle and mocking. "You're getting angrier and angrier. You are!"

"You're trying to make me, aren't you? To me, you haven't become what you promised to be when you were a kiddie, but the opposite. You were a warm-hearted child. You used to give your spending money away to the first snotty-nosed little brat you saw crying in the street. I used to see generosity in you, and kindness. Where's it all gone?"

"It hasn't gone. That's why I'm what I am."

Mick uttered a grunt of disgust. "Away with you! You talk to me about grown-up motives, purpose, intelligence, and then I see you roll that boy for his money with as little scruple as some rotten old dockside trot friskin' a drunk for his wallet. It's not what you did with Jack's money that I'm caring about. It's what it shows up in you, your bloody cold, hard arrogance. It's like polished granite. I can't even scratch it. You just can't see that anything's wrong so long as it serves your purpose."

"Mick, is this a quarrel?"

"Maybe. It will be if that smile stays on your face. Maybe not. We'll see."

"I could face it, Mick. Though I'd be sorry."

"So should I."

She let the little ice-points of attack melt from her eyes. "You know," she said quietly, "you're building up a great deal from a very little thing. Yes, don't interrupt, it is a very little thing. I only acted on an impulse. Not that I regret it, but that's how I am. Our newspaper was in a pretty bad jam. It's the most important thing in the world for us. It's there to help everybody, Jackie Agass included, if he only knew it. And we had to raise the money quickly. I stripped myself to the last farthing, and so did every friend I went to. Whatever I did was entirely off my own bat. Nobody told me to. They might even have disapproved, if they'd known how I'd gone about it." She pulled a little face. "I wouldn't like to tell you how often I've been told off, for being opportunist, and reckless, and erratic, and all sorts of other things. Anyway, if I'd had the time, I might even have got around to paying him back. In fact I might even have got that watch you gave me out of pawn. I am still human, you know, whether you're prepared to believe it or not."

"It's a bit late in the day to tell me all this. You didn't think of it when we were tearin' each other up last night, and you didn't have the good grace to say it to Jackie Agass."

For a second she seemed to blaze up again inside. "I will *not* make excuses for myself! Let them think what they like!"

Mick's manner was easier now. "D'you know what beats me about you, Rosie? What absolutely defeats me? It's that granite certainty. You're right. You're always right. Everything you do is right. Your newspaper is doing good. You've no doubt of that. There's no glimmer of fear in your mind that it might be doing harm. The

355

truth is whatever you happen to tell other people. Anything they say to you is just a noise in your ears while you're deciding what to say next. Rosie, nobody knows the outcome of what they are doing. I don't speak from books. I only have sixty years of life to go from, but that's a great deal more than you have. What we strive for is never what comes to pass. Nobody on earth has the right to be absolutely certain."

"We have."

"You imagine you have. An' I don't mind admitting, that's your strength."

"I know we have. We're the first people on earth to discover the laws of history. We've learned to control its speed and direction. Against all the so-called brains that have run the world so far, the people that are trying to stop us, we're like astronomers compared with astrologers. We don't claim to know everything, far from it, but it's us who's the scientists, and all the rest are guessers and whistlers in the dark. We know as much about the process of social birth and death as a doctor knows about birth and death in his hospital ward. The world is pregnant, it's writhing with pain, and we're prepared — I've no purpose in hiding it — we're ready to be as ruthless in bringing about a quick and healthy birth as a doctor is when he has to bring a child from a diseased and dying mother. And our end is just as humane as his, whatever we have to resort to, on the big scale or on the tiny little personal scale, to attain it."

Mick preserved a daunted silence for a few moments. Then he said, "Well, I've never seen any personal gifts in you. Perhaps — I might as well be frank — that's what's wrong with you and others like you, having ambition but no talents, wanting to ride up to the top merely by turning the world upside down. Grabbing for the prize you can't earn, and won't drudge for. Anyway, your clever friends have certainly taught you one gift, and that's the gift of the gab."

Rose's smile returned. This time it was friendly. "If I've

got it from anyone, you old blarney-monger, it's you. Give me a drink."

Mick brought her a glass of brandy, and when she had finished it she relaxed peacefully back into her armchair, gazing reflectively up at the ceiling as if the liquor had stilled her agitation. "I've told you often enough what made me what I am," she said. "It wasn't any 'clever friends'. It was my life. This dreadful little street — oh, I know it's not a slum, but it's a slum of the spirit. People in streets like this grow up like plants in cellars, away from the sunlight. They could flower into something beautiful, but they don't. They could grow up to a wonderful stature, but they remain stunted. They are born and die without knowing what life might be. My mother stifled in this street. You've said yourself she was made for a life a thousand times better. I think, in a different world she could have found some place that would have allowed her to give to — oh, to everybody — what she gave to us. She wouldn't have been locked in by ignorance and fear — yes, poor dear, I love her ten times as much as when she was alive, but she was an ignorant woman, and it wasn't her fault, it was her inheritance. And in a different world there wouldn't have been the war that killed her. Did she deserve that? And there wouldn't have been the life that gave our Chris the consumption and denied him the conditions for getting better. You," she said, "you're the one to talk! You cared for her, didn't you? But you can't see farther than the end of your nose because you've got a vested interest in Lamb Street staying as it is. Oh, you're the great man, you're the good neighbour, aren't you? Everybody's friend. But you've been nice and comfortable this last thirty years, in your nice, warm pub, with a better living coming in than anyone else in the street ever saw, and never the dole to fear as they had for years. It suits you all right when they all come flocking into your saloon bar every night to swill your gin, and your mild-and-bitter, all trying to forget the blankness, and the aimless drudgery, and all the other

357

things they're frightened of outside."

"You're very hard on me, old girl. You're pretty snooty about them, too, considering that they're your own people."

"Oh, I don't blame you, and I'm not sneering at them. You're all prisoners. What's more, I know it's in them to be different. You don't have to tell me about all the good in them. I haven't forgotten it. And I've seen them show their strength, too, though they haven't seen it themselves. When we used to go collecting for Spain, and in the war, and when they put Labour in. They can break out of their slum when they all learn to use their strength together, with everyone else like them. So for heaven's sake don't keep telling me that I don't care about them, and that I only want to do myself a bit of good. If you think you know me, then please believe in me, and believe that I live for others as well as myself."

It was Mick's turn to smile. "I could deny that, you know. I could remind you of the little girl who wouldn't stay in one job long enough to learn it. I could remind you of the girl who couldn't see anything wrong in borrowing a dress off the hook in the shop where she worked, just because she fancied it. I could remind you of the kid who gave herself airs and dreamed of being a princess. I could tell you that you're just a self-appointed saviour, that you really think yourself better than those you want to lead, and that they don't want to have people like you marching them in column of fours wherever *you* want them to go. I could ask you why you've never taken the chance of doing good in some humble and anonymous way — if you're so keen to help others, you could do it on the quiet, nursing, or teaching, or doing welfare work, or going out to help the blacks —"

"What, me?"

"Listen to that ring in your voice! You couldn't bear it, could you? I could tell you that you're the worst little snob I know, that your one aim in life has been to escape from Lamb Street and live the kind of life that pleased you better. I've been watching you all this morning. You've had your nose in the air as if it was a sewage farm you were walking through, not the street your mother was content to live in. I could ask you why you think the life you lead — your flat, and your smart friends — very smart, from what you tell me, considering they're supposed to represent the underdog — and your parties, and your love affairs, and your discussions about culture and whatnot — why d'you think it's any less shabby than the poor old Lamb Street mums coming in here to knock back their bobsworths of gin? I could tell you that in my Church there are proud priests and humble priests, and the proud priests aren't priests at all."

She was flushing now, and sitting upright. He put his glass down, and gave her a reassuring grin, as if he were able at last to feel some mastery over her. "But I won't. I'll assume you're the genuine article. In that case, there's only one thing wrong with you. You're still young. Not enough has happened to you yet. When you've been bashed around a bit by the years, you'll know you can't change the world, because the world's made of people, and people aren't only made of flesh and bone and hope, but of savagery and envy and fear. All your lot'll be able to do, even if you do win, is to pummel and pound the world around till you've changed the shape of it, but it'll be the same world, with the same human beings in it, and the same yeast of good and evil breeding and bubbling among them. Why don't you leave 'em alone? All right, they're bloody cannibals sometimes — I haven't forgotten Barmy — but that's how it's always been. Speaking for Lamb Street — I can't tell about the rest — we don't face up to the whole filthy muddle of it too badly. We manage to make a bit of a life out of it, and that's an achievement, believe you me!"

Rose sat for a moment, still flushed, with her head to one side, as if listening for echoes. Her lips were pursed. Mick asked, "Another drink?"

"I'll get it myself." She crossed to the sideboard, filled

359

her glass and, leaving it where it stood, began to pace restlessly back and forth with her arms hugged across her chest. "You say what's wrong is that I'm young." She was not looking at Mick, but was frowning at the carpet. "Perhaps yours is that you're old. You're a defeatist. You don't believe people can be changed for the better. I do." She turned to face him, and stood looking proudly down at him. "Look here, I'll tell you something. You had a jolly good slam at me, didn't you? Well, I'll do something you've not been willing to do — I'll concede you a point. I'll admit I've got my faults, and I'll admit you've put your finger on some of them. It's true I'm ambitious. It's true I've got no special ability. It's true I want the best out of life. What do you want me to do, love the whole human race and leave myself out? But this is what you don't understand — the road I've taken is the only one that can help me get the better of my faults. Any other way — go on, tell me any other way a girl like me, poor and pretty, tries to get out of the rut — any other way, my faults would have got the better of me, and double-quick, too, I can tell you! How many girls have gone to the bad, who were like me at sixteen? Plenty, and you know it. I could go down on my knees and thank the Party for what it's done for me. And I know this, too, that the harder I work to change the world for the better, the quicker I'll change myself for the better. When you see tremendous achievements and tremendous sacrifices, it's easier not to be vain. When you see real hope for everybody you don't want so much to grab for yourself. The world opens out wider every day, and there's more to look at than yourself in the mirror."

"By God!" Mick thumped his knee. "Look who's talking!"

"Well, that's my answer to you, Mick Monaghan, and in time you'll see that I'm right. And the same goes for everybody else. You walk about the streets of this town, and ask yourself what's wrong with it. I don't suppose you ever did. I do. See the people swarming in the streets, pushing and shoving and jostling each other off the pavements, look into all those white miserable faces, all hurrying and worrying. See the dirt and the ugliness, all those catchpenny adverts screaming at you, and the kids at the corners learning how to waste their time — that's all they'll ever have to do, except work, till they die. Everybody's a stranger. Nobody cares about his job, it's just eight hours a day taken from him, a third of his lifetime. You see them all crawling about as if they've lived for generations cap in hand, and so they have, begging for the jobs they hate. Go and watch them flocking to the dog tracks, and queuing up in the drizzle for rotten Yankee films. Think of all the joy that's stored up in books and plays and pictures and music, it might not exist for all they know. How many of them will ever see the Lakes, or the Avon, or the Dales, or the Cotswolds, before they've lived out their poor starved lives? No wonder it's a nightmare!"

"So it is," Mick said. "The bloody place is too big. God didn't make us to live packed like fleas in a barrel."

"That's not the point of it. It's the sheer terrifying, miserable, dreadful lack of purpose that poisons life. That's the horror. It matters more than material conditions — they're bad enough, though they keep improving, but they're not the root of the matter. It's the emptiness, the lack of meaning, having nothing more to do once you're born except while away the time as painlessly as possible till you die. Give life a meaning, and everything changes. Listen — one day, when people walk this city, they'll be the owners of everything they look on. Every day, when they go to work, they'll know they're working for their own good and the common good. Then they'll walk the streets as if the streets belong to them. Their faces will be changed, because their minds will be changed. The word 'neighbour' won't just mean the man next door, but everyone they pass in the streets, the crowds won't be made up of strangers and rivals any more. People will be secure at heart, because their jobs will be secure and peace will be secure — and it will be, we've won half the world already and we're going to win the other half. No more penny arcades. Children will be educated to enjoy life to the last drop, not just to be office boys and fill in the pools coupon. The world won't end at the end of your street — people will travel, and they'll come back richer in heart. That's how we'll change people. Well," she ended a little truculently, "what have you got to say to that?"

Mick studied her with a sombre and compassionate smile. "Drink up your brandy, girl. If that's what you really believe, I'm not going to say a thing. You talk as if you don't know about all the people before you who've dreamed the same dream as you, and to get it they've built and built, organised and organised, disciplined and disciplined, punished and punished, and then they've woke up to find themselves in a prison twice as grim as the one they were in before."

She turned back to get her drink. "You're old," she mocked, "your eyes are getting dim."

"They can still see farther than yours, thank God! I'd like to think you'll wake up from this dream before it's too late. You've done it before, you know. You've chopped and changed, put your heart and soul in something, and forgotten it a year later. I fancy you haven't changed so much. You're still restless, you still stride about and look about you as if there's something you haven't found yet. Don't be so sure what you'll be in a few years time."

"No!" The intensity of her protest was almost agonized. She clenched her fist and banged it on the sideboard again and again. "No, no, no! Not now! Not this time! You don't know what it used to be like. Every day that passed, I felt I'd lost a chance to do something tremendous. Every single morning I woke up, I used to say, 'What is it, where is it, what's the thing that I have to do, how do I come to life?' It used to gnaw at me. Not any more," she cried, her expression one of distress. "I have certainty now. I have confidence. I tell you this is for keeps."

Mick nodded, and left her to herself till she had recovered. A little later he said, "To change the subject, when are you going to marry again?"

"Why should I?"

"It might bring you down to earth. What's stopping you?"

"Where's the man?"

"What man are you looking for?"

"The man I can respect."

He was smiling again, but gently. "There you go again. There's nothing to be done with you. There's no such animal. Don't get me wrong, girl. It's not because you're too good for them, it's because you're too conceited. Well, don't leave it too long. Ten years go quickly, especially when you're having a good time, and all of a sudden you'll find you're going hard. You'll start turning into one of those handsome hags I've seen too often — the dashing young women of yesterday. All wit and no laughter. Everlastingly busy outside and a bit lonely inside. You watch out, my old girl."

"A pretty picture," Rose laughed. "I'm terrified. You'd better give me another drink to reassure me." She went back to her chair. "What would you like me to do? Marry Jack Agass?"

"I wouldn't advise that. Not for your sake or his. He'll be happier with the one he's got."

"With her? I wish him joy. Imagine going to bed with that female suet pudding!"

Mick grinned. "Don't be so sure. If she's anything like her mother, he's got a warm time ahead of him."

"Oh? And what do you know about her mother?"

"A gentleman never tells."

"Oh, Mick, Mick, you old ram!" She lay back in her chair, quivering with merriment. "I can't help loving you. Is there any woman in this street you haven't been at?"

"Quite a few, unfortunately. But I reckon I've got ten good years ahead of me yet."

Laughter made her cough. She steadied herself, and

363

raised her glass. "We'll drink to that. To your ten good years!"

"And I'll drink to you! Which 'you' is the real one, the one you see or the one I see? Here's hoping I'm wrong!"

Rose's eyes were bright. "Idiot! Oh, what a pair we are to be lecturing each other!" Father and daughter touched glasses and drank.

Chapter 5

JACK SPENT THE NEXT WEEK AT HOME recovering from his burns. He went several times to the hospital, to have his dressings changed and to visit Bernie, who was making good progress but who would require some minor plastic surgery before he was ready to face the world again.

Visitors thronged the Wakerell house every day. Relatives called to sympathise and congratulate, and to bear back to their own homes the excitement of having had tea with someone whose name had been mentioned (to the extent of four lines in a column of 'news briefs') in the newspapers. Neighbours came, bringing fruit, milk, cigarettes, eggs, magazines and lamb chops for Jack. They all subscribed lavishly to the collection, launched by Mick, for a wedding present; and, fulfilling Mick's prediction, they gave even more generously to buy a huge wreath for Barmy's funeral. On the night of his burial there was such a warmth of sentimental recollection generated in the saloon bar of The Lamb that twice the usual quantity of beer was called for to assuage it. Several of the women became maudlin, and many a soulful tribute was uttered, until Mick Monaghan was callous enough to turn all the mourners out ten minutes before closing time.

Jack was diffident and resentful at the public homage but Joyce revelled in it. Her accounts of Jack's heroism to the girls at work grew more fervid every day, and she came home early every evening after informing Madame Sophie, "I must be by his side. He needs me," as if he were hovering between life and death. Her mood towards him had finally thawed. She was loving, but there was none of the anxiety or pleading in her attentions that there had once been. She walked with him wherever he went, or stood behind his chair when he received visitors, with something of her mother's haughty serenity of carriage. Alone with him she was affectionate, sometimes gleeful, but never humble. When they discussed the final plans for their wedding she listened to his ideas attentively but lazily, and announced her own point of view with the calm certainty that it would prevail. To her mother — who throughout the week was beside herself with glory, ushering in visitors, bragging to them, pouring tea for them, drinking innumerable nips of gin with them and popping more lumps of sugar into her mouth than she had consumed in the last month — she displayed a patronising friendliness that sealed Mrs. Wakerell's defeat in the household.

Now that the quarrel was receding in Jack's memory, his remorse evaporated and he was no longer abject to Joyce. The old boisterousness crept back into his attitude to her, but beneath it there was always a hint of apprehension, expressed in ostentatious gestures of respect.

Inwardly he felt empty and saddened, but relieved. He discovered, with a vague wonderment, that he loved Kate no less for what he now knew about her. She had been a holy picture in his memory, an image worshipped but flat and unreal. Now she lived there as a woman, and he was warmed by the sense of all she had given him, as a man is when he realises what of himself has been the gift of women. He felt her loss more sharply than before. He even had moments of elevation when he wanted to see the world through her loving eyes. But he was free of her, for the warmth in him had awakened him to Joyce, the living woman, and through Joyce to the living world. The past had stood between him and the present. He had taken refuge in illusive memory, and its drugging comfort had

made the present, with its problems and tribulations, yet harder to face. It had given him false standards and a false vision of people. Disillusioned now, his only conscious awareness was of loss and an inability to focus, but even in his emptiness of heart there was the feeling of freedom, of a burden lifted.

One evening, in the darkened parlour, he asked Joyce, "D'you reckon we'll get on all right?"

"Oh!" The exclamation was full of scorn. "There's a silly question!"

"It's a fine time we've picked to get married, you know. All sorts of trouble on the way."

"There always is. I reckon the sky'd fall in if there wasn't."

"Wars an' all that." He studied her unmoved profile in the darkness. "You don't seem worried."

"Why should I? Everything's going to be lovely."

"How do you know?"

"Because."

"Because what?"

"Because my Easter bonnet with all the ribbons on it. You think too much. Brains fry well with breadcrumbs. That's all they're good for."

"Go on, you're daft."

"Well, that makes two of us."

Jack drew the curtains, shutting the lamplight, and the street noises, and the world, and the future, out of their thoughts. What was to be, they could not tell. All they knew was that, in alliance, they would always be able to make the best of a bad job. That was what made their world go round.